KERRY BARRETT was a bookworm from a very early age and did a degree in English Literature, then trained as a journalist, writing about everything from pub grub to *EastEnders*. Her first novel, *Bewitched, Bothered and Bewildered*, took six years to finish and was mostly written in longhand on her commute to work, giving her a very good reason to buy beautiful notebooks. Kerry lives in London with her husband and two sons, and Noel Streatfield's *Ballet Shoes* is still her favourite novel.

Also by Kerry Barrett

Bewitched, Bothered and Bewildered
I Put a Spell on You
Baby It's Cold Outside
I'll Be There For You
A Spoonful of Sugar
A Step in Time
The Forgotten Girl
The Girl in the Picture

The Hidden Women

KERRY BARRETT

ONE PLACE. MANY STORIES

HQ
An imprint of HarperCollins*Publishers* Ltd
1 London Bridge Street
London SE1 9GF

This paperback edition 2019

2
First published in Great Britain by
HQ, an imprint of HarperCollins*Publishers* Ltd 2019

ISBN: 9780008323035

MIX
Paper from
responsible sources
FSC
www.fsc.org   FSC™ C007454

This book is produced from independently certified FSC™ paper
to ensure responsible forest management.

For more information visit: www.harpercollins.co.uk/green

Typeset by Palimpsest Book Production Ltd, Falkirk, Stirlingshire
Printed and bound in Great Britain by
CPI Group (UK) Ltd, Croydon, CR0 4YY

For Petrova Fossil, the original Attagirl

Prologue

Helena

April 2015

'I thought you'd be pleased,' I said, watching Greg's stony face for any sign of happiness.

'Well I'm not.' His expression softened, just a bit, and he sat down next to me on the sofa and took my hand.

'It's just too soon,' he said.

'We've been together for five years, Greg,' I snapped. 'It's not like we just met.'

He had the grace to look at least slightly ashamed.

'I meant for me, not us,' he said. 'It's too soon for me. And you. We're still young. We should be out having fun, not at home with a squawking baby.'

'We're in our thirties; we're not kids,' I said, resting my head against the sofa cushions. I felt sick and I didn't think it was just because of my unexpected pregnancy.

I'd done the test that morning, and showed Greg the unmistakeable dark line as he brushed his teeth.

'It's positive,' I'd said, feeling a tiny shiver of excitement mixed with fear. 'I'm pregnant.'

Greg had glanced at the plastic stick and then kissed me, his breath minty fresh.

'I need to run,' he'd simply said. 'We'll chat tonight.'

And now we were chatting and it wasn't going the way I'd thought it would.

'I thought we were set,' I said. 'I thought we were a team.'

'We are a team,' Greg said. 'You and me.'

'You and me and our baby,' I said.

Greg winced. He tried to cover it up by pretending to cough, but I'd seen it.

'I don't want to have a baby, Helena,' he said. 'I'm sorry, but that's just how I feel.'

I couldn't speak.

'There's a clinic,' Greg said. 'Max at work told me about it. His girlfriend went there a while back. He gave me the card, hang on …'

He dug about in his pocket while I let my fingers drift down to rest on my stomach.

'I need some air,' I said, ignoring his outstretched hand clutching a business card. 'I'm going for a walk.'

I grabbed my jacket from the arm of the sofa, and stumbled my way out of the front door.

'H,' Greg said. 'Don't be like this. It's hormones; you're not thinking straight.'

I didn't answer. I walked a little way down the road and then I sat at a bus stop and took my phone out.

'Miranda?' I said, when my sister answered. 'I need your help. I'm having a baby and I think I've just left Greg.'

Chapter 1

Helena

May 2018

'Here?' I said, staring at my boss Fliss in astonishment. 'Jack Jones is coming here?'

'Yes, here,' she said, resting her hand on her computer keyboard as though to warn me I was about to lose her attention. 'Apparently he's very interested in social history and he wants to know how you work. It's no biggie.'

'But I've got a system,' I said, knowing it was no good protesting when Fliss had decided something. 'I don't want him to mess it up.'

'He's not taking over, Helena, he just wants to know how you're getting on.' Fliss sounded impatient. 'He'll be here after lunch.'

I forced a smile. 'Fine,' I said. 'I'll get some stuff together.'

I wandered back to my desk feeling wrong-footed.

'What's with the face?' asked my colleague Elly as I sat down. 'Did Fliss tell you off?'

I wiggled my mouse to wake up my screen. 'No,' I said

gloomily. 'She told me Jack bloody Jones is coming in this afternoon to see how I'm getting on with my research.'

'Shut. Up,' said Elly, spinning round in her chair to face me. 'Shut. Up.'

I blinked at her. Did she really mean me to be quiet?

'Jack Jones is coming here? THE Jack Jones? We never get to meet the celebs,' Elly was beginning to babble. 'I've worked on this show for five years and I've never met one single person whose family history I've researched. Have you met anyone?'

'No,' I said. She was right. I'd not worked on *Where Did You Come From?* as long as Elly had, but I'd researched the family trees of lots of celebrities and not been so much as introduced to anyone.

'And it's Jack Jones?' Elly went on. 'Jack. Jones.'

I nodded. 'It's an interesting one, actually. His great-grandfather was at the Somme ...'

I trailed off as Elly waved her hand to shush me.

'He's gorgeous,' she said. 'Properly handsome. And I've heard he's going to be in that new superhero film soon so he'll be a massive Hollywood star.'

I nodded again. I knew who Jack Jones was of course – star of the latest Sunday night detective drama that was wowing audiences, and tipped for superstardom – and Elly was right, he was gorgeous. In any other circumstances I'd love to meet him. But I had a certain way of working, and a system, and a process, and I didn't appreciate interference or anyone checking up on me, however handsome they were.

'Will you come with me?' I asked Elly. 'To the meeting?'

She gaped at me. 'Seriously?' she said. 'The meeting with Jack Jones?'

I couldn't help laughing at her face. 'Yes, the meeting with Jack Jones,' I said. 'I could do with the help.'

Elly was getting up from her chair. She pulled on her coat and picked up her bag as I looked on in confusion.

'Is that a no?' I said.

'It's a yes,' she threw back over her shoulder as she headed for the lift. 'I'm going to buy a new top and get my hair blow-dried.'

Chuckling to myself I turned back to my screen. We worked on more than one celebrity story at a time and I was currently tracking the maternal line of a breakfast TV presenter. I'd got right back to the early 1800s and I thought I might be able to go further if I was clever about it.

I clicked on to the census web page I used, intending to get back to work, though I couldn't concentrate on Sarah Sanderson properly with the news that Jack Jones was coming into the office weighing on my mind. I absolutely loved my job and I considered myself to be really lucky that I'd landed this role on *Where Did You Come From?* Social history may have been my passion but it wasn't exactly well paid – so making the jump into television was brilliant for me – and I enjoyed the research as well as seeing the process of the show being made. My colleagues were lovely, and Fliss was very understanding when it came to having to rush off on time each evening to collect Dora from nursery, or working from home when she was ill.

Spinning round in my chair, I surveyed my shelves of neat brown folders, each with the name of the celebrity written along the spine and arranged in alphabetical order. I ran my finger along them until I found J and pulled out the Jack Jones file. I'd found out quite a lot about his family already so I had things to tell him. But today I was supposed to be working on Sarah Sanderson's family history. Giving up an afternoon to Jack Jones was going to throw everything out.

I opened the folder and looked at the picture of him clipped to the front cover. I liked to have a photo of each person so I knew whose family I was researching – especially for those celebs I didn't really know much about. It helped them become real for me, and then their families became real, too.

Elly was right, Jack Jones was really handsome. He had glossy brown hair that was longish and curlyish and flopped over his forehead, and a smile with a hint of mischief. I felt a brief flicker of excitement. Though I wasn't a massive fan of the whole celeb thing – I couldn't name the Kardashians or the members of One Direction – I had really enjoyed the detective series that Jack had starred in. I wondered if it would be weird to discuss the cryptic ending with him and decided it would be a bit fangirl. Mind you, I thought, not as fangirl as Elly getting her hair done.

I picked up my phone, smiling at the picture of Dora wearing my sunglasses on my home screen, and took a photo of Jack's picture, then added it to my siblings' group chat.

'Guess who I'm meeting this afternoon ...' I typed.

Almost straight away, my baby sister Imogen replied. 'OMG!' she wrote. 'Is that Jack Jones? I love him!'

I grinned. Before I could reply, a message arrived from my other sister, Miranda. 'I have no idea who that is,' she wrote. 'But he's easy on the eye.'

I smiled again. My sisters were nothing if not predictable.

'Has anyone heard from Andy?' Another message pinged through from Miranda. 'I can't see if he's getting these. Immy manages to reply all the way from Africa and he can't be bothered to keep in touch from Scotland.'

I made a face at my phone. I adored my big sister Miranda but she could be a bit of a mother hen. Not surprising, I supposed, when you thought about what she'd had to take on when we were kids, and I'd never forget how she'd been there when I needed her when Dora was born.

'He's probably not on Wi-Fi,' I typed. Andy was on an archae-ological dig somewhere on a windswept island in the North Sea – hardly hanging out in a coffee bar in Glasgow as Miranda obviously thought. 'He'll check in when he can.'

I threw my phone into my bag and pulled out my make-up. If Elly was dolling up to meet Jack Jones, then perhaps I should do the same.

Chapter 2

Jack Jones was nothing like I'd expected. For a start he arrived by himself. No entourage, no publicist, not even a driver. He just got off the tube and sauntered into the office, scruffy bag thrown over his shoulder and hair unwashed. Elly was not impressed by his distinctly un-starry appearance. She went down to reception to meet him, giddy with excitement, while I went into the meeting room, laid out some biscuits on a plate and made sure the coffee machine was working.

I put my folders of research on to the table and waited for them to arrive, nervously tapping my fingers on my knee. What if he messed up my notes? What if he questioned my methods? I wasn't comfortable about this at all.

'This is your researcher, Helena Miles,' Elly said, standing at the door of the room and ushering Jack Jones inside. 'I'll leave you to it.'

I stood up.

'Pleased to meet you,' I lied, holding out my hand for Jack Jones to shake. Wait. Elly was leaving us to it? What? I caught her eye over Jack Jones's shoulder. She wrinkled her nose up at his back and flicked her newly blow-dried hair in a disdainful shrug. Jack Jones obviously didn't live up to her expectations. Horrified at the idea of entertaining a bona-fide celebrity by myself, I widened my eyes pleading with her to stay, but she spun round and headed back to her desk.

'Is everything okay?'

I dragged my eyes from Elly's retreating back and looked at Jack Jones, who was still holding my outstretched hand.

'Oh,' I said, awkwardly, dropping his hand like it was hot. 'Sorry, Mr Jones. Sorry.'

Jack Jones smiled at me. 'Call me Jack,' he said. 'Is it okay if I call you Helena?'

I liked the way he said my name in his clipped, period-drama accent.

'Of course,' I said.

He smiled at me again, a sort of wonky, half-smile that crinkled the corners of his eyes. He looked straight at me and I looked back and my stomach flipped over. He was gorgeous. At least his face was. For the first time I took in what he was wearing – scruffy jeans, battered trainers and a scuffed leather jacket. His brown canvas bag was slung across his body and his hair was a mop of dirty curls, very different from the hair that artfully fell across his forehead in the picture at the front of his file.

Unable to help myself, I glanced down at the photo on the folder. Jack saw me looking and grinned again.

'Photo shoot Jack,' he said, pulling out a chair and sitting down. 'Not my real self.'

Embarrassed that he'd caught me looking and still feeling weak at the knees thanks to his smile, I collapsed into the chair next to him and moved it ever so slightly further away.

'So,' I said, all business. 'I understand it's your dad's family you're interested in?'

He nodded. 'I didn't really know them,' he said. 'My dad was around a bit when I was little, and apparently I did meet my grandparents a couple of times, though I don't remember. But they've passed away now, and then Dad died last year – though I'd not seen him since I was ten.'

'Oh, I'm sorry,' I said. His story sounded painfully familiar to me, making me think of Greg and how he'd not seen Dora more than a handful of times.

Jack shrugged. 'He was like a stranger to me,' he said. 'It was just me and Mum when I was growing up.'

'No brothers or sisters?' I asked. Again I was struck by how similar his story sounded to Dora's – and how different it was from my own chaotic, busy childhood home.

He shook his head. 'Just me.'

I looked at his impish face, and felt so sad for the little boy he'd once been that I almost threw my arms round him and hugged him. My sister Imogen would have done. But thankfully, I remembered I was Helena Miles who did not do things spontaneously, unless you counted walking out on my boyfriend when I was pregnant.

Instead I opened the folder and showed Jack his rough family tree.

'So, this is your dad's family,' I said, tracing the line with my forefinger. 'Your grandfather was a pilot in World War Two, and your great-grandfather fought at the Somme.'

Jack was looking at me in wonder. 'Really?' he said. 'Tell me more.'

Putting all thoughts of Sarah Sanderson's maternal line out of my head, I sat with Jack all afternoon and explained what I'd found out so far. I always did the initial research, then passed my findings on to specialists – in Jack's case we'd send him off to speak to an expert on World War One about his great-grandfather. And I was in the process of tracking down someone to speak to about his grandad too, who'd been too short-sighted to join the regular air force but who'd flown for the Air Transport Auxiliary, transporting planes from factories to airfields all over Britain. It was a great family story all round.

Jack was thrilled. He asked all the right questions and wrote endless notes in his scrawling handwriting, on a notepad he pulled from his tatty bag. At one point, he got so excited talking about the trenches that he threw out his arm and knocked over his cup of coffee. I leapt for the folder he had been reading and got it out of harm's way just in time.

He was very sweet and enthusiastic and every time he smiled he made my hands tremble. But oh my goodness, he was the clumsiest, scruffiest, bulldozer of a man I'd ever met. My carefully ordered notes were pulled out of the folders and spread across the table as the edges of the papers folded over and curled. There was the coffee incident, as well as biscuit crumbs scattered everywhere, and a similar hairy moment when Jack's biro leaked all over his hand and he left sticky blue fingerprints on a photocopy of his great-grandfather's service record.

Eventually, to my absolute relief, Jack looked at his watch – which appeared to have Mickey Mouse on it – and stood up.

'I'm late,' he said. 'I have to dash.'

'Okay,' I said, possibly a bit too eagerly. 'I'll show you out.'

Jack pulled on his leather jacket and surveyed the table, which was covered in notes and screwed-up tissues where he'd wiped the biro off his fingers, and biscuit crumbs.

'God what a mess,' he said. 'I'll help you clear up.'

'No need,' I said, desperately wanting him gone. 'I'll do it.'

But I was too late. He was already scooping up all my notes – no longer in any sort of order – and stuffing them back into a folder.

'Really,' I said, gritting my teeth. 'I can do it.'

I went to take the folder from him and there was a small tug-of-war as we tussled over it for a second, then it fell to the floor scattering papers everywhere.

I closed my eyes briefly and when I opened them, Jack was on his hands and knees picking up bits of paper.

'Ooh look,' he said, flinging one sheet at me from his position down on the floor. 'This says Lilian Miles on it. Have you been doing your own family tree and got them mixed up?'

I looked at the paper he'd given me. It was a document about the Air Transport Auxiliary.

'No, it's yours,' I said, bristling at the suggestion that I'd get papers muddled. 'Frank Jones is mentioned – look.'

I pointed at the bottom of the page, where I'd highlighted Jack's grandfather's name.

'It's saying he'd been cleared to fly the class of planes that included four-engine bombers,' I said.

'And so had Lilian,' Jack said, showing me the name at the top of the page. 'No relation of yours?'

I chewed my lip, thoughtfully. 'Perhaps,' I said. Then I shook my head. 'It must just be a coincidence.'

Which was exactly what I said to my parents about what I'd seen at our regular Friday evening family dinner.

'And there, right at the top, was the name Lilian Miles,' I said, helping myself to more pilau rice – we always got takeaway on Fridays because neither of my parents could cook and Miranda, my sister who'd done all the cooking when we were growing up, was usually knackered from work.

'I thought it had to be a coincidence,' I carried on. 'But isn't it strange?'

Dad shrugged. 'No idea,' he said. 'Like you say, probably just a coincidence.'

'But what about Great-Aunt Lil?' Miranda fixed Dad with a look that told me she wasn't impressed with his response.

Mum smiled at the mention of Lil. She was very fond of her.

'Yes, what about Lil?' she said.

'What about her?' Dad asked, snapping a poppadom in half with a crack and scattering crumbs across the table. I fought the urge to sweep them up with my hand.

'Could the Lilian Miles on the list be our Lil?' Miranda asked.

'It won't be her,' I said. 'There were lots of women named Lilian back then; trust me, I've seen a million birth certificates in my time.'

'But not lots of women named Lilian Miles,' Miranda pointed out.

'Is it just a coincidence?' Mum said. She looked thoughtful. 'Robert, what do we know about what Lil did in the war?'

Dad had just shovelled some more rice into his mouth but he sat up a bit straighter when Mum spoke.

'Planes,' he said eventually, once he'd swallowed. 'Definitely something to do with planes. I remember her buying me a toy when I was a kid.'

'Do you think it could be her, Nell?' Miranda said, using my childhood nickname. 'Maybe you could investigate?'

Mum and Dad exchanged a glance. Just a quick one and I had no idea what it meant. But I saw it and it intrigued me.

I shook my head. This was exactly what I'd been worried could happen.

'We're not allowed. We can't use company time or resources to research our own families. I had to sign a thing, when I joined, saying I wouldn't do it. And we can only access all the genealogy sites from work.'

'But how would they know what you were looking up?' Miranda said. She was like a dog with a bone when she got something in her head.

'They'd know,' I said darkly, though I thought she was probably right. Fliss could check what searches we did. In fact, we could all see everyone's searches because we all shared a login. But we never paid much attention to what the others were researching and I supposed no one would know whether I was looking up my own family or someone else's. 'More naan?'

The conversation moved on. And if it hadn't been for that look between my parents, I'd probably have forgotten all about the mention of Lilian Miles in my research. But that little glance, and the way Dad had suddenly sat up when he remembered Lil had done something with planes, stayed with me. I wondered what it meant and why it had captured his interest so much.

12

Chapter 3

Lilian

June 1944

'That's your brother isn't it? And is that his wife?'

Rose was peering over my shoulder at the photograph I kept stuck on the inside of my locker.

'He looks like you, your brother.'

I gave her a quick, half-hearted smile and reached inside my locker for my jacket.

'And is that their little lad she's holding?' Rose went on, undeterred by my lack of responses. 'What a sweetheart. He looks like you as well. You've all got that same dark hair.'

Rose was one of the most infuriating people I'd ever met. Back when we'd been at school together my mum had told me to be nice.

'She just wants to be your friend,' Mum would say. 'She's not as good with people as you are.'

Back then, I'd been one of the class leaders. Confident and a bit mouthy. Able to make anyone laugh with a quick retort, and to perform piano in front of all sorts of audiences. But that was before.

I'd not seen Rose for a few years and I was finding her much harder to deal with now. For the thousandth time I cursed the luck that had sent my old school friend to join the Air Transport Auxiliary, and at the same airbase as me.

I pulled my jacket out with a swift yank and slammed the locker door shut, almost taking off Rose's nose as I did it.

'Got to go,' I said.

I shrugged on my jacket, heaved my kitbag on to my shoulder, and headed through the double doors at the end of the corridor and out into the airfield. It was a glorious day, sunny and bright with a light wind. Perfect for flying. I paused by the door, raised my face to the sun and let it warm me for a moment.

The airfield was a hubbub of noise and activity. To my left a group of mechanics worked on a plane, shouting instructions to one another above the noise of the propellers. Ahead of me, a larger aircraft cruised slowly towards the runway, about to take off. It was what we called a taxi plane, taking other ATA pilots to factories where they'd pick up the aircraft they had to deliver that day.

My friend Flora was in the cockpit and she raised her arm to wave to me as she passed. I lifted my own hand and saluted her in return. A little way ahead, a truck revved its engine, and all around, people were calling to each other, shifting equipment and getting on with their tasks. I smiled. That was good. It was harder to organise things when it was quiet.

Glancing round, I saw Annie. She was loading some tarpaulins on to the back of a van. Casually I walked over to where she stood.

'Morning,' I said.

She nodded at me and hauled another of the folded tarpaulins up on to the van.

'I'm going to Middlesbrough,' I said, dropping my kitbag at my feet. I picked up one of the tarpaulins so if anyone looked over they'd see me helping, not chatting. 'Finally.'

She nodded again.

'I've left the address in your locker with my timings,' I went on. 'She's waiting to hear from you so send the telegram as soon as I take off.'

'Adoption?' Annie said.

I nodded, my lips pinched together. 'Older,' I said. 'Three kids already. Husband's in France.'

Annie winced. 'Poor cow.'

'I know,' I said. 'Her mum's helping.'

'How far along is she?'

'About seven months. She reckons she can't hide it much longer. I've been waiting for one of us to be sent up there.'

Annie heaved the last tarpaulin on to the van.

'Best get going then,' she said.

I gave her a quick smile.

'Thanks, Annie,' I said.

A shout from across the airfield made me look round. 'Lil!'

One of the engineers was waving to me from beside a small single-engine Fairchild.

'Looks like mine,' I said to Annie.

She gave my arm a brief squeeze. 'It's a good thing you're doing here,' she said.

'You're doing it too.'

Without looking back at her, I picked up my bag and ran over to the plane.

'Am I flying this one?' I said. We all took it in turns to fly the taxi planes, but I did it more often than some of the others; I loved it so much.

The engineer – a huge Welsh guy called Gareth who I was very fond of – patted the side of the plane lovingly.

'You are,' he said. 'She's a bit temperamental on the descent so take it easy.'

I rolled my eyes. 'Gareth,' I said. 'I know what I'm doing.'

I opened the cockpit door and flung my bag inside.

'Right,' I said. 'Take me through all the pre-flight checks.'

I'd been in the ATA for two years now, and I was cleared to fly every kind of plane – even the huge bombers that many people thought a woman couldn't handle, but I never took anything for granted. I always went through checks with the engineers and did everything by the book. I liked feeling in control and I didn't want to put my life in anyone else's hands. Not again.

The taxi flights were quick – normally twenty minutes or so as we headed to the factories to pick up our planes. Today was the same. So it wasn't long before we'd landed at South Marston, and I was ready to take off in the Spitfire I was delivering to Middlesbrough.

I climbed up into the plane and checked all the instruments, even though I'd flown hundreds of Spitfires and it was as familiar to me as the back of my own hand.

I loved flying. I loved feeling the plane doing what I asked it to do, and the freedom of swooping over the countryside. I'd spent two years hanging round the RAF base near where I lived in the Scottish borders before I joined up. I'd learned everything I could about flying, without actually piloting a plane myself. And then, as soon as I was old enough to sign up I'd applied to the ATA. I'd loved it straight away and I knew I was a good pilot. I'd raced through the ranks and completed my training on each category of plane faster than anyone else.

And yet every time I went on one of my 'mercy missions' as Flora called them, I was risking it all.

Putting all my worries aside, I focused on the plane. I watched the ground crew as they directed me out on to the runway, then thought only of the engine beneath me as I took off northwards.

Once I was up, I relaxed a bit, and took in the view. The day was so clear, I could see the towns and villages below. I imagined all the people going about their lives – hearing my engine and looking up to see me as I passed. Because it was a brand new plane, there was no radio, no navigation equipment – nothing.

I liked the challenge that brought. It meant my brain was always kept active and I had no time to brood.

Middlesbrough was one of our longest flights and by the time I landed it was afternoon and the heat of the summer day was beginning to fade.

I slid out of the cockpit and headed to a man with a clipboard, who appeared to be in charge.

'Spitfire,' I said. 'Made in South Marston.'

He nodded, without looking at me. 'Where's the pilot?' he asked. 'I need him to sign.'

'I'm the pilot,' I said, through gritted teeth. 'Do you have a pen?'

Now the man did look up. He rolled his eyes as though I'd said something ridiculous and handed me a pen from his shirt pocket.

I scribbled my signature on the form he held out. 'Is there a flight going back?'

'Over there,' he said, gesturing with his head to where a larger Anson sat on the runway. 'But there are a few of you going. Be about an hour?'

I breathed out in relief. An hour was more than enough. 'Fine,' I said. 'Can I grab a cuppa?'

He pointed his head in the other direction. I picked up my bag and went the way he'd indicated. But instead of going inside the mess hut, I slipped round the side of the building and out towards the main gate. I hoped the woman would be here – I didn't want to risk missing my flight back; that would lead to all sorts of trouble.

'Just going for some cigarettes,' I told the bored man on the gate. He barely acknowledged me as I sauntered past and out on to the road. It was quiet with no passing traffic. Across the carriageway, a woman stood still, partly hidden by a tree. She was wearing a long coat, even though it was summer, and she was in her late thirties. Her hair was greying and she had a slump to her shoulders that made me sad. She looked at me and when I raised my hand in greeting, she smiled a cautious, nervous smile. Confident she was the person I was meant to meet, I ran across the road to her.

'April?' I said.

She nodded, looking as though she was going to cry.

'I'm Lil.'

'Lil,' April said in a strong north-east accent. 'I need to go. I went early with my others and I'm sure this one's no different. I can't be here when the baby arrives. I can't.' Her voice shook.

I took her arm. 'I've got a family in Berkshire,' I said. 'Lovely woman. She's wanted a baby since they got married ten years ago but it's not happened. Her husband's a teacher – so he's not off fighting. They've got a spare room for you.'

April flinched and I looked at her.

'He was a teacher,' she said. 'The man. The baby's father.'

I stayed quiet. Sometimes mothers wanted to talk and sometimes they didn't but whatever they wanted, it was easier for me to stay silent.

'He was so nice,' April went on. 'Charming. Kind to my boys. Helpful to me. You know?'

I nodded.

'And then one day he wasn't so nice,' she said. 'And I know I should have told him to stay away, that I was married. I should have made it clearer. But I missed Bill, you see. And I know it's my fault.'

She paused.

'It's my fault.'

'It's not your fault,' I said, wondering how many times I'd said that and why it was easy to tell others that and not myself. 'And it's not the baby's fault.'

I unzipped my bag and pulled out an envelope.

'Your train tickets are in here,' I said. 'And the name and address of the family. You need to change at Birmingham and they'll meet you at Reading station – they know what train you'll be on.'

Looking a bit stunned, April took the envelope. 'Why do you do this?' she asked. 'What's in it for you?'

I shrugged. 'It's the right thing to do,' I said.

April looked doubtful but she didn't argue.

I glanced at my watch.

'I have to go,' I said. I took her hand and squeezed it. 'Good luck.'

Chapter 4

Helena

May 2018

After dinner I cornered Miranda in the kitchen as we washed up.

'What was all that about?' I asked her.

'Should we club together and buy the parents a dishwasher,' she said, squirting washing-up liquid into the sink.

'I can't afford it,' I said. 'And they wouldn't use it anyway.'

Miranda frowned. 'True.'

I elbowed her in the ribs as I passed her a stack of dirty plates.

'Miranda, focus. Did you see Mum and Dad look at each other when I mentioned Lil?'

She elbowed me back like we were still ten and twelve, not thirty-four and thirty-six.

'That was a bit weird, wasn't it?' she said.

'What was weird, darling?' Mum wandered into the kitchen clutching two empty wine glasses. 'Is there another bottle?'

I thought Miranda might burst with the effort of not rolling her eyes. 'In the fridge,' she said, through gritted teeth. 'You watched me put it in there.'

Mum blew an air kiss in her direction. 'Don't get snappy, Manda,' she said, mildly. 'What was weird?'

'Work stuff,' I said. 'Manda was telling me about some really important deal she's doing. Worth millions. Trillions even.'

Miranda was the youngest ever head of international investment at Ravensberg Bank and also the first woman to do the job. I was fiercely, wonderfully proud of her and in total awe of her skills. Our anti-capitalist parents, however, thought it was terrible. They always appeared faintly ashamed of Manda's money, which I thought was ironic considering she'd honed her financial management skills by organising the family budget before she hit her teens. And she still invested both of our parents' erratic income wisely and made sure they never ran short.

In fact, thanks to Dad composing the scores for huge blockbuster films since the Nineties, and Mum's enthusiastic love of art history earning her spot as an expert on an antiques valuation television show, my parents were both pretty wealthy. Not that they'd ever admit it. If they even knew. They shared a vague 'it'll all work out' approach to money and mostly ignored anything Miranda said about it.

'Urgh,' said Mum, predictably. 'It all sounds so immoral somehow, finance chat.'

I grinned at Miranda over Mum's shoulder and she scowled at me.

'Take the bottle into the lounge,' she said to Mum. 'We'll be in when we're done.'

'Is Dora asleep?' I asked. Friday nights were dreadful for my daughter's carefully crafted routine. She absolutely adored my parents and tended to run round like a mad thing for the first half of the evening, then drop.

'Curled up on the sofa like an angel,' Mum said, soppily. The adoration went both ways.

'And Freddie?'

'Playing piano with your father,' Mum said.

Freddie was Miranda's seven-year-old son who could be adorable and vile in equal measures but who had apparently inherited Dad's musical talent – much to our father's delight.

Mum opened the fridge, took out the bottle and retreated. I turned to Miranda, who'd finished the washing up.

'So, you saw the look, right?'

She nodded.

'What do you think it meant?'

Miranda shrugged. 'Probably something completely unrelated, knowing them,' she said. 'They were interested though. Dad especially. Do you think it is our Lil?'

'No,' I said, though I wasn't as sure as I sounded.

'Where did you see her name?' Miranda asked. She pulled out the wooden bench that lived under the kitchen table and sat down with a sigh. 'I'm exhausted. Freddie was up half the night.'

I didn't want to talk about Freddie; I wanted to talk about Lil.

'On a list of people approved to fly bombers,' I said.

'Did women fly planes in the war?'

I nodded. 'I don't know a whole lot about it, but it seems so. Not in combat, obviously.'

'Obviously,' said Miranda drily. 'It's funny that Lil's never mentioned this because it sounds amazing. Flying bombers?'

'Not just bombers,' I said. 'The records I found are from something called the Air Transport Auxiliary. They flew all the planes. Took them from the factories where they were built to wherever they were needed.'

'And it was women doing this?'

'Mostly,' I said. 'But men did it too. Jack Jones's grandad did it because he was too short-sighted to join the regular RAF, which is faintly terrifying.'

Miranda chuckled.

'But yes, mostly women. They called them the Attagirls.'

'I like that,' Miranda said. 'It's clever. And only a tiny bit patronising.'

It was my turn to laugh. 'They were really impressive,' I said.

'What's incredible,' Miranda said, shaking her head, 'is that I've never even heard of these women.'

'I've not heard much about them either,' I admitted. 'And it's literally my job.'

'If it was our Lil, I can't believe she's never talked about it,' said Miranda. 'It strikes me as something you'd want to talk about. It sounds wonderful.'

'She's always been vague when I've asked her about the war. Never really told me what she did.'

'She'd have only been about to turn sixteen when the war started,' Miranda said. I was impressed; I'd been sneakily counting on my fingers trying to add it up. 'And only twenty-one at the end.'

'Old enough to be doing something,' I pointed out. 'I had an idea she did office work.'

Miranda screwed up her nose. 'I can't believe we've never been interested enough to ask her for the details,' she said. 'That's terrible of us. You're a historian, Nell. You should be ashamed of yourself.'

I stuck my tongue out at her. 'I've asked her lots of times,' I said. 'She's always told me how boring it was and how she couldn't wait for the war to finish so she could travel.'

'Sounds like she was trying to make it sound dull enough so you wouldn't keep asking,' Miranda said.

I blinked at her. 'Oh God, it actually does sound like that,' I said. 'Do you think she saw some awful stuff? Or did some really brave things?'

'Lil?' Miranda said with a glint in her eye. 'Brave? I'd say so, wouldn't you?'

I thought about our great-aunt, who'd been the only person to step in when things were really tough for us back in the Nineties. Lil, who hated being in one place for long, but who'd stayed in London until she knew Miranda and I were okay and that our family wasn't about to fall apart. Lil, who regularly phoned Dad throughout our childhood and reminded him about parents' evenings, and exams, and even birthdays. I smiled.

'Definitely,' I said.

I perched on the table next to where Miranda was sitting on the bench, and put my feet up next to her. She frowned at me and I ignored her.

'The ATA girls flew every kind of aircraft,' I said. 'Massive bombers, and tiny fighter planes, and everything in between.'

'Do you think they got a hard time from people who didn't think they were capable?' Miranda asked, well aware of what it was like to be a woman in a man's world. 'I have lost count of the times someone's asked me to take minutes in a meeting, or fetch coffee.'

'Because you're the only woman?' I said, shocked but not entirely surprised. 'What do you say when that happens? Do you go?'

'It doesn't happen now because I'm in charge.' Miranda allowed herself a small, self-satisfied smile. 'But when I was starting out, I used to just do it – go and get the drinks, or hand round the biscuits.'

I winced. 'And when you weren't just starting out?'

'Once,' said Miranda coolly, 'I asked if I was expected to take the minutes with my vagina.'

'No, you didn't.'

'I did,' she said, laughing. 'That was one chief exec who never asked me to do that again.'

I was amazed by her bolshiness and said so. 'You definitely share that with Lil,' I pointed out. 'I expect she had to be bolshie if she was flying planes all over the place, just like you had to be a bit gobby to make it in your job.'

'She's definitely bolshie, our Lil. But I suppose we don't even know for sure the Lilian Miles on this list of yours is her,' Miranda said. 'It actually could be a coincidence, like you said.'

We both stayed quiet for a second, then Miranda spoke again.

'We should ask her,' she said.

'Ask her?'

Miranda nodded. 'Ask her.'

Chapter 5

Lilian

June 1944

It was late when I finally landed back at base. The sunny skies that had made flying such a joy were now chilly and as I slid out of the back of the Anson, I scanned the horizon. It was a clear night, which meant a good view for German bombers, and I wondered if there would be a raid later.

Once I'd signed the plane in and reported to the officer on duty, I picked up my bag and headed off towards the entrance of the airfield. I was tired and I wanted to get back to the digs that I shared with Annie and Flora. We needed to go over all the details of April's case, and I wanted to check if anything else had come up today.

'What's in your bag?'

The voice made me jump. I squinted into the lengthening shadows round the side of the mess hut.

'Who's there?'

'It's me.' The shadows changed into the shape of a man and out from the side of the building came Will Bates – one of the

RAF mechanics who worked on the base. He was funny and charming and I knew Rose was quite sweet on him.

'Hello, Will,' I said, gripping my bag slightly tighter. There was nothing incriminating in it; I'd given everything to April, but his level stare was making me nervous.

'You're always carrying a load of stuff,' he said. 'I just wondered what you were lugging around the whole time.'

We all carried overnight bags whenever we went on a trip because sometimes we couldn't get back to HQ. But the way he said it made me feel uncomfortable. I raised my chin.

'Been watching me, have you?'

To my surprise, Will looked a bit sheepish. 'I have as it happens,' he said.

I narrowed my eyes and stared at him. 'Why?'

He coughed in a sort of nervous way and I relaxed my grip on the straps of my bag, just a bit.

'Because you're pretty,' he muttered. 'And you look fun. I thought you might like to go dancing one evening, when we've both got the same day off.'

I closed my eyes briefly, feeling relief flood my senses.

Will smiled at me. He was a good-looking chap, with dark red hair and deep brown eyes. When he smiled, I got a glimpse of the little boy he'd once been – probably thanks to the sprinkling of freckles across his nose. I couldn't help but smile back.

'Dancing?' I said.

'Dancing.'

I leaned against the rough wall of the mess hut and took a breath.

'Will,' I began. Oh, how to even start explaining the mess my head was in, and the difficult feelings I had about men and women and the relationships between them.

'I'd like that,' I said. 'But maybe we could go as part of a group?'

Will studied me closely. 'A group,' he said.

'At first, at least.'

He grinned again. 'You're on,' he said. 'See you later.'

He pulled a packet of cigarettes out of his pocket and lit one, the flare from the match shining on the curl of his lip and the twinkle in his eye.

'Bye, Lil,' he said, sauntering away across the airfield.

I watched him go. 'Bye,' I said.

But as I turned towards the barracks, he stopped.

'Oh, Lil,' he said, with that boyish grin again. 'I know you're up to something.'

Unease gripped me, but I pretended I hadn't heard. I shifted my bag up my shoulder and carried on walking away from him. I didn't look back.

* * *

'He said what?' Annie said, when I told her about the conversation.

'That I was up to something,' I said. I was lying on my bed in my nightgown, even though it was still early. Missions like tonight's always exhausted me, and Will's appearance hadn't helped.

'You are up to something,' Flora pointed out. She was on my bed too, sitting by my feet. She had a sheaf of paper on her lap.

'That's why I'm so nervous,' I said. 'Between Rose sniffing around and Will Bates lurking in the shadows, I'm worried people are starting to suspect.'

'I am positive Will Bates knows nothing,' Annie said. 'He's just teasing you. Flirting.'

I scowled at her.

'I'm positive,' she repeated. 'He may be pretty …'

She paused to give Flora and me time to appreciate Will's handsome face in our imaginations.

'… but he's not the sharpest tool in the box.'

28

I smiled at Annie's bluntness. She certainly told it how it was and she did not suffer fools gladly. Her sharp brain made her a real asset to our little group, while Flora's organisational skills kept the whole thing running smoothly. I'd lost count of how many times I thanked my lucky stars that they'd both joined the ATA instead of using their skills in the War Office or behind a desk somewhere.

The first time we'd helped a woman, it was just by chance. Back in 1942 when we'd been doing our training in Luton there had been a girl in our pool called Polly. One evening we'd all been out – it was fun there, and there were a lot of army regiments stationed nearby, lads doing basic training just like us. Their presence always made for a good night. But that one evening, Polly didn't come home. She eventually arrived, much later, with her dress torn. She hadn't told us what had happened – she didn't have to. Quietly, me and Annie gave her a bath and cleaned her up, and tried not to wince at the bruises on her thighs.

A few weeks later, Annie caught Polly being sick in the toilet and realised she was pregnant.

'What am I going to do?' Polly had hissed at us in the bathroom that day, her face pale and her forehead beaded with sweat. 'I can't have a bloody baby.'

She'd gagged, just with the effort of speaking.

'I didn't even know his name.'

'We need to help her,' I told Annie.

'But what can we do?'

I'd shaken my head. 'I don't know,' I'd said. 'But we need to do something.'

I'd not known Annie long at that time, but I already knew she was someone I'd trust with my life.

'Someone helped me once,' I'd admitted. 'Not like this, not …'

Annie's eyes had searched my face. I'd squeezed my lips together in case I cried.

'And now you think we should help Polly?' she'd said.

I'd nodded.

'We'll find a way.'

And that's where Flora came in. She knew someone in Manchester. Someone who'd helped a friend of her sister. A doctor. At least, that's what he said he was and we never checked. Flora made the arrangements, Annie and I worked out the logistics and the transport, and Polly went off to Manchester just a fortnight later. She came back even paler, but after a couple of days' rest – we told our officers that she was having some women's troubles and they didn't push it – she was fine again.

We had thought that was it. But it wasn't. Polly told someone what we'd done for her, and quietly, word got round. Turned out there were women all over the place who needed help of one sort or another and it seemed we were the ones to help them. Gradually we built up a network of people, all over the country. Truth was, the network had existed long before we came along. We were just lucky that we could put people in touch with each other. Doctors who could do what we needed them to do, women desperate to adopt a baby, others willing to shelter a pregnant woman for a few weeks – or nurse someone who'd picked up an infection after their, you know, procedure.

We criss-crossed the country delivering planes, and sharing information or arrangements with women while we did it. In two years, we'd helped eleven women – April was number twelve. We'd seen five babies born and adopted and the rest, well, they'd been sorted. And we'd had one death, a young woman called Bet who lost too much blood after her op, and who'd been too scared to go to hospital in case she got into trouble. We didn't use that doctor again and we'd made sure we checked out new places now, but we were all haunted by Bet's death. Never thought about stopping though. Not once. And if losing one of our women wouldn't stop us helping others, nor would Will Bates and his clumsy flirting.

30

I sat up in bed and looked across at Annie, who was lying on her own bed next to mine.

'April's going to let us know when the baby comes,' I said. 'Don't reckon it'll be long.'

Annie nodded. 'Glad we got there in time.'

Flora was opening letters. We had a box at the local post office where people could contact us.

'Too late for this one, though,' she said, scanning the paper. 'She wrote this last month and she says she was already eight months gone then. She'll have had the baby by now.'

Annie shrugged. 'Can't help 'em all.'

But I wished we could.

Chapter 6

Helena

May 2018

It seemed Miranda and I weren't the only ones to be thinking about Lil. On Monday morning, just before lunch, the office receptionist phoned me to say I had a visitor.

'This is a nice surprise,' I said as the lift doors opened and I saw it was my dad. 'Are you working nearby?'

We were based in Soho, and Dad often worked close by when a film he'd composed the music on was in post-production. It wasn't unusual for him to pop by and say hello when he was in the area, but he normally phoned first.

Now he gave a vague nod over his shoulder. 'Nearby,' he said.

'I'm a bit busy at the moment but we could go for lunch in about half an hour if you like?'

But Dad shook his head. 'I wanted to ask you something,' he said. 'Could we nip into another room, perhaps?'

Behind his back, I saw Elly studiously bashing away at her keyboard, pretending not to be listening.

'Of course,' I said, a flicker of unease in my stomach. 'Follow me.'

I led him into the meeting room where I'd met Jack Jones the week before, and shut the door.

'Are you okay? What's the matter? Is Mum okay?'

Dad smiled. 'Nothing's the matter,' he said. 'We're both fine. Fit as fiddles.'

He gave a little skip as though to prove how fit he was even though he was approaching eighty. Mum wasn't far off seventy.

I raised my eyebrow at him and he pulled out a chair and sat down. I did the same.

'So what's up?'

'I wanted to ask you a favour,' he said.

'Go on.'

'I know you said you weren't supposed to do your own research, but any chance you could have a quick look into this Lil stuff for me?'

'Dad, no,' I said. 'I can't.'

'It's important.'

I stared at him. 'Why?' I said. 'Why is it important?'

Dad looked at his hands. 'No actual reason that I can put into words,' he said. 'I'd just like to know more about my family. Before it's too late.'

He took a breath.

'I never really asked my parents much about the war, and that generation just didn't talk about it, did they?'

I shook my head. More than once I'd come across the most amazing stories in the course of research that had never been mentioned in the family.

'I think the war was so awful, more awful than we could ever imagine, and those who lived through it found it hard to talk about,' I said.

'My father – your grandfather – was in the RAF.'

'I know,' I said. 'I've seen his medals.'

Dad nodded. 'Never mentioned it, not really,' he said. 'Not to us, at least not often. He had some old air force friends I remember him meeting up with, and I imagine they talked about what they'd done.'

'Their own version of group therapy,' I pointed out. 'Must have helped.'

'I wish I'd asked him more about it,' Dad said. He looked really sad and I thought suddenly that even though my grandpa had been dead for more than twenty years, he must still miss him.

I reached out and took his hand. 'He might not have talked, even if you'd asked,' I said. 'Did Grandma ever say anything?'

'Not about Dad in the air force,' Dad said. 'But, of course, I remember bits about the war. Not much, because I was very small. But I remember living with Mum, and not really knowing Dad when he came home.'

He paused.

'And I remember Lil,' he said.

'What do you remember?' I asked, intrigued by this little insight into my own family history.

'I remember her wearing a uniform,' Dad said slowly. He tilted his head to the left and looked far away over my shoulder. 'I remember sitting on her lap and playing with a toy plane and her arm round me felt scratchy, the material I mean. It was a uniform.'

'How old were you?'

He shrugged.

'About four, perhaps? I loved that plane.'

'Was that the one Lil brought you?'

'I always thought my father gave it to me,' he said. 'But now I really think about it, I seem to remember Lil bringing it. It's such a long time ago.'

'Uniforms and toy planes sound to me like that was our Lil on my list,' I said.

34

Dad nodded. 'That's what I thought.'

'Give me a minute,' I said.

Leaving him in the meeting room, I dashed back to my desk and found the Jack Jones file – now with all the papers back in the correct order.

'Everything okay?' Elly said, super-casually.

'Dad worked with Jack Jones,' I said, sort of truthfully. Dad had indeed done some music for the TV show Jack had starred in – though he never met the actors as a rule. 'On that detective thing. He wanted to check something.'

Elly looked dubious but she didn't say anything.

I took the folder back to the meeting room and showed Dad the list with Lilian Miles on it.

'So, she flew planes?' Dad said in awe. 'Bloody hell.'

I nodded. 'Amazing, right?'

'Could you check her records?'

'Dad,' I said, in a warning tone.

'There must be service records,' he said, not put off by my frown. 'Surely they'd help us find out if it's her? We know her date and place of birth; it shouldn't be hard to cross-reference.'

'I can't, Dad,' I said. 'It's completely verboten to do our own research. I could lose my job.'

I grinned at him.

'You could do it, or Mum. She knows about research. Though it's expensive to subscribe to some of the databases.'

Dad shook his head. 'Oh, Nell, you know what we're like with computers. We just don't have the skills,' he said. 'I'm not bad on the email business but anything more complicated just flummoxes me. I'm no spring chicken.'

I patted his hand reassuringly. 'You do brilliantly,' I lied, knowing he was right. He and Mum struggled to work their television.

'What about if you did it outside work?'

'I don't know,' I said. 'It just feels so wrong because I found

35

the information at work. It's not right to use company resources for personal searches. I could get into trouble.'

'Your boss wouldn't know, Miranda said,' Dad pointed out.

I shrugged. 'I can't,' I said again. 'Why are you so interested?'

'I told you, I just want to know about my family,' Dad said. But he didn't meet my eyes when he said it. What was he hiding?

'There is something we can do, though,' I said, watching him carefully.

Dad looked hopeful. 'What?'

'We could ask her.'

'Ask her,' Dad repeated, just as I'd done when Miranda suggested it.

Before I could continue, there was a knock on the door of the meeting room and Fliss stuck her head round, her long blonde hair swinging.

'Sorry, Helena,' she said. 'I thought I'd booked this room?'

Guiltily, I gathered up the Jack Jones papers I'd been showing Dad and smiled. 'Just an unplanned meeting,' I said. 'We'll get out of your way.'

I went to hustle Dad out of the room, before Fliss realised I'd been mixing up work and personal stuff, but it was too late. She was looking at Dad curiously.

'Fliss Hopkins,' she said, holding out her hand for him to shake.

'Robert Miles.'

She beamed at him. 'Helena's father?'

'Indeed,' said Dad giving her a dazzling smile. He was such a charmer.

'I was just going over some Jack Jones research when Dad popped in to see if I was free for lunch,' I said.

'But Helena tells me she is far too busy to join me, so I will bid you farewell,' Dad said smoothly making me wonder if he'd always been such a good liar.

'Nice to meet you,' said Fliss.

36

She stood back to let us leave the room then entered herself, leaving the door open.

'Let me think about it,' I said as I showed Dad to the lift, hoping Fliss hadn't realised I had been showing Dad my Jack Jones research and that she didn't decide to have a look at it herself. 'I can't search Lil's records, not without putting my job at risk, but I'll have a think about what else we can do.'

Dad kissed me goodbye. 'Thanks, Helena,' he said. 'It means a lot to me.'

Chapter 7

Lilian

September 1939

I cycled as slowly as I could through the village, wobbling on my bike because I wasn't going fast enough to keep my balance.

'Morning, Lil,' Marcus the postman called. 'Mind how you go.'

I ignored him, concentrating on keeping my legs going round. I had an ache in my stomach and my limbs felt heavy and hard to control.

'By lunchtime it'll be over,' I whispered to myself over and over as I cycled. 'By lunchtime it'll be over.'

I could see the house up ahead, squatting at the end of the village like a slug, and growing bigger as I approached. I slid off my bicycle and chained it to the fence, and then, dragging my heels, walked up the path to the front door. Before I could knock, it opened. My piano teacher's wife stood there. She was dressed to go out, wearing her hat and holding her gloves in one hand and her handbag in the other. I wanted to cry.

'Lilian,' she said, beaming at me 'How nice to see you. He's in the music room – go on through.'

I forced a smile. 'Thank you, Mrs Mayhew,' I muttered, slinking past her. She was so pretty and fresh-looking in her summer dress. I felt her eyes on me as I went and wondered if she knew. If she could tell. I felt dirty. No, not dirty. Filthy.

At the music room door, I paused. Then I lifted my hand and knocked.

'Come,' said Mr Mayhew. Taking a breath, I went.

Mr Mayhew was sitting at the piano, making pencil notes on some sheet music that was on the stand.

'Ah, Lilian,' he said. 'You're late.'

He turned round on the stool and gave me a dazzling smile. My breath caught in my throat. Always when I wasn't with him, he became a monster in my head. Then, when I saw him again – saw his dark, swarthy good looks and his broad shoulders – I wondered what I had been worrying about.

'Come and sit,' he said, shifting over on the padded stool. 'Let's play something fun to get warmed up.'

I put down my music case and settled myself next to him. I felt the warmth of his body as his thigh brushed mine when I sat, but I couldn't move away because the stool was too small.

Mr Mayhew – I couldn't call him Ian, even though he'd told me to – moved a sheet of music to the front of the bundle on the stand. It was a Bach piece that had been one of my favourites, long ago when I was still a child.

He turned to me, his face just inches from mine. I smelled coffee on his breath and tried not to recoil as nausea overwhelmed me.

'Ready?' he said.

I nodded, putting my hands on to the keys.

'Two, three, four ...' he counted us in.

I knew the music by heart, so as I played I shut my eyes and imagined I was anywhere but in this stuffy room, with Mr Mayhew's body heat spreading through my thin cotton frock.

39

At the end of the piece, Mr Mayhew stood up and I felt myself relax. Slightly.

'Good,' he said, strolling over to the window and gazing out into the garden. 'Now let's go through your examination pieces. Start with the Brahms.'

I relaxed a bit more, realising he wanted to concentrate on music today.

'Could you open a window, please?' I asked. 'It's very warm.'

He nodded and pushed the sash upwards. 'Are you feeling well?' he asked me, his brow furrowed in concern. 'You're very pale.'

I swallowed. 'I'm fine,' I said. 'It's just the heat.'

Mr Mayhew came over to where I sat and stood behind me. Gently, he reached out and stroked the back of my neck.

'Lilian,' he said gruffly. 'Is something wrong?'

I froze. My stomach was squirming and I wasn't sure I could put how I was feeling into words. How could I tell him I'd wanted his approval for months, so badly that I almost felt a physical ache when I played a wrong note. That when he smiled at me my heart sang with the most beautiful music. That when he told me I was special to him, I wanted to throw myself into his arms and stay there forever. And yet, as spring had blossomed into early summer, and he had kissed me for the first time, I'd gone home feeling confused and guilty. When, just a week later, he had put his hand up my skirt while I played, his fingers probing and hurting, I'd gasped in fear and he'd nodded.

'Like that?' he said, his voice thick. 'I thought you would. I knew what you wanted from the day you walked in here.'

I'd stayed still, not understanding what he was doing. Not wanting to upset him by asking him to stop. Because I had wanted this. Hadn't I?

Now, after our lessons he would kiss me, and touch me – and make me touch him too. I didn't know how to say no. Because

40

I'd started this, hadn't I? And sometimes he came to school to meet me at the gate and give me music he'd copied for me by hand – see how much cared – and we walked home the long way through the woods. And he'd take me by the hand and lower me into the soft moss below one of the trees and unbuckle his belt and …

I found that by imagining playing the piano I could pretend it wasn't happening. And then when it was over, Mr Mayhew would always be so kind. He would brush leaves from my hair, and tell me how precious I was. I never cried until I was alone.

Now, feeling his fingers on the back of my neck, I waited for what he would do next.

'Are you cross with me?' he murmured. 'Because I wanted you to play first?'

'No,' I said. 'I want to play.'

'You tease me,' he said. He trailed his fingers over my collarbone and down to my bust, and I closed my eyes.

And then the front door banged shut and he pulled away as if my faded cotton dress was prickly.

'Ian,' Mrs Mayhew called. 'Ian, are you there?'

She came into the music room without knocking, which she never did. Mr Mayhew was very strict about that. Not a surprise, I supposed, given what we were often doing instead of playing piano.

Mrs Mayhew's hat was askew and her hair was escaping from its roll. She had a streak of dust across the front of her dress and her forehead was beaded with sweat. I'd never seen her look so flustered; she was normally perfectly groomed.

'Oh, Ian,' she wailed. 'Ian, have you heard the news?'

Mr Mayhew stiffened next to me. 'He's done it, has he?' he said. 'He's bloody gone and done it?'

A tear rolled down Mrs Mayhew's face, leaving a clean track in the grime on her cheek.

'I ran all the way from the village,' she said. 'They were talking

41

about it on the street. Mrs Armitage was sitting at the war memorial, just weeping.'

I felt sicker than I had moments before. Mrs Armitage had lost both her sons in the Great War. The war we'd been told would end all wars. The war that my own father never talked about.

'What does this mean?' I stammered. 'Is it Hitler? What has he done?'

Mr Mayhew patted me on the head distractedly, his full attention on his wife.

'He's sent his troops into Poland,' he said. 'And Mr Chamberlain promised that if he did that, then …' His voice trailed off.

'I need to go home,' I said. 'I need to find Bobby.'

Mrs Mayhew looked at me for the first time. I didn't think she'd even realised I was there before then.

'Bobby,' she said vaguely. 'Who is Bobby?'

I was already halfway out of the door. 'He's my brother,' I said over my shoulder. 'I need to find my brother.'

Chapter 8

Helena

May 2018

Work was crazily busy for the next few days and I didn't have any time to think about Lil for a while. Until Jack Jones turned up at the office again – much to my surprise.

'I'm sorry to bother you,' he said when I went down to reception to see him. 'I was having lunch with my agent nearby, and thinking about everything you'd found out and I wanted to see how you were getting on.'

I gave him a small, forced smile. 'Yeah, all good,' I said vaguely. I was getting on pretty well with his research, but I wasn't happy about him checking up on me in this way.

'Oh God,' he said. 'Does this look like I'm checking up on you?'

He was so close to what I was thinking that I stared at him in horror.

'It does a bit,' I admitted, unable to think of anything else to say but the truth. 'The celebs aren't normally this interested.'

He grinned at me, pushing a lock of his curls out of his dark eyes, and I felt myself melting, just a bit.

'I'm being a nightmare,' he said.

'It's fine.' I was feeling slightly odd. 'Do you want to come upstairs?'

I took him up to the office and we sat in the same meeting room as before. Elly was at lunch, thank goodness, else she'd have been hovering to see what Jack wanted.

I offered him a coffee and tried to disguise my relief when he turned it down.

'I had an early start today so I've had more than enough caffeine already,' he said, with the same cheeky grin. 'It makes me a bit bouncy.'

'I wish you'd bounce my way,' I thought to myself and then blinked in surprise. What was happening here? I'd barely looked at a man since Greg and I had fallen apart. Being a heartbroken single mother hardly made me a catch. And yet, here I was, fluttering my eyelashes at a real-life celebrity who was as likely to fancy me back as – well, as Greg I supposed.

I swallowed. 'I've found out quite a lot about your grandparents, and your great-grandparents,' I said carefully looking away from where his T-shirt hugged his broad chest. 'It's relatively simple to research just one or two generations back.'

I leafed through my folder to find the right documents.

'Do you not know any of this already?'

Jack shook his head.

'My maternal grandparents came over from Jamaica in the Fifties,' he said. 'They had one daughter already, and my mum was the first of their children to be born here. She's the middle child – I've got two aunties.'

I nodded, interested. We'd not researched his maternal family at all so this was all new to me.

'My grandad was a bus driver and my gran was a nurse. They worked really, really hard and they wanted a better life for their kids – my mum and my aunties.'

I nodded again.

'And then Mum decided she wanted to be a writer, which wasn't really in their plan,' he said with a smile. I could see he was really proud of his family and my heart swelled a tiny bit more. 'But they were so supportive of her. And she worked all the way through university to pay for herself.'

'They all sound amazing,' I said.

'Then Mum met my dad,' Jack said. 'And it all went a bit wrong for a while.'

'Wrong, how?'

'He wasn't a bad bloke, by all accounts. He seemingly loved Mum and they planned to get married. But she found out she was pregnant and he got scared, I think.'

I rolled my eyes. 'Same old story,' I said sharply.

Jack looked at me with interest. 'Sounds like you mean that,' he said.

I gave him a grim smile. 'Happened to me,' I said, wondering why on earth I was sharing my story with him and yet somehow unable to resist.

'My boyfriend legged it when I got pregnant,' I said. 'Well, I legged it actually but only after he'd given me a brochure for an abortion clinic.'

'Ah,' said Jack.

'Ah.'

'And did you, erm …?'

I smiled properly this time and showed him the photo on my phone. 'Dora's two,' I said. 'And she's not seen Greg for more than a year. He took a job in Canada.'

Jack winced. 'What a douche,' he said.

I suddenly felt uncomfortable, sharing so much with a stranger. 'It's fine,' I said. 'We're fine.' I smiled. 'Show me a family that doesn't have a baby born with the whiff of a scandal and I'll show you a family that knows how to keep secrets.'

45

Jack nodded sadly. 'My dad's family were quite traditional and a mixed-race grandkid born out of wedlock didn't really work for them.'

I patted his hand, trying hard to fight the temptation to gather him up into my arms. He looked so sad.

'I met them a few times, and my dad was around a bit when I was younger, but he got married to someone else and his visits got less and less frequent. By the time I was ten, I never saw him at all.'

'Did you miss him?' I was fairly sure Dora never gave Greg a second thought but I worried she would as she got older.

He shook his head. 'I'd never had a proper relationship with him.'

'How did you find out he'd died?'

'Solicitor,' Jack said, shrugging. 'He left me some money.'

'So he was thinking about you after all.'

'I think that makes it worse,' Jack said. 'Because he could have just rung, you know? And I'm doing okay, in my career. I didn't need his money – but I needed a dad.'

I breathed out. This was so sad. I hoped he'd be as honest with the camera crew when they filmed his story – it would make a great episode.

'And you want to know more about his family now?'

'I know lots about my Caribbean side. I know everything. I've met everyone. I know the recent history and I know further back – the murky bits. The nasty, horrible, slavery bits.'

I nodded again.

'And I'm really aware that I can only go so far back on that side of my family. We will never be able to go much further than a few generations because no one kept records. I don't know where we came from, or what my ancestors did, and I will never be able to find out.'

'So now you're filling the gap on the other side instead?' I said, understanding now where his drive to discover his family came from.

'That's the plan.' He gave me a little sheepish smile. 'Sorry to be so demanding.'

I smiled back at him and for a second we stayed that way, eyes locked, smiling at each other, until I dropped my gaze. What was I doing?

'I don't mind at all,' I said honestly. 'Happy to help.'

'Did you find out anything about your own family mystery?'

I didn't understand what he was talking about. Did he mean Greg? I knew where he was. I looked at him blankly. 'What mystery?'

'Your Lilian Miles,' he said.

'Oh, Lilian. No, not really. I don't think there's anything mysterious about it all …'

'But?'

'But there was a look between my parents, when I mentioned what I'd found.'

Jack sat up a bit straighter. 'And?' he said.

'And my dad turned up here and asked me to research her some more.'

'Interesting,' said Jack, raising his eyebrows.

'I chatted about it with my sister …'

'You've got a sister?'

'I've got two,' I said, finding the way his mind darted between subjects a bit disconcerting. Maybe he had drunk too much coffee. 'And a brother.'

'Awesome,' Jack said. 'So what did your sister say?'

'She said I should ask my great-aunt what she did during the war and whether this Lilian Miles is her.'

'Seems reasonable enough.'

'I suggested that to Dad,' I went on.

'And what did he say?'

I frowned. 'He didn't really say anything because we were interrupted. He was very keen for me to research her, though. I don't understand why.'

'I understand,' Jack said.

I stared at him. 'You do?'

'I understand what it's like not to know about part of your family,' he explained. 'Maybe your dad feels the same.'

'Perhaps,' I said, doubtfully. 'But he knows all about Lil. She even lived with us for a while. She's hardly an enigma.'

Jack grinned. 'But you don't know about her war.'

'Well, no …'

'So she is an enigma. At least part of her life is.'

I shook my head, feeling like he'd just backed me into a corner. 'Dad was hiding something,' I said thoughtfully, almost to myself. 'It was like he didn't want to tell me the real reason he was so keen.'

'You have to find out more,' Jack said.

Eagerly, he took my hand and I felt a jolt like the electric shocks I always got off the dodgy lift buttons in the office. Surprised, I pulled my hand away and he looked embarrassed.

'Sorry,' he said. 'I shouldn't have done that.'

'No, don't apologise,' I blustered. 'I just got an electric shock is all.'

He smiled at me. 'Sorry,' he said again. 'Next time I take your hand, I'll warn you in advance so you can earth yourself.'

'Next time,' I said, sounding robotic and as though I didn't really understand the words, like Eleven from *Stranger Things*.

We smiled at each other and I felt myself flush.

'So, yeah,' I said briskly, to break the awkward moment. 'Dad wants me to look at the service records but I explained I'm not allowed. Fliss is very strict about us not researching our own family history at work.'

'Use my research,' Jack said.

'I beg your pardon?'

'Use my family as a cover. Find Frank Jones in the ATA and look up Lil while you're at it.'

'I really don't think that's a good idea,' I said. 'It's too risky.

We can all see each other's searches. What if someone twigs I'm looking up my family? I can't lose my job.'

Jack shrugged. 'Just an idea,' he said. 'No need to decide now. Why not think about it?'

I smiled despite my misgivings. 'Okay, then,' I said. 'I'll think about it. But for now, I'm just going to talk to Lil.'

Jack grinned again. His smile was infectious.

'Great,' he said. 'Let me know how you get on.'

Chapter 9

I thought about how best to approach the subject with Lil all weekend. Several times I picked up the phone to speak to her in her care home down in Surrey, then changed my mind. I'd go and see her in person, I thought. And anyway, I didn't know for sure yet that she was the Lilian Miles on the ATA list. The only way to find out was to double-check the service record – under the cover of checking Frank Jones of course. If – and it was a big if – I decided to go down that road, I couldn't do it until I was back at work on Monday and had access to all the databases.

Work, as always, was busy that week. Filming was starting on the next series of the show and it was all hands on deck to check the last few details. I was kept busy all day Monday and most of Tuesday going over the royal connections of a Sixties' pop star who was a distant relation of Lady Jane Grey, while Elly raced round trying to find a historian who was an expert in prostitution to talk to a celebrity chef whose ancestor ran a high-class brothel in Victorian Manchester.

Late on Tuesday afternoon, the phone on my desk rang.

'Helena?' I recognised those clipped tones immediately.

'Jack,' I said, ignoring the way my heart thumped. 'Hello.'

50

Next to me, Elly raised an eyebrow.

I spun round in my chair so I had my back to her.

'What's up?' I asked Jack.

'I've been doing a bit of research,' he said. 'Thought you might like to see it.'

'Research?' I said, sounding a bit stupid. 'What kind of research?'

'I tracked down my uncle. My father's brother.'

'You did? That's wonderful. Was he pleased to hear from you?' I could hear Jack smiling at the other end of the phone.

'He actually was,' he said. 'Turns out he's a big fan of *Mackenzie*.'

Mackenzie was the detective show Jack starred in.

'I'm so pleased,' I said. 'Are you going to meet up?'

'We are. He says he's got some photos to show me.'

'That's great,' I said, honestly. 'Do you think he'll chat to you on camera? It's always good to get social history from people who have actual memories.'

'I'm sure he'd be game,' Jack said. I scribbled down a note to mention it to the director of his show.

'... service records,' Jack was saying.

'I'm sorry, I missed that,' I said. 'What was that about service records?'

'I thought we could check them together, to find out more about my grandfather's time in the ATA,' he said. Then he lowered his voice, even though no one but me could hear him. 'We could see if my grandad knew Lilian Miles. Maybe they worked together. Have you spoken to her yet? Did you find out if she's one of your relatives? Wouldn't that be utterly amazing?'

'You are the keenest celebrity I've ever worked with,' I said.

Jack laughed. 'I'm sorry.'

'Don't apologise – it's nice,' I said. 'And I understand why you're so eager. It's just unusual.'

'So did you speak to her?'

'Not yet,' I said. 'But I'm planning to.'

I paused, aware of my colleagues – especially Elly of course – all around me.

'What you said, about the service records,' I said, choosing my words carefully. 'Perhaps we could check them.'

'Of course.' Jack sounded pleased. 'I'm guessing it will be better for our cover story if we do it together.'

'I agree,' I said cautiously, still nervous about the plan. Was I going to regret this? Especially considering the chaos he'd brought with him when he came to the office last week. Though, I thought, he'd been far less disruptive when he came in the second time. And I found I really wanted to see him again.

Mentally I started checking my plans for the week. I'd finished with the Sixties' pop star now, so tomorrow and Thursday was more Sarah Sanderson research, and I'd planned to set aside Friday to look into Jack's research. Maybe Jack could pop by the office late on Friday afternoon and we could look it all up together, and have a sneaky look at Lilian Miles while we were at it. I could duplicate all our findings and make him his own file to take away, so he wouldn't mess up my own folders. And I could get Mum to collect Dora from nursery and take her back to theirs for our Friday dinner.

'How about Friday afternoon?' I said. 'About fourish?'

'Sorry, no can do.' Jack sounded genuinely fed up. 'I'm filming on Friday.'

'Oh that's a shame. I can email you anything I find out …'

'Are you free now?'

'Now?'

'Let's do the research now. Unless you're snowed under?'

Elly prodded me in the back and when I glanced over my shoulder at her, she made a kissing face. I stuck my tongue out at her.

'Erm,' I said. 'I suppose so.'

'I can be there in half an hour?' Jack said.

'Great,' I said, feeling a little bit railroaded. 'See you then.'

It was more like an hour and a half later when Jack strolled into the office. Most of the researchers, including Elly much to my relief, had gone home, and I'd had to call Mum in a panic and ask her to get Dora for me. I was, for the gazillionth time, thankful that I'd chosen to live so close to my parents when Greg and I split up. It may have seemed a backwards step – though not as backwards as staying in Miranda's annexe while she was between au pairs had seemed – but it had been a good decision.

Jack looked completely different from how he was last week. His hair was swept back off his face, and he was wearing good jeans, a black T-shirt, and a nice leather biker jacket. He really was gorgeous. I felt slightly wobbly when he grinned at me as he approached my desk. Then his face fell as he clocked that there was no one else around.

'God,' he said. 'Am I making you work late?'

'No,' I lied. 'I had some things to do anyway.'

Jack peeled off the jacket, bundled it up and threw it down on the floor under Elly's desk. I itched to shake it out and hang it up, but I didn't. Then he sat down in Elly's chair and spun round so he was facing me.

'What do we do first?' he asked.

My head was spinning – and not just from the way he looked or the smell of his aftershave. He was like a whirlwind, coming into my carefully ordered space and throwing everything around, metaphorically and literally I thought as his elbow caught a book that was on my desk and sent it crashing to the floor.

'Oops,' he said. He picked it up and put it on Elly's desk, then turned his attention back to me.

'How come you've not spoken to your aunt yet?'

Completely unable to think straight with his eyes trained on me, I opened my mouth like a guppy and nothing came out.

'Your Aunt Lilian?' Jack said carefully. 'You were going to speak to her.'

'I've not really had a chance,' I said. 'I've been busy.'

Jack sat back in Elly's chair and put his feet up on her desk. He looked at me with a cheeky smile and said: 'Sounds like there's something holding you back. Tell me everything.'

So I did.

Well not everything. But I explained that Lil was very special to me and my siblings, so it was strange we didn't know she'd been a pilot. Jack listened intently.

'Miranda – that's my sister, remember I mentioned her before? She's very black and white and she can't see why I won't just ask Lil,' I told him. 'Dad's the same. But I'm worried this could be something traumatic for her. If she is the Lilian Miles on the list, there has to be a reason for her not mentioning it for over seventy years. She's quite frail now and I don't want to upset her.'

'You want to make sure it really is her before you go to her,' Jack said, nodding. 'I get that.'

'There could be something in the records that gives us a clue about why she might not have mentioned it,' I said. 'Sometimes we find reports of actions that might have been upsetting. Maybe someone died – as far as I know some of the ATA did die. Amy Johnson, for one.'

'I've heard of her,' Jack said in delight. 'She was in the ATA was she?'

I nodded. 'Crashed in bad weather,' I told him. 'Obviously Lil didn't die, but maybe she lost a friend? Or was in some sort of accident? It could be anything.'

'You're very caring,' Jack said.

He pulled his chair closer to mine and I got another whiff of his aftershave.

'You look different,' I said, unable to resist commenting, and wanting to shift his attention off me.

'I was doing a press conference for the new series of *Mackenzie*,' he said, pulling at his T-shirt self-consciously. 'My agent always makes me dress up for them.'

He leaned closer to me.

'I just wear what she tells me to wear,' he said, in a low voice even though there was no one around to hear him. 'I'm hopeless with fashion and stuff. She gets a stylist to buy me clothes.'

He looked down at himself and then back at me with a funny, embarrassed grin. 'What do you think?'

'Of the clothes?' I stammered. 'Oh, nice. You look, erm, great.'

Jack smiled properly now. 'So do you,' he said.

I felt a blush crawl up my neck and on to my face so I turned away. 'Service records,' I said hurriedly. Thank goodness I never met the celebrities if I developed thumping big crushes like this one on them all.

'Service records,' Jack echoed.

We had access to so many databases, that it was hard to keep track. We used most of the Second World War ones often, but I'd never had the need to search the ATA archive before. I hoped that meant none of my colleagues checked it very often either and no one would notice me searching for a Miles family member.

It took me a while to find the right site, then check the folder where we stored all our shared logins and type it in.

When the site eventually loaded, I breathed out in relief. It was formatted exactly like most of the Forces sites. 'It's all very easy,' I explained. 'We just need to search for the name and the dates. Your grandfather …'

'No, do Lilian first,' Jack said. 'Go on – I really want to know if she's your aunt.'

With hands that trembled slightly, knowing I was doing something wrong and that Fliss would be furious if she caught me, I typed *Lilian Miles* and *1940–45* into the search bar and pressed return.

It took a while, but it brought up just one result. *Lilian Miles*, it said, *15/10/23, Air Transport Auxiliary*. I gasped.

'That's her,' I said. 'That's Lil's date of birth.'

'Click on it,' Jack urged.

I shook my head, wobbling again over what I was doing. 'I

don't need to,' I said. 'We know it's her now. We don't need to know any more.'

'You said you might be able to work out if there was anything upsetting from looking at the records,' Jack pointed out.

'I don't want to,' I said.

But Jack leaned across me and clicked on Lil's name, and the screen filled with details. It had Lil's personal information – her date and place of birth, her age when she joined up, and where she did her basic training.

I glared at him, but I wasn't really cross. It was too interesting.

I scanned the page, trying to take it all in. Lilian had done so much when she had been so young. And then, right at the bottom of the screen was what I assumed was the reason for Lil never mentioning her time in the ATA.

Jack saw it at the same time as I did.

'Ah,' he said.

There, in large capital letters, it said: DISHONOURABLE DISCHARGE.

Chapter 10

Lilian

June 1944

I stayed stock-still as Flora drew a line up the back of my calf.

'It tickles,' I giggled.

'Don't move,' she warned. 'I've got very steady hands but I can't keep it straight if you wiggle. There, done.'

I twisted round so I could see her handiwork. I'd covered my legs in gravy browning. Flora's addition – which was more gravy browning, but made up to a thicker paste – made it look like I was wearing nylon stockings.

'Not bad,' I said, approvingly. 'Shall I do you now?'

'Make sure it's straight,' Flora said. She hitched up her skirt and I took the narrow brush from the pot and started to draw.

'Are you excited?'

I concentrated on keeping the line straight. 'I love dancing,' I said. 'You know I love music.'

'Maybe you can get up on stage with the band.' Flora chuckled. 'Show them all how it's done.'

'Maybe,' I said, wishing I could. I missed playing piano more

57

than anything else. There was a church hall in the nearby village with a rackety old upright in the corner and sometimes I sneaked in there, but it wasn't the same.

'When this bloody war is over, I'm going to play the piano every single day,' I told Flora.

She smiled over her shoulder at me. 'I'm going to wear stockings that dogs don't want to lick,' she said.

From across the hut, Annie joined in. 'And I'm going to wear clothes that fit,' she said, hitching her belt a notch tighter. Our rations didn't seem to be going as far any more and we were all far skinnier than we'd been when the war started.

'All done,' I said, finishing Flora's seams.

She peered over her shoulder and clapped her hands in pleasure. 'Gorgeous, darling,' she said. 'Are you sure you don't mind us tagging along with you and Will?'

I shook my head vigorously. 'Not in the least,' I said. 'He seems nice enough, but I don't want to be getting into romance and complications. Not here. Not now.'

Flora turned round and gazed at me, her blue eyes unblinking. I thought she was going to ask me if I was being completely honest, but she didn't and I was grateful. Instead she squeezed my hand.

'We'll stick together,' she said. 'Like the Three Musketeers.'

I grinned. 'One for all and all for one,' I said. I threaded my arm through hers and then through Annie's and we walked to the door, ready to go and meet Will.

He was waiting by the mess hut, laughing with a couple of other mechanics and smoking a cigarette.

'Evening, ladies,' he said, straightening up as we approached. 'Lilian.'

I nodded to him. 'Will,' I said.

We fell into step as we walked down the short road to where the dance was being held. We could hear the music as we got closer and my spirits lifted a bit.

'Like dancing?' Will said.

I smiled. 'I love it.'

Inside the hall was pulsing with life. We'd all been flying non-stop for weeks, getting planes in position for the landings on the beaches in France. We'd not known what was happening of course – we only found out afterwards. But we were proud to have played a part in something so important. The hard work of the last few weeks, though, meant everyone was desperate for some fun – and from the look of the hall they were already having it.

The men mostly wore RAF uniforms. They were jiving with girls in bright red lipstick, their hair shining and, I saw with a relieved smile, gravy browning on their legs. There were a few GIs; I guessed they were passing through. They were getting a lot of attention with girls flocking round them like bees round a honey pot. Some of those girls, I couldn't help noticing, wore actual Nylon stockings. On the stage was a small band with a pianist, a drummer, a trumpet player and a female singer. Like I always did – and knowing I was being stupid – I scanned their faces, pausing a second longer on the pianist, just in case.

Will steered us over to a table in the corner. 'Have a seat,' he said. 'I'll get some drinks.'

'Want to dance?' Flora said.

I shook my head. 'Not yet, I just want to sit here and soak it all up.' It was ages since there had been a dance near enough for us all to go to. 'You go – I'll be fine.'

'Sure?' Flora looked concerned.

'I'm sure,' I said. 'Will's just gone for some drinks and you'll be right over there.'

Flora, Annie and Will's friends swirled off to the dance floor and I sat drinking in the atmosphere. I loved everything about it. The heat coming off the dancers, the cloud of smoke from people's cigarettes, the buzz of conversation fighting with the music from the band. Everything. I thought I'd like to play in a dance band one day. If I ever got tired of flying.

'You look happy,' Will said, handing me a glass of something.

I smelled it – cider I thought – and took a suspicious sip. It was sweet and slightly fizzy.

'I love this,' I said to Will as he drew up a chair next to me. 'I love how the music just makes everyone forget about their worries and throw off their responsibilities.'

'The music and the cider,' Will said, with a wink.

I laughed.

'So, Lilian Miles,' Will carried on. 'Tell me your story.'

I blinked at him. What did he mean?

'Not much to tell,' I said airily.

'How did you end up in the ATA?'

'Oh, just thought it sounded fun,' I said vaguely. 'My brother's in the RAF and I didn't think he should be the only one who got to fly.'

Will looked impressed. 'Must be in your blood,' he said. 'You've certainly got the knack.'

I bristled, just a little bit. 'I've worked hard.'

'Course.' Will caught the edge to my voice and changed the subject.

'Let me tell you about something Gareth did earlier ...' he began.

As he told the funny story, I started to relax. Will was very easy to be with – he had a sharp eye for people's quirks and a funny way of telling stories. I laughed as he told an anecdote about some of the RAF officers on the base. He was a lovely man, I thought.

'Dance?' he eventually suggested and I nodded. He took my hand and led me out to the floor, swinging me round as another jive track started. He wasn't the best dancer but what he lacked in skill he made up for in enthusiasm, whirling me backwards and forwards across the floor until I was breathless and giddy.

'Having fun?' Annie spun past me, on the arm of one of Will's friends, called Frank.

'Lots of fun,' I gasped. I was happier than I'd been for ages. Months. Years, perhaps. Not for the first time in my life, I marvelled at just how wonderful music was at making everything seem better.

'Come with me,' Annie said, grabbing my hand. 'Will, you get us some more drinks.'

Will saluted Annie jokingly and, giggling madly, Annie, Flora and I crowded into the lav where two women were checking their hair at the mirror.

'So?' said Flora, craning her neck to check her seams were still in place on the back of her legs.

'So what?' I looked at my reflection. My hair was coming loose and my cheeks were flushed.

'Do you like him?'

'Will?'

'No, Father Christmas. Of course, Will,' Annie said.

I leaned against the wall. 'He's lovely,' I said. 'He's so funny, and charming. And he loves to dance.'

'Uh-oh,' said Flora. 'I think someone has a crush.'

I felt myself blush. 'That's just the thing,' I said with a sigh. I waited for the two girls who'd been doing their hair to leave so it was just the three of us. 'I don't.'

Annie looked at me. 'Really?'

I shook my head, sadly. 'Nothing,' I said. 'I wish I felt something – a spark or something – but I don't.'

Flora draped an arm round my shoulder. 'Darling Lil,' she said. 'I know you play your cards close to your chest.'

'And a lovely chest it is,' Annie drawled. She sat up on the sink next to me and lit a cigarette as Flora nudged her to be quiet.

'When I joined up, I never thought I'd be lucky enough to meet two girls like you,' Flora went on. 'I was so bloody scared and you made it better.'

I smiled at her. I felt the same.

'And I know you don't want to talk about what happened to you,' she said. I dropped my eyes from hers. It was too hard to think about and I was grateful the girls knew something was wrong inside of me, but never pushed me to elaborate. Flora squeezed me a bit tighter. 'But I also know that we are all a bit damaged. Some more than others. That's just life. And if you don't want to be with Will, then don't force it. Maybe it'll happen later, maybe it won't. It's fine either way.'

I felt tears heavy behind my eyelids and blinked them away. 'Thanks,' I whispered.

Annie jumped down from the sink. 'Thank God none of us are flying tomorrow,' she said, stubbing out her cigarette. 'I'm more than a bit tiddly.'

'It's a shame, though,' Flora said. 'Because if one of us had been on that trip to Newcastle, we could have …'

'Shh,' said Annie covering Flora's mouth with her hand. She nodded towards the cubicles. The one at the end was shut. Flora's eyes widened in shock.

'Bloody hell,' I breathed. None of us had noticed that someone else was in the lav with us.

We all stared at each other for a second, grateful Annie had noticed when she did and stopped Flora before she said anything incriminating.

'Let's go home,' I said.

As we turned to leave the tiny toilet, we heard whoever it was in the cubicle pull the chain.

'Let's go,' I said again, suddenly desperate to be out of there. 'It's past my bedtime.'

Chapter 11

Helena

May 2018

I was too surprised to do anything but stare at the screen. Above the red stamp declaring that Lil had been dishonourably discharged, it also said Lil had been court-martialled and found guilty of contravening standing orders. It was completely bewildering and I wasn't sure what to do. Luckily, Jack took over.

'This is a shock,' he said. 'Do you need to get back for Dora?'

I shook my head, touched he'd remembered her name.

'She's with my mum.'

'Well, how about we print this out, take all the info we've got to the pub, and chat about it all over a drink?'

I felt shaky. What had Lil done that deserved a court martial? Had she broken the law? Had she gone AWOL? I shook my head again, more vigorously this time.

'None of this makes sense,' I said. 'This doesn't sound like Lil.'

Jack was bustling around me, stuffing pieces of paper into

the folder. I found I didn't even care that he was putting them in upside down and back to front. Instead I just stared at the screen.

'It must be a mistake. Lil has always been a bit of a free spirit, but she's not a bad person.'

Jack paused in his gathering. 'Come on,' he said. 'Let's get out of here and you can tell me all about her. She sounds interesting.'

'Oh, she's interesting, all right,' I said. I looked at him standing there, clutching the folder, with bits of paper hanging out of it, and smiled. 'Thanks. You're being very nice.'

'I feel like it's all my fault,' he admitted. 'You'd have been none the wiser if I'd not turned up and started poking around your research.'

He wasn't wrong, but somehow I was pleased. Finding out more about Lil's war felt like the right thing to do – even if she'd kept it a secret all this time.

Jack grinned at me and I squinted at him.

'Can you go to the pub?' I said. 'Like a normal person?'

He frowned.

'I am a normal person.'

'I mean, you're famous. Won't you get mobbed?'

'Nah,' Jack said. 'No one ever thinks it's me. I think it's because I'm so scruffy. People usually just tell me I look like Jack Jones.'

I laughed and gestured to his immaculate T-shirt. 'But you're all dressed up,' I said.

With a grin, Jack pulled a tatty hoodie out of his bag and shoved it over his head. Then he jammed a faded baseball cap on top of his curls, balled up the beautiful leather jacket and squished it into his rucksack – much to my distress – and looked at me in triumph.

'Better?' he said. 'I'm in disguise.'

I laughed again because he looked so pleased with himself.

'Better,' I agreed.

'So let's go,' Jack said. 'I'm dying to know more about Lil.'

'If you want to know more about Lil, you really need to meet my sister Miranda,' I said. 'Mind if I give her a ring?'

It wasn't a total lie. If I adored Lil, Miranda adored her even more and she could definitely talk about her until the cows came home. But I could do that myself, so I didn't need Miranda to paint a good picture of our aunt. Instead I thought I wanted her there as a kind of shield. My attraction to Jack seemed to be growing by the second and I wasn't completely comfortable with being alone with him. I thought having Miranda there might force me to be more professional and stop gazing at him with my tongue hanging out like a thirsty puppy.

Unfortunately, Miranda's reaction was predictably similar to mine. She arrived in the bar at a trendy hotel near the office just after we did. Jack was ordering the drinks and I was sitting in the semi-circular booth he'd chosen.

'We'll have more room here to spread out all the papers,' he'd said when we arrived, turning round to catch a waiter's eye and knocking the folder off the table with his bag. I'd caught the file before everything fell out and put it back on the table top without him noticing. 'Stay here, I'll get some drinks.'

Miranda slid in next to me.

'Is that him?' she said, watching Jack at the bar with ill-disguised longing. 'Oh, my.'

I elbowed her, hard. 'Stop it,' I said. 'You're married. And too old for him.'

'Window shopping,' Miranda said. 'And I am not too old.'

Then she stopped looking at Jack and turned her stare to me instead.

'Hang on,' she said. 'This isn't just banter, is it?'

'Jack's getting wine, I think.'

'Don't ignore me. You like him.'

I felt myself flushing again. 'He's nice,' I muttered. 'And handsome.'

'Ohhhh,' Miranda breathed. 'You've got a crush.'

I gave her a fierce look. 'Have not,' I said.

'You are allowed,' she said. 'It's not a crime. It's ages since you broke up with Greg. It's definitely time to get back on that horse.'

'Jack is not a horse.' I frowned at her, to warn her he was approaching. 'And it's unprofessional to have a crush on someone I'm researching. And how can I date anyone? I've got Dora to think about.'

'Lot of excuses, there, Nell,' Miranda said. 'Protesting too much, I think …'

She stopped talking as Jack approached. He put a tray of drinks down, slopping some of his beer on to the table, and beamed at Miranda.

'Hello, hello, hello,' he said, gleefully shaking her hand. 'I've heard lots about you from Helena.'

Again with the way he said my name. I imagined him saying it to other people. '*Have you met my wife – Helena?*' and smiled to myself.

'Nell,' Miranda said, giving me a shove. 'Are you with us?'

I blinked, startled out of my daydream. 'Sorry,' I said. 'I was just thinking about Lil.'

'Oh yes, tell me more,' Jack said. He began taking the drinks off the tray and I helped him, trying to make sure he didn't spill any more than he already had. I handed Miranda a wine glass and a napkin to wipe up splatters and poured some Pinot Grigio for us both.

'Is Lil your dad's sister?' Jack drank a mouthful of beer.

'No, she's Dad's aunt, actually,' Miranda said. 'Our parents are both only children. But Lil was the baby of her family, so she's not really that much older than Dad.'

'You said she was very special to you?' Jack prompted.

Miranda and I looked at each other. We didn't often talk about when we were growing up.

I took a breath. 'We had a bit of an unconventional childhood,' I began.

'And you have two other siblings, am I right?'

He'd remembered what I'd told him. Miranda, obviously impressed, smiled. 'That's right,' she said. 'There's Andy and Imogen, too.'

'Andy's nearly thirty, and Immy's twenty-six,' I added.

Jack nodded. 'I always wanted brothers and sisters when I was growing up,' he said. 'I'd like to have lots of kids.'

Miranda gave me a meaningful look and I spluttered on my wine. Jack thumped me on the back.

'Easy there,' he said. 'No need to gulp.'

Miranda, looking chic and businesslike in what seemed to be a very expensive suit, with her curly hair pulled back into a neat twist, leaned back in the booth and carried on talking while I wiped my mouth with the napkin Jack offered.

'Our parents are both creative and a bit scatty,' she said.

I snorted. 'Scatty,' I said. 'Forgetful, more like.'

'When we were growing up they weren't great with money,' Miranda went on. 'Bills often went unpaid. The electricity would go off. They weren't poor. Just disorganised.'

'But when we were really small, it was all fun,' I said. 'We were too little to know any different and all we knew was they loved us.'

'But when Mum had Imogen, things changed,' Miranda said. 'Postnatal depression, I guess. Though it took a while for it to really get a hold of her.'

Jack nodded. 'I have a friend who has depression,' he said. 'It's like a gradual creeping up with him.'

'That's it exactly,' Miranda said. 'She didn't just wake up depressed one morning, it was more like a downward spiral.'

I let Miranda talk. She was two years older than me so she remembered it better.

'Once, Mum left Andy in my classroom when she dropped me

at school, instead of taking him to nursery,' she continued. 'When my teacher noticed him, she rang Mum to come and get him. She was so upset.'

'Andy wasn't remotely bothered of course,' I added, wanting to make Mum sound less awful.

'But that's when things started to go downhill. Mum wasn't really functioning and Dad – well, like I said, he was "scatty".' Miranda made quote marks with her fingers. 'Things got a bit messy for a while.'

Jack smiled at me. 'Did your mum work?' he asked.

'She still does,' I said. 'In fact, you might know of her – she's an art historian.'

'So that's where you get it from,' Jack said to me. I felt like a flower opening up in sunshine as he turned his gaze to me.

Miranda butted in and I almost tutted because I was enjoying having Jack's attention.

'She's an expert in Victorian painting and she's often on those daytime antiques shoes. She's brilliant, actually, on screen. She's so enthusiastic and because she's been a university lecturer forever she explains things really well. She writes books, too. We're very proud of her, because it's not been easy for her.'

Jack was staring at Miranda. 'I know her,' he said, excitedly. 'She's got hair just like you but in a cloud round her face, right?'

Miranda laughed. 'That's her,' she said. 'And she wears glasses like Helena's.'

I pushed my black-rimmed specs up my nose and grinned. 'I don't have the hair,' I said, gesturing to my own poker-straight style. 'But I did inherit the dodgy eyesight.'

I felt we were giving Jack an unfair picture of our mother so I carried on. 'Mum's wonderful. She's a brilliant grandmother to Dora, and Miranda's little boy. She's helped me out so much. I wouldn't have been able to go back to work without knowing she was round the corner.'

Miranda nodded. 'She is fab,' she said. 'We're lucky she got over her depression and that it never came back – not like it was.'

'And what about your dad?'

I felt a bit like Jack was researching us rather than me him, but somehow I didn't mind.

'Dad's a composer,' Miranda said. 'He writes music for films and TV shows, and adverts sometimes too.'

I shifted in my seat. 'He did some of the music for *Mackenzie*,' I said, wondering if I should have mentioned this before. 'Not the theme but some of the incidental music.'

He gaped at me in astonishment. 'No,' he said. 'My *Mackenzie*?'

'The very same.'

Jack chuckled. 'Isn't it a small world, eh?'

'Isn't it,' said Miranda. 'Dad's career was just taking off in the Nineties, when we were growing up. He worked long hours. And when Mum got ill, he wasn't completely able to cope with four kids.'

Jack nodded. 'And Lil?'

'She was a musician, like Dad,' I told him. 'Piano, mostly, but she's the sort of person who can play anything. She was a session musician and she travelled all over the world playing with different bands or singers. Six months on a cruise ship here, a year in a jazz club in New York, there. Recording an album with the Rolling Stones one day, hanging out with Fleetwood Mac the next.'

'Sounds incredible.'

'She's got some brilliant stories,' I agreed.

'But when we were kids and Mum was poorly,' Miranda said, 'Lil stepped in and made sure we were being looked after.' She drained her wine glass. 'I'm not sure what we would have done without her.'

'Blimey,' Jack said, topping up Miranda's empty glass. 'You are really close?'

I nodded. 'I thought so,' I said. 'And yet she's never mentioned her time in the ATA.'

I looked at Miranda. 'Manda, we found Lil's service record.' I picked up the folder Jack had brought with him, which was now splattered with beer and something that looked like tomato ketchup, even though we'd not eaten. 'Look at what happened.'

I handed her the sheet of paper and watched as she read the lines at the bottom.

'Oh shit,' she said. 'Dishonourable discharge?'

'What do you think, Manda?' I said. 'Do you still think we should speak to her about it?'

Miranda made a face. 'I'm going to Paris on Friday for a week,' she said. 'So I can't help. But yes, I think you should go and see her. Find out what it was all about.'

'She might not want to talk,' I said. 'What if it upsets her? She's really old.'

'She's tough as old boots,' said Miranda. 'I really think you should try to talk about it. We can't pretend that we don't know now – she'd see through that in a flash.'

I nodded. That was true.

'All right,' I said. 'I'll go and see her at the weekend.'

Chapter 12

The following Saturday, Dora and I sat on a train heading out through the leafy suburbs of south-west London to see Lil. She was ninety-four now and very frail, so she lived in a care home. It was an amazing place, funded by an entertainers' charity. All the residents of the home had once made their living as performers of one kind or another and now saw out their days reminiscing together and – too often for my liking – providing their own entertainment. They had mostly been jobbing actors, or, as Lil had been, session musicians, but there was the occasional recognisable face and they all loved to put on a show.

I normally phoned ahead when I visited, but today I'd not told Lil I was coming. After everything we'd found out, I was nervous about seeing her, which was strange considering how much I loved her. And for some reason I didn't want to warn her – though quite why I needed to be so sneaky about it all, I wasn't sure. It wasn't like I was expecting to walk in and catch her piloting a Spitfire around the residents' lounge.

What I actually found, when we walked into the residents' lounge, was one of the actors – a man who once trod the boards at the RSC and had been a regular on the West End stage –

standing in the middle of the room, reciting a speech from *A Midsummer Night's Dream*.

I paused by the door, scanning the room for Lil and clocked her sitting in the corner watching the ageing actor with barely disguised amusement. Our eyes met and she smiled.

'Hello,' she called, ignoring the fact that the actor was still going. 'I wasn't expecting you today.'

Dora jumped up and down. She loved Lil. 'Hello!' she shouted. ''Lo, Lil!'

Like a small bullet, she swerved the gesturing arms of the Shakespearean chap, and hurtled over to my aunt. I followed and sat down next to her.

'Surprise!' I said. 'Careful of Lil's legs, Dora.'

Dora clambered up on to my knee and beamed at Lil. ''Lo, Lil,' she said again.

'Hello, my darling girl,' Lil said to her, twirling one of her curls round her finger. 'I think you've grown again.'

'Do you want to stay here?' I asked Lil, looking at the actor with suspicion.

'Oh God, please, please, take me out of here,' she hissed. 'I can't bear to listen to this for a second longer. He's such a nice chap until he gets all overexcited about sodding Shakespeare.'

I grinned. 'I couldn't possibly interrupt such a cultural afternoon,' I teased.

Lil gripped my hand with a strength I didn't know she had. 'Take me out of here,' she said, 'or I'll tell him your name and the names of your siblings.'

I sighed. Mum and Dad had named us all after Shakespearean characters – Miranda from *The Tempest*, Imogen from *Cymbeline*, and Andy – Lysander – and me from *A Midsummer Night's Dream*. I liked all of our names individually – even Lysander's – but I did think that all together they were a bit, ooh what's the word, pretentious? And I had a feeling the actor, who was now starting on something from Hamlet, would bloody love it.

'Let's go,' I said to Lil.

She was in her wheelchair – she could walk but she was frail and had broken her hip a year or so back, and she was a bit wobbly – so it was easy to perch Dora on her knee, and then back her out of the lounge's large French windows and round to her room, which was also on the ground floor.

Lil had a corner room, overlooking the garden. It was as homely as it could be with lots of her books piled on shelves and a poster featuring a jazz band that she'd once played with in Paris. Lil hadn't ever accumulated a lot of stuff because she'd moved round so much in her life but the few things she had, she'd brought with her. She had a guitar in the corner of her room, though I hadn't ever known her to play it often, and the lounge had a piano for her to play whenever she felt the urge. And if none of the other residents had got there first.

I pulled out some colouring and a selection of My Little Pony toys to keep Dora amused. She plonked herself on the floor and started arranging the ponies into a long queue.

'Traffic jam,' she cooed. 'Bloody, bloody traffic jam.'

I made a mental note to watch my language when I was in the car with my sponge-like daughter and rolled my eyes at Lil.

She chuckled. 'Make us some tea, darling,' she said.

She had a kettle on a table in the corner of the room, with a small fridge underneath for milk. I filled the kettle from the tap in her bathroom, switched it on and produced a box of pink wafer biscuits – her favourite – from my bag.

She grinned. 'You always remember,' she said. I made the tea and put her cup next to her, studying her as I did. Lil had never been big – we were all fairly dainty in our family and Immy especially was teeny – but now Lil was very delicate, like a baby bird. Her hair, which had once been as dark as mine, and similarly straight, was now pure white and thin. She wore it cut short, and

I could see her scalp in places. But her eyes were alert and, despite her frailty, she was still as smart as anything.

'So why are you here?' she said, as I sat down.

I blinked at her. 'Just wanted to see you,' I stammered, surprised by the direct question.

'Oh bollocks,' she said. 'You always tell me when you're coming, and Miranda's normally with you, and Freddie. Why are you here on your own with Dora?'

She stared at me in an accusing fashion.

'With pink wafers,' she added, like Hercule Poirot revealing the culprit. 'You only bring pink wafers when you want something.'

'Oh for heaven's sake,' I said, folding at once. I would be terrible in any sort of interrogation. 'I do have something I want to ask you, but I was going to build up to it gradually.'

Lil smiled at me in triumph. 'Spill,' she said.

I pulled my folder out of my bag – the clean, orderly version without Jack's beer splatters – and took a deep breath.

'I've been researching a family for work,' I began. 'The family of the actor Jack Jones.'

Lil looked unimpressed. She'd never been interested in celebrities, which oddly was why so many of the fame-obsessed fellow residents in the home thought she was wonderful.

'Jack's grandfather was in the Air Transport Auxiliary,' I went on, noticing her stiffen slightly as I said it. 'And while I was looking for his records, I found this.'

I handed her the copy of her own service record. She glanced at it, without interest, and then put it on the side table next to her cup of tea.

'Lil,' I said. 'I didn't mean to find this, but I did. And now I can't pretend I didn't see it.'

She nodded, taking a bit of a wafer. 'Who's the grandfather?' she said.

I blinked at her.

'Jones? Did you say?' She looked thoughtful. 'Frank Jones?'

I smiled. 'That's the one. Do you remember him?'

'Nice chap,' she said. 'Brilliant at impressions – he used to have us all in stitches taking off the officers and the ground crew. Such a performer.'

I was thrilled – maybe that's where Jack got his acting talent from.

'Was he a pilot?' I asked. 'Frank?'

Lil nodded, helping herself to another wafer. 'Weren't many men, funnily enough. It was mostly …'

She trailed off, as her eyes went misty from memories.

'Mostly women?' I finished for her. 'Like you?'

I laid my hand on the service record.

'Lil, it says you went to a court martial,' I said. I watched her expression close down as I changed the subject, but I carried on regardless. 'And that you were dishonourably discharged from the ATA.'

Lil nodded again. 'That's right.'

'So, I wondered if you could tell me any more about it,' I said. 'Not necessarily about the discharge, but about the ATA itself and what you did there. It would be really helpful for Jack's story …'

I trailed off as I realised Lil was shaking her head.

'No?'

'I don't think so, darling,' she said. 'It was a long time ago and I don't remember much.'

I looked at her and she looked back, her pale blue eyes wide with innocence.

'You don't remember much about the war?'

Lil shrugged. 'I've done a lot of things since then.'

'You remembered Frank Jones.'

She stayed quiet.

'Lil,' I said, more forceful now. 'You flew Spitfires. How can you not remember?'

She said nothing, her lips pressed together in a tight line.

'Was it all the flying during the war that made you want to travel? Did it give you the bug?'

Again, Lil stayed silent.

'Did you ever want to get in a plane again, after the war had ended?' I went on. I had so many questions and my words were falling over each other in my urgency to ask them. But I was getting nowhere.

'Why did you join the ATA? What made you want to fly?'

Lil closed her eyes.

'Lil,' I wailed. 'Surely you can tell me something?'

She opened her eyes again and looked at me. 'Nothing,' she said. 'I'm sure it all happened just as you said, darling, but I can't tell you anything.'

I sat back in my chair, disappointed. 'Lil, surely you can remember something?'

She looked at me briefly then glanced away, her eyes flickering to the folder on the table. She took a breath and she sat up a bit straighter.

'It's not that I can't remember, Helena,' she said, speaking slowly and clearly as though she wanted to be very sure I was understanding her. 'It's that I don't want to remember.'

I stared at her. Was that it? Was that all she had to say?

'I'm very tired now. It was lovely to see you both.'

'Oh,' I said, surprised. My visits normally lasted longer than this.

'Thank you for the wafers.'

I stood up, picked up my bag and stuffed the service record back inside the folder.

'Come on, Dora,' I said. 'Let's go and get on the train.'

Obediently, Dora stood up. 'Bye bye, Lil,' she said. She trotted over and gave Lil one of her little ponies. 'Present,' she said. 'For Lil.'

'This is yours, darling,' Lil said.

But Dora shook her head. 'Present,' she said fiercely. 'Bye, Lil.'

Smiling, I bent down and gave Lil a kiss.

'Bye then,' I said, hoping she'd say, '*Stop, stay longer*'. But she didn't.

She smiled back at me, but it was an odd smile. One without any happiness in it. 'Bye, Dora,' she said. 'Bye, Helena.'

Chapter 13

Lilian

September 1939

I skidded to a halt at the garden gate and jumped off my bicycle, ignoring it as it clattered to the ground behind me. I hurdled the small wall and raced up the path, just as Ruth, my sister-in-law, opened the door.

'Have you heard?' I panted.

She nodded, stony-faced.

'Is Bobby here?'

She nodded again, and stood aside to let me in to the small cottage.

'He says he's going to join up,' Ruth said. Her voice wobbled. 'He says it's best to go before they call you up.'

I squeezed her fingers then, still trying to catch my breath, I went into the front room where my brother Bobby was fiddling with the wireless.

'Damn thing just won't pick up the signal,' he was muttering.

'Bobby …' I began.

He looked up. 'Oh, Lil,' he said. 'Lil.'

I went to him and rested my head on his chest. Ruth was behind me and I felt her reach past me and wrap her arm round Bobby's waist. We stood there for a second, in a strange three-way hug. Then I raised my head.

'Do you remember? What it was like before?'

Bobby was ten years older than me, so he'd lived through the Great War. The war that had broken our father.

'Sit down,' Bobby said. 'Ruth, can you make some tea?'

Ruth gave me a quick smile and headed to the kitchen.

I turned my attention back to Bobby. 'Do you remember?'

He shook his head. 'Not properly,' he said. 'I remember when Dad came home, of course. He actually came back a little while before Armistice Day, because of his hand.'

Dad's hand had been badly burned by a rifle backfiring. He always kept it tucked in his sleeve now.

'I was terrified of him,' Bobby carried on. 'I didn't know who he was – not really. And I remember going into town for the celebrations and how worried Mum was after.'

'She thought you'd get ill?' I said, remembering the stories of the Spanish Flu epidemic that had swept through people who'd been squashed into Trafalgar Square.

Bobby leaned back against the cushions. 'She was so worried I'd get poorly, she didn't really think about poor Dad and how he was coping,' he said.

I thought of our dad. I'd only ever known him as he was now – prone to dark moods with a hatred of loud noises. I couldn't imagine him being any other way.

'Ruth says you're talking about joining up,' I whispered. 'Please don't, Bobby. Please don't.'

He pressed his lips together and I studied him. He looked so like me with his dark hair and narrow face.

'Bobby, please,' I said again. 'We need you here. Mum needs you. Ruth needs you. And me, I need you.'

Bobby shook his head. 'They'll call me up anyway,' he said.

'This way at least I get to choose what I do, and where I go, and who with.' He straightened up. 'And it's the right thing to do,' he said.

I slumped in my seat. I knew there was nothing I could do to persuade him otherwise. Bobby was such a good man. He'd never shirk his duty or stand aside while others fought. No matter how much I wished he would.

'What do Mum and Dad think?'

I blinked in surprise. It hadn't even occurred to me to go home. Bobby and Ruth's house was where I felt most welcome.

'Dunno,' I muttered. 'I was at my piano lesson when Mrs Mayhew came home and told us.'

Bobby's expression darkened slightly at me mentioning my lessons. He didn't have much time for Ian, though I'd never said anything about our … whatever it was. Romance? Love affair? I shuddered to think what Bobby would say about that.

'I suppose I should go,' Bobby said, getting up. 'Mum will be in bits, bless her. And Dad? Who knows how he'll react.'

I groaned. 'Can I stay here?'

Bobby smiled at me, indulgently. 'Course,' he said. He lowered his voice. 'Actually, could you make sure Ruth's all right? She's been a bit odd the last few days.'

I stood too and went up on my tiptoes to kiss him on the cheek.

'Tell Mum I'll be home in time for tea,' I said.

He picked up his jacket and went out the front door, while I went the opposite way into the kitchen at the back of the house. Ruth was standing at the sink, staring unseeingly out into the tiny yard.

'Ruth,' I said. She didn't answer. 'Ruth,' I said, a bit louder this time, and she jumped.

'Oh, Lil,' she said, giving a fake sort of laugh. 'I didn't see you there.'

I took a step towards her. 'Are you all right?'

I loved Bobby, of course – he was my brother – but Ruth was the one I really adored. She and Bobby had been sweethearts since they were at school so I'd known Ruth almost as long as I could remember. She was so pretty, with her curly red hair and freckles, and her smiley face. But she wasn't smiling now. Her green eyes were filling with tears.

'Lil,' she said. 'Oh what are we going to do?'

I pulled her in for a cuddle. 'Bobby will be fine,' I said, hoping I was right. 'He'll be fine. He's strong as a horse, that one.'

Ruth sniffed and wiped her eyes. 'I hope you're right,' she said. She took a breath. 'I, erm, I thought I was expecting.'

I froze. Ruth had wanted a baby for so long. Bobby wanted one too, and I thought they would make wonderful parents. But each time Ruth fell pregnant, she started bleeding just a few weeks later. One terrible time, a year or so before, she'd got further along. Even started to show. But the baby came much, much too early and the little scrap of a thing – so tiny they couldn't tell if it was a boy or a girl – didn't even take one breath. Just like my dad, Ruth had been changed by all the heartache and I thought the light had gone out of her eyes.

Now I looked at her, and saw those eyes were still sad. I bit my lip.

'I thought I was, but then I started bleeding,' Ruth said. She brushed a stray curl off her forehead, tucked it behind her ear and gave me a forced smile. 'Still, probably for the best, eh? Given everything that's happened.'

I squeezed her arm, at a loss for words. 'You sit down,' I said. 'I'll make the tea.'

Later, when I was back home, I thought about Ruth and how much she wanted a baby. In fact, babies were all I thought about all the way through dinner.

'You're very quiet,' Mum said to me, as she handed me a glass of water.

81

I gave her a reassuring smile. 'Just worried about what will happen if there's a war,' I said.

Mum shuddered. 'Shhh,' she said, tilting her head towards the front room, where Dad was eating his dinner on his lap, listening to the news on the wireless. 'Don't let your father hear you talk like that. He's fretting that Bobby will get called up.'

I stayed silent, thinking of Bobby and Ruth – and Ian. Would he get called up? War seemed inevitable now; at least that's what Mr Chamberlain had said. My brother would be heading off to fight; he said he wanted to join the air force. Would Ian go too? What would I do if he went away? Could I go with him? Maybe I could join up too – I was almost sixteen. Was that old enough?

After dinner, I went upstairs slowly and lay on my bed, counting backwards in my head, over and over. Eventually, I sat up and found my diary and leafed through it, going back through the months. I hoped I was wrong, that I'd counted wrong, that the diary was wrong. But it seemed I wasn't. I was late. Really, really late. Ten weeks late, according to my dates. Ten. Weeks.

Feeling dizzy, I locked the bedroom door, and slid out of my cotton dress. Then I pulled off my brassiere and girdle and stood in front of the mirror. My breasts, which were usually small and round, looked fuller and my nipples were dark. And my stomach, normally flat, was slightly curved. I breathed in sharply. How had I not noticed this before? I turned sideways and examined my reflection more carefully, cupping my hands round my small round tummy. There was a definite bulge to my abdomen.

'Lord,' I said to myself. 'Oh Lord.'

Unable to look at my reflection a moment longer I pulled on my nightgown and got into bed, even though it was still early. Staring at the ceiling I thought about what this meant. Ruth, my lovely, kind, caring Ruth, wanted a baby so badly and couldn't have one. And here I was. Fifteen years old. Not even finished with school. Unmarried. Carrying on with my piano teacher, who I seemed to love and hate in equal measure. And undoubtedly, undeniably, pregnant.

'What am I going to do?' I muttered. 'What the bloody hell am I going to do now?'

Chapter 14

Helena

May 2018

'She really doesn't remember anything?'

I leaned back in my chair, twirling the cord of my desk phone round my hand and trying to pretend that Elly wasn't glued to every word of my conversation with my father.

'She said she didn't at first,' I said. 'But I didn't believe her.'

'It was a long time ago.'

Dad sounded disappointed and I sighed.

'No, it's different,' I said. 'Later she said she didn't want to remember, not that she couldn't.'

'You think she knows exactly what happened and she just …' Dad trailed off.

'Doesn't want to talk about it.'

There was a pause on the other end of the line.

'Could be something awful,' he said.

'Has to be.' I'd done nothing but go over and over what could have happened to Lil and drawn a blank. I wasn't completely clueless; I understood why people were dishonourably discharged

– going AWOL for one, or committing some sort of crime – but I couldn't make that fit with the Lil I knew.

'Doesn't it make you curious though?' Dad said. 'You're a historian, Nell. You solve mysteries and here's one dropped into your lap about your own family.'

'Dad,' I said. 'It's not a mystery, it's Lil. Our Lil.'

'Doesn't it make you wonder what she's hiding?'

'No,' I snapped. 'It makes me wonder what awful thing happened to her back then that saw her dishonourably discharged and refuse to talk about it more than seventy years later.'

Dad sighed. 'You're right,' he said. 'I forget how elderly she is. We're all getting on a bit.'

'Speak for yourself,' I said, softening towards him again now he'd stopped haranguing me.

'I worry,' Dad began. 'I worry that this is part of our family story and Lil won't be around to tell it, and it will be lost.'

'I know,' I said. 'And heaven knows I understand how awful it is to lose a bit of family history. But I don't know what we can do. She's an old woman. We can hardly strap her to a chair and shine a light in her eyes until she tells us what happened.'

'This is very important to me,' Dad said.

I paused. 'Dad, is there something you're not telling me?' I said. 'Why are you so desperate to find out about what Lil did in the war?'

He gave a funny little laugh. 'Of course not,' he said. 'It's just curiosity.'

'Really?' I said, not believing him. 'It's hardly just a passing interest, Dad. This is curiosity that could cost me my job, and upset an old lady. And not any old lady, one who looked after us when we were little, and made sure our family all stayed together.'

Dad made a funny swallowing sound. It almost sounded as though he was fighting back tears. 'I'm sorry,' he said. 'I have to go.'

He hung up and I stared at my phone in confusion. Had Dad been crying? What on earth was going on?

'Problems?' said Elly.

'Family,' I said. I suddenly felt close to tears myself. 'Oh, Elly, I don't know what to do.'

'Tell me all about it,' she said. 'We'll sort it out.'

Briefly I filled her in.

'So, in a nutshell, your dad wants you to find out more, your auntie won't talk about it, and Jack Jones says you can use his research as a cover story?' Elly said when I paused for breath.

'That's the long and short of it,' I said. 'But it just seems so important to Dad. I really thought he was going to cry just now.'

Elly made a face. 'That's odd,' she said.

I ran my fingers through my hair in despair. 'There's got to be more to it than Dad's letting on, but I don't want to push him. I'm stumped. Lil doesn't want me to do this research, and Dad does. If I don't do it, I'll upset him. If I do it, I could upset Lil – and piss off Fliss.'

I lowered my voice, even though Fliss was in her office.

'You know she's got a thing about people doing their own research and she can see what I'm looking up, if she fancies checking.'

Elly looked thoughtful. 'Did Lil actually tell you not to do any research?'

'She made it quite clear she didn't want to remember,' I said.

'No, but did she actually say that you weren't to do the research?'

I shook my head. 'No,' I said. 'She didn't say very much at all.'

Elly shrugged. 'There you are then. If she really didn't want you to know, she'd have said so, wouldn't she?'

'Are you saying I could do the research anyway?'

Elly smiled. 'That's exactly what I'm saying. She doesn't need to know, does she?'

'It seems a bit sneaky.'

'Oh, it's totally sneaky, but I don't see what harm it would do.'

'What if she did something awful and us knowing changes the way we feel about her?'

'I don't think that's very likely,' Elly said. 'Look, she probably just had an ill-advised bunk-up with a superior officer, or a scandalous romance with another woman. I hardly think she's some master criminal.'

I smiled. 'She's wonderful, our Lil,' I said. 'I simply can't imagine she did anything bad.'

'There you are then.'

I made a face. 'But the fact is, she doesn't want me to know. Even if it was just a – what did you call it? An ill-advised bunk-up?'

'Just carry on as you were. Don't tell her what you've found out, do tell your dad. Boom. Everyone's a winner.'

'I suppose,' I said.

Elly leaned past me and picked up Jack's folder. She put it in front of me so I could see his face.

'He said to use him as a cover, right?'

I nodded.

'So, use him. Keep all your Lilian research in your Jack folders; put Jack's story as the reference. No one will check. It means you can do your research without Fliss sniffing around and you get to spend more time with Mr Hottie here.'

'True.' It was definitely tempting. 'And Lil did know Jack's grandfather, so it's not entirely unrelated research.'

'Phone him,' she said. 'There are no losers in this situation.'

'This is very much letting my heart rule my head, which is something I never do,' I pointed out.

Elly pushed my phone towards me. 'It's not a big deal, Helena,' she said.

'I'm not over Greg,' I said desperately.

'Greg who?'

I paused, struggling for a second to remember Greg's surname. Elly almost jumped out of her chair in triumph.

'HA!' she squealed. 'You're completely over Greg.' She looked at me sympathetically. 'Listen, Helena,' she said. 'Do you think Greg's moping around in Toronto, or wherever?'

'Ottawa,' I said. 'He works for the government.'

She gave me a look that told me she definitely did not care about that. 'He's probably out every night, romancing …' she trailed off, 'whatever the female version of Mounties is.'

I smiled, despite myself. 'I think they're Mounties, too.'

'The point is he's having fun,' Elly said, 'and he doesn't even deserve it. You do.' She gave my phone another shove. 'Just dial the number and tell him you want to do the research. Be sexy.'

With a groan, I picked up my phone and hit his number. He answered on the first ring.

'Oh,' I said. 'That was quick.'

Elly threw her head back in despair. 'Sexy,' she hissed at me.

I spun round in my chair so I couldn't see her.

'I've decided I'd like to do some more research into Lil's time during the war,' I said. 'But I'll need to use your grandfather as a cover, if you're willing. Will you help me?'

I swear I could hear Jack smiling on the other end of the phone. 'I'd love to,' he said. 'Are you busy for lunch?'

I thought about it. I was supposed to be meeting Miranda but she wouldn't mind rearranging.

'Nope,' I said. 'Not busy at all.'

'Great,' Jack said. 'How about we go for a drink somewhere quiet and have a chat about what we do next?'

'I'd like that,' I said. I couldn't stop smiling. My cheeks hurt with the sheer grinniness of it all.

'Me too,' Jack said. 'I'm glad you phoned.'

Out of the corner of my eye, I saw Elly punch the air.

'See you later,' I said.

Chapter 15

Lilian

June 1944

I had a headache the next day. Too much cider, I thought. Not to mention a night spent tossing and turning, worrying about Will and how we'd been so careless about chatting in the lav without checking if anyone else was in there. We'd not said anything we shouldn't have, but it still made my blood run cold. We couldn't afford to be so lazy.

I wasn't flying that day. It was nice to have some time off after the hectic few weeks we'd had when we'd been flying two or even three different planes every day. I was still on duty, though, so I spent the morning helping Gareth with one of the taxi planes that wasn't running properly. I remembered Will's impression of him and smiled to myself. Will really was a nice man. He'd be a lovely boyfriend. Just not for me, I thought sadly. Maybe once upon a time, but not now. I thought about Flora saying we were all damaged. Maybe we were, but I knew my cracks ran deep.

'Spanner,' Gareth was saying. I looked at him, confused. What did he want?

'You're trying to unscrew a screw with a spanner,' he said. I looked down at my hand and gave him a rueful grin.

'Sorry,' I said. 'Bit of a late night.'

He nodded to the mess hut. 'Go and get yourself a cuppa,' he said. 'Might wake you up a bit.'

'Thanks,' I said, grateful for a break. 'Shall I bring one back for you?'

'That'd be nice,' Gareth said.

I stood up and brushed the dust from my overalls. 'Won't be long.'

Sauntering across the field, I felt a bit happier. Flora was right. I didn't owe Will anything. It wasn't my fault if he liked me and I didn't have to do anything I didn't want to do. Not this time. I didn't want to upset him, though, so I hoped I'd be able to cool things off without him being hurt.

I took a tea from the urn and sat down at one of the long tables to drink it. The mess hut was quiet and I was pleased to be able to have five minutes' peace. It didn't last long, though, because after a few minutes Rose slid into the chair opposite me.

'Hello, Lil,' she said.

I gave her a forced smile. 'Rose,' I said.

'Saw you at the dance last night,' she said. I wrinkled my nose. I'd not seen her. She didn't wait for me to answer, though, just carried on.

'Saw you with Will,' she said.

'A gang of us went together.' I slurped at my tea, wishing she'd leave me alone. 'It was fun.'

'Will was sweet on me for a while,' Rose said. There was a sharp edge to her voice.

'We're friends,' I told her. 'Nothing else.'

She gazed at me, her eyes wide with innocence. 'That's not what everyone's been saying.'

I felt a flush of anger. I hated gossip more than anything else.

It was gossip that had made things so hard, before. 'Well maybe don't listen to tittle-tattle and we'll all get on better,' I snapped.

Rose winced. 'Don't worry, I know you're only friends. Do you know how I know?'

I wanted to get up and walk away, but I also wanted to know what she'd heard. 'How?' I said.

'I heard you,' she trilled. 'I heard you, Annie and Flora chatting in the lav.'

I rolled my eyes. 'It was you in the cubicle,' I said. 'Then you know that there's nothing between Will and me. You're welcome to him.' I knew I was over-simplifying my relationship with poor Will, but I just wanted Rose to go away.

Rose's eyes filled with tears. 'But it doesn't work like that, does it?' she said. 'It's always the same way. Girls like you come along and take the men from under our noses.'

I snorted. Where on earth had this come from? 'I told you, there's nothing between us.'

'Doesn't matter,' Rose said, matter-of-factly. 'Because whatever you think of him, he's sweet on you all right. He's all doe-eyed when you walk past, with your neat waist and your raven hair.'

I stared at her in utter surprise. 'Rose,' I said, trying not to laugh. 'Are you blind? I'm wearing bloody overalls. I've got oil on my face. And my raven hair, as you put it, is covered in dust and tied up in a hanky. What is it you're seeing here?'

Rose looked back at me, unblinking.

'Rose,' I said again, more gently this time. I was beginning to wonder if she was having some sort of funny turn. 'I don't want to be Will's girlfriend. I just wanted to go out dancing and have some fun. If you want to make a move on Will, go right ahead.'

She gave me a tight smile. 'It's too late,' she said. 'You've got your claws into him now.'

Exasperated, I got up. 'I've got work to do,' I said. 'You're bonkers, Rose.'

I took my empty mug over to the counter and asked for another cup to take back to Gareth. Behind me, I could sense Rose's eyes boring into my back but I ignored her.

As I walked away, holding Gareth's mug carefully, I heard her call out. 'It's funny,' she said in a singsong voice, 'what you can learn from tittle-tattle.'

I slowed down but I didn't stop walking. What did she mean?

'People talked when you left, you know,' she said.

This time I did stop. What was she trying to say?

'There was nothing to talk about.'

'Maybe so,' she said. In one quick move, she got up from the table and headed out of the door at the other end of the mess hut. I stayed where I was, frozen to the spot. What was she trying to tell me? Did she know why I'd moved away from Kent? Surely not. No one knew. Did they? Mother had no idea, and Mr Mayhew wouldn't talk.

Even if Rose had somehow found out … I stifled a gasp. Even if she had found out, she couldn't be sure. We'd been so careful.

I shook my head. No. It was almost five years since I'd left home. She couldn't possibly know anything. Too much time had passed. And the war meant lots of people coming and going in the villages. Rose was just being, well, Rose. She obviously had an enormous crush on Will and she wanted me to step aside. Well, I'd happily do that if it meant she left me alone.

My mind whirling, I pushed open the door that led to the airfield and walked back to the bomber where Gareth was waiting.

'Tea's up,' I said, handing him the mug. He took it and gulped it down.

'You've got an admirer,' he said.

My heart sank. 'What have you heard?' I was shorter than I'd intended to be.

'That Will was looking for you.' Gareth grinned at me.

'We're just friends,' I muttered. 'I don't … I'm not really in the market for an admirer.'

Gareth was looking at me oddly. 'Are you all right, Lil?' he said. 'You've gone a bit pale.'

'I think I might be coming down with something,' I said.

'You go home and have a lie-down,' he said, his face furrowed with concern. 'I'll tell Annie to come and see you're all right when she gets her break, shall I?'

I forced myself to smile. 'Thanks, Gareth,' I said.

Without looking back, I left the airfield and headed back to our digs, quiet in the middle of the day with no one around. I stripped off my overalls and climbed into my narrow bed, pulling the blankets over my head. I'd thought I'd be fine here. Safely away from whispers and nosy neighbours, but I'd been wrong. Just one evening dancing with Will and all my demons were crowding in on me again. I'd pulled away from him on the walk home from the dance because I was terrified he would try to kiss me and I didn't know how I'd react; no one had kissed me since Ian. I'd thought I was healing, but perhaps I wasn't. Perhaps I never would.

And now Rose was sniffing round too. And if she'd overheard our conversation about Will, then she'd have heard us mention Newcastle. What if she put two and two together and worked out what Flora, Annie and I were doing. The whole thing could come tumbling down around us – and goodness knows what would happen to the women we were trying to help. And to us. Would we be court-martialled? Sent to prison? Shot, even? I didn't know. Shaking like a leaf, I buried my head into the pillow so my sobs didn't echo round the room, and I cried and cried.

Chapter 16

Helena

May 2018

I could hardly believe I was throwing caution to the wind, rearranging plans, and going to have lunch with Jack without planning the meeting to within an inch of its life.

Generally speaking, I was what I believe people call tightly wound.

'You're clenching,' Miranda said to me on an almost daily basis. And I usually was. I liked to be in control of my world, and my flat, and my desk at work. I was no psychologist but I understood that this was down to our chaotic childhood. Whereas Immy and Andy had embraced the unpredictable nature of our upbringing, Miranda and I were more, well, clenched, about the whole thing. Miranda ran her home and the bank she worked for with similar military precision – just as she'd taken over running the family home when we were kids. I didn't so much as buy a new tube of foundation without researching it to death first. I had a system for everything. And I never did anything spontaneously. Yet, here I was, racing through the streets of the West End to meet Jack, wearing Elly's bright red lipstick.

'You can't go on a date without lipstick,' Elly had said.

'It's not a date,' I'd replied. 'It's a lunch meeting. A business lunch meeting.'

She'd raised one eyebrow at me and I'd ignored her.

Jack was waiting for me outside the bar. I saw him before he saw me, so I could take a minute to admire his broad shoulders and the curls that fell across his forehead. He was reading a book – an actual book – which made my heart sing, though I frowned to see he'd folded the pages right back on each other. Didn't he care he was breaking the spine?

As I got closer, he looked up and smiled and I felt my legs wobble in what was becoming a familiar fashion. He had such an effect on me; it was crazy. And terrifying.

'Business meeting, Nell,' I told myself inwardly. 'Stay calm. Stay professional.'

'You look amazing,' Jack said, kissing me on the cheek and stuffing the book into his pocket at the same time.

'Professional,' I said.

Jack looked at me in surprise.

'I was trying to look professional,' I blustered. To hide my embarrassment, I reached into his pocket and pulled the book out. It was a battered copy of an Agatha Christie mystery. I straightened out the pages and smoothed the cover.

'Bag?' I said.

Jack held out his backpack and I carefully put the book inside.

'Sorry, Miss,' he said.

Laughing at his contrite expression I followed him inside.

We ordered a bottle of red wine, even though I never did lunchtime drinking.

'They do great tapas here,' Jack said. 'Let's chat first, then we can order?'

I nodded, feeling slightly wrong-footed. This wasn't a date. Was it?

'So, fill me in,' Jack said, pulling a notebook out of his bag. 'What do you need me to do?'

Ah, no. Not a date. I was both relieved and disappointed.

'I don't really need you to do anything,' I said. 'I just need to know you wouldn't mind if I pretended to be researching your family, log all my searches under your file, while I was researching my own.'

'You don't need me to look anything up?' Jack looked disappointed and I laughed.

'It's my job,' I pointed out. 'They make it look like you're doing the research on camera, but it's all already done.'

'I was looking forward to it,' Jack said. He looked so glum, I laughed again.

'You can help if you like,' I said. 'It's always good to have another pair of hands.'

'Great.' Jack grinned at me and again I felt that tingle in my stomach. He had so much charisma. 'I'm looking forward to hearing more about Frank, too.'

'He was a bit of a performer apparently,' I told him.

Jack looked at me, astonished. 'You spoke to your aunt?'

'I did.'

'And she remembers my grandfather?'

I nodded. 'She said he was a mimic. Kept everyone amused with impressions of the officers.'

'Ha!' Jack said, delighted. 'So perhaps I'm not the only actor in the family after all.'

'Perhaps not,' I said, pleased to have pleased him.

'What else did she say?' Jack said. He brandished his pen as if he was about to write down every word I said.

'She said nothing.'

'Nothing?'

I filled him in on Lil's reluctance to talk, and Dad's desperation to know more.

'I feel like I'm in a very awkward position,' I said. 'But Elly convinced me to do what Dad wants. She reckons Lil can't have done anything that bad, and I don't need to tell her that I'm researching her.'

Jack made a face. 'Tricky,' he said. 'On the one hand, I totally understand your dad wanting to know more about his family. On the other, Lil sounds so special to you …'

'I don't want to upset her,' I said.

There was a pause.

'Do you know what we should do?' Jack said suddenly.

'What?'

'Eat. We can't think on an empty stomach.'

So we ordered a whole bunch of tapas and wolfed them down almost as fast as the waiter brought them to our table.

I felt so comfortable with him; I could almost feel myself unclenching as we chatted over tapas. He was funny and clever, and unashamedly fond of reality TV and football.

'Tell me about your family,' I said, chasing a garlic mushroom round my plate with a piece of bread. 'You said it was just you and your mum?'

Jack's eyes softened. 'Just us,' he said. 'Like how it's just you and Dora.'

I smiled again at him remembering my daughter's name.

'She's a writer, my mum,' he carried on.

'Yes, I remember you saying. What does she write?'

He smiled. 'TV shows. Soaps, mainly.'

'Ahhh,' I said. 'In the business.'

He took a sip of wine. 'She had me quite young,' he said. 'She was just starting out in the industry and she was grafting, you know? Putting in the hours. So when she had me, she just took me with her.'

'To the TV studios?'

He nodded. 'I spent a lot of time in writers' meetings, and story-lining conferences, and in dressing rooms,' he said, smiling.

'I loved it. I used to hang out on sets with the actors – it's what made me want to be part of it all.'

'Sounds unconventional,' I said.

Jack nodded. 'It sounds it, but I'm not sure it was. I was in the studios a lot when I was tiny, but by the time I was at school, Mum's career was more established and she could work from home a lot. She was so strict about me doing my homework, and going to bed on time. I never missed class, or anything like that.'

I looked down at my plate. It was silly – I'd sort of hoped Jack's mum had been more like my own, but actually she sounded more like the mum I'd always wanted. The mum I was trying to be.

'Mum knew having me young could have been the biggest mistake of her life,' Jack went on. 'But she was determined it wasn't going to stop her living her dreams. And she wanted me to have choices too.'

'She sounds amazing,' I said truthfully but not without a certain amount of envy.

'I owe her a lot.'

My stomach twisted slightly, as I thought about how much Miranda and I owed Lil. I said as much to Jack.

'Tell me more about what she did for you?' he said. 'When your mum was ill.'

I shrugged. 'She was there when we needed her,' I said.

I took a breath and picked up my glass of wine.

'Mum had days when she wouldn't be able to get up,' I said. 'She'd be okay and then there'd be periods when she was struggling. Some of the time she'd shut herself in her study, and when things were really bad, she'd stay in bed.'

Jack's eyes were fixed on my face. I tried to smile.

'It wasn't her fault,' I said, my voice wobbling a bit. 'Like I said, she was a brilliant mum before then. And since then. She just had that bad patch, and it made things tricky for a while.'

'How long?'

'A couple of years,' I said, looking into my wine. 'Five, perhaps. At the most.'

'That's quite a long time,' Jack said gently. 'Especially for kids.'

I nodded. 'Dad tried so hard,' I said. 'But there were a lot of us, and he was trying to keep his career going, plus he's rubbish with money.'

'Lil helped?'

I smiled at the memory. 'Miranda phoned her. She was only twelve, but she just took control. Mum was in a very dark patch – the worst, I think, it had ever been. Immy was about two, and Andy would have been six. Dad had just got his first big film job, so he was trying really hard to keep on top of things but it was all a bit messy.'

'Go on.'

'Lil didn't like staying in one place for long,' I explained. 'She was almost seventy then, but she was still travelling. She was doing a lot of cruises by then. She liked being out on the ocean, she said. When Miranda phoned her, she'd just finished a cruise and she was supposed to be heading off again. But instead, she came to stay.'

I remembered Lil turning up one morning, her suitcase covered in stickers from the countries she'd visited – did you still get those? I wondered – and dark circles under her eyes. She'd kissed us all, and then gone upstairs to see Mum, who was in bed. A little while later she came down again, nodded at me and Miranda, and went outside to Dad's studio, which was at the bottom of the garden. Miranda and I sat quietly in the kitchen, waiting for her to reappear. And when she did, she looked more than a little bit cross.

'I've had a word with your father,' she'd said. 'And I'm going to stay here for a while. Immy will have to share Andy's bedroom.'

I'd felt such relief I wanted to cry. Instead I just grinned at Miranda, who smiled up at Lil.

'Andy won't like that,' she said. 'Immy farts in her sleep.'

And that was that. Lil moved in and like some 1990s version of Mary Poppins, she slowly changed our lives.

'Lil knows everyone,' I told Jack now. 'She's met so many people over the years and everyone adores her. She called in a lot of favours for us, I think. Dad couldn't persuade Mum to get help, but Lil just invited an old friend round – and that friend happened to be a doctor, and then there was another friend who was a counsellor … She was sneaky but it worked.'

Jack topped up our wine glasses. 'She sounds brilliant,' he said. 'What else did she do?'

'Taught us to cook,' I said. 'And when she realised Miranda was good with numbers, she helped her get to grips with the family finances. My parents were making money but they weren't spending it wisely. Miranda took over – she still looks after their cash for them, even now.'

Jack chuckled. 'I could do with Miranda organising my bank account,' he said.

'Don't ever say that when she's in earshot,' I warned. 'Because she'll actually do it. She phones me every April to remind me to open a new ISA.'

'And do you?'

I scoffed. 'No,' I said. 'But please don't tell Miranda that.'

'What else?' Jack said.

'Silly things,' I said. 'Tiny things that don't seem important but actually made such a difference. She bought a big calendar for the wall and made us all write things on it, and she reminded Dad about parents' evenings, and sports days, and even birthdays. She got a cleaner, so the house wasn't dirty any more, and invited our friends round for tea. She forced Dad to eat dinner with us, instead of working through meals, so we got to spend more time with him.'

I paused.

'It was Mum that she helped the most, though.'

'Are they close?' Jack asked.

I made a face. 'They have a bit of an odd relationship,' I said. 'It's almost like Mum is embarrassed about what happened, which is crazy but I suppose understandable. She never talks about it and she sort of rolls her eyes at any mention of Lil, but she's very protective of her. Massively so. She was the one who found the home for her, and she's the one who makes sure she has everything she needs. She visits all the time, too.'

Jack nodded. 'That's sweet,' he said. 'I'd like to meet her.'

'Mum?'

He laughed. 'Lil, you doofus.'

Then his expression changed slightly.

'But I'd like to meet your mum, too.'

There was a flicker of something between us, like a charge of electricity. I shifted in my seat a bit to break the tension.

'I feel bad that I'm choosing Dad over Lil,' I said.

Jack reached across the table and took my hand. I moved my wine glass out of the way just in the nick of time and actually smiled at his clumsiness. What was happening to me? Our fingers fitted together exactly. He gave my hand a reassuring squeeze and then let go.

'Let's do a bit of research and see where it takes us,' he said.

My hand felt hot where he'd touched it, and cold now he'd let go.

'Okay,' I agreed, wondering if I'd regret it. 'Let's see where it takes us.'

Chapter 17

Lilian

September 1939

Once I realised I was pregnant, I did nothing at all. I was suspended, like vegetables in aspic, unable to act or even think. I stayed quiet. I went to school and came home and read my books. I avoided Mum and Dad, and I kept away from Mr Mayhew. I didn't want to see him. I dropped a note through his door saying I was needed at home and couldn't come to my lessons, and I didn't hear anything from him.

It was harder to avoid Bobby. When war was declared, just a couple of days after my realisation, I wanted to go and see my brother, to ask what he'd decided to do. But instead I waited for him to come round and break the news that he'd joined up and he was, as he'd planned, heading into the air force. It was the first time I'd ever seen my father cry.

Ruth sought me out. She was wretched at the prospect of Bobby joining up. She had two brothers of her own, who'd also joined up, and she was feeling sad and scared and she wanted me to comfort her. But I was stricken with guilt. I couldn't get things straight in my head. I knew now that I was expecting a baby. A real baby. And I knew that I couldn't tell Ruth about it. She would hate me. And I didn't blame her.

My head was a tangle of thoughts and emotions. I loved Mr Mayhew and I hated him. I wanted to be with him and I never wanted to see him again. I wanted to tell Ruth the truth and I wanted to be far away from her, so she wouldn't guess. I lay in bed at night and wished my baby away. I wished that I would bleed like Ruth had. And then I cried because I remembered Ruth's little scrap of a child and how sad she was, and I knew I was a terrible, awful, bad person. I cried when I thought of Mrs Mayhew and how much she loved Mr Mayhew and how she didn't know what he was doing when she wasn't there. I cried when I thought of my father, and of Bobby going off to fight the Nazis … I cried all the time.

I stopped eating. I found I couldn't stomach much anyway, and it seemed wrong to nourish my body when it had done so much that was bad. I didn't have much meat on my bones at the best of times, but after a week or so of barely eating, I was already growing thinner, and my skin had taken on a grey tone. I caught Mum and Bobby talking about me in the kitchen when they thought I was upstairs and couldn't hear. I lurked by the door and peered at them through the gap.

'Is it me?' Bobby had asked, his face etched with worry. 'Is she worried about me going away?'

'I think it's everything,' Mum said. 'The war, your father …' She paused. 'She's not playing the piano. She hasn't been to her lessons and even when I ask her to play something for me, she won't.'

Bobby sighed. 'Is she going to school?'

'Far as I know. That headmistress would be round to complain fast enough if she wasn't, I'm sure.'

Mum folded the tea towel she was holding and hung it over the edge of the sink.

'Oh, Bobby,' she said. 'Are you doing the right thing? Do you have to go?'

Bobby shrugged. 'You know I do,' he said. 'I just wish the timing was better. With Lilian the way she is, and Dad, and Ruth …'

Mum stroked his face, like she did to me when I was little and I felt poorly.

'I'll take care of Ruth,' she said. 'Don't you worry.'

Standing in the dim hallway, I felt a crushing sadness. More than anything at all I wanted to be little again. I wanted to climb on to my mother's knee and cuddle up, while she stroked my face – just as she'd done to Bobby – and told me everything was all right. I didn't feel like an adult, despite Mr Mayhew telling me I was a beautiful woman. I felt like a little girl. A silly, naughty little girl who'd done something terrible and was going to pay the price.

I let out a sob, and stifling it so Bobby didn't realise I was there, I turned and ran upstairs before he and Mum caught me listening.

A day or so later, when my stomach was starting to swell and I'd thanked my lucky stars my school uniform was a pinafore dress and not a skirt, I came out of school and found Ruth at the gate.

I stopped for a second, then carried on walking. 'I can't stop,' I called. 'I have chores to do.'

Ruth hurried after me and took my arm. 'I spoke to your mum,' she said. 'She wants you to rest. No chores today. Come and have a chat with me.'

'I can't,' I said dully. 'I really can't.'

Ruth pulled my arm so I turned to face her. 'You bloody well can,' she said. I stared in surprise. She never so much as snapped at me.

'There is something going on with you, Lilian Miles, and I don't know what it is. But your mum and Bobby and me, we're all worried out of our minds. And with Bob going away and your dad in the state he is, worrying about you is the last thing we need. So you'll come with me, Missy, and you'll tell me what's going on.'

I opened my mouth to protest then shut it quickly when I saw the expression on her face. 'Fine,' I said. 'I'll come.'

We walked into the centre of the village, and sat down on a bench by the war memorial. There were fresh flowers at the bottom and I shuddered, wondering if there would be more names added before too long.

'Right then,' said Ruth. 'Spill the beans.

I didn't know what to say. I couldn't tell her the truth, but I had to tell her something or she wouldn't leave me alone. I took a breath. 'I think I'm in love,' I said.

Ruth stared at me. 'In love?' she said. She started to laugh. 'You're in love? No wonder you're such a mess.'

I tried to laugh along with her, but I couldn't.

'Who is it?' Ruth said. 'A lad from school? Is it that lad who plays clarinet? Gordon whatsit?'

I shook my head. I couldn't speak.

Ruth nudged me. 'Come on,' she said. She seemed relieved that it wasn't anything more serious.

'It's not someone from school,' I managed to say. 'He's older than me.'

'Older?' she said, teasing me. 'Handsome is he?'

I thought of Mr Mayhew's swarthy looks. For the first time I wondered if he was Jewish. I'd never seen him or Mrs Mayhew at church, though they weren't the only people in the village who didn't go. I nodded.

'Handsome,' I whispered. I screwed my face up. 'And married.'

Ruth looked shocked, but I could tell she was pretending.

'Married, eh?' She chuckled. 'And you've got a crush on him? Ah, lovey, it's hard when you fall for someone who doesn't feel the same way. But you just need to pick yourself up and get on with things. You'll meet someone else. Someone your own age.'

I looked at her sweet, kind face and I longed to throw myself into her arms and cry and tell her everything.

'It's Mr Mayhew,' I wanted to say. 'And I thought I loved him, and that he loved me, and I wanted him so badly I felt it like an ache in my belly. But when it happened, it wasn't like I expected it to be. It hurt and it made me feel sad and sore. And now I'm pregnant and I don't want to be.'

But I knew I couldn't say those words. Not now. Not ever.

'Oh, lovey,' Ruth said again, obviously seeing my stricken face. 'It's all going to be all right.'

She put her arm round me and pulled me close.

'It's looking like this war isn't going to be nearly as bad as we all thought it was going to be. They're saying it'll be over and done with by Christmas. Bobby's packing and getting ready to go off to training, and I reckon he won't even get past London before they send him back again. And I know your mum will be pleased about that because she's worried about him flying those planes. And I can't blame her. Your dad will be fine. He's been through worse than this, bless him.'

She kissed my temple and gave my plait a gentle tug.

'And your silly heart will heal,' she said. 'You'll get over this, my darling. And you'll find someone new. Everything is going to be fine.'

I rested my head on Ruth's shoulder as a tear rolled down my cheek. I wanted to believe everything she was saying but I knew it was all just platitudes. Who knew how long this war would last, or whether Bobby would make it home. I feared even the distant rumble of planes or guns would shred Dad's remaining nerves to pieces, and that Mum would crumble if he did. And I knew that my heart would possibly never heal. How could it? When I was carrying Mr Mayhew's baby and I had no idea what to do about it?

'Everything is going to be fine,' Ruth said again. But she didn't sound very sure.

Chapter 18

Helena

June 2018

The actor was in the same position in the lounge as he'd been the last time I'd visited. This time, he seemed to be telling stories about his career. A group of elderly women were listening, hanging on his every word.

'And then of course, there was the time I played a guest role on the sitcom *Family Fun* …' he was saying. One of the women near him – who I recognised as being one of the former stars of that very show – pointedly raised an eyebrow and picked up a magazine, and I chuckled to myself as I sneaked past to find Lil.

She was in her room today. She was lying on her bed, eyes closed, listening to an Elton John record that was spinning on the turntable she'd brought with her from home.

'Oh, I can't bear all this modern rubbish,' I said. 'Why can't you listen to some proper music?'

She opened one eye and looked at me. 'Get with it, Grandma,' she said. 'All the kids are into Elton John now. He's going to be the next big thing, just you wait and see.'

I laughed. 'Are you feeling okay? It's not like you to have a lie-down during the day.'

'I'm fine,' she said. 'I just didn't sleep very well last night and while I adore Hugh most of the time, when I'm tired and he goes off on one I find it hard to bite my tongue. Thought I was better off in here. I'll sit up now you're here and we can chat.'

As I helped her into her chair, I told her about the sitcom actress in the lounge and she chuckled.

'Where's Dora today?' she asked.

'With Miranda,' I said.

'I like that you girls help each other out,' Lil said approvingly. 'It's how it should be.'

I smiled, and we shared some small talk about Mum and Dad, and Immy's latest project, saving elephants in a remote part of Africa. Lil showed me a postcard she'd received from Andy from his archaeological dig in Shetland and she asked lots of questions about what he was doing, and the time period he was interested in – none of which I could answer because, frankly, I never paid that much attention to Andy's digs until they were finished and I could see what he'd found for myself.

The whole time, I watched her like a hawk, wondering if there was anything else – any other important memories – that had slipped from her mind. But as far as I could tell she was the same Lil. Guarded and slightly distant, admittedly, but funny, sharp, and with absolutely no time for anyone who annoyed her.

'You look different,' she said, eyeing me carefully. 'Have you changed your hair?'

I shook my head. 'I never change my hair,' I pointed out. I'd had the same long, straight style with a blunt fringe, since I was ten.

But Lil wasn't giving up. 'New glasses?'

'Nope, had these a while.'

'Different outfit?'

I was wearing jeans and a plain black T-shirt. It wasn't exactly

108

quirky or out of the ordinary. I shook my head again and Lil gasped.

'I know what it is.'

I looked down at myself, wondering what she'd seen.

'You look happy,' she said. There was an accusatory edge to her voice. 'Are you happy?'

I giggled in a very un-Helena girly fashion. 'I am,' I said. 'But it's not like I was unhappy before.'

Lil narrowed her eyes. 'Have you met someone?'

'God, you're like the Spanish Inquisition,' I said, grinning. 'No, I've not met anyone.'

'Really? Because you look giddy.'

'Giddy?'

'Don't be coy. It's about bloody time if you ask me. It's ages since you got shot of that awful Greg.'

'He got rid of me,' I pointed out. 'And Dora.'

Lil rolled her eyes. 'Tell me,' she said.

'It's just a crush,' I said, feeling myself blush. 'It's totally one-sided.'

'If it helps you move on, then that's fine,' said Lil. She was always so sensible and she was right. I'd been brooding over what had happened with Greg for too long, and Jack was a very welcome distraction.

'He's someone I met through work. He sort of arrived in my life and created chaos. And I don't seem to mind.'

Lil chuckled. 'Your life could do with a bit of chaos, if you ask me.'

'I think you might be right, there,' I said. 'It's crazy, though, Lil. Nothing's happened between us – he took my hand for about five seconds once, and he kissed me on the cheek last time we met. But I can't stop thinking about him. I just want to spend all my time with him.'

'Don't lose yourself,' Lil said, her tone sharp. 'Don't spend all your time with him.'

'I won't.' I was a bit taken aback by her negative reaction when she'd started out so positive. 'But we're working together. On a … sort of project.'

'What sort of project?'

'He's one of the celebs we're researching, actually,' I said, feeling a bit silly, like this thing I had with Jack really was just a schoolgirl crush.

Lil raised her narrow eyebrows. 'What's his story?'

'His great-grandfather fought at the Somme,' I said, telling the truth and lying all at once. I couldn't exactly mention his grandad being in the ATA.

'And that's keeping you busy, is it?'

I made a face. I could see where she was going with this. 'Pretty busy.'

Lil gave a brisk nod. 'Good.'

'Jack – that's his name.' I stopped short of saying his surname in case she put two and two together and came up with Frank Jones and the ATA. 'He was in that detective thing Dad did the music for.' I felt like I was babbling and I didn't really know why. 'I'm seeing him later. We're going bowling. He's invited us both, me and Dora, bless him. I have no idea why he chose bowling or why I agreed. I don't think I'm very good at bowling …'

Lil was sitting very still in her chair. 'This has nothing to do with the questions you had last time?' she said, interrupting my rambles about bowling shoes.

I felt like a weasel as I assumed what I hoped was an innocent face. 'Questions?' I said, lightly. 'Oh, the ATA stuff? No, nothing to do with that.'

There was a pause as Lil studied me.

'I just thought it might be fun to check out some of my own family history, as I spend so much time researching other people's,' I said, trying not to sound like I was making this up as I went along. 'But actually, I'm so busy now with work – and with Jack – I don't have time to research the poor Miles family.'

I sent silent curses to my father for putting me in the position of lying to Lil, and hoped she'd believe me.

There was a beat of silence, and then Lil gave me one her dazzling smiles. 'Tell me who else you're researching, darling,' she said. 'I love hearing your stories.'

With a sigh of relief, I started telling her about the Sixties' pop star who was related to Lady Jane Grey. It seemed I was off the hook. Lil believed me when I said I wasn't doing any digging into what she did during the war, so I was free to carry on.

'I just don't know why she is being so secretive,' I told Jack later. We were indeed going bowling – that bit hadn't been a lie. Jack had sent me a text earlier saying he thought I was stressing over Dad asking me to do the research and that I should have some fun. Another text had arrived almost straight away.

'Bring Dora,' he'd added. 'I'd love to meet her.'

I'd almost said I was busy, but suddenly I couldn't face another evening alone at home watching Netflix so I'd agreed. And here we were, at the bowling alley. I'd not been bowling for about twenty years.

'She changed completely when I told her I'd stopped researching my own family – went from sullen and negative to her usually smiley self,' I told Jack.

'Was that awkward?'

'God, it made me feel like a worm,' I said, 'knowing I was lying to her.'

'Are you intrigued?' Jack said with a sly grin. 'Is your interest piqued?'

I groaned. 'Completely,' I admitted. 'Dad is so desperate to know more and I have to admit I am interested to find out what she's hiding. And then I remember she's our Lil and she must have her reasons.'

We were queuing up at a retro bowling alley in the centre of town. It was done out like a 1950s American diner, and I felt like I was in *Grease*. Dora, predictably, had gone to sleep in her pushchair, which I was pleased about, even though I knew it meant I'd have a hellish bedtime when we got home.

'It definitely has more than a little whiff of mystery about it,' Jack agreed.

'Dad's completely obsessed,' I said. 'He's been messaging me so much I've had to mute him.'

'Why do you think he's so interested?' Jack said.

'Ah, well that in itself is a mystery. He got quite emotional when he asked me to do the research – begged me really. But then he downplays it and says it's just something he wants to know more about.'

'No ideas what it could be?'

I shrugged. 'Nothing concrete. Some secret from long ago? Something he knows that Lil doesn't, or vice versa? But I can't think what it could be.'

Jack made a face. 'All families have secrets,' he said.

'And thank goodness they do, or I'd be out of a job,' I joked.

'Do you reckon it's all to do with this dishonourable discharge?'

'I don't know,' I admitted. 'It seems strange to have two secrets in one family but I can't for the life of me see how they're connected.' I shook my head. 'But they have to be, don't they? Otherwise why would Dad be so desperate for me to find out more? All I know is Lil did something wrong and she doesn't want us to know about it.'

'But you don't reckon it was that bad?'

I shrugged again. 'It's Lil, isn't it? How bad can it be? Elly says it's probably just that she had an affair with her boss, or with a woman,' I said, taking the shoes the woman at the counter handed me, as Jack gave her his credit card. 'And that I shouldn't feel guilty about finding out more because it won't change anything.'

Jack took his own shoes, and turned to face me. 'What do you think?' he said. 'Do you feel guilty?'

I made a face. 'Truthfully?' I said, gazing up at him. He was much taller in real life than he looked on the TV and, I thought, much more handsome. I took a breath. 'I think Elly's right. Dad's so desperate to know more, and it won't change anything for Lil.'

'So we'll carry on?' Jack said. 'You'll carry on, I mean?'

'I know that in theory it's going against Lil's wishes, but I can't really see it's that bad,' I said. Was I talking Jack into it, or myself? I didn't know.

Jack nodded thoughtfully. 'You could be right,' he said.

Then he grinned. 'I'm pleased you said you'd come tonight.'

My stomach flipped over. 'It was kind of you to think of me,' I said politely, not wanting to misjudge the situation.

'I wasn't being kind,' Jack said. He dropped the bowling shoes he was holding on to the floor, then he took mine out of my hands and dropped them too.

'Jack?' I began.

'They're getting in the way,' he said. He gathered me into his arms, bent his head down and kissed me. Right there, in the reception area of the bowling alley with me holding on to Dora's buggy with one hand.

'Your lane's ready,' the receptionist said behind us and we broke apart, grinning like lovesick teenagers at each other. Jack scooped up the shoes and we headed over to start the game.

'That was unexpected,' I said, my head still spinning. It was a long time since anyone had kissed me like that.

'Thought we should do it first,' Jack said. He handed me my shoes and started pressing buttons on the screen that controlled the game. 'Then it's not hanging over us all evening and we won't be worrying about it.'

I laughed. 'Very practical,' I said. 'And really, very lovely.'

Lovely was an understatement. It had woken all sorts of feelings inside me that I'd thought I'd locked away.

Jack grinned at me. 'We can have another go later,' he said. 'There, all ready.'

He hit one of the buttons and our screen flashed up with our names. Sort of. He'd written Heleeena and Jcak.

'Oh,' he said.

'Let me.' I reached past him, relishing the feeling of his body next to mine, and corrected his dodgy typos.

He put his arm round me and squeezed me tight. 'Helena,' he said. 'I know this sounds crazy, but I want to spend a lot more time with you. I don't want to come on too strong, though, or scare you off.'

I couldn't stop smiling. 'Jack,' I said. 'You create havoc everywhere you go. You've turned my whole life upside down, and you've not even been inside my flat yet. If you haven't scared me off so far, I think we're okay.'

He kissed me again and I melted into his arms.

'Right,' he said, eventually. 'Now that's sorted, I think we should start the game.'

Jack turned back to the screen. 'Now, what do I press to get things going?' he said.

He whacked one of the buttons with a flourish, there was a beat and suddenly all the lights began to flash and an alarm started buzzing on every lane.

I collapsed into giggles once more. 'Oh Jack,' I said. 'What have you done?'

Chapter 19

Lilian

June 1944

'Lil, over here!' I glanced round at the sound of my name, and groaned. It was Will, waving wildly at me from behind the propeller of a Spitfire.

'Hello!' I called, carrying on walking. I wanted to clear a request for leave with one of the officers, and I really didn't want to stop and chat with Will, who was becoming increasingly difficult to avoid.

Will, though, wasn't getting the message. I heard his footsteps behind me.

'Lil,' he panted. 'I'm glad I caught you.'

I paused and smiled politely. 'Will, I've got a lot to do and I need to catch Flight Captain Rogers. I don't have time for a chat.'

I turned to go, and Will caught my arm.

'Lil,' he said again. 'I just wanted to say I had a really nice time, at the dance. And I'd love to do it again some time.'

He took a step towards me and I caught my breath.

'Maybe just the two of us next time?'

He looked so hopeful, squinting as he looked into the sun, and giving me that little boy smile, that I felt completely wretched. I couldn't string him along. It simply wasn't fair.

'Will,' I said. 'I do have to speak to Flight Captain Rogers but then I'm free for a bit. Can you meet me for a quick cuppa in the mess hut? Twenty minutes?'

Will looked thrilled and I felt awful. But I had to tell him the truth. It wasn't right to lead him on and let him think we might become an item.

'Twenty minutes,' he said.

I walked away, feeling his eyes on me.

'I love to watch you leave,' he joked. I knew I was supposed to give him a wink over my shoulder, or swing my hips in a coquettish fashion, but instead I pretended I hadn't heard. I wasn't like other girls, and the sooner he realised that, the easier things would be for both of us.

Flight Captain Rogers cleared my request for leave, but before I could get ready for my time off, I had to speak to poor Will.

He was already in the mess hut when I got there, sitting at a table by himself. He jumped up when I entered and he smiled at me.

'I got you a cuppa,' he said.

'Thank you.' I sat down opposite him and took a slurp, more to put off talking than because I was thirsty.

'Will,' I said at the same time as he said: 'Lil …'

We both laughed and I looked down into my mug of tea.

'Lil,' Will said again. He looked very nervous and his voice was a bit funny. 'I think you're marvellous. You're everything I'd want in a girl and more.'

'Oh, Will,' I said. I screwed my face up. 'You're not so bad yourself. You're handsome, and funny, and a wonderfully terrible dancer.'

He smiled at that and I smiled back.

'And I think you're sweet and kind … and you'd be a lovely husband one day.'

Will's expression had changed from smiling to frowning. 'But not for you?' he said.

I groaned. This was so hard. I tried again.

'I like you very much,' I said. 'This isn't about you. It's about me.'

Will looked disbelieving and I felt terrible. I didn't want him to be hurt. I wanted him to understand that I was damaged. Broken. That I couldn't be the kind of girl he wanted me to be.

'Something happened to me,' I started slowly. 'A few years ago.'

Will watched me, not speaking.

'I had my heart broken, I suppose, in a way. But it wasn't just that. It was more.'

'Bad boyfriend?' Will said, sympathy showing in his eyes. 'Did he hit you?'

I shook my head. 'No, not that. It was just wrong.'

Will took my hand. It took all my willpower not to snatch it away.

'Did he …' He lowered his voice. 'Did he force himself on you?'

My eyes filled with tears. How could I explain? How could I put it into words?

'It's complicated,' I whispered. 'But it's left me …' I shook my head again. 'It didn't just break my heart,' I said, 'it broke me.'

Will looked confused and upset. 'Lilian,' he said. 'What happened?'

'I can't talk about it,' I said, so close to tears now. 'I really can't. Please don't ask me.'

'All right,' Will said. 'It's all right.'

'It's not all right,' I said. I closed my eyes briefly to stop the tears falling. 'But I can't make it better. All I can do, is tell you that I can't be your girlfriend. I can't be anyone's girlfriend. I'm broken and I can't be fixed.'

Sweet, sweet Will put his mug of tea down and came round the table to sit next to me. He patted my shoulder and offered me his hanky.

'Lilian Miles,' he said, 'I don't know what's gone on in your life, but strikes me you're one of the bravest girls I've ever met and if it's upset you then it must be bad.'

I gave him a weak, watery smile.

'If you don't want to talk about it, that's fine,' he carried on. 'But you should know that I am a good listener and if you ever want a shoulder to cry on, I'll be right there. In a heartbeat.'

I gave him a stronger smile this time. 'You're the most wonderful man,' I said, grateful that he wasn't going to try to persuade me or talk me into anything. 'I wasn't sure you'd understand. This is the first time ... you're the first man who's wanted to be more than friends since ... you know.'

Will nodded. 'It might get better,' he said hopefully. 'You might find that in a couple of years you want to step out with a fella again.'

I screwed my nose up but I didn't want to throw his kindness back at him. 'I might,' I said. 'Time is a great healer.' I blew my nose on his hanky. 'Don't wait for me, Will. There are hundreds of girls out there who'd be glad of a fella like you. Thousands of them.'

'Not as nice as you, though.'

I waved away his protests with a hand that trembled slightly.

'Rubbish,' I said. 'I'm nothing special. Think of all the brave women up and down this country of ours, doing wonderful things in munitions factories, and hospitals, and army bases and farms. They're all fine girls and every one of them would make a lovely sweetheart for you.'

I smiled at him. 'And they'd be very lucky to have you.'

Will looked crushed. He stared at me for a fraction too long, and then his expression softened. 'There's really no chance?' he said.

'I'm sorry.'

'And it's nothing I did?'

'Nothing whatsoever.' I gazed out of the window so I didn't have to look into his hurt eyes. 'It's me, Will. It's all me.'

On the airfield, I could see Rose talking to one of the other mechanics. She turned to go and swung her hips as he watched her walk by, just as I should have done when Will had been watching me.

'Rose likes you,' I said. 'She likes you a lot.'

Will looked in the direction I was staring. 'She's pretty,' he said.

'See.'

'But she's not the whole package. You're the real deal, Lil.'

'Don't be too quick to write her off,' I said, warming to my role as matchmaker. 'Rose is gorgeous. She's clever, too. And one of the best pilots on the base.'

'She is?'

I had no idea, but I felt if I convinced Will to woo Rose instead, I might not feel so awful.

'And she's got a great figure,' I said, with a cheeky smile.

Will raised an eyebrow and I stuck my chest out and looked downwards and then back at him.

'Great,' I said.

Will shrugged. 'Maybe I'll take her out for a drink,' he said half-heartedly. 'But not yet.' He nudged me gently. 'I need a couple of weeks to get over you.'

I nudged him back. 'I am sorry, you know,' I said. 'I wish things were different. I wish I could be your girl. But I can't.' I stood up, still clutching his hanky. 'I'll get this washed.'

He waved his hand. 'Keep it.'

I picked up my kitbag, and started to walk towards the door.

'Lil,' Will called. 'Is it over?'

I looked at him. 'Is what over?'

'Your romance with this other lad. This bad bloke. Is it over?'

I thought that perhaps it would never be over, at least in my head, but I nodded. 'Over and done with long ago,' I said. 'Over and done with.'

Chapter 20

Helena

June 2018

I was moping. Moping like a lovesick teenager.

'What's the matter with you?' Elly asked, as I slumped at my desk, listlessly scrolling through a census document. 'Had a row with Jack?'

'Nope,' I said, bashing the return key haphazardly. 'Not spoken to him.'

'Ha!' said Elly in triumph. 'I knew it was to do with Jack. I can read you like a book.'

I gave her a withering look and carried on scrolling.

'You're missing him,' Elly said. 'Phone him.'

I sighed. 'Can't. He's filming. In New York.'

In fact, I'd not seen Jack since our evening in the bowling alley almost a fortnight ago. He'd said he was busy, but I'd not really grasped exactly how busy he was. His life was a whirl of rehearsals and screen tests and voice-overs and interviews. The superhero film he'd been linked with wasn't happening, so his agent was sending him to read for all sorts of other parts – sometimes with

121

just a few hours' notice. He did message me a lot, which was great, but he wasn't here. And now he was in New York filming a guest role in an Emmy-winning drama, which his agent thought might lead to a part. It was hectic and exciting and it was annoying me enormously.

'What's he filming?' Elly asked. She was totally over-invested in my relationship with Jack but I didn't mind. I loved talking about him. And thinking about him. And daydreaming about him …

I filled Elly in on the guest role, and what his agent had said, and what his career plans were, until I saw her eyes starting to glaze over and realised I'd perhaps gone on too much.

'I just want to see him,' I muttered.

'How are you getting on with the research?' Elly asked. 'Have you found out anything about your aunt?'

I shrugged. I'd not done anything really, despite Dad's endless messages. I'd even avoided our usual Friday night family dinner, pretending I had something else on. I was still hopelessly torn between wanting to please Dad and to protect Lil.

'Why don't you do a bit of digging?' Elly said. 'It'll snap you out of your mood and, you never know, you might find something so juicy that Jack can't resist meeting up to hear all about it, even if he's supposed to be in Hollywood.'

'New York,' I said.

Elly rolled her eyes. 'Look Lilian up on the 1939 census,' she said. I nodded. It was where we normally started with wartime stories so it made sense.

'They lived in Kent back then,' I said. 'My grandad Bobby and grandma Ruth, Lil, and my great-grandparents. They all lived in the same village. I can't imagine there's much to tell.'

'It's a start,' Elly said.

Realising I wouldn't be able to settle to what I was supposed to be doing, I pulled up the 1939 census and logged in, thinking for the millionth time how easy the internet made searches like these. I typed in Lilian Miles and pressed enter. It brought up one entry for someone in Manchester who was seventy-five in 1939. That wasn't her.

I tried again, spelling Lilian with two Ls in the middle in case it had been entered differently – it sometimes happened. But this time it came back with no results. How strange.

'Odd,' I muttered. This time I typed in Robert Miles – my grandad, who Dad was named after – and got a hit. It brought up his address in the village in Kent called Fairbourne, where I knew he and Lil had grown up. Then I tried my grandma, Ruth, but just like with Lil, there was no mention of her.

'Elly,' I said. 'She's not showing up.'

Elly peered over my shoulder. 'Weird,' she said. 'Maybe she'd left by then? Joined up?'

I shook my head. 'Can't have, she was only fifteen when war broke out. There's no mention of my grandma either.'

'Evacuated?' Elly suggested.

'From Kent?'

Elly shrugged. 'I don't mean officially, like the kids from the East End. But all the planes flew over Kent on their way to bomb London – maybe they went somewhere else to keep them safe? I've come across lots of families who moved away.'

A light bulb went on in my head and I counted on my fingers. 'My dad was born in February 1940,' I said. 'Grandma would have been pregnant when the war started.'

'And where was your dad born?'

I grinned. 'Scotland,' I said. 'He was born in Scotland. He says Grandma went up there to live with a friend when the war started because she didn't want to be near London.'

Elly looked triumphant. 'Told you,' she said.

I shut the England and Wales census and opened the Scottish version instead, typing in my grandmother's name, Ruth Miles.

Immediately it came up with an entry. I clicked on it and it opened.

'*Ruth Miles, 25,*' I read. '*Jemima Thorogood, 53 (widow of Donald Thorogood). Lilian Miles, 15.*' The address was Kelso, which I knew was in the Scottish Borders.

I gasped in surprise. Lil had been in Scotland with my grandmother. Ruth had apparently gone to Kelso to stay with this Jemima and taken Lil with her. I had no idea who Jemima was – I'd never even heard of her – and I had no idea why Ruth would have gone to stay with some random woman.

I said as much to Elly, turning my screen so she could see the entry.

'Maybe she was a family friend or a godmother or something,' I said. 'There has to have been a link.'

'So why would Lil go with her?' Elly asked.

I tapped my fingers on my desk, thinking. 'My great-grandfather served in World War One,' I said. 'Had a tough old time of it I think. The way Dad and Lil tell it, sounds like he had shell shock.'

Elly made a face. 'Poor bloke,' she said.

'Perhaps another war was too much for him and he had a bit of a breakdown.'

It was something we'd come across more than once in all of our research – the men who'd come home from the trenches reacting badly to the outbreak of another war.

'Maybe he was taking up all my great-grandmother's time and energy,' I said. 'And Lil went with Grandma so she could help her when she had the baby, and Grandma could keep an eye on her in turn.'

Elly nodded. 'Makes sense,' she said. 'What will you do next?'

I thought for a moment. I had lots of things I could do. I could find my father's birth certificate, which I didn't remember ever seeing. I could find out more about Jemima Thorogood, or her dead husband Donald. I could have a look at my great-grandfather's records from the First World War and see if I could discover anything that would have left him shell-shocked and unwell. I could try to find out some more about Fairbourne in Kent during the war to see if it was under the flight path of the planes heading to bomb London, or I could research Kelso to see if there were any local history records that mentioned a link to my great-grandparents, or Ruth and Lil, or Jemima. I could check the RAF bases for any that were located near Kelso that might have inspired Lil's choice to join the ATA Girls.

I had lots of different paths I could follow and any one of them could lead to me finding out the truth about what happened to Lil later on in the war. But, slightly hating myself, I didn't do any of them. Instead I sent Jack a message telling him I'd found out some interesting info about Lil and I wasn't sure what to do next. I told him I'd value his opinion and that perhaps when he got back to London we could meet up to chat it through.

'I'm pathetic,' I said, pressing send.

'Totally,' said Elly cheerfully. 'But he's worth it.'

Almost straight away my phone buzzed with a reply.

'Exciting!' it said. 'At JFK on my way home. Can we meet tomorrow? Or the next day? Jx'

I read it out to Elly and she high-fived me.

'See?' she said. 'Worth it.'

'I'm basically pretending not to know how to do my job, and risking upsetting my favourite auntie just to get close to a slightly chaotic actor,' I said.

'And to help your dad,' Elly said.

I nodded.

'And Jack is not just a slightly chaotic actor, he is a completely hot actor,' she added. 'Who is totally into you.'

'I suppose …'

'It's worth it,' Elly said firmly. 'You know I'm right.'

I grinned. 'I know,' I said.

'Helena?' I jumped as Fliss appeared behind my desk. 'Can I have a quick word?'

I raised my eyebrows at Elly as I followed Fliss into her office and sat down.

'How is the Lady Jane Grey research going?' she said.

I felt a pang of guilt. I knew I hadn't been giving it the attention it deserved.

'Not bad,' I said. 'I'm waiting to hear back from a Tudor historian from Oxford.'

That was true but there was plenty I could have been doing in the meantime.

'And Jack Jones?' she said.

My heart thumped simply at the mention of his name. 'Erm, yes. Not bad,' I said. 'I've handed over the stuff about his great-grandfather to Percy …'

Percy was our First World War specialist. He'd go through all the information about the Somme that I'd found and take things from there.

'And his grandfather?'

'He was in the ATA,' I said, hoping I didn't look as guilty as I felt.

'Interesting?'

'Actually, really interesting.' Now I didn't have to lie – it truly was fascinating. 'He was one of very few men who were in the ATA. It was mostly women.'

Fliss smiled. 'Great,' she said. 'That's a nice angle. How come his grandfather joined up then?'

'He was too short-sighted to join the regular RAF,' I said.

'Christ.'

I chuckled. 'I know, right.'

Fliss smiled again. 'Sounds like you're on top of things,' she said. 'I was just worried you'd seemed a bit distracted and I wanted to check everything was going okay?'

'It's fine,' I said. 'I had a bit of family stuff happening but everything's fine.'

'Dora okay?'

'She's great,' I said.

'Good,' Fliss said. 'It was nice to meet your dad the other day.'

I gave her a tight smile, hoping she wouldn't ask any more. 'He said the same,' I said.

'Just shout if you've got too much to do,' Fliss said. 'I can always take some research off your hands.'

'Honestly, I'm fine,' I said. 'But thanks.'

Fliss nodded at me and I scarpered back to my desk, my cheeks flaming. Did this mean she was keeping an eye on me? I knew I had to be careful if there was a chance she could look at my searches. While my family were supportive and Miranda had taken me in when I was pregnant and homeless, I couldn't rely on them being a safety blanket forever. I was, after all, a grown-up woman in my thirties with a child to support. This job was really, really important for me and for Dora and I couldn't risk losing it.

Chapter 21

Lilian

September 1939

Time was passing and I knew I had to do something but I had no idea what. I lay in bed at night, sleep eluding me, wishing I didn't exist. There was no way out, as far as I could see. I even thought about taking my own life, but I wasn't sure how to do it. Or what the consequences would be if I failed. Instead, I simply carried on, going through the motions of everyday life.

In many ways, everyone was doing the same thing. I was carrying on despite my condition, and England was carrying on despite the war. In fact, not much had changed since war had been declared almost three weeks ago. Some people – Mr Vincent from the post office and Albie, the butcher's son – had volunteered to be air raid wardens and been given tin helmets. But after the first few nights when they officiously patrolled the village after dark, they put their helmets aside again. The war didn't seem real, though we knew things were happening in Europe. My father listened to every news bulletin and read the newspaper from cover to cover every day. And then Bobby got his call-up papers.

He was told to report for his induction at RAF Uxbridge at the beginning of October, which meant he had two weeks left at home. Lots of the men in the village were going. A few to the RAF like Bobby, two brothers to the navy, and the rest into the army. The call-up papers were coming thick and fast. So Marcus the postman told me as I walked to catch the school bus one morning. He had a sheaf of letters in his hand and he waved them at me.

'Your brother's going to have some company,' he said.

I looked at the envelopes without interest. I had blocked out the thought of Bobby leaving, just as I was blocking out everything else.

'Couple going to the air force, so they'll be with your Bobby,' Marcus was saying. 'But most of these are army papers.'

He leafed through them.

'I've got one here for Paul Benjamin, another for his brother – their mother will be upset to have them both go so early – one for Ian Mayhew, one for Gerry Carter …'

'What did you say?' I wanted to be sure I'd heard correctly.

'Gerry Carter?' he said, giving me a quizzical look.

I wanted to grab him and shake him. 'Before that.'

'Ian Mayhew,' he said. 'And the Benjamin brothers.'

But I was off, racing to the Mayhews' house. I'd spent the last few weeks avoiding Mr Mayhew, but suddenly I knew that if he was going to join up, then I had to tell him. I had to tell Mr Mayhew that I was expecting his baby. He was, after all, what I considered a grown-up whereas I was most definitely not. He would know what to do. He would make all this horrible torment go away.

I ran through the village and up the path to the Mayhews' house, then I hammered on the door. Mr Mayhew answered, looking grumpy.

'Lilian,' he said. 'What's the emergency?'

'You volunteered,' I said breathlessly. 'Marcus has your papers.'

Mr Mayhew glanced behind him nervously. 'Winifred is here,' he said. 'Let's walk.'

He went back into the house, and I heard murmured voices from the kitchen, then he came back out with his jacket over his arm, and shut the front door behind him.

'Bus stop?' he said.

I shook my head. I couldn't go to school, not now.

'Church hall, then,' he said. 'You can play me something on the piano.'

Obediently, I started walking towards the centre of the village. I longed to take Mr Mayhew's hand, and wondered what he would do if I did. Then his fingers brushed mine and I recoiled. What was wrong with me? I was a swirling mess of confusion at every turn.

'Where have you been?' Mr Mayhew asked, as we walked.

I shrugged. 'School,' I said. 'Home. Dad's not taking things very well.'

'Did your brother join up?'

I nodded. 'RAF.'

Mr Mayhew breathed in. 'I'm joining the army,' he said. 'I wasn't sure if they'd take me. I'm almost thirty, after all.'

'They probably need all the help they can get, even from old men,' I said, viciously, wanting to wound. He didn't react.

'I've missed you,' he said. 'I will miss you when I go. Will you write?'

I shook my head, turning my face away from him so he wouldn't see that I was crying.

We were close to the church hall now and I could see a group of elderly ladies heading inside. We couldn't chat if they were there.

I veered off the pavement and into the churchyard. After a second, Mr Mayhew followed me. I perched on a bench under a tree and he sat next to me.

'I expect they'll need more space in here,' I said, gazing at the rows of graves. 'Once the fighting starts properly. Lots of men won't come home alive.'

I didn't know what I was doing. Why was I saying such terrible things?

Beside me, Mr Mayhew flinched. 'What's going on, Lilian?' he asked. 'What's the matter?'

I pulled the end of my plait over one shoulder and held on to it tightly, as though it might bring me luck.

'I'm pregnant,' I said. It was the first time I'd said the words. 'I'm having a baby.'

I started to cry, trying to get the words out between gasping sobs.

'And I thought you should know, because of the war. You might not come home. But you should know. I wanted to tell you. And I don't know what to do.'

I looked up at Mr Mayhew, desperate for some words of comfort. Aching for him to take me in his arms and tell me things were going to be all right, that he'd look after me now. That somehow we could make this work. That I wouldn't bring shame on my parents, and break Ruth and Bobby's hearts, and watch my whole life – my hopes and dreams of being a musician – crumble into the dust.

But he didn't. He sat, straight-backed, on the bench and watched me cry. As I gathered myself, and my sobs grew less frequent, he stared straight ahead. A muscle flickered in his cheek but otherwise he was perfectly still.

'What does this have to do with me?' he said.

My head spun. What did he mean? 'The baby?' I babbled. 'The baby is yours.'

Mr Mayhew glanced at me in disdain. 'So you claim,' he said. 'But I would be a fool to believe anything a little slut like you says. Wouldn't I?'

Completely wrong-footed by his reaction, all I could do was stare at him, open-mouthed.

131

'You girls, you're all the same. Giving me the big eyes, and the little laughs. Pressing your bodies up against me when I'm just trying to show you how to play a piece correctly. And then pretending it's a surprise when I respond. Like you don't want it.'

He turned to face me. 'You wanted it,' he spat. The fury in his expression made me shrink back against the bench.

'Girls?' I whispered. 'Girls?'

I'd thought I was special. That we'd had something precious. But had I – all along – just been one of many?

Mr Mayhew stood up and brushed invisible dust from his trousers. I had a feeling he was actually brushing me off, rather than any dirt. Perhaps that was how he saw me – as a speck of dust to be removed from his life.

'This has nothing to do with me,' he said coldly. 'Please stay away from me and my wife. I don't want her upset when I'm leaving so soon. If you come near us, I will inform the police.'

He walked away through the churchyard, without looking back. Dizzy and nauseous, I tried to follow but found myself doubled over as my stomach cramped and I vomited bile – I'd barely eaten for days so there was nothing to bring up.

'Mr Mayhew,' I croaked, but he was gone.

Scared and feeling more alone than I'd ever been before, I staggered in the direction of the road, using the gravestones as support. The stone was cold against my hot hands. My stomach was twisting and I had to stop to retch again before I made it on to the street.

I looked in both directions, but I couldn't see any sign of Mr Mayhew. He must have walked home even faster than his usual brisk pace. I didn't know where to go. Sweat beaded my forehead, and my stomach was sore. I couldn't go to school in this state and I didn't want to go home and face my mother's questions and my father's gloomy face. I'd go to see Ruth, I decided.

Slowly, holding on to the fence to help me stay upright, I

walked past the church hall. One of the women we'd seen earlier – an elderly lady who knew my mother from the Women's Institute – was coming out of the door. She saw me and called my name.

'Lilian,' she said. 'Why aren't you at school? Are you ill?'

I turned towards her and she gasped.

'Oh, my dear girl,' she said. 'You look terrible. Shall I fetch your mother?'

'I'm fine,' I said. 'I just need to lie down.'

And then the ground came up to meet me and everything went black.

Chapter 22

'Lilian, can you hear me?'

I opened my eyes. My head ached and I couldn't make out what I was seeing. Shapes loomed over me. I shut my eyes again.

'Lil, open your eyes.'

This time I recognised the voice. It was Bobby.

'Bobby,' I said.

'I'm here.' Someone – Bobby, I supposed – took my hand. 'Ruth's here too. And the doctor.'

I blinked as the room came into focus. I was in Ruth and Bobby's lounge on the settee with a blanket over me. Bobby was sitting next to me, Ruth behind him, and Dr Gilbert was hovering by the door.

'Food,' Dr Gilbert said. 'Proper meals, lots of sleep and a bit of TLC. I'll come back later to check on her.'

'Thanks, Doctor,' Ruth said. She followed him out of the room and I heard muffled conversation and then the front door opened.

'What happened?' I said to Bobby, though I was beginning to remember. 'I fainted.'

Bobby looked sombre. 'You fainted at Mrs Elliott's feet,' he said. 'Gave her quite a shock. Why weren't you at school, Lil?'

I wriggled on the settee so I could sit up a bit. 'Had something to do,' I muttered.

Ruth came back into the room and sat down on the floor by my head. She stroked my hair gently. I saw her exchange a look with Bobby and it made me nervous.

'Lilian,' she said carefully. 'Mrs Elliott said you were clutching your tummy before you passed out.'

I shut my eyes. I didn't want to look at her.

'Dr Gilbert examined you, to check you didn't have appendicitis,' Ruth carried on.

I squeezed my eyes shut even tighter.

'Lilian,' she said. 'Dr Gilbert thinks you're expecting a baby.'

Her voice shook a bit on the last word and I felt her hand, still resting on my head, tremble.

Bobby took over. 'Tell us the truth, Lilian,' he said. 'We can help you.'

I shook my head, eyes still tightly closed, and a tear dripped down on to the cushion beneath my head. 'I can't,' I whispered. 'I can't.'

'Darling girl, you can tell us,' Ruth said. 'We're your family and we love you. But we can't help you unless you tell us what's happened.'

'Are you hungry?' Bobby said suddenly. 'You're so thin, and Dr Gilbert thinks you've not been eating properly. How about some toast and a cup of tea, and we can have a proper chat about all this. Get it all sorted out.'

Suddenly I realised I was absolutely ravenous. I opened my eyes. Bobby and Ruth were both bent over me, their faces worried. I threw myself into Bobby's arms and hugged him tight.

'Help me,' I begged him. 'Please, please help me.'

And he did.

First, he made me some toast and a pot of tea and Ruth helped me sit up on the couch with the blanket over my legs like an old woman. And then, once I'd eaten and drunk, and I felt a bit better, though still very shaky, they each sat on either side of me and held my hands.

'Are you pregnant?' Ruth said.

I nodded my head. 'I think so,' I said.

She bit her lip. 'How far along?'

I looked up at the ceiling. 'I don't know,' I whispered. 'I'm not sure how you tell. But I think maybe three months? Four, perhaps?'

Ruth breathed in sharply and I thought perhaps her last pregnancy would have been the same, if she'd not started bleeding. How unfair the world was. How awful and unfair.

'Lil, who is the father?' Bobby asked, his expression dark and guarded. 'Whose baby is it?'

'I can't tell you,' I said. 'I can't. Please don't ask me.'

Bobby and Ruth looked at each other again, this time a more knowing glance.

'Is it that bastard Mayhew?' Bobby hissed.

Hearing his name in such a way felt like a slap. I winced at the words Bobby was saying and he nodded.

'I knew it,' he said. 'I bloody knew it. I told Mum not to send you there. I'd heard stories about why he left his last school. She said not to listen to gossip.'

'He's done this before?' Ruth said, staring at Bobby in horror as I thought about Mr Mayhew saying 'girls' in the churchyard.

'He's done it before,' I said, simply. 'He told me.'

'What did he do?' Bobby said, looking sick to his stomach. 'Did he …?'

I took a breath. 'I love him,' I said. But as I said the words, I realised they weren't true. Had they ever been? I wasn't sure.

Ruth squeezed my fingers. 'He took advantage of you, Lil,' she said. 'How old were you when this started? Fourteen?'

'Almost fifteen,' I said, like that made all the difference.

She shook her head.

'I knew what I was doing,' I said, still determined to defend Mr Mayhew, despite his cruel words. 'I wanted him.'

'You're too young,' Bobby said. He was simmering with anger. 'He's an adult and you're just a kid. He's a filthy, disgusting …'

'Bobby,' Ruth said, warning him. 'Calm down.'

'Does he know?' Bobby said. 'Did you tell him?'

I couldn't speak. Though my feelings about Mr Mayhew were confusing and conflicted, I knew that telling Bobby how he'd reacted when I told him about the baby wouldn't look good. Did Mr Mayhew's reaction prove he was a bad person? I was afraid it did.

'Did you tell him?' Bobby asked again.

'I told him,' I said quietly. I started to cry again. 'He said I was a slut and that he didn't think it was his baby.'

Bobby stood up. 'That bastard,' he said. 'I'm going to bloody kill him.'

Ruth grabbed his arm. 'Bobby, don't you dare. That's not going to help anyone.'

She was calm. Much calmer than I'd expected her to be. And her eyes were shining with purpose. 'If you hit him, everyone will know there's a problem between you,' she said. 'We need to keep this quiet.'

'It'll make me feel better,' Bobby muttered, but he sat down again.

Ruth was looking at me intently. 'Lilian,' she said. 'Do you want to have a baby?'

'No,' I wailed. I didn't even have to think about it. 'I don't know what to do with a baby. I'm too young to be a mother. I just want to play the piano.'

'I've got an idea,' said Ruth.

Bobby was watching his wife, a strange look on his face – admiration mixed with fear. 'Ruth?' he said. 'Really?'

She nodded. 'Think about it,' she said to Bobby over my head. I had no idea what she was talking about. I just wanted my big brother to mend things. Put them right. I trusted him and her more than I trusted my own parents.

'Are you sure?' Bobby said.

Ruth nodded again. 'If you are,' she said.

He reached across me and gripped her hand and something passed between them. A strength. A determination. I waited.

'We'll take your baby,' Ruth said. 'We'll love that baby so much, Lilian. We'll care for it and cuddle it and tell it stories at bedtime. And you can be involved if you want. As much as you want. Or as little.'

I looked at her. My sweet, kind, selfless sister-in-law. Whose heart had been broken and whose eyes had been dull and sad and were now shining with hope.

'You'd take my baby?' I said, hardly able to believe what I was hearing. 'You'd look after it? You'd be its mum and dad?'

Bobby smiled. 'We'd be honoured,' he said.

'But how?' I said. 'People would know it was my child.' I pulled my school dress tight over my swelling stomach. 'It's going to be obvious soon.'

Ruth was thinking, drumming her fingers on her leg. 'I told your mum,' she said, more to herself than to Bobby and me. 'I told her I thought I was pregnant a while ago. But I never told her I'd started bleeding because that was when Hitler invaded and your dad started with his crying and that …'

'So you could tell her you're expecting,' I said, seeing where she was going. 'Instead of me.'

The relief of not having to break my mother's heart was enormous.

'But we'd have to go away,' I carried on. 'How can we go away? Where on earth would we go?'

Ruth was smiling. 'My godmother Jemima lives in Scotland, near the border,' she said. 'She married a farmer and he died a few years ago. It's not easy for her, on her own, and she's had a few troubles of her own. We could go and stay with her. Help her out.'

'Mum wouldn't let me go,' I said.

'There's a war on,' Bobby pointed out. 'It would be for your own safety. We could say Ruth's pregnant and I want her to be somewhere safe. And you're going with her to help.'

'Mum will want to come.'

'She can't leave Dad,' Bobby said. 'She can visit when the baby's born.'

I felt more hopeful than I'd felt for weeks. Could this possibly work?

'And what about your godmother?' I said to Ruth. 'Will she go along with this mad idea?'

Ruth bit her lip. 'Jemima's had a difficult time herself,' she said. 'I'm not sure what's gone on with her, but I know she won't stand by if someone needs help.'

'Would the baby call you Mum and Dad?' I said.

Ruth took a breath. 'I think so,' she said. 'We'd be the baby's parents. If we're doing this, we need to do it properly. Have us on the birth certificate.'

'Would you mind?' Bobby asked gently.

I imagined a little girl, with my dark hair, climbing on to Ruth's knee and calling her Mamma. I tested how my heart felt about my daughter – or son – calling my brother Daddy. And I discovered I didn't mind at all. It felt like a gift. A gift they were giving me – to take my baby and bring it up as their own. To love it as they loved me.

I shook my head. 'I wouldn't mind at all,' I said.

'We need to be fast,' Ruth pointed out. 'We can't stay here for too long.'

Bobby stood up and took a pad and a pencil from the mantelpiece, then he sat down again and started scribbling notes.

'You go to the post office and send a telegram to Jemima,' he said to Ruth. 'I'll go and find Mother. I'll tell her you're poorly, Lil, and that you're staying here tonight.'

I was pleased; I didn't want to go home.

'Once I've heard back from Jem, we can tell your parents that

139

I'm pregnant,' Ruth said. 'And we can say that it'll do you good to get away, because you've been ill.'

'What about school?'

'We can work something out,' Bobby said.

'And does she have a piano?' I asked. 'Does Jemima have a piano?'

Bobby smiled at me. 'If she doesn't, I'm sure you'll sniff one out somewhere.' He paused. 'What shall we tell Mayhew?'

'He's been called up,' I said. 'He's going away.'

'Let's hope he gets shot,' Bobby said viciously.

'Bobby, don't,' Ruth said.

'He won't care,' I said, seeing clearly for what seemed to be the first time in well over a year. 'He doesn't care about me, and he won't care about the baby. If anyone tells him we've gone, he'll probably just be relieved. He won't make any trouble.'

'Is it settled then?' Bobby said.

I let my hand drift downwards and rest on my small rounded belly. Then I put my other arm round his waist and rested my head on Ruth's shoulder.

'It's settled,' I said. 'You're going to be the best Mum and Dad this little mite could ever wish for.'

Chapter 23

Helena

June 2018

'Oh are you a sight for sore eyes,' Jack said as he opened the door. 'I'm so pleased to see you.'

I smiled at him, feeling slightly self-conscious. I'd never been to his house before and it felt really intimate.

'Are you wearing good underwear?' Elly had asked as I left the office earlier.

'Elly,' I'd said, laughing despite myself. 'I am not going to sleep with him.'

She'd raised her eyebrows at me, not surprisingly. I had, actually, arranged for Dora to stay over at Miranda's. And I thought I probably would sleep with Jack if the opportunity arose (oh please, let the opportunity arise) but that didn't mean I wanted to discuss it with Elly.

So, I was wearing good underwear, even though I was just wearing jeans and a casual shirt in a 'oh, this old thing?' kind of way.

'You look great,' Jack said. 'I love your shirt.'

'Oh, this old thing?' I said, and he laughed.

'Come on in,' he said.

Jack lived in a pink-fronted house in a row of pastel-coloured terraces in Notting Hill. It wasn't big but I thought it probably cost several times what my little house was worth.

'This is nice,' I said, taking off my leather jacket and handing it to him. He hung it on a peg, where it fell off again.

'It's fine,' he said. 'I'm not here very much.'

I bent down to pick up my jacket and hung it up again.

'Give me a tour?'

'There's not much to see,' he said. 'But follow me.'

The house had a largish living room with a table at one end, a roomy kitchen extension on the back, and two bedrooms upstairs. Both were so messy it was impossible to tell which room Jack used.

'I sleep in this one and use the other one for packing and unpacking,' he said sheepishly, gesturing towards the pile of clothes on the floor. 'I'm always coming and going.'

'It must be hard,' I said sympathetically. 'Not spending much time at home.'

Jack grinned. 'I don't really consider this home. Home is my mum's house.'

'That's sweet,' I said, feeling a twinge of envy again at his happy family life.

I glanced at the untidy bedroom and quashed my instinct to start picking things up. I couldn't really imagine having a night of unbridled passion here, despite my lovely underwear.

'Shall we go downstairs?' I said, before I began picking up T-shirts.

'Itching to tidy up?' Jack said, wrinkling his nose at me.

'A bit.'

Jack tilted his head and looked at me.

'Totally,' I admitted and he laughed again.

'Let's go into the kitchen,' he said. 'I have a cleaner who keeps that to your standards.'

Thankfully he was right. The kitchen was gleaming – it was obvious he didn't cook very much. Jack poured some wine and I perched at the breakfast bar while he dug about in a drawer looking for takeaway menus.

'There's one place that's really good,' he said as a ball of string fell out of the drawer and rolled across the floor. I bent down to retrieve it and wound the loose end round and round.

'Order online,' I said. 'There's an app.'

'Brilliant,' said Jack. 'Let's do that.'

He pushed the drawer closed, shoving in all the bits that were poking out, and turned to smile at me. I felt my stomach turn over with a delicious mixture of happiness, laughter and lust. He really was special.

'You do the order,' he said. 'And tell me all about Lil.'

It was a lovely evening. After the food arrived we took our wine into the living room and sat together on the soft sofa, our curry laid out on the coffee table in front of us.

'Lil went to Scotland with my grandmother, early in the war,' I explained. 'A place called Kelso.'

Jack nodded. 'In the borders?'

'Have you been?' I was surprised.

'No, but I met a girl from there once.'

I felt a tiny twist of envy. 'Ex-girlfriend?' I said super casually.

'Ex make-up artist,' he said with a smile.

I filled him in on Ruth and Lil moving up north, and my theory that my great-grandfather may have been struggling with the outbreak of another war.

'Makes sense,' he said. 'What's our next move?'

I smiled at him using 'our'.

'I thought I might find out more about Kelso and the airbase that was nearby,' I said. 'I did a bit of research and discovered it was called Charterhall. It might have been the reason Lil joined the ATA.'

Jack nodded. 'She probably watched the planes from where she was living,' he said.

'Exactly.' I took a mouthful of wine. 'And she probably knew lots of pilots, too.'

Jack raised an eyebrow. 'Maybe she had a romance with one of them?'

'Perhaps,' I said. 'But she was only just sixteen.'

'Oh come on. I bet you had romances when you were sixteen.'

I made a face. 'No, I didn't,' I admitted. 'But I was a bit of an oddball. Immy definitely had boyfriends when she was that age, and so did Miranda.'

'Then it's not an outlandish suggestion,' Jack said, a touch of triumph in his voice. 'Would your dad remember? How old was he?'

I shook my head. 'He was born in Kelso, actually,' I told him. 'I thought that might have been another reason for Lilian to have gone with my grandmother – to help with the baby.'

'Your grandfather had signed up?'

I nodded. 'I still think it's odd,' I said. 'To go so far away, when my grandmother – Ruth – would have had all sorts of support in Kent.'

'I think you should ask your dad,' Jack said, offering me the last piece of naan.

I shook my head no – both for the bread, and for asking Dad. 'He was a baby,' I said. 'He won't remember.'

'But did they stay there for the whole war? If so, he'd have been a little boy when they left. He's bound to remember some things. Maybe he can shed some light on why they moved up there.'

I felt silly. 'I can't believe I don't know these things,' I said. 'I don't know if Dad was in Scotland for the whole war, and I don't know what he remembers.'

I thought for a minute. 'I've seen a photo of him as a baby in a terrifying-looking gas mask that covered his whole body,' I said.

'And he's talked about how, because he was in the country, they weren't really bothered by the bombs too much. I've always assumed that was in Kent but it could just have easily been in Kelso.'

'You should ask him,' Jack said. 'I bet he'll surprise you with how much he remembers. And he'll be keen to help you, presumably, given how you're doing all this for him.'

I winced, remembering something. 'Fliss called me in to her office,' I said. 'She said she was worried I was doing too much and she could help out.'

'That's nice of her,' Jack said.

'Hmm.' I made a face. 'Not sure.'

'You think she's got wind of what you're doing?'

'I don't see how, but I need to be a bit careful,' I said. 'More work in work time, and less personal stuff. I need to keep her away from checking on what I'm researching.'

'Sounds like a plan,' Jack said. 'Though surely you wouldn't get into much trouble, even if she did know what you were doing?'

I wasn't sure. I said as much, then changed the subject. 'What do you remember?' I asked him. 'About when you were little?'

'We lived in Manchester for a while when I was about four,' Jack said. 'Not for long according to Mum but to me it felt like forever. She was working on a soap – *Rosamund Street* – then. It was a big break for her writing career and she wasn't going to let being a single mum stop her.'

'She took you with her?'

He smiled. 'I remember my grandma saying she'd look after me and I was worried about that because Grandma made me eat peas and I hated peas,' he said. 'So I was pleased I could go with Mum. We stayed in a house near a canal and I went to work with her every day and watched them filming.'

'Amazing,' I said. 'No wonder you're an actor – you've been learning your craft for thirty years.'

'I was young,' Jack said. 'Really small, because I'd not started school yet. Younger than your dad was when the war ended. And I remember all sorts from back then.'

I nodded thoughtfully. 'You're right,' I said. 'I should speak to Dad. See whether he remembers living in Scotland.'

'Can I come?' Jack said. 'When you ask him? Will it be at one of your family dinners?'

I blinked at him. 'Probably,' I said. 'I see a lot of my family but we really only get a chance to properly chat at our dinners.'

'So can I come?' he said. 'This Friday?'

'They're boring,' I said. 'Just Miranda nagging Mum about money, and Dad whingeing about the film industry.'

'I can whinge about the film industry,' Jack said eagerly. 'And I'd like to meet your dad anyway – I loved the music on *Mackenzie*.'

I sighed. 'Fine,' I said. 'But I still don't really understand what the appeal is.'

Jack turned to me and took my glass of wine from my hand. 'Helena,' he said patiently. 'It's you.'

'What's me?'

'You're the appeal.'

He took one of my hands in his, and with the other he gently pushed my hair back from my face. My skin fizzled at his touch.

'I think you're wonderful,' he said. 'And I want to know all about you. I want to meet Dora properly – when she's awake. I want to meet your parents and your siblings and I am desperate to meet Lil. I want to spend lots and lots of time with you and if that means coming to a family dinner, then I'm in.'

I felt weak with longing. 'Okay,' I said faintly.

Jack pulled me closer to him and kissed me. 'I'm in,' he murmured.

Chapter 24

Lilian

July 1944

Will was beginning to annoy me. Just a little bit. He was treating me like I was some sort of fragile ornament. I couldn't go anywhere on the base without him suddenly appearing to open a door for me, offering to carry my bag, or getting me a cup of tea. It was unsettling and, like I said, beginning to get on my nerves.

'I just want him to leave me alone,' I told Annie, who was finding the whole thing hilarious. 'I can't bear him following me round like a puppy.'

'You're off to Scotland tomorrow, aren't you?' she said. 'A couple of days away might do the trick.'

I was indeed going up north. I'd had my leave signed off, and Flight Captain Rogers had agreed to find me a delivery in Scotland so I could visit Ruth. I was excited at the thought of seeing her and her little Robert. He was a proper boy now – not a baby any more – and I enjoyed seeing how he'd changed every time I visited.

We were in our bedroom, Annie reading some letters we'd received and me just lying on my bed, staring at the stains on the ceiling, thinking.

'I shouldn't have told him anything about what happened to me,' I said. 'I hate people knowing too much.'

'Don't worry about it,' Annie said. 'He's on your side – totally on your side. He's not going to spread rumours about you.'

"Spose,' I said. 'I just hate being treated like a victim.'

Annie looked at me over the top of a letter. 'I know,' she said, sympathetically. 'And I know you don't like talking about it all. But you did the right thing, telling him. It's good to be honest.'

'Rose knows something,' I said.

'So maybe it would be a good thing if they get together,' Annie said. 'Will might calm her down a bit, make her understand that you didn't do anything wrong.'

'Maybe,' I said, though I wasn't convinced. 'Anything we can help with in those letters?'

Annie nodded. 'One,' she said, handing it to me. 'An adoption, and the mother lives quite near a base.'

I sat up to read the letter, all my worries gone. I found it so satisfying when we actually could help people and we often couldn't. We were getting so many requests for help now that we'd talked about getting someone else to come on board, but that was risky and I wasn't keen. Instead we just did what we could, when we could. Last week Flora had sorted an abortion for a woman in Edinburgh, and now we had an adoption to arrange.

'Norwich,' I said, thoughtfully. 'Easy enough for us to get to her – there are lots of bases over that way. Who do we know over there?'

'Madge,' Annie said. 'She's the nurse at the women's hospital, remember?'

'Oh yes, Madge.'

We had built up a network of sympathetic women. Madge was

a friend of a friend of Flora's. She knew all the families locally that were struggling to have children and had helped us – and them – before.

'Far enough away?' I asked. It was often better if the mothers could move away for a while, so they didn't have to hide their bumps.

'Possibly,' Annie said. 'If not, Madge has contacts all over.'

'So, we need to see Madge,' I said, scanning the letter for the woman's story. Same old, same old. She'd had her head turned by a soldier and discovered too late that she was expecting. She said there was no chance of passing the tot off as her husband's as he'd not been home for a year.

Annie grinned. 'I'll check the rotas,' she said. 'One of us is bound to be heading that way soon.'

East Anglia was brimming with bases as it was so handy for planes flying to Europe. We flew there often, delivering all sorts of aircraft.

'I reckon within the week,' I agreed. 'Probably won't be me, though, if I'm off up to Scotland.'

Annie shrugged. 'Fine,' she said. 'Flora and I can handle it.'

I grinned at her. 'Course you can,' I said. I swung my legs off the bed and stood up, handing her the letter. 'I have to go – I've got to find out what I'm taking up to Charterhall.' I dropped a kiss on Annie's head. 'You're a good person,' I told her.

She grinned at me. 'You too,' she said.

Feeling happy – we were helping another woman, and I was looking forward to seeing Ruth and Robert – I wandered down the road to the airbase. I wanted to find Gareth, who I knew would have a heads-up about which planes were going up north. Sometimes we delivered planes we'd never flown before so we had a little handbook we could refer to. I liked to have advance warning whenever it was possible and Gareth seemed to know everything.

'Need a hand?'

I jumped as Will appeared next to me.

'I'm not doing anything,' I said, a bit more snappy than the jokey tone I'd intended. 'I'm not carrying anything, I'm not opening anything, I'm not lifting anything. I'm fine.'

Will didn't so much as flinch. Instead he smiled at me. 'Am I fussing?' he said. 'My sister says I'm a terrible fusspot.'

Instantly my irritation vanished. He really was a nice bloke.

'You are a bit,' I said. 'I really am all right, you know.'

Will gave a little chuckle. 'Sorry,' he said. 'Going to find Gareth?'

I nodded. 'I'm taking a plane up to Scotland tomorrow,' I told him. 'And I've arranged to see my sister-in-law while I'm there.'

'Ah that'll be nice. Is she the one with the little lad?'

I felt a bit nervy at his mention of Robert, but I managed to smile. 'My nephew,' I said, nodding. 'He's four.'

Across the runway, I saw Rose watching us. For once I was grateful for her lurking as it gave me an opportunity to change the subject.

'There's Rose.' I nodded my head slightly in her direction, which was behind Will. He went to turn and glance over his shoulder and I stopped him with a pat on his arm. 'Don't make it obvious you're looking, silly.'

He made a funny face at me and I carried on.

'In a minute, walk past her, all casual, and then say: "Oh hello, Rose, I didn't see you there," like you've only just noticed her.'

'Right,' said Will, looking vaguely bemused.

'And then compliment her on something – her hair probably; she has nice hair.'

'Not as nice as yours,' Will said and I scowled at him.

'And then walk away,' I said undeterred. 'Leave her hanging.'

Will sighed. 'She's pretty, that's for sure, but I'm not sure she's the girl for me.'

'Give her a chance, Will,' I said. 'For me.'

'All right,' he said. 'For you.'

I squeezed his arm. 'Go on then,' I said. 'Go and say something nice.'

Casually I waved goodbye to him and, watching Rose and Will all the time, I sauntered over to where Gareth was sitting on a bale of hay reading some paperwork.

Now Will and I were no longer chatting, Rose was heading back towards the huts. So she crossed paths with Will as he walked in the opposite direction. He stopped her with a tap on her arm – just like the one I'd given him – and I saw him give her the full beam of his little-boy smile. She smiled back, ducking her head and looking up at him through her eyelashes. Oh, she was good. He said something to her and she flushed, patting her hair as he walked away. This was great. Maybe they would hit it off and he could get her to leave off me a bit.

'Lil,' Gareth said, obviously not for the first time judging by his irritated expression. 'What are you staring at?'

'Nothing,' I said, turning to give him my full attention. 'I'm all yours. Any idea what I'm going to be flying tomorrow?'

Chapter 25

The flight up to Scotland was long and not much fun thanks to a nasty rainstorm that followed me up the coast. It was a dreadful summer; it felt more like autumn had arrived already. I had to concentrate so hard the whole way, I wondered if I'd be any good when I got to Jemima's house – I felt like I would simply collapse into bed and sleep for a whole day.

But as soon as I landed at Charterhall I felt like I'd come home. The farm, where Ruth and I had moved to not long after the war started, was nearby. Watching the planes take off and land from there had inspired me to sign up for the ATA.

I did my post-flight checks, handed over the plane to the ground crew without even a grimace when they asked me, again, where the pilot was, and then with a spring in my step, I headed off the base and down the road to catch the bus to Kelso. Even the horrible weather didn't dampen my good mood and seeing Ruth and Robert peeking out of the window of the farmhouse as I arrived was wonderful.

'Auntie Lil,' Robert called. He'd grown so much since I'd last seen him. He'd lost his toddler podginess and looked like a proper little lad now. As I always did when I saw him, I tested my feelings to see if I felt like his mother. Which, of course, I was.

Biologically, if not in any other way. To my relief, once again, I knew I still wanted to be Auntie Lil. I hoped it would stay that way.

I waved wildly at him and grinned as Ruth flung open the door.

'Come in,' she said. 'It's such an awful day. Are you soaked?'

'Not too bad,' I said, peeling off my coat.

Robert hung off my arm. 'Auntie Lil, will you play the piano?' he asked. 'Play now, Auntie Lil.'

'Oh, Robert, give Lil a chance to get dry,' said Ruth, scooping him up into her arms and ruffling his dark hair. Robert looked so much like Bobby now that I knew no one would ever question whether Ruth was his mother. She smiled at me over Robert's head and I smiled back. I owed her so much.

Robert ran off to play with his train set and I followed Ruth down the corridor into the snug farm kitchen.

'Where's Jemima?'

'Harvesting potatoes,' Ruth said. 'She's become a hero to all the Land Girls around here. She's teaching them all sorts.' She looked at me and smiled. 'You look well. Happy.'

'I am happy.'

'I'm glad.'

Robert ran in and climbed on to my knee, showing me the train he was holding. I cuddled him close, enjoying his little boy smell.

'I could teach you how to play the piano,' I said. 'And then you can enjoy the music when I'm not here.'

'Yes, yes, yes,' he said. He looked at Ruth. 'Mamma, Auntie Lil is going to teach me.'

Ruth gave him such a doting smile that my heart ached. 'You are very lucky to have such a talented aunt.'

I didn't play the piano much at the base, though I did sometimes wander into town and play on the rickety old upright in the church hall. Jemima's piano had been tuned just for me when

153

we came to live with her, and she'd obviously kept it in good condition when I'd left. Robert led me through to the living room, his little hand sticky in my own, and we sat together on the stool.

It was a lovely afternoon, Robert perched on my knee, picking out the notes I taught him and – to my utter joy and pride – showing he had a good ear for music. Ruth sat on the sofa, watching us and filling me in on how Bobby was doing and other news from home. My father had almost died in 1942 when he'd had a stroke, so now my mother spent her days caring for him. Ruth wanted them to come up to Scotland but Mother didn't think Dad would make it through the journey. Bobby was part of Bomber Command now, based out of Yorkshire. Our paths crossed every now and then. Not as often as I would have liked.

'Do you worry about Bobby?' I asked. 'Constantly?'

Ruth shook her head. 'You remember when the war first started and he went away, I spent the whole time just watching out of the window and wondering when the telegram would come?' she said.

I nodded.

'But then Robert was born and he took up all my time, and the war just went on and on, and it became the new normal.' She grinned at me. 'I don't even worry about you so much any more.'

'I'm fine,' I said. 'I'm a very good pilot and it's not as though I'm in combat. I'm not doing anything nearly as dangerous as the boys flying the bombers, or the fighter pilots.'

'It's not the flying I worry about,' Ruth said.

I kept my eyes on the piano keys. 'This one,' I said to Robert, putting his little finger on middle C.

Ruth knew what Flora, Annie and I did and though she was quietly supportive, I knew she would rather we didn't take such risks.

'That's fine too,' I said.

154

Wanting to change the subject, I started to tell her about Will and how he was trying his hardest to woo me, and I was tempting him with Rose.

'Oh, Lil, you should give him a chance.' Ruth laughed.

'I'm really not interested,' I said, but Ruth had stopped giggling. She was staring out of the window, her face pale.

'What is it?' I turned to see the telegram boy walking up the path and I swear my heart stopped beating for a second. 'Oh, Ruth,' I said.

'Stay with Robert,' she said dully. She got up and walked out of the room. I pulled Robert close to me, pretending to admire his piano playing, but really listening to Ruth's muffled conversation.

'Lil,' she called. 'Lil, it's fine. It's fine. The telegram is for you.'

'Oh, thank God,' I breathed, tickling Robert and making him chuckle and squirm on my lap. But why did I have a telegram? Was it something to do with the ATA?

I slid Robert on to the piano stool and followed Ruth's path to the front door.

'Lilian Miles,' the telegram boy said, handing it over.

I tore it open. *'Emily Page,'* it said, followed by an address in Edinburgh. *'Needs help. Can you arrange? Annie.'*

'Shit,' I said. 'Sorry, Ruth.'

'What's the matter?'

'Someone we – you know – sorted out, last week. Sounds like she needs help.'

'What can you do from up here?'

I showed her the telegram. 'She's in Edinburgh,' I said. 'I need to go to her.'

Ruth looked like she was going to protest but instead she nodded. 'I'll get Jemima,' she said. 'She can drive you in the van. Do you have petrol coupons?'

'My ration book's in my bag.'

Ruth was pulling on her coat. 'You need to get changed – you can't go in uniform. Take a dress out of my wardrobe and put it on. I'll be back in ten minutes – be ready to go.'

'Ruth,' I said, horribly aware that I could be risking being arrested. Abortions were always dangerous and I didn't even know if Emily Page would still be alive when I got to Edinburgh. 'You don't have to do this – I can get the train. It's fine if you don't want to be involved.'

Ruth opened the front door. 'It's the right thing to do,' she said.

Chapter 26

Helena

June 2018

'Miranda's the oldest ...' Jack said as we walked down the road towards my parents' house that Friday. He'd already gone through all my siblings about five times, but he was super keen to hear all about them. 'I can't imagine having one brother or sister, let alone three,' he kept saying. 'You're so lucky, Helena.'

'Miranda's the oldest, then me, then Andy, and Immy is the baby,' I said now.

'And Andy's the archaeologist?'

I nodded. 'He's doing a dig somewhere on some Scottish island,' I said, smiling as I thought about my brother. 'He was always digging stuff up when we were kids. The garden was covered in holes.'

'And Immy?'

'She's a singer at heart, but she's also a conservationist. She's working on a game reserve in South Africa.'

'Blimey,' said Jack, taking my hand. 'You Miles kids aren't exactly run of the mill, are you?'

I made a face. 'Miranda and I aren't special,' I said.

Jack nudged me. 'Miranda's raising a son, while running that bank, single-handed, by the sound of it,' he pointed out. 'And her husband … whose name I've forgotten …'

'Pietr,' I said. 'He's German.'

'Pietr,' Jack said. 'Pietr has an equally high-flying job.'

'The same job, actually,' I said. 'Just at a different bank.'

'Bloody hell,' said Jack. He looked a bit worried. 'Is he coming tonight?'

'Nope,' I said. 'Miranda's got some corporate thing tonight so it's just you and me.'

'And your mum and dad.'

I shuddered. 'Yes, them too,' I said. 'More's the pity.'

Jack laughed at my nerves. 'I'm looking forward to meeting them,' he said. 'I can't wait to get all the gossip from your dad about the films he's worked on.'

'He doesn't go on set much,' I warned him, steering him up the overgrown path that led to the peeling front door, still painted the same colour as when I was growing up. 'We're here.'

I took a breath, preparing myself to knock on the door, when it was flung open.

'Helenaaaaaaaaa!' shrieked a voice and I jumped in surprise.

'Immy!'

My baby sister stood in the doorway, looking gorgeous in cut-off denim shorts, and a vest with a checked shirt over the top. Her curly hair was longer than I'd ever seen it and trailed down her back in loose waves, and her freckled nose was sunburned.

'What are you doing here?'

'Visa shit.' Immy waved her hand like international borders were of no consequence to her. 'I had to come home to renew something.' She threw her arms round me. 'It's so nice to see you.'

I hugged her back. I may have trash-talked them to Jack but

I adored all my siblings with a fierce protective love and I was very pleased to see Immy.

Jack was waiting patiently on the doorstep.

'Oh, Immy,' I said, untangling myself from her tanned limbs and gesturing to Jack. 'This is my, erm, my er, my Jack. This is Jack.'

Jack gave her a dazzling smile and came forward to kiss her on the cheek. Immy's jaw dropped and I thought it might be the first time I'd ever seen my talkative little sister properly speechless.

'Jack,' she stammered. 'Jack Jones.'

Jack grinned. 'That's me. Shall we go through? We brought some wine – let's get it open.'

Laughing at Immy's still-startled expression, I led the way into the kitchen where Mum and Dad were arguing with Miranda, and Freddie was playing on an iPad.

'Hello, darling,' said Mum. 'There's wine in the fridge. Miranda, I simply don't understand why you won't accept that capitalism has had its day.'

Miranda gave me a weary glance over Mum's head.

'Thought you weren't coming,' I said, opening the fridge door and topping up her empty glass.

'Thank you,' she said. 'I wasn't, but Immy called and said she was at Heathrow so I cancelled my meeting.'

'Where's Pietr?' I said in an undertone.

'Lounge,' she said. 'He said he had to make an important phone call. I think he's watching the football and occasionally shouting in German to make us all think he's doing something terribly difficult.'

I chuckled and turned to Jack. 'Drink?' I asked, then in a low voice I added: 'Sorry, sorry, sorry. I thought it would just be Mum and Dad.'

But Jack looked thrilled by the chaos. 'It's fine,' he said. 'It's great.'

'Hey, Fred,' I said, ruffling my nephew's hair. 'What's up?'

He barely looked up. 'I'm building a castle but pigs keeping getting in,' he said.

I looked at him blankly, but Jack plonked himself down next to Freddie and grinned.

'Oh brilliant,' he said. 'Why don't you dig a hole to trap the pigs?'

'Will that work?' Freddie said doubtfully.

'Worth a try, right?'

Freddie looked at Jack for a second then nodded. 'Will you help me?'

'Absolutely.'

'You're both weirdos,' I said, laughing.

'Minecraft,' Jack told me over his shoulder. 'Billy taught me all about it.'

Billy was his ten-year-old co-star on *Mackenzie*. I started to say something, but Jack had turned his attention back to Freddie, so instead I poured us both a glass of wine, and sat myself down next to Immy to hear all her news.

As she regaled me with talk of elephants and lions, I watched my family through Jack's eyes. I saw Miranda good-naturedly telling Mum to stop talking about stuff she didn't understand, as Mum ranted about the FTSE. And Dad screwing his face up as Freddie told him the zombies were attacking his village and pretending to be one of the zombies' victims. And Immy, twisting her hair up out of her way while she acted out a dramatic confrontation between two of the volunteers she worked with. Pietr eventually reappeared and took Miranda's teasing about his 'important' phone call in good humour.

And I realised that Jack was right – I was lucky to have them. In all their messed-up, unconventional glory. I smiled and as I did, Jack looked up and caught my eye.

'Okay?' he said. I loved him checking in on me. I nodded.

'Hungry,' I said. 'Shall we order?'

Later, after we'd all eaten, Jack charmed the pants off both my parents by admiring – completely honestly – all Dad's music and all of Mum's documentaries; and he won Immy's heart by saying he would put a link to her conservation project on all his social media. (He had well over a million followers on Instagram. An actual million. I had sixty-four.)

He raised an eyebrow at me. 'Ask your dad about Scotland,' he said in an undertone.

'He won't remember,' I said.

Jack shrugged. 'Worth a go, though.'

Miranda was helping a very tired Freddie into his coat. 'What's worth a go?'

'Lil was in Kelso, at the start of the war,' I said to Dad.

'Visiting?' he asked, his eyes sparking with interest. 'Or living there?'

'I don't know,' I said. 'I found the 1939 census and she's on there. Did she live with you?'

'I don't remember much about it,' Dad said, sweeping Freddie into a hug and then kissing Miranda on the cheek and giving Pietr a manly slap on the back. 'Goodbye, young man. Bye, Miranda. Bye, Pietr.'

Mum walked to the door to show Miranda and her family out, and Dad offered us all more wine.

'I was very young,' he said. 'I remember her visiting but not actually living with us.'

'You lived with Grandma Ruth up there?' I said.

Dad nodded. 'And her godmother; I called her Jemmy,' he said. 'Nice woman. It was her house, actually. She died when I was a teenager.'

'Why were you in Scotland? Do you know?'

'It was safer, I suppose. Kent was often bombed when the Germans were heading to and from London. And my grandfather was in a bad way, I believe. Shell shock. I think it was better that we stayed out of the way.'

I resisted giving Jack a triumphant look.

'Lil wasn't around much then?' I said. 'I guess she signed up when you were too small to remember.'

Immy was watching me and Dad with curiosity. Mum wandered back in and watched too.

'Aunt Lil?' Immy said. 'I didn't know she lived with you when you were little, like how she lived with us?'

Mum and Dad exchanged a glance again. Just like they had that first night when I'd found Lil's name in my notes.

'What?' I said. 'What aren't you telling me?'

Mum shrugged. 'Nothing, Nell,' she said. 'Your dad was tiny when the war ended, and just a baby at the beginning. You can't expect him to remember much.'

Dad looked sheepish. 'Your mother doesn't want me to do this research into Lilian,' he said.

'I'm doing the research,' I pointed out and Mum smiled at me.

'I worry about her,' she said. 'She's not as young as she was. She said you'd been asking questions about the war and she was quite upset about it.'

I was horrified. 'Oh God, was she really?'

'I didn't mean to cause trouble,' Dad sighed.

'Well you did,' Mum snapped.

Immy and I looked at each other. Our parents hardly ever bickered.

'Should I leave it?' I said. 'I'd be glad to, if I'm honest. It's already causing ructions at work.'

'Things are fine as they are,' Mum said. 'Leave it be.'

Immy looked bewildered, but I just nodded.

'I will,' I said. 'I promise.'

Satisfied, Mum turned her attention to Immy, and over her shoulder Dad caught my eye. He gave a tiny shake of his head and I closed my eyes for a second. Did he really want to carry on, even knowing Lil had been upset?

I raised my eyebrows questioningly, and he put his hands together in a begging gesture. Bugger it.

I shrugged and Dad smiled. There was definitely more to this than he was letting on, and briefly I considered tackling him about it. There had to be a reason he was so desperate to find out more.

But no. I was determined this wasn't going to upset my Lil. I'd pretend to Dad that the trail had gone cold, I thought. Anything rather than stir up trouble in my fragile family. That's what I'd do.

Chapter 27

Lilian

November 1939

'Feeling better?' Ruth smiled at me as I wandered into the kitchen after taking an afternoon nap.

I nodded. 'I was just tired,' I said. I looked over her shoulder and pinched a piece of apple from her chopping board. 'And hungry. Are you making apple pie?'

'It's for dinner,' Ruth said. 'But I can boil you an egg if you're starving?'

'Yes please,' I said. I was permanently starving at the moment and thanked my lucky stars daily that thanks to Jemima, her green fingers and her chickens, we didn't ever go hungry.

I sat down at the kitchen table and smoothed my dress over my growing bump. 'The baby is kicking,' I said. 'Want to feel?'

Ruth put a pot of water on the hob to boil and came over.

'Here,' I said, guiding her hand. Obediently the baby gave a wiggle and then a hefty kick that made me breathe in sharply.

'Uncomfortable?' Ruth asked.

I shook my head. 'Not so much uncomfortable as odd,' I said. I gave her a sad smile. 'The whole thing is odd.'

'I know, lovey,' Ruth said. She was still standing next to me with her hand on my tummy so I rested my head against her apron-clad front and let her stroke my hair. 'Not much longer.'

I was about six months pregnant now and we'd been staying with Jemima for several weeks. She'd been gratifyingly pleased to see us when we turned up.

'Thank bloody God,' she'd said, gathering Ruth to her as soon as we'd got off the train. 'I've been so absolutely bloody lonely.'

Jemima had been our saviour, really. Welcoming us into her home – and putting us to work – and helping with our deception. I'd played some piano for the local Sunday school, while Ruth worked in the kitchen garden at the farm, growing all sorts of vegetables under Jemima's guidance. We had been lucky, in a way, that the weather was miserable; we bundled up in sweaters and thick coats and no one noticed my bump – or Ruth's lack of one – when we walked into town.

Ruth even wrote weekly letters to my mother, telling her all about my pregnancy symptoms as though they were her own, and she sent regular updates to Bobby, who was now finished with basic training and learning how to fly bombers.

Now my pregnancy was getting harder to conceal, I spent more time on my own. Jemima had dusted off her old piano and had it tuned for me, which I was pathetically grateful for. But even with music as a companion I wasn't completely happy. I was really tired now and feeling pretty wretched about the whole thing. More than anything in the world I wanted *not* to be pregnant. I knew Ruth saw my baby as the answer to all her prayers, and perhaps he or she would be. But I just saw it as a weight pulling me down. I was listless and completely miserable.

I missed Mr Mayhew dreadfully, and hated myself for missing him. When we'd first moved to Kelso, I'd spent many evenings crying on Ruth and Jemima, trying to explain my conflicted feelings for him.

'I loved him so much,' I'd sobbed. 'And I thought he loved me, too.'

Ruth had wrapped her arms round me and rocked me as though I was the baby. 'I know, sweetheart,' she'd cooed. 'I know.'

'You were too young,' Jemima had said fiercely. So fiercely, in fact, that I wondered if she'd had similar experiences to mine, but even so I bristled at her dismissing my feelings for Mr Mayhew.

'What does my age have to do with anything?' I'd snapped back at her. 'I knew what I was doing.'

Jemima's eyes had filled with tears and she'd shaken her head.

'No, you didn't,' she'd said. 'You felt like you were a woman, that you were in charge, leading him on. But you weren't, Lil. He was in charge the whole time.'

I'd sat dumbly, realising that what she was saying was true.

'You were – you are – just a kid,' Jemima had continued. 'And he took advantage of you and made you think it was all your fault. This Mr Mayhew of yours is a bad man.' She'd smiled at me. 'And I can tell you that without even meeting him. He's a bad man – and you're well shot of him. You've had a lucky escape, my girl.'

But even though I knew Jemima was right, and even though I knew Mr Mayhew was no good, I still missed him.

'I'm going to go for a walk,' I said to Ruth now. 'Might wake me up a bit.'

She looked alarmed. 'Into town?' She glanced at my swollen belly.

'No, I'm going to walk across the fields, get some air,' I said.

Ruth smiled. 'That's a great idea. The sun's shining, even if it is freezing out.'

Ruth helped me wrap up warmly and even guided my feet into my boots – I was finding it hard to bend over now. Then she kissed me on the forehead. 'Don't stay out too long,' she said. 'And don't get cold.'

Pleased to be out of the house, I waddled off down the lane and out into the fields.

The countryside round Kelso was beautiful and Ruth had been right – it was a beautiful crisp winter's day. Jemima said she thought it might snow, and I wondered if it would. The hills around would look lovely with a covering of white.

I trudged in a fairly ungainly fashion across one field, looked at the stile to get into the next one, which was the way I normally went, and thought better of it. I was too big to be climbing over stiles now. I'd go a different way. I followed a small path round the edge of the field, through a wooden gate, and past a small clump of trees. I was feeling warmer now and I unwrapped my scarf and pulled my hat from my head. Up ahead the path snaked upwards to the top of a small hill. I'd walk up there, I thought, rest for a while, and then walk home again.

I was quite breathless by the time I reached the top, even though it wasn't too high. The baby was filling my abdomen and squeezing the air out of my lungs, according to Ruth who seemed to know all about pregnancy and babies and childbirth. I certainly felt the air squeezing out of me now, as I puffed and panted my way up the hill, my breath making little fluffy clouds in the cold air.

'Ohhhh,' I gasped as I made it to the highest point. 'Goodness.'

In front of me, the land fell away to a valley. It was such a clear day, I could see for miles – I thought I could even see the sea on the very far horizon. I wondered where the border was. We were only just inside Scotland in Kelso, and I knew the line that divided the countries wiggled about a bit.

'They should mark it with trees or something,' I murmured to myself. 'Then everyone would know.'

I turned slightly away from the sea and gasped again. This time I was looking at an airfield, way below me. I could see little toy planes moving about on the runway and thrillingly one looked like it was about to take off. I watched it speed along and then just as I thought it was going to overshoot and crash into the woods at the end, it lifted off the ground and gracefully swooped up into the sky.

I felt a warmth in my bones that I'd not felt for a long time. I wondered who was flying the plane and what kind of aircraft it was. I'd often thought of Bobby flying but it seemed different to actually see the planes. Was the pilot I was watching alone up there, or with a crew? I envied him so much it felt like an actual pain in my heart. The freedom of being up there, by himself, flying like a bird through the crisp blue sky.

I ignored the voice in my head that pointed out he was probably going to fight a German and risk his life in the process. I just thought it looked amazingly, wonderfully, enviably free. A million miles away from me – so fat I could barely walk, stuck in the house away from other people in case anyone realised I was pregnant, trapped in Ruth's wonderful yet suffocating concern, my wings clipped before they'd even had time to grow.

'I'm going to fly,' I said to myself. 'I want to fly.'

And then I laughed because it was such a ridiculous suggestion. As if to remind me who I was and why I was there, the baby kicked me hard and I realised I needed the toilet, again. With a sigh, I gave the airfield one final glance, and started the waddle back down the hill to Jemima's house.

'I'll come back tomorrow,' I said, talking out loud again. My mother had always said speaking to yourself was the first sign of madness. Which was ironic, because it was when Daddy stopped talking that we really knew he was struggling.

As I lumbered down the hill, hurrying a little because the baby was wriggling in a way that was making my need for the lav even more urgent, I thought about the little plane and wondered where it was now. I felt that sharp pang of envy again. I was determined to come back and watch the airfield some more.

Chapter 28

Helena

July 2018

'What's going on with you and Dad?' Immy asked me on Monday. We were in the pub around the corner from my house – close to my parents, who were looking after Dora again. I thought if this thing with Jack turned into, well anything really, I'd have to find some other babysitters; I didn't want to take advantage of my parents. Miranda was on her way, too. I'd considered inviting Jack but thought my sisters might be annoyed if my, erm, whatever he was, gate-crashed our catch-up.

'I stumbled on some info about Lil when I was researching Jack's family for work,' I explained. I brought her up to speed, just as Miranda arrived, looking uncharacteristically flustered.

'Sodding husbands,' she said, shrugging off her jacket.

'What's Pietr done now?' For all Pietr ran a multimillion-pound department and spoke three languages, he was surprisingly hopeless at everyday tasks. I had a suspicion he did it on purpose just so Miranda would take over. I couldn't blame him – I did that myself sometimes.

'Breathed,' she said. 'Existed.'

Immy giggled.

'And forgot to pick Freddie up from school.'

'Shit,' I said.

She shrugged. 'It's fine,' she said. 'It was just a miscommunication. I thought Pietr was doing it, because Lotta was at college late.'

'Who's Lotta?' asked Immy.

'Au pair?' I said. It was hard to keep track of Miranda's ever-changing stream of students.

'Lotta was at college, and I'd told Pietr, but he got his weeks mixed up. It was fine, in the end. Freddie's friend's mum rang me and she took him home with her until Freddie's idiot dad showed up.'

Her lower lip trembled ever so slightly. 'It's fine,' she said again. 'It was just a mistake.' She took a breath. 'It just reminded me,' she said. 'Of when Immy was a baby.'

I patted her hand sympathetically. 'It's not like that,' I said. 'It's not.'

She smiled at me gratefully.

'In a way, it's worse,' I said. 'Because Mum was ill so it wasn't her fault. But you married Pietr so it is your fault.'

There was a pause and I wondered if I'd misjudged how upset she was, but fortunately she laughed.

'Sod off, Helena,' she said. 'Let's get drunk.'

A bottle and a half later, Immy remembered what I'd been telling her when Miranda arrived.

'So what do you think the big secret is, with Lil?' she said.

'Elly at work thinks she had some illicit affair with a married colleague,' I said. 'Maybe a woman.'

Immy, who I suspected played for both teams herself though she'd never said as much, looked impressed, but Miranda shook her head.

'Dishonourable discharge?' she said. 'Surely that's too serious a punishment for just falling for the wrong person?'

I shrugged. 'Different times,' I pointed out. 'But I can put in a request for the court martial documents. It's easy enough to find out. If I want to.'

'Do you want to?' Miranda and Immy said in unison. They both fixed me with their gazes. I looked away.

'Not really,' I said. 'I'm intrigued of course, but Lil clearly doesn't want me to.'

'Mum said she was upset,' Immy told Miranda, who made a face.

'We're hardly a conservative bunch,' Immy said. 'We'd not be remotely bothered by Lil having an affair with a man or a woman, or both.'

I nodded.

'So why doesn't she want you to know?'

'It doesn't really matter why, does it?' I said. 'The fact is, she doesn't want me to.'

Immy made a face, and Miranda frowned but I ignored them.

'I don't want to,' I said again. 'It's not worth the fallout – Lil being upset, my job being at risk.'

'What about Dad?' Miranda said. 'He wants to know.'

'That's what I think is so weird,' I said. 'Why does he want to know? I'm not even sure *what* he wants to know. He keeps making out it's just idle curiosity, but he is willing to upset Lil, and go against what Mum thinks, to find this out. What's going on?'

We all sat in silence for a minute, wondering what could be driving Dad's determination to dig deeper into this mystery.

'So this was all happening when he was a kid,' Immy mused. 'Maybe it's something to do with his childhood? His parents? Perhaps Lil's troubles affected him in some way.'

I felt a glimmer of sympathy for my dad, but not enough to change my mind. 'He'll have to ask Lil himself,' I said firmly. 'I'm out.'

Miranda shrugged. 'You can tell him,' she said. 'He's just walked in.'

Surprised, we all turned to watch as Dad looked round the pub until he saw us, then rambled over to our table in his familiar shuffly way.

'Hello, girls.'

'Everything okay?' I said. 'Is Dora okay?'

'She's fine,' Dad said. 'I just thought I'd come and have a drink with my favourite daughter.'

It was an old joke but we all smiled just the same.

'Which one?' we chorused.

'You know,' Dad said, tapping his nose meaningfully, in his well-rehearsed response. He sat down.

'Why are you really here, Dad?' I said.

He looked sheepish. 'That obvious, eh?'

We all nodded.

'I've not been completely honest with you,' he said.

I rolled my eyes. 'I worked that out. In fact, we've just been talking about you. Are you going to tell us what's going on?'

'Shall I get us all another drink?' he said.

'I'll go,' Immy said in a hurry, sensing my rising irritation.

She went to the bar, and spoke to the barman, pointing at our table and then came back and sat down again. 'He's going to bring them over,' she said. She looked at Dad. 'Now spill.'

Dad took a deep breath. 'I think Lilian could be my mother,' he said.

All three of us stared at him.

'Dad …' I began.

'I know it sounds crazy,' he said, talking over me. 'But I've had my suspicions for a while. Years, probably.'

'Why on earth do you think that?' I said, bewildered. Obviously in my time on the show, I'd uncovered more than one family secret along these lines, but I'd never once considered it could have happened in our family.

'When I was about nine, I heard my parents arguing,' Dad said. It sounded like he'd practised what he was saying and I

172

wondered how long he'd been rehearsing telling someone this story. 'They hardly ever exchanged cross words so it was unusual. Mum was saying that I deserved to know the truth about my parents, and Dad said it was too difficult.'

I nodded. 'So you thought you might be adopted?' I said. 'I thought that too for a while. After I'd read *Anne of Green Gables*.'

Miranda nudged me. 'As if,' she said. 'You look exactly like the rest of us. Carry on, Dad.'

Dad smiled at her. 'It was the family resemblance that confused me,' he said. 'I used to look at my dad's face and see how much I looked like him. How could I be adopted if I looked just like my father?'

Dad paused.

'It should have been enough to convince me that I was indeed my parents' son. That I wasn't adopted, and that I'd misunderstood what I'd heard. But ...'

'Go on,' Immy said.

'That little niggle remained,' Dad said, a faraway look in his eye. 'As I got older it stayed with me.'

'But what made you think Lil could be your biological mother?' Miranda asked.

'When I was growing up, Mum and Dad – your grandparents – were always very keen to include her in my life,' Dad said. 'They sent her programmes from recitals I'd played in, and kept her up to date on my education and whatnot.'

I shrugged. 'That doesn't mean anything,' I said. 'She could just be a doting aunt.'

'Of course,' Dad said. 'And I didn't think anything of it back then.'

He paused. 'She had a way of looking at me,' he said, almost to himself. 'She'd take my face in her hands and stare right at me. When I was little, I thought it was funny, but she kept doing it when I was older; she still does it.'

We all nodded. Lil did do that to Dad, but not to any of us. I'd never questioned it.

'It was like she was looking for something in my face,' Dad said.

'Still doesn't prove anything,' Miranda pointed out.

Dad shook his head. 'I know,' he admitted.

'So when did you start thinking there was more to your relationship?' I asked, still not convinced.

'Years ago, I was writing the music for a TV show. The story was similar – the main character had found out he was adopted and the person he thought was his sister, was really his mother. I read the script and it was like a light going on in my head.'

'And you never mentioned it until now?' Miranda said.

'I spoke to your mum about it,' he said. 'But I never wanted to rock the boat with my parents. I couldn't upset them.'

'You never said anything to Grandma?' Immy asked.

Dad bit his lip. 'I loved my parents very much,' he said. 'They were wonderful people.'

'Wonderful enough to adopt you?' I said.

Dad nodded slowly. 'My father,' he said. 'Bobby, I mean. He was very protective of Lil. I'm sure he'd have done anything to look after her. And my mother adored her. They were a tight little family unit.'

'If Lil was pregnant in 1939 it all makes sense,' I said, running with the idea now. 'She couldn't have had a baby – she was just a teenager and who knows who the father was. Perhaps you're right, Dad. Maybe Grandma Ruth and Grandad Bobby brought Lil's son – you – up as their own.'

Immy sat up a bit straighter. 'Maybe Grandma took Lil away, to Scotland. She had the baby – she had Dad – and Grandma pretended Dad was her son.'

Dad was sitting quietly, listening to us speculate.

'I've never seen your birth certificate, Dad,' I said. 'Do you have it?'

'I do,' he said. 'But your grandma and grandad are listed as my parents. I'm not sure how they'd have got round that.'

Immy flapped her hands at him. 'Lil is very enterprising; she'd have come up with something.'

'They never had any other children,' Miranda said. I'd been thinking along the same lines.

'Maybe they had fertility problems and that's why they volunteered to take Lil's baby,' I agreed. 'Perhaps it was their only chance to have a child.'

'Possibly,' Dad said, blinking slightly as we all fired our ideas at him.

'Lil had Dad, she had you, I mean, in 1940, then she handed you over to Grandma and went off to fly planes a couple of years later when she was old enough,' I said. 'Except something went wrong in 1944, and she got court-martialled.'

'Maybe they found out she'd had a baby out of wedlock,' said Immy, who was obviously loving this drama. 'On the wrong side of the blankets.'

'That's the obvious conclusion,' I said.

'Helena,' Dad said. 'You need to request the court martial papers.'

'No,' I said. 'Absolutely not.'

'Please, Nell.'

'No. God, Dad. No.'

'But …'

'This isn't just a TV show, like when I do research for other people,' I said. 'This is our lives. Our family. It's our lovely Lil, who looked after us when we were in trouble.'

'But what if Lil is Dad's biological mum?' Immy said. 'You can't blame him for wanting to know the truth.'

I looked at Dad. 'If you want to know the truth, then you need to speak to Lil,' I said. 'No more sneaking around.'

Immy tutted but Miranda squeezed my hand, letting me know she was on my side.

175

'It's not our story,' she said. 'It's not our secret. We don't have any right to poke about in Lil's past.'

Dad looked upset but I wasn't going to let him talk me into this.

'I can't, Dad,' I said. 'It's not even that it could cause trouble at work. Imagine if Dora decided to track down Greg behind my back when she's older. I'd be devastated. But if she came to speak to me about it, then it would be fine.'

Dad nodded. 'You're right,' he said.

'We're a family,' I said, quite fiercely. 'We shouldn't keep secrets. If you want to know if Lil's your biological mother, then you have to ask her.'

'So no court papers?' Dad said.

'No,' I said. 'No court papers.'

Chapter 29

Lilian

July 1944

Nothing fazed Jemima. Nothing. Not Ruth and I turning up on her doorstep with barely a week's notice. Not me being pregnant when I was unmarried and wasn't even quite sixteen. Not Robert's birth one clear, cold wintry night. And not even Ruth claiming to be the mother of my baby raised an eyebrow.

Though she never really talked about it, I got the impression she was more relieved than sad when her husband died and from some things she'd mentioned it seemed he'd never treated her very well. Jemima was quiet and watchful, and – I knew – scathing about a society that would punish a woman for a man's misdeeds. Ruth told her what happened between Mr Mayhew and me and she never once judged me, or criticised me, instead she was endlessly sympathetic and supportive. More than once I'd wondered what we'd have done without her. But she'd said the same to me – she'd been lonely up in Kelso, miles from her family, and had been thinking of moving away when war broke out. And then Ruth had got in touch and she'd decided to stay.

Now she pulled up outside the house in the battered van she drove and leaned out of the window. 'Come on then,' she called. 'Best get going.'

I straightened Ruth's dress, which was too long for me but hopefully didn't look too much like a little girl playing dress-up, and stuffed the telegram into the pocket of my borrowed coat.

'We'll hopefully be back for supper,' I said, kissing Ruth on the cheek and ruffling Robert's hair.

It wasn't a long drive to Edinburgh, but it felt endless. I wasn't sure what sort of trouble Emily Page was in, or what state we'd find her in. Abortions were so risky – physically and legally – that her asking for help could mean she was bleeding or locked up. I wasn't sure. I'd simply replied to Annie saying I was on my way, and now I was hoping we could be of assistance.

'Do you think she's been arrested?' Jemima said, giving voice to my worries.

I'd been going over it in my mind since the telegram arrived, but now I shook my head. 'I don't think so,' I said slowly. 'Because Annie gave me her home address.'

'Infection then?'

I nodded, pinching my lips together tightly. I was terrified about what might have happened to Emily in the hours since she'd contacted Annie.

'Lucky you were up here,' Jemima said. We were into the outskirts of Edinburgh now, and she was peering through the windscreen looking for landmarks – it was hard to navigate without road signs.

I nodded again, checking the telegram for the address. 'It's one of these streets, I think,' I said, pointing out of my window. 'Yes, this one.'

Jemima swung the van left and we pulled up outside one of the Edinburgh tenement blocks that towered over us.

I jumped out of the van, almost before Jemima had turned

the engine off and walked quickly down the street trying to find the right flat.

'It's this one,' I called as I found the bell with Page written above it. But when I pulled the iron knob, and heard the ringing upstairs, no one answered.

Jemima had come up behind me. 'Try one of the neighbours,' she suggested. I rang the bell for the ground-floor flat and, to my relief, I heard the door open. An elderly man stood there in battered brown carpet slippers.

'So sorry to disturb you,' I jabbered. 'My friend lives upstairs. She is ill and we need to get to her.'

Jemima was already halfway up the stone stairs. I followed, leaving the man standing staring at us from down below.

The door to Emily's flat was on the latch. Jemima pushed it open and we both walked in.

'Emily,' I called. 'It's Lilian Miles. Annie sent me.'

The small flat was full of the detritus of shared womanhood and it reminded me sharply of the digs I shared with Flora and Annie. This could have been any of us living here. There were stockings drying on a clothes horse in the hallway, piles of unopened post on the floor by the door, and a half-empty bottle of gin on the sideboard in the living room.

'Emily,' I called again. This time I heard a quiet moan. I ran into one of the bedrooms and found Emily, chalky-faced, curled up on her bed.

'Jemima, she's here,' I said. 'Emily, I'm Lilian Miles.'

She looked up at me, fear in her eyes.

'Annie sent me,' I added and Emily started to cry.

'I'm so scared,' she said quietly.

I sat down on the edge of the bed and took her hand. 'Where are your flatmates?'

'Work,' she whispered. 'Factory.'

'Are you bleeding?' I asked.

She nodded without lifting her head from the pillow.

'Can I look?' Jemima asked.

Emily nodded again, and Jemima gently lifted the blanket. The sheet beneath Emily, and her nightie, were soaked in bright red blood. I felt sick. Would she die?

Jemima looked grim. 'We need to get her to hospital,' she said in my ear.

I let out a juddery breath. I knew she was right. 'Emily, we have to take you to the hospital,' I said, stroking her hair. Her forehead was clammy but her skin was cold.

'No,' she said. 'No.'

'It's fine,' I said. 'We'll say you've had a miscarriage. They won't know.'

Emily closed her eyes.

'Emily,' I said louder. 'Emily don't go to sleep.'

Moving quickly, Jemima pulled Emily's dressing gown from the back of the door and I found her slippers under the bed.

'We need to go,' I said. Together, we sat Emily up – she was so weak and droopy that it was like putting clothes on a doll and for a moment I was reminded of how Robert had been when he was a tiny baby. I'd been so fortunate to have Ruth's help back then, and not to have ended up in the same situation Emily was in now. Jemima pushed Emily's arms into the dressing gown, and I put the slippers on her feet. Carefully we lifted her off the bed, taking care not to let her see the blood-soaked sheet in case she panicked, and half carried her out of the flat and down the stairs. The old man was still standing there.

'Oh, Miss Page,' he said, as we came down. 'Oh, hen, what's happened?'

'Where is the nearest hospital?' Jemima said.

I could see blood running down Emily's leg and I felt icy cold as I realised she could die right here, and we'd probably be to blame. At least, Annie, Flora and I would be.

The old man gave Jemima surprisingly clear directions and we bundled Emily out into the cold street and into the van.

'This isn't your fault,' Jemima said, reading my mind as I covered Emily with a blanket. 'You did the right thing.'

I felt sick.

'Here, put this on her finger.' Jemima handed me a plain gold band she wore on her right hand. 'Her ring finger.'

Carefully I pushed the ring on to Emily's finger.

'We'll tell her to use a fake name,' Jemima said. 'It's just easier if everyone thinks she's married.'

'Thank you,' I said. 'You're a good person.'

Jemima put her foot down on the accelerator and the van sped through the deserted Edinburgh streets.

'So are you,' she said.

It only took a few minutes to get to the hospital. Once more we half carried Emily and then Jemima drew back.

'I'll wait in the van,' she said. 'It'll get confusing if I'm here, too.'

I smiled at her gratefully as she ducked out of the door, then called to a passing nurse for help.

'My friend is pregnant,' I lied. 'I think she's losing the baby.'

I stayed with Emily until she'd been admitted. I filled in a form giving her name as Mrs Emily Smith and told the nurse she was a widow. When the doctor came, he gave me a long look but I held his gaze without flinching.

'She's miscarrying,' I said and he didn't argue.

As people began bustling round me, I bent to whisper in Emily's ear. 'Mrs Emily Smith, remember,' I said.

She nodded weakly. 'Thank you,' she said.

Jemima was quiet on the drive home, at least while she negotiated the cobbled streets of Edinburgh. Then, when we were out into the countryside she took a breath. 'Does that happen often?' she said.

I bit my lip. 'Often enough for it to be a constant worry,' I admitted. 'Depends on the pregnancy I think and who's … doing it.'

181

'Was it Katie? Who helped Emily?'

Jemima was watching the road, but her shoulders were tense. Katie was her friend, a midwife who'd helped me and had delivered Robert.

'No,' I told her and watched her relax a tiny bit, knowing her friend wasn't responsible for leaving Emily bleeding alone in her flat.

'The horrible thing is it all comes down to money,' I said. 'Some girls can pay for a doctor and some girls can't.'

'And Emily?'

I leaned my head against the window of the van and watched the verge whizz past.

'Emily couldn't afford a nurse either,' I said.

Jemima breathed in sharply.

'There are women who will help, and we try to make sure they're all right, but it's not easy to vet something that's illegal.' I sounded a bit desperate, like I was trying to justify the choices we made. Which I was. 'They're cheaper, but sometimes things go wrong. Sometimes things go wrong when the doctors do it, too. But they can usually put it right again.'

Jemima nodded, her lips pressed together.

'Emily was unlucky,' I went on. 'But I still believe what we're doing is right. If this wasn't illegal, then women wouldn't be put in this position.'

'Maybe things will change, after the war,' Jemima said.

'Maybe,' I said. 'Maybe not.'

We were quiet for a while. It was getting dark and I wanted to be back at the farm more than anything. To sit in the warm kitchen with Ruth and Robert and talk about silly things.

'That could have been me,' I said suddenly. 'Bleeding, in hospital.'

Jemima stayed quiet.

'I didn't know what to do, when I realised I was pregnant,' I said. 'And I didn't really have any choices because I was just a child. I had no money. I couldn't have done that even if I'd known about it. But still, it could have been me.'

'But it wasn't,' Jemima said.

'Because of you,' I pointed out. 'You and Ruth and Bobby.'

'And Katie,' she said.

I nodded. 'And that's why I want to help other women. It's why I do what I do.'

'It's why I did it too,' Jemima said.

I stared at her, not understanding. In the years I'd known her, she'd never really opened up about why she'd taken us in.

'My husband was a drunk and a bully,' she said, matter-of-factly. 'And I didn't want to marry him, but my dad wanted me off his hands. And Donald had money so he seemed like a good match.'

I didn't say anything. I wanted to let her tell her story.

'I never wanted to sleep with him but he didn't let that stop him,' she said, snorting with disgust. 'I despised him. I hated him so much. And when I realised I was pregnant, I just wanted to get rid of it. Katie helped me. And she helped me make sure I never got pregnant again. Long time ago now.'

'Oh,' I said helplessly. 'And that's why you helped me?'

Jemima nodded, never taking her eyes off the road. 'And now you help others. It's like a chain.'

I smiled. 'A strong chain,' I said. 'Unbroken.'

But I was wrong.

Chapter 30

Helena

July 2018

'This is huge,' Jack said. 'Enormous.'

'I know. It's crazy.'

'You never suspected that Lil might be your biological grand-mother?'

'No, not an inkling,' I said. 'Dad says he's thought as much for years, though. He never let on, mind you. And he's got nothing concrete to base it all on – just a feeling, and the way Lil looks at him.'

We were in my kitchen, just a couple of days after Dad's revelation. Jack had volunteered to cook me dinner, and I'd asked if he could do it at my house so I didn't need to find a babysitter. I'd put Dora to bed before he arrived, so we could have time for the two of us.

Jack was unpacking the shopping he'd brought with him.

'That's quite sweet,' he said. 'Like they've got a bond.'

I rolled my eyes. 'I don't want to research Lil any further,' I said. 'Like you say, it's huge. It's too huge. I told Dad he has to speak to her.'

'I think you're right,' Jack said. 'It's not fair of him to ask you to do this.'

I smiled at him, feeling the sheer loveliness of having someone in my corner.

'What does Miranda think?'

'She agrees with me,' I said.

'Uh-huh?' Jack glanced at me over his shoulder then carried on staring at the dials on my fairly basic cooker.

'She thinks it's a can of worms,' I said. 'And she's absolutely right. Have you ever used a cooker before?'

Jack turned round fully and gave me a sheepish grin. 'Not as such,' he said.

I raised an eyebrow. 'I normally just microwave stuff.'

I laughed and he joined in.

'I'm never home,' he said. 'And I quite often get stuff delivered. My personal trainer sorts it all out.'

'Oh, the hard life of a fabulously famous actor,' I teased, pretending to fan myself. 'Having all these staff at your beck and call. To cook for you, and clean for you, and buy your clothes for you …'

'I bought dinner,' Jack said, gesturing at the Waitrose bags on the side.

'You did,' I agreed. 'But cooking it seems to be a bit tricky …'

'Can you show me how to turn it on?' Jack said.

'I might.'

'Helena, you are infuriating,' he said, chuckling. 'Would you just show me how to turn the damn oven on already?'

I stood up, sauntered slowly across the small kitchen and turned the two dials that operated the oven.

Jack pulled me to him and kissed me. 'Maybe this was just a ruse to get you closer to me,' he said.

'And maybe you're just hopeless in the kitchen,' I said. 'And I am starving to death.'

It was amazing how comfortable I was with Jack. I was beginning to see that Miranda was right when she said he liked me. But I still couldn't quite believe it. He was so busy all the time, and it was a fact that the women he worked with were goddesses compared to average old me. I couldn't believe that given the choice he'd prioritise me over drinks with a Bond Girl, or a party with a BAFTA winner – but it seemed that, at least for now, he was.

Somehow, Jack managed to cook the very basic pasta, sauce and garlic bread he'd bought, with only a few mishaps. And really it didn't matter that the bread had fallen on the floor more than once, because it was still in its wrapper, and it was only a little bit bashed. And the splatters from the sauce all over the worktop could be wiped off. Like the red-wine stain.

We ate at the small kitchen table and I talked some more about Dad and Lil. 'Dad asked me to get the transcripts of the court documents,' I said. 'But I said no. I just really don't feel comfortable with it.'

'You did the right thing,' Jack said. He slurped up some spaghetti, ignoring the splatters on his shirt. 'I'd do the same.'

I smiled at him.

'It's funny, isn't it? Dad said he suspected his parents might not be his real mum and dad before they died. But he never wanted to upset them by raising it. He prioritised their feelings over his own.'

'Not funny at all,' Jack said.

'I always thought blood was thicker than water,' I said. I gestured to the ceiling with my fork, roughly in the direction of Dora's bedroom. 'I've always worried Dora would be drawn to Greg, because of their shared biology.'

Jack shook his head. 'Absolutely not,' he said. 'At least that's not my experience. I've told you about my dad. He was a stranger to me. I didn't know him at all. Of course, I'd have liked to have known him – but I don't feel like there's a gap in my life.'

'Really?'

'In my opinion, biology doesn't matter,' he went on. 'Your grandparents were your father's real mum and dad. They raised him. They loved him.'

I nodded. 'You're right,' I said.

'My mum found a new partner when I was fourteen,' Jack added.

I was surprised. He'd never really mentioned having a stepdad. 'Was that hard for you?'

'Not as hard as you'd think it would be,' he said. 'His name is Jon. Huge bloke – fills a room. Looks like a boxer, but he's actually an artist.'

I grinned. 'Sounds as though you like him.'

'I really like him,' Jack said. 'He moved in just after I'd done my GCSEs. He never really tried to be my dad, but somehow he became one anyway.'

'That's nice,' I said.

'So what I'm trying to say is, I can understand your dad putting his parents' feelings ahead of his suspicions.'

I nodded, looking up at the ceiling again.

'Are you thinking about Dora?' Jack said. 'She'll know that you were the one who was there for her, even if Greg does decide he wants to be a dad.'

I nodded. 'I would never stop Greg seeing her,' I said. 'I want them to have a relationship. I just don't want her to love him the way she loves me, purely because of biology. God, that sounds so pathetic.'

'It sounds nice,' Jack said.

He stood up, shoving his chair back and making his wine glass wobble precariously because it wasn't on the coaster properly. He came round to where I sat, crouched down and threw his arms round me, squeezing me tight.

'You're nice,' he said. 'Lovely in fact.'

He let me go so he could look at me. His face was so close to mine I could feel his breath warm on my lips. My stomach curled with lust and something else that I thought might be, could just possibly be, the very beginning of love.

He kissed me and I kissed him back, clinging on to him to stop him falling backwards because he was still crouching by my chair and despite all his personal training sessions, I knew his legs would be wobbling.

'I'm really sorry,' he said eventually. 'I'm desperate for a wee.'

I giggled. 'Up the stairs, the door on the left,' I said. 'You just need to lift the latch on the stair gate at the top.'

He stood up, shaking out his legs, and headed upstairs.

I cleared the table and put the plates in the dishwasher, and wiped away all the splatters from Jack's spaghetti. I put the coffee machine on, and I peeked in the bag and discovered a rather delicious-looking lemon tart, which I put in the oven to warm up, and a tub of melted ice cream, which I put in the freezer to cool down.

And then I realised Jack hadn't come back from the toilet. I wondered where he had disappeared to. My house was only tiny – just the lounge and kitchen downstairs, and two bedrooms and a bathroom upstairs.

I wandered into the hall.

'Jack?' I called up the stairs. 'Are you okay?'

'Up here,' he called back.

Oh God, had he taken himself to my bedroom? I wondered. It wasn't a horrible idea, but it wasn't something I'd been planning.

But no. When I went upstairs, I found him sitting on the floor next to Dora's little toddler bed, his long legs bent up in front of him. He was reading *The Gruffalo* and a very wide-awake Dora was sitting up in bed, gripping the cuddly monkey she slept with, and listening, enthralled.

'Dora called out when I came up to the loo,' he said. 'Hope you don't mind.' He made a face at me. 'I knocked over the towel rail and I think the clatter might have woken her up. Sorry.'

I chuckled.

'Mamma,' Dora said, holding out her little arms to me for a cuddle. 'The man is reading.'

I went to her, sitting on her bed and letting her snuggle on to my lap. I kissed the top of her curls. 'The man is called Jack,' I said, smiling at him over Dora's head.

'Jack,' said Dora. She clapped her hands at him. 'Read,' she demanded.

'Whoa,' said Jack. 'She knows her own mind.'

'READ,' said Dora.

So he did. He read the whole story, doing different voices for the characters, and making me and Dora laugh.

When Dora's eyes began to close, I whispered: 'You go downstairs and sort out dessert, and I'll tuck her in.'

Quietly – well, as quietly as he could manage – Jack crept out of Dora's room. I kissed her on the forehead and her eyes opened.

'I like Jack,' she said sleepily.

I kissed her again. 'So do I, darling,' I said.

Feeling happier than I'd felt for ages, I tiptoed away and went downstairs to find Jack. He'd found the tart and the ice cream and was busy dishing it up.

'More wine?' I asked.

He nodded. 'Sounds good.'

As I opened the fridge to get another bottle, my phone buzzed with a message. I pulled it out of my jeans pocket and I swiped it to open it. It was from Elly.

'Forgot to say I was doing some legal requests last week,' she'd written. 'Saw you wanted a court martial transcript so I added that in too.'

My heart lurched. Shit. I'd written the date of Lil's court martial and the verdict on a Post-it and stuck it to my computer screen. I'd never thought for one minute that Elly would see it and request the transcript.

'Just got the email.' Elly went on. 'It's a corker. Printed it out for you and it's on your desk. See you in the morning.'

I stared at the small screen of my phone in horror. How could this have happened? After making the decision not to find out anything else, it was suddenly taken out of my hands.

'Shit,' I said, showing Jack the message. 'Shit.'

'Shit,' he echoed as he read.

'What am I going to do?' I said. 'I don't want this information. I was absolutely clear with Dad that we shouldn't do it this way.'

'But now you have it,' Jack said. 'What are you going to do?'

'I know what I should do,' I said. 'I should ignore it.'

Jack looked dubious. 'Can you ignore it?'

I shrugged. 'I could get Elly to shred it and delete the email,' I said half-heartedly.

'But …'

'But she's read it,' I said. 'She said it was a corker.'

'She did,' Jack said.

'What does that mean?'

'I have no idea,' he said.

'Is a corker bad or good?'

'Again, no idea,' Jack said.

'How can I sit next to Elly every day, knowing she knows, and not ask for more information?'

'You're going to read it aren't you?' Jack said.

'Is it awful if I do?' I said. 'Am I a terrible person?'

Jack grinned. 'I think you're human,' he said. 'But keep in mind, there will be consequences.'

'I will,' I said. 'There are always consequences.'

Chapter 31

Lilian

July 1944

I was fit to drop by the time I got back down south the next day. I'd not slept well after our trip to Edinburgh, seeing Emily's blood-soaked sheets every time I closed my eyes. Then Robert had woken me up early asking to play planes, and though I was exhausted, I couldn't resist his little face.

Sometimes we got trains back after delivering planes which was time-consuming and tiring; other times we got a taxi flight from the airfield where we'd dropped the plane back to our base in Maidenhead. But this time I'd been roped in to fly a big transport plane, a type I'd never flown before, straight back down to Berkshire for some repairs. I was pleased I could head straight home but with the weather still bad I'd been forced to concentrate hard the whole way. When I finally landed it was getting dark and all I could think about was shovelling some food into my mouth and collapsing into bed. Plus I knew I had to find Annie and Flora and fill them in on what had happened with poor Emily.

I did all my post-flight checks, signed the log in a daze, picked up my bag and headed towards the mess hut, starving hungry and desperate for a cup of tea.

Standing by the door to the hut, looking worried, was Annie. I waved to her and she rushed towards me.

'Oh, Lil, you're back,' she said, grabbing my arm.

'It's fine,' I said. 'It was touch and go for a while, but we got Emily to hospital and she's going to be fine. It's lucky you managed to get a telegram to me so quickly.'

Annie looked relieved. 'Thank God,' she said.

I nodded.

'Bugger,' Annie said. 'I forgot to tell you, something else happened …'

I was so tired, I could barely follow her frantic train of thought. 'Something else has happened to Emily?'

'No, not Emily. Forget Emily.' Annie paused, obviously cross with herself for saying such a heartless thing. 'But she's going to be all right, is she? She's on the mend?'

'I don't know,' I told her honestly. 'I hope so. But she was in a bad way when we got there.'

'You did well,' Annie said. 'But, Lil …' She took a breath. 'There's a man here to see you.'

I blinked at her. 'Bobby?' I said, my heart lifting.

'No, not Bobby,' she said. 'He said his name is Ian Mayhew.'

I felt myself sway slightly, whether from shock or fatigue, I didn't know.

I'd never really spoken to Annie or Flora about what happened to me. Annie, bless her heart, hadn't a clue who Ian Mayhew was, and yet my reaction obviously told her that this strange man turning up would be difficult for me. She steered me to a bench and sat me down.

'He's not here,' I said, shaking my head. 'There must be a mix-up.' I could hear the words Annie was saying, but somehow I couldn't understand them. Mr Mayhew was in the army. He was in France. Or Africa. Or the Pacific. He wasn't here.

But Annie was holding my hand, tight, and looking straight at me.

'Is he …?' she began. 'Did he …?'

After a tiny hesitation, I nodded.

Annie pinched her lips together. 'He wants to see you. But if you don't want to, I can go and tell him you're stuck out on a job.'

I didn't speak. I didn't know if I wanted to see him.

But Annie hadn't finished. 'He's hurt, Lil. Pretty badly.'

'Where is he?'

'He's in the office. He's alone. I said I'd find you.'

I looked, stupidly, in the direction of the office and then back at Annie.

'Do you want me to come with you?' Annie said.

I pulled my bag off my shoulder and handed it to her. 'No,' I said, taking a deep breath. 'I'll be fine. Can you put my bag on my bed for me?'

I walked towards the office, feeling queasy. I'd not seen Mr Mayhew since the day I'd told him about the baby and he'd told me about the other girls. I'd hidden out at home until we went to Scotland and he'd obviously tried his hardest to avoid me. I couldn't for the life of me understand why he'd turn up here now.

He was sitting on a plastic chair in the deserted outer office. Because it was dark now and the office was lit with harsh strip lighting I could see him through the window without him seeing me. He looked terrible. He was in uniform but it was hanging off him, he was so thin. His hat was on the table in front of him and I could see his hair was receding and grey. He looked old, I thought with surprise.

He looked up and I froze, worried he'd see me, then realised he was actually looking at his own reflection in the window. And my goodness, now I saw what Annie had meant. His face was puckered down the left side, pitted and drawn with scarring from – I assumed – burns. His left arm hung limply against his torso, his hand wizened and wasted. And I saw now that he was using crutches. They were resting against the chair at his side. He'd obviously been badly injured. I felt a rush of something – love? sympathy? horror? – as I looked at the pulled, shiny skin on his scarred face. I realised now how cruel he'd been to me, but that didn't mean I wanted to see him like this.

I breathed in deeply, then before I could change my mind, I pushed open the door to the office.

'Ian,' I said. It was the first time I'd called him anything other than Mr Mayhew.

He looked up at me, then pushing himself up with his good hand, he staggered to his feet. 'Hello, Lil,' he said. 'Sorry to drop in unannounced.'

He was talking like we were acquaintances who were politely making small talk. I hoped he wouldn't try to kiss me, so I took a step backwards and gazed at him in confusion.

'You look wonderful,' Mr Mayhew said. 'Grown up.' With his good hand he gestured to his own body. 'I'm fucked,' he said.

I winced at the harsh word, but I didn't reply. I wasn't sure what he was doing here or how he'd know I was here. My mouth was dry and I licked my lips.

'What do you want?' I croaked.

Mr Mayhew smiled. It pulled the puckered skin taut and made him look more like his old self. 'Can we sit?' he said. 'I find I get uncomfortable quite quickly if I stand for too long.'

'What happened?' I asked. He backed into the chair he'd been sitting in before, and I sat down next to him, leaving an empty chair between us.

'El Alamein,' he said. 'Minefield.'

I was impressed, despite myself. 'Brave,' I said.

Mr Mayhew shrugged. 'Not like some.'

We sat quietly for a second, then he carried on.

'I was in hospital for a long time, then a convalescent home, and then I went back to Kent for a while.'

'I thought you'd moved away?' I said. 'You and …' I swallowed the bile that rose up. 'You and your wife?'

'She went to America, to be with her sister,' Mr Mayhew said dismissively. 'I don't think she'll be back.'

Silently, I wished Mrs Mayhew well with her new life. She deserved to be happy, I thought. But Mr Mayhew was still talking.

'While I was in Kent, I saw your mother.'

I closed my eyes briefly.

'She was very kind. Saw me one day in the market square when two planes went over – dogfight. I heard the guns and it brought it all back. I had a bit of a funny turn and she was walking by. She sprang into action, calmed me down. Made sure I was all right.'

'Like she did with Dad,' I muttered. 'She looked after Dad.'

'And she was chatting away to me, talking about everything and nothing. Trying to distract me while I started to breathe normally again, and she mentioned her daughter was flying planes now.'

Mum had been fairly discreet about what I'd been doing in the war. She knew all about keeping her cards close to her chest, thanks to Dad's struggles, and she was always very much of the opinion that what went on in our family was no one else's business. I wondered if she'd ever suspected that Robert was my son, but she seemed to accept Ruth's stories of pregnancy without question.

I knew what Mr Mayhew meant, though. I remembered when Dad had one of his episodes, especially at the start of the war when things were really bad, Mum would bustle round him, chatting inanely, giving him something to focus on other than imagining the awful things he'd seen in France. I could imagine her babbling about me and how I had swapped pianos for planes, not realising that Mr Mayhew would tuck that knowledge away.

'What do you want?' I said again, clearer this time. 'I'm really tired and I'm flying again tomorrow.'

'I wanted to see you,' Mr Mayhew said. 'I miss you.'

I stared at him. 'You don't miss me.'

Mr Mayhew, to my horror, had tears in his eyes. 'I miss our life before,' he said. 'Before all this.'

'When you were cheating on your wife and fucking me and Lord knows how many other girls?' I said, knowing I was being crude and not caring one jot. 'When you could charm any woman into bed? Or should I say, any girl.' I spat the word at him.

Mr Mayhew nodded. 'You're right to be angry,' he said pathetically. 'But I've been punished, Lil. Punished enough. I've lost my wife, and my looks, and my hand. I can't even play the piano any more.'

'Good,' I said. 'I'm glad. You deserve it.'

'Lil, please,' he said. He reached out and took my hand. I didn't pull away, even though I wanted to.

'Did you think you could come back here and I'd tell you everything was all right, and we'd be together forever?' I said. 'Pick up where we left off?'

He had the grace to look sheepish. That was obviously exactly what he'd thought.

'I probably don't even do it for you any more, do I?' I patted my hair, which was escaping from my hat. 'Now I don't have my plait or my school uniform?'

'You're beautiful,' Mr Mayhew said. He pulled me towards him and kissed me. For a second – just a second – I kissed him back and then I jerked my hand away and stood up.

'I don't want to see you again,' I told him. 'You have to leave. I'll get some of the mechanics to show you the way out.' I was thinking about Gareth and his friends, who were big lads and always willing to help me.

'Lilian,' Mr Mayhew said. 'I love you.'

'Hah,' I practically shouted. 'No, you don't. You don't love anyone except yourself.'

I turned to go, then turned back. 'You didn't even ask about the baby,' I said in despair at his selfishness. 'You didn't even ask.'

He looked up at me. 'Did you have it?' he asked, pathetic again. 'Am I a father?'

'No,' I said, lying without even thinking about it. 'You're not a father. The baby died.'

I pushed open the door and walked out, hearing Mr Mayhew start to sob behind me.

A movement round the side of the hut caught my eye, and I jumped. 'Annie?' I called quietly, wondering if she'd come to see if I needed help. But there was no reply.

Slowly, I tiptoed round the side and jumped as I saw a couple entwined. They were leaning up against the wall of the hut, kissing.

'Sorry,' I said, as I backed away, but not before I recognised them. It was Will and Rose.

'Sorry,' I said again, feeling sick at the thought that they might have seen me and Mr Mayhew together.

I took one last glance through the window at Mr Mayhew, who was sitting in the plastic chair, head in his hands, and then I went to find my friends.

Chapter 32

Helena

July 2018

I got to work early the next day. Part of me wanted to ignore the transcript that would be sitting waiting for me on my desk, but another part wanted to read it as soon as I could.

I'd phoned Jack that morning and begged him to come with me to work but he'd laughed at me.

'I can't come with you because it's weird for a grown-up to take her boyfriend to work, nice as it sounds,' he said, while I did an inner dance because he'd called himself my boyfriend. 'And also, I've got a rehearsal.'

'Nervous?' I asked him. I already knew how worried he got when he was starting something new. Today was his first read-through for a new ITV drama tipped to be the next *Line of Duty*, and then he was heading off to New York again.

'Bricking it,' he said. 'How can I play a police officer? What do I know about crime fighting?'

'You'll be great,' I said. 'Dora, eat your Cheerios, darling. When do you get your uniform? Do you get to bring it home?'

'Uniforms?' he said. 'Really?'

'Well, not uniforms in general. Just you in uniform,' I said.

'Jack,' said Dora, banging her spoon on the table and waking me from my daydream of Jack in a uniform. 'Jack read the book.'

'Dora wants you to read to her again,' I told him.

'I definitely will,' he said. 'But right now, I have to go. And so do you.'

'Come with me,' I wailed again. 'I don't want to read it without you.'

'Then don't read it,' he said. 'Or wait until later and we'll read it together.'

I rolled my eyes at the very idea of waiting hours and hours with the transcript just sitting there. 'That's not going to happen,' I said.

'Then go, read, and ring me if you want to talk,' he said. 'Go!'

I'd hung up, raced round getting Dora ready for nursery, dropped her off, and headed to work in a fluster, pausing only to text Jack a good luck message for his audition as I arrived at the office.

But now, as I pulled off my coat and sat down at my desk, I thought I needed luck more than Jack. What was going to be in this transcript?

I briefly – briefly – considered going to get a cup of tea from the kitchen before I started reading, but I was already turning the pages and opening the printout.

I read it quickly at first, scanning the pages for anything that would give me a clue about Lil's discharge. Then I read it again, more slowly this time, really taking in the enormity of what I was seeing.

'What do you think?' Elly's voice made me jump and I looked up. The deserted office was filling up and there was a buzz of conversation around me. I'd not even noticed anyone coming in through the doors behind me, because I'd been so engrossed in all the court documents.

Elly pulled up her chair and handed me a cup of tea. She'd obviously been in the office a while and I'd not realised.

'Corker, right?'

I nodded. 'Oh. My. God,' I said. 'This is amazing.'

'I can't believe she was punished,' Elly said, frowning. 'I think she should have been given some sort of medal.' She looked wistful. 'You know what? This would be amazing telly. It would be a whole programme on its own.'

'Oh wouldn't it?' I said. 'It would be incredible.'

'What are you going to do?' Elly said. 'Are you going to speak to Lil?'

I looked through the printout again. I wasn't really sure what to do with it. 'I need to tell Miranda,' I said.

Luckily Miranda was free that evening. So, I raced over to her house after work and Lotta, Miranda's au pair, put Dora to bed in the spare room. I'd lift her into the buggy and hope she didn't wake up, later.

Then we sat down in Miranda's lovely – very neat – living room and I told her what I'd learned.

'So the first thing you need to know is that I did not request these documents,' I said.

'Okayyyy,' Miranda said, doubtfully.

'I absolutely meant it when I told Dad this was the wrong way to approach it,' I said. 'But Elly saw I'd written the info down, and because she was requesting some documents herself, she did mine too. She thought she was doing me a favour.'

'So you got the court documents accidentally?' Miranda said. I nodded.

'You could have deleted them,' she pointed out.

I snorted. 'Yeah right,' I said. 'Would you have deleted them?'

'Yes, I think I would have,' she said, lifting her chin. 'You knew there would be consequences of carrying on this investigation and you should have made the decision not to find out any more.'

I grinned at her. 'I'll go then,' I said. 'And not tell you what I found out?'

I went to stand up and Miranda grabbed my arm.

'Don't you dare,' she said. 'Spill.'

With the faintest air of triumph, I took a breath. 'Lilian was accused of running a network across the country, using contacts she made when she was flying planes,' I said.

Miranda looked confused. 'A network of what? Black market stuff? Smuggling? Lil?'

I smiled. 'No, nothing like that,' I said. 'If this is true, then she was amazing, Miranda. She is amazing.' I picked up the documents. 'She was charged with contravening standing orders,' I said.

'What does that mean?'

'Not much, to be honest. As far as I can tell it's just a vague charge when they can't make anything more specific stick.'

'Riiight,' said Miranda. 'So what had she done to contravene these orders?'

'Lil was accused of running a network organising abortions for women all over the country.'

'Illegal abortions?'

'Shut your mouth, Miranda,' I said, laughing at her shocked reaction. 'Yes, illegal abortions.'

'She was making money out of women in trouble?' Miranda said. 'That doesn't sound like Lil.'

'She didn't make any money out of it; the documents are very clear about that. In fact, there was very little evidence as far as I can see. No financial gains, no testimony from anyone she'd helped.'

'Did she admit it?'

'Nope,' I said. 'Well, ish. She admitted helping a friend get an abortion.'

'But you think there's more to it?'

I gripped the court documents tighter. 'I do,' I said. 'Don't you think it all makes sense?'

'It does,' Miranda said cautiously. 'But it seems so implausible. When was this?'

'Towards the end of the war. Late summer of 1944.'

'So she'd not even have been twenty-one? And she did all this by herself?'

I wrinkled my nose up. 'Hmm,' I said.

Miranda sat up a bit straighter. 'What do you mean?'

'Lil was the only one who was arrested and the only one who was discharged. But some of the notes mention two other women – Annie Armstrong and Flora Stewart. Lil, though, swore she was the only person involved. That she'd arranged that one abortion and that one only, and that she'd acted alone.'

Miranda whistled through her teeth. 'This is incredible,' she said. 'And the verdict was guilty?'

'Yes and no,' I told her. 'Lil admitted arranging that one abortion in court. If the network did exist …'

'… and you think it did,' Miranda added.

'If it did exist, Lil covered its tracks so well that there just wasn't enough evidence. So instead Lil was charged with contravening standing orders for arranging one abortion for a friend.'

'What a bloody woman,' Miranda said.

'I know.'

We sat for a moment in silence thinking about Lil and what she might have done. And then I voiced what we were both wondering. 'Do you think this proves that Lil is Dad's real mum?'

Miranda made a face. 'You think her own experiences as a teenager made her want to help other people in the same situation?'

'Makes sense. The two things link with each other.'

'I think you're probably right,' Miranda said thoughtfully. 'Imagine being fifteen, pregnant, terrified …'

'No idea what to do for the best,' I added. 'Maybe the father was fifteen too – what could he do to help? Or if he was older, he'd have been off to fight.'

'And then someone stepped in to help.'

'Grandma Ruth,' I said. 'She stepped in. She and Lil went to Scotland, Lil had the baby, and Grandma Ruth adopted him.'

'This is huge,' Miranda said.

'That's what Jack said. I think it's wonderful.'

'Wonderful for us seeing it through twenty-first-century eyes,' Miranda pointed out. 'Not so wonderful for Lil who went through it.'

Since I'd read the documents, I'd been wondering about what to do next, and now I thought I knew. 'I want to talk to Lil,' I said.

'What if it upsets her?'

'I don't want to talk about Dad, or about her going to Scotland,' I said. 'I want to talk about the court martial. She did an amazing, brave, innovative thing and she was punished for it – unfairly, in my opinion. She should have some recognition. If not officially, then at least from us.'

Miranda nodded slowly. 'I suppose,' she said. 'Just don't upset her.'

I gathered up the papers, pleased to have got to the bottom of it all. 'I won't,' I said. 'I'll congratulate her. Tell her what an inspiration she is. How brave she was. I'm sure she'll realise it's a good thing that we know … oh …'

I stopped and Miranda looked at me.

'What?' she said.

'I suppose we should tell Dad first.'

Chapter 33

I left Dora sleeping at Miranda's and walked round to my parents' house, clutching all the court transcripts to my chest.

Mum and Dad were pleased to see me, as they always were.

'I've got the documents,' I told Dad as I went into the lounge.

He turned off *Only Connect*, and turned to look at me in surprise.

'The court documents?' he said. 'But I thought ...'

'I know,' I said. 'And I meant it. Elly at work requested them accidentally – and then I couldn't help but look at them.'

Mum and Dad both looked up at me, nervous and hopeful.

'Does it prove anything?' Mum said. She took Dad's hand and squeezed it. 'Does it prove that Lil is Robert's biological mother?'

'Not exactly,' I said. 'Have a read.'

I waited for them to find their reading glasses. Mum found hers in Dad's pocket, and Dad found his perched on top of his head. Then infuriatingly slowly, they read through the documents. Mum read them twice, pointing out parts to Dad for him to reread. Finally, as I was about to scream with impatience, they were finished.

'Nothing,' said Dad, with a sigh.

'What?' I said. 'That's not nothing.'

Mum's eyes were bright with tears. 'What a woman,' she said, just as Miranda and I had done. 'Knowing Lil as we do, it seems obvious to me that she was covering up for a whole crowd.'

'Amazing, isn't it?' I said. 'If it all happened as we think.'

'Incredible,' Mum agreed.

'I remember when I told her I was having Dora,' I said. 'I went down to see her and I cried. I was in bits, do you remember?'

Mum nodded. 'Of course,' she said.

'I told her I was pregnant first and she was so pleased,' I said. 'And then I started to cry and I told her Greg wasn't happy, that he didn't want to have a baby, and that I was pretty sure I was going to end up doing it alone. And she was so angry – I could see it in her face.

'But then she took my hand, and she said that whatever I decided to do would be for the best. She said she would be there to support me whatever I decided.' I was welling up just thinking about it. 'I think she was doing what she'd done all those years ago,' I said. 'Doing it for me this time.'

Mum gave me a hug. 'She's wonderful,' she said.

'But there's nothing,' Dad interrupted, leafing through the documents once more. 'No mention of any baby.'

'There are lots of mentions of babies,' I said, wryly. 'Just not the one we expected.'

'I honestly thought the discharge would have been because she'd had a baby,' Dad said, looking confused. 'But this is a whole other level.'

'I've got an idea,' I said.

Dad looked at me expectantly.

'I think – Miranda agrees – that while this doesn't give us any concrete proof that Lil is your biological mother, it does sort of back it up.'

Mum was nodding. 'It does, Robert, do you see? Lil was helping other women the way she was helped.'

'Exactly that,' I said.

'I see,' Dad said. 'I do see. But I just thought that this would prove one way or another if she was my real mother, and I could put the whole thing to bed.'

I shook my head. 'Dad, I'm so sorry, but without Lil's name on the birth certificate, I'm fairly sure there won't be any proof. Nothing written down, anyway. As far as documentation is concerned, your parents were Ruth and Bobby.'

Dad looked glum.

'You know what I'm going to say?' I said, softly. 'If you're determined to know one way or another, then the only way to find out is to talk to Lil.'

Dad pushed his glasses up on to the top of his head and sighed. 'I know,' he said. 'You're absolutely right. I just really, really don't want to have the conversation.'

'It won't be easy,' I said. 'You'll have to decide whether your desire to know outweighs your desire not to talk about it.'

'I'm very worried that I might be wrong,' he admitted.

'You could be,' I said. 'We've got no proof.'

'Imagine if I bowled in there, all guns blazing, and told her I'm her son,' Dad said. 'And she looks at me, completely bewildered, and says no I'm not?'

'She could, you know,' I said. 'That could happen.'

'And how would she feel then?' Dad said. 'I'd have unsettled her, and probably upset her, and dragged her good name through the mud ...'

'Hardly,' Mum snorted. 'It's not the 1940s now, you know.'

Dad ignored her. 'And worst of all, I feel the whole time I'm wondering about this, I'm somehow dishonouring my parents,' he said.

'I understand.' I patted him on the hand.

'Lil adored my father,' Dad went on. 'And my mother – oh she thought the world of my mother. So if I feel like I'm dishonouring them just by thinking these things, what will Lil say?'

'Dad,' I said. 'You need to calm down.'

'I know,' he said, gripping Mum's hand tightly. 'It's just such a … what's that word Imogen always uses? Headfuck. It's such a headfuck.'

I blinked in surprise. 'It's definitely that,' I said, chuckling at his choice of words. 'Listen, Jack was telling me about his father and stepfather the other day and he said something I think might help you.'

'I said that I'd always thought blood was thicker than water, and he said I was wrong. He said he would have liked to have known his father but he doesn't have a gap in his heart where he should have been because he has a wonderful mother, and a loving stepdad.'

Dad nodded.

'He said that biology doesn't matter, it's really just about love.'

'He's right,' Mum said. 'And haven't I told you that myself when you've been fretting about Greg?'

I smiled. She had told me. Many times.

'Finding out the truth won't change the way you felt about your parents,' I said. 'And it won't stop them being your parents. Bobby will always be your dad, and Ruth will always be your mum. And Lil's your auntie. Your favourite auntie. And if it turns out she gave birth to you, then so much the better. Because she's your favourite auntie, and your biological mum. But it won't stop Ruth being your mother. How could it?'

'Goodness,' said Dad. 'When did you get to be so wise about family secrets?'

'Dad,' I said witheringly. 'It's literally my job.'

He smiled. 'So it is.'

'I understand that you want to know the truth,' I said. 'And I still think you should talk to Lil. But don't feel guilty about it. And don't expect her to suddenly become a mum to you, because that won't happen either.'

'I'm almost eighty,' Dad said. 'I don't need a mum.'

'Everyone needs a mum,' I said. 'But have a think about whether you're going to speak to her.' I stood up. 'I need to go and get Dora from Miranda's. I'm going to see Lil this weekend – I really want to talk to her about these documents. I won't mention anything to do with you, Dad. Not yet.'

'Be careful, Nell,' Mum said. 'She didn't want us to know, remember? Just be a bit cautious.'

'I will,' I said. 'I'll tread carefully.'

Chapter 34

Lilian

July 1944

'I'm the pilot,' I told the ground crew, unsmiling, as I signed the papers they handed me. I ignored the smirk the mechanic gave his mate and checked my watch. I had to be quick. I'd taken off much later than I'd hoped, thanks to a fog that had rolled in this morning and taken ages to clear, which hadn't helped the dark mood that I'd been struggling with since Mr Mayhew had turned up. I felt strange, having seen him. Like a chain had been broken – and I was free. But despite knowing he'd never try to find Robert, or – I hoped – contact me again now, I still felt a sense of loss and I thought perhaps we'd always be linked. It was an odd feeling; it had plunged me into a kind of gloom and the horrible flight had added to my woes.

When I'd been flying, I'd heard a strange thud in the back of the plane and almost considered turning round to check, but in the end I'd decided it must have been a bird, and carried on. I knew there was a woman waiting for me. She was meeting me in the nearby town and she'd have already been waiting for an hour. I just hoped she'd still be there.

Papers dealt with, I hurried down the side of the mess hut. I had four hours before I had to take another plane back. More than enough time to get into town and meet the woman.

'Thought I'd take a look round,' I said casually to the chap in the security office. 'Can I get a bus into town?'

'Jeff will take you,' he said, tilting his head in the direction of a grocer's van parked close to the entrance to the base. A man was loading empty crates in the back. 'Room for a little one, Jeff?'

Jeff gave me a broad, toothless smile. 'Jump in,' he said and I climbed into the passenger seat.

It was a short trip to the town centre, and I was grateful for the lift that meant I'd reach my contact faster. Though the journey felt longer thanks to Jeff's questions about which planes I could fly.

'Spitfires, yes,' I said, nodding and staring out of the window.

'And bombers?'

'All the bombers,' I said.

'Never Lancasters?'

'I've not flown many, but I'm cleared for them,' I said.

'Lancasters? Really? A little lass like you?'

I smiled at him letting his words wash over me. 'Is this the town centre?' I asked. 'Can I jump out here?'

Jeff pulled up at the kerb and I thanked him and climbed out, leaving him shaking his head and muttering 'never Lancasters' as I looked round to see where we were meeting.

Under the clock, had been my instruction, and straight ahead of me was a church with a tall clock tower. Beneath it was a bench, and sitting on the bench was a young woman, about my own age, looking pale and worried.

Forcing myself not to run and draw attention to us, I strolled over. 'Mary?' I asked.

210

I startled the woman, who was lost in her thoughts. She jumped and gasped. 'Oh, Lilian?'

I nodded and she stood up and threw her arms round me.

'I thought you weren't coming,' she said. 'Thank God.'

'Shall we walk?' I asked her. 'It's easier to talk.'

She looped her hand through my arm. 'We can go into the churchyard,' she said. 'It's quiet.'

We strolled through the gates together. I thought we would look like two friends chatting, should anyone pay attention to us. In my experience, no one really noticed anything – they were all too worried about themselves to pay attention to anyone else.

'I bet you hear all sorts of stories,' Mary said as we walked.

I shrugged. 'You don't have to tell me anything,' I assured her. 'I'm not here to judge you.'

'I was stupid,' she said. 'Believed the things he was telling me. Thought he loved me. Same old story.'

I snorted. 'We've all been there.'

Mary groaned. 'And oh God, he was so handsome, Lilian. Dark skin, amazing accent …'

'GI?' I said, interested.

She nodded. 'Gone now, of course.'

'Killed?' I gasped.

'Nah, well maybe, I suppose. But gone into Europe somewhere. Probably chatting up all those French girls with that accent.'

Mary steered me round the side of the large church. 'And he left me a reminder of our night together, didn't he?'

I nodded. 'There's a woman, in Lincoln,' I said. Lincoln was only a few miles from where we were. 'She's a nurse. I've not met her, but my friend has. Her name is Lizzie Wells and she's expecting you on Monday.'

Mary stared straight ahead. 'Monday?' she said. 'Right.'

'You work in a factory?'

She nodded.

'Parachutes,' she said.

'You'll need time off. Can you say you're sick?'

'How long?'

A picture of Emily wrapped in her bloodied sheets flashed into my mind and I pushed it away. 'A week, probably,' I said. 'You'll have to play it by ear.'

Mary looked horrified. 'What should I say?'

'Something infectious is best, then they'll leave you alone. Dicky tummy?'

Mary nodded again. 'Fine,' she said. 'That's fine. My friend Elaine knows what's happening. She can cover for me.'

I opened my bag and took out a sheet of paper.

'This is Lizzie's address, and all the details you'll need,' I said, handing it over. 'Don't contact her before or after. If anything goes wrong, send me a telegram. My details are on there too. Don't keep the paper. Read it now, memorise it, and then rip it up, and chuck it. And it might be best to get yourself a cheap wedding ring beforehand. Just in case.'

'In case?'

'Sometimes there's bleeding,' I said, carefully. I wanted her to know the risks, but I didn't want to scare her. 'And if you need to go to the doctor you're going to want to give them a false name. Say it's a miscarriage.'

Mary bit her lip. 'Will it hurt?'

I shook my head. 'I don't know,' I said honestly. 'You don't have to do it, you know. You can change your mind any time.'

'I won't change my mind,' Mary said. 'I can't have a baby. I don't want a baby. And I definitely don't want *this* baby.'

I gripped her hand and smiled at her. She was very pretty, with shining red hair and perfect make-up.

'Good luck,' I said. 'When … when it's all done and you're back at work, could you drop me a letter and let me know how you are?'

'Course,' she said. She smiled. 'Why do you do this? Risking your own neck to save other people?'

'I had a baby,' I said honestly. 'And I didn't want a baby either. And someone helped me.'

Mary's blue eyes searched my face. 'You're young,' she said. 'Who helped you?'

'My sister-in-law.'

'And the baby?'

'She's his mum now.'

'Happy?'

'He's very happy.'

Mary laughed. 'I meant you. What about you? Are you happy?'

I thought about it for a minute. Back when I'd realised I was expecting Robert, I'd thought I would never be happy again. But now I was. Not all the time. There was a sadness inside me that I sometimes thought might be there forever. And sometimes – like when Mr Mayhew turned up at base last week – that sadness was nearer the surface. But sometimes, when I was flying, or when I was laughing with Annie and Flora, or when I was watching Ruth playing with Robert, I was happy. No question.

'I'm happy sometimes,' I said. 'As long as I keep moving.'

'I'm glad.'

We'd walked all the way round the church now and reached the gates again. Together we strolled back out into the town square and Mary turned to face me. 'I owe you,' she said.

'Pay Lizzie, not me.'

She laughed again. She had a nice laugh, low and melodic, and I was glad she was still finding things funny despite her predicament.

'I meant I owe you metaphorically,' she said.

I waved my hand. 'We all help each other,' I said. 'Just make sure you're there for someone else one day.'

Mary leaned forward and gave me a kiss on the cheek. 'Goodbye, Lilian,' she said. 'Thank you.'

'Bye, Mary. Good luck.'

I turned and walked away without looking back. I hoped she was going to be all right.

Chapter 35

Helena

July 2018

I looked round my bedroom in despair. Jack's T-shirt was slung across my dressing table. It had knocked over the pot I kept my make-up brushes in and they'd spilled on to the floor. One of my pillows was squished down the side of the headboard, and the framed print from an Audrey Hepburn exhibition that hung on my wall was wonky. It looked like Jack and I had spent the night in the throes of passion, throwing our clothes off and shaking the walls. In actual fact, I'd been watching an old episode of *Gilmore Girls* and picking at some pasta, when he'd rung from a cab.

'I've landed and I'm jet-lagged and fed up and I miss you,' he said. 'Can I come over? I promise I'll leave before Dora wakes up in the morning.'

'Now?' I'd said in horror, glancing at my beautifully tidy flat. 'You want to come here?'

'I don't want to go back to my house,' he wailed. 'Because you're not there.'

How could I resist?

Jack had pulled up outside about forty-five minutes later, hanging with fatigue. He'd been doing another guest appearance on the US show and he'd had to squeeze it in between filming started for the new series of *Mackenzie* back here.

He'd kissed me, glanced at the TV screen and commented that he'd 'met her once in LA' and she was 'really, really nice' – I had no idea which of the actresses on screen he meant – then he'd curled up with his head on my lap and gone to sleep. When I woke him up to get him to come upstairs to bed, he'd peeled off his clothes and crawled under the duvet without a word – which is when the whole T-shirt/make-up brushes thing must have happened.

Now I was alone in bed, and I could hear Jack in the shower. I shut my eyes so I couldn't see the carnage in my room, and listened to his muffled singing through the wall. I was pleased to see him, even if I'd not really seen him. I just hoped he wouldn't wake Dora. I wasn't ready to have her seeing him share my bed. Not yet.

When Jack came back into the room, hair wet and wearing just a pair of jeans, I couldn't hide my smile.

'You're awake,' he said. 'And looking very pleased about it.'

'Pleased to see you,' I said. 'Even though it's extremely early.'

'Jet lag,' he said. 'Sorry.'

'How was the show?'

Jack made a face. 'Hard work,' he said. 'But brilliant. There's talk of extending the guest role.'

'Really?' I was impressed. 'That will be great.'

'I'd have to be in New York for longer,' he said. 'Few months probably.'

I was alarmed by how much that thought alarmed me. But I forced a smile. 'So, Dora and I will come and stay with you for a while,' I said.

Jack was looking round for his T-shirt and I pointed to the wrecked dressing table.

216

'You could come with me for the whole time,' he said. 'Oops, did I do that?'

He looked at the skew-whiff print on the wall and I nodded. 'It's fine,' I said. 'Just leave it …'

Jack pulled on his T-shirt – inside out – then tried to straighten the picture. He stood back to check it was right, and there was a pause and then it dropped down the wall and hit the floor with a crack. I winced.

'Oh bugger,' Jack said. 'I'll get it reframed for you.'

I closed my eyes again. Jack was definitely worth the chaos he brought with him, but man there was a lot of chaos.

'I have to go,' he said.

'Stay a bit longer.'

'What about Dora?'

'She's still asleep.'

Jack shook his head. 'I can't, more's the pity. I'm working.'

'Again?' I said. 'It's the weekend. Why are you working?'

'I don't know, ask my agent,' he said, giving me his best grin. 'Can we catch up later?' He crawled up the bed and gave me a lingering kiss. 'We can continue this later too,' he said. 'What are you doing today?'

'Going to see Lil,' I said. 'I want to speak to her about every-thing I've found out.'

I'd filled Jack in via email while he was away, so he knew as much as I did.

'Oh, I wish I could come,' he said. 'Can I come?'

'You're filming,' I reminded him. I ruffled his hair. 'And you're going to be late.'

'They'll wait for me,' he said confidently.

'They won't.'

Jack screwed up his face. 'No, you're right. They won't,' he said. 'Must go.'

He gave me one last kiss and disappeared out of the door. I heard him thump down the stairs, missing the last step and

217

thumping extra hard, and then open and close the door. Smiling to myself I stretched out in bed, wiggling my toes in delight at how lucky I was to have met him.

Then I got up and started to pick up my fallen make-up brushes. I straightened everything on my dressing table, retrieved the pillow from behind the headboard and plumped it up, made my bed, and then looked in dismay at the Audrey Hepburn print. It had landed on its end and the glass was cracked diagonally all the way across. I decided to leave it where it was, leaning against the wall, in case the glass fell out when I moved it. I didn't want Dora to cut herself.

'Lucky it wasn't a mirror,' I said to myself with a shudder. 'Don't want seven years' bad luck now when everything is going so well.'

Singing softly to myself, I got Dora up and dressed and we ate toast while making silly faces at each other.

'We're going to see Lil,' I told her, and she smiled happily.

'Lil, Lil, Lil,' she cooed. 'Pony?'

'Go and find them, then.'

I helped her down from the table and she ran off into the lounge to search for her little ponies. I bustled about packing a bag for her with snacks and nappies and spare clothes and all the other stuff a two-year-old girl needed to leave the house.

When the doorbell rang, I was annoyed, thinking it was Mum or Miranda come to interfere in my visit to Lil's, but even that didn't stop my good mood.

I ran down the hall and threw open the door. There, looking exactly the same as he had the last time I'd seen him, more than a year before, was Greg. To his side, slightly behind him and gripping his hand with both of hers, was a tall blonde woman – almost as tall as he was – with straight white teeth and tanned skin.

'Helena,' Greg said. 'Hi.'

I stared at him not sure what to say. 'Hi,' I managed.

'This is Kimberley,' he said, turning slightly to the blonde woman.

'Hi,' she said.

We stood there awkwardly for a second.

'Could we come in?' Greg said, politely. 'We won't take up too much of your time.' Like he was selling double glazing or something.

I stepped back and let them come in, then I remembered Dora was in the lounge so I stood like a sentry by the door to stop them going that way.

'Kitchen,' I muttered.

I didn't offer them a drink, and I didn't sit down. I stood by the worktop, while Greg and the woman – Kimberley – perched at the table.

'What do you want?' I said rudely. 'Only, I'm busy.'

Greg took a breath. 'I wanted to see you,' he said. 'Because I'm home for a visit, and well, some things have changed, and I thought I should come in person because I didn't think you'd answer if I called …'

I rolled my eyes so hard it hurt. 'What do you want?' I said again.

'We're getting married,' Greg said. 'Me and Kimberley.'

'Lovely,' I said. 'Congratulations. See yourselves out.'

Kimberley gave a funny little laugh. 'Helena,' she said. She was Canadian, judging by her accent. I glared at her. 'This is my fault in a way. You see, Greg told me about your daughter, Dora, and I suggested he come visit her.'

Greg smiled at her in an indulgent way. A way he'd never smiled at me.

'It was more than a suggestion,' he said. 'It was an ultimatum.'

'I don't care,' I said.

Greg shifted on his chair awkwardly. 'No, of course not,' he said. 'Long story short, Kimberley told me she wouldn't marry

219

me unless I reached out to you, and tried to form a relationship with Dora.'

Despite myself, I was impressed. I looked at Kimberley. 'You said that?'

She nodded and I nodded back.

There was a pause.

'Great,' I said. 'Fabulous. So, you've "reached out",' I made the words heavy with sarcasm. 'Now you need to go.'

'Helena,' Greg said. 'Please.'

'How long are you here for?' I said. 'Are you staying?'

He shook his head. 'Just a month this time,' he said. 'But there's a possibility I could be transferred back to London in the future.'

'Yay,' I said. I found a piece of junk mail that was lying on the side and handed it to him with a pen.

'Write your number on there,' I said. 'I'll think about it.'

Obediently, Greg wrote his phone number and an address on the envelope. 'We're staying in an Airbnb,' he said. 'It's not far from here.'

I shrugged. 'I've got a train to catch,' I said. 'You need to go.'

'Is Dora here?' Greg said. He looked round as though he was expecting her to jump out of the fridge.

'She's in the lounge,' I said. 'Please go away.'

Greg and Kimberley exchanged looks and then, obviously deciding it wasn't worth arguing, they both stood up and trailed down the hall to the front door.

As they stepped out of the front door, Dora appeared in the lounge doorway.

'Mamma,' she said. I scooped her up in case Greg tried to talk to her.

'Go away,' I said again. 'I'll call you.'

They walked down the path and I shut the door behind them. Then I buried my face in Dora's curls, hardly able to believe that Greg had just been here after so long.

'Come on then, baby,' I said to her. 'Let's forget about that silly man.'

'Silly man,' she echoed, as I'd known she would.

'We need to go and see Lil.'

Lil would know what to do.

Chapter 36

Lilian

July 1944

Back at the base, I had time for a cup of tea in the mess hut, and then I found the taxi plane that was taking me back to Maidenhead.

'It's all ready,' one of the ground crew told me. He had bright ginger hair that stuck up on top of his head in a tuft, and an infectious smile. 'There's just you and the pilot today. You can check her out, if you like?'

I climbed into the cockpit and did the checks because there was still no sign of the pilot, and then I realised I'd left my bag on the ground outside the plane. I tutted to myself. I was tired and not thinking straight, feeling a bit emotional after meeting Mary, but that was no excuse to be so slack.

I jumped down and picked it up, just in time to see a pair of legs disappearing into the back of the plane.

'Excuse me,' I called, assuming it was the pilot. 'Is there a problem?'

I walked round to the back of the plane. It was a Wellington, so it was big and there was plenty of room inside. I called out again but there was no reply. Perhaps I'd imagined it? And when I saw the pilot climb into the cockpit, it seemed I had.

The ginger-headed mechanic walked past and I called out to him. 'Is there someone still working on the plane?' I asked.

He shook his head. 'No, you can go,' he said. He gave me a cheeky smile. 'Unless you'd rather stay here with me?'

I rolled my eyes but I smiled – his grin really was infectious.

'I thought I heard someone inside,' I explained. 'Can I check it's clear to put my mind at rest?'

'No time,' he said. 'You're cleared for take-off and the pilot's there. You need to go.'

On cue, the engine started, so sighing, I climbed into the cockpit next to the pilot and introduced myself.

The flight home was uneventful, but as soon as we landed back in Maidenhead, I jumped down from the cockpit and raced round to the back of the plane.

I put my arms up and pulled myself through the open hatch, waiting for my eyes to adjust to the dim light inside.

And there, perched on one of the long benches used by the bomber crew, sat Will Bates and Rose Smythe.

Will, to his credit, looked horrified that I'd found them. Rose, however, looked at me in defiance.

'Found us then?' she said.

I couldn't speak. I was so surprised to see them there that I couldn't find the words. 'What?' I muttered. 'Why?'

'Lil, I'm so sorry,' Will said. 'I didn't mean for any of this to happen.'

'What?' I said again. 'What happened?' I sat down on the bench opposite them and stared at them. 'Would someone explain what's going on here?'

Rose lifted her chin. 'I'll explain,' she said.

I made a flourish with my hand. 'Please do,' I said.

'I knew you were up to something,' she said. 'You and those

friends of yours. I heard you talking in the lav at the dance and I've seen you whispering and sneaking about. I thought it was black market stuff you were trading, or selling, and I wanted to know what you were doing.'

She paused. 'I was doing my bit for the war effort,' she said.

'Pah, no you bloody weren't,' I said. 'You just wanted to annoy me.'

Rose didn't take my bait. 'The black market is destroying Britain's efforts to fight Nazi Germany,' she parroted. 'It was our duty to find out what you were doing.'

I looked at Will. 'And she told you all this, did she?'

He nodded, looking at his feet. 'She said we had to find out what you were doing because it was definitely illegal. And I was angry with you,' he said. 'Because you lied.'

My head was spinning. 'Lied?' I said. 'Lied about what?'

'About your bloke.'

I shook my head, completely confused.

'I saw you with him,' Will said. 'I saw you kiss him.'

'Mr Mayhew?' I said. 'You saw me?'

I made a fist with one hand and punched the other palm. 'Bloody hell, Will. I heard you outside, but I thought you two were just having a kiss and a cuddle. You were spying on me?'

'You were kissing another bloke.'

'I wasn't,' I said. 'He kissed me.' Then I gathered myself. 'And even if I had kissed him, it's none of your business.'

Will scowled at me, making his little boy face look ugly and twisted. 'You told me you didn't want to be with me, because something bad happened to you,' he said. 'And you told me it was over.'

'I told the truth,' I hissed at him. 'But I owe you nothing.'

Rose jumped in. 'Will told me what you'd said, and I remembered all the rumours about you and Ian Mayhew back home,' she said. 'When he turned up at the base, I realised it was all true.'

'This has nothing to do with you,' I said, still bewildered. 'Why do you even care?'

'Because why should you get away with it, when nobody else does?' Rose said. 'Why should you get to do whatever you want with no consequences, when we don't?'

I laughed without humour. 'Oh, there are consequences,' I said. 'Believe me, there are consequences.'

'There will be,' Rose said.

I shrugged. 'I'm not involved in the black market,' I said. 'Do whatever you need to do.'

Rose leaned forward on her elbows. 'I know you're not involved in the black market,' she said.

I looked at her closely. Why was she smiling?

'I know what you and your horrible friends are doing. You're arranging illegal abortions for women with no morals. And probably being paid handsomely for it, too.'

My stomach plummeted into my boots. Shit. Shit. Shit. She did know. She and Will must have followed me to meet Mary, and eavesdropped on our conversation.

'I'm not sure which bit is the worst,' Rose went on. 'The illegality of it. The fact that these women might die. Or the fact that these women don't really deserve anyone's help. If they've got themselves into trouble, then why shouldn't they get themselves out of it?'

'It's not like that,' I said, through gritted teeth. 'That's not what it is.'

Will spoke up. 'When I thought you were involved in the black market I felt bloody awful,' he said, looking stricken. 'But this is much, much worse. This is people's lives you're playing with, Lil. It's not just a few cigarettes that have fallen off the back of a lorry, or a couple of bottles of bootlegged booze.'

'It's important,' I began, then I stopped. What was the point? They'd never understand why we did the things we did.

'What are you going to do?' I asked.

225

'We're going straight to Flight Captain Rogers and telling her,' Rose said firmly.

But Will shook his head. 'Anonymous, you agreed,' he said to Rose.

Rose sighed. 'Fine. We'll find a way to tip her off anonymously,' she said. 'It doesn't really matter how we do it. The important thing is we do it. She can't be allowed to get away with this, Will. She really can't.'

'I'm still here, you know,' I said. 'Still here, listening to what you're saying.'

Will was shaking his head. 'It's not right,' he said. I felt a tiny glimmer of hope and I smiled at him.

'Oh for goodness' sake,' Rose said, infuriated. 'I'll do it if you don't want to. I'm not scared of her.' She tipped her head in my direction.

Will looked right at me. 'Scared of her?' he said. 'I'm not scared of her. I …' He trailed off and Rose scowled at him.

'You're in love with her?' she said, disgusted. 'Still? After everything?'

Will shrugged. 'I wish it wasn't true,' he said. 'But I can't help it.'

I looked straight at him. 'I'm sorry,' I said and he nodded.

'I'm going to report this,' Rose said. 'She's not getting away with it. Even if you are in love with her.' She spat the words out and I shuddered.

'Do what you need to do,' Will said.

He got up and slid out of the hatch on to the runway. I watched him walk away without looking back. Then I followed him. I had to get to Annie and Flora before Rose did whatever it was she was planning.

'Enjoy your time while it lasts,' Rose called after me. 'You're not going to be here much longer.'

I pretended I hadn't heard, but I had an awful feeling she was right.

Chapter 37

Helena

July 2018

On the way down to Surrey on the train, Dora went to sleep on my lap so I reread the court martial documents, even though I almost knew them off by heart now I'd read them so many times. I wanted a distraction so I didn't think about Greg.

I would ring him, I thought. I couldn't keep him away from Dora, despite how rubbish he'd been in the past, and Kimberley had struck me as a nice enough woman.

But I was shaken by his timing – when all these family secrets were coming out of the woodwork, and just as I was getting into something with Jack. Suddenly I felt like the ground had shifted beneath my feet, and the happy person I'd been that morning seemed a long way away.

I drummed my fingers on the court documents. I was a bit apprehensive about telling Lil what I knew, but I thought she'd be relieved it was out in the open. I imagined she had kept quiet about what she'd done because of the illegality of abortions back then. Could she even get into trouble with the law now for things she'd done back then? I wasn't sure. Plus of course there were the moral questions that remained even now. I thought if I told her how amazing we all believed her to be, she'd be pleased, and hopefully even see that she had done a wonderful thing back then, no matter what the law had said.

There was a celebratory feel to the lounge today. There was bunting up on the walls and the remains of a cake on the table – and Lil was playing the piano. I grinned to see her sitting straight-backed on the stool, bashing out some boogie-woogie with all the energy of someone half her age.

Watching her with barely disguised adoration was the old sitcom actor. He winked at me when I walked in, and said something to Lil, who stopped playing and turned round on the stool to see me.

'Darling Helena, and my gorgeous Dora, how nice to see you,' she said.

'Are we too late for the party?'

'We had cake for Jeanie's birthday,' Lil said. She got up from the stool and I offered her my arm as support. 'She's ninety-five.'

'Ooh, she's older than you are,' I said. 'Will you get cake for your birthday?'

'I bloody hope so,' she said. 'Shall we go to my room? It's a bit raucous in here. Jeanie used to be a Tiller girl – she's been threatening to show us all her high kicks.'

The lounge was indeed more lively than I'd ever seen it. Clearly a birthday was the only excuse all the residents needed to unleash their inner performers. I giggled at the sitcom actor, who was beginning to tell an anecdote about the time he charmed Judi Dench.

'Oh, he's not so bad, you know,' she said, seeing me look. 'He's got a good heart.'

I raised an eyebrow at her, and she ignored me as we walked down the corridor, Dora running ahead, and into her room.

'Chair or bed?' I asked.

'Chair today. I'm feeling good.'

I helped her into her chair and arranged the cushion behind her, then I sat down in the chair facing her.

She showed Dora the little pony that Dora had given her.

'I keep it next to my bed,' she said. 'To remind me of you.'

'So,' I said, casually. 'Greg showed up this morning.'

'He never did?'

'Just bold as brass on the doorstep, with his Canadian fiancée.'

Lil shook her head. 'The cheek of that man,' she said.

'He wants to reach out to Dora.'

Lil snorted. 'What did you say?'

I smiled, slightly. 'I threw him out.'

'Ha!' Lil gave a bark of laughter, but then she looked serious. 'You should give him a chance though. Family is important.'

'I know,' I said, feeling wretched. I looked at Dora, prancing her little horse along Lil's bedspread. 'What if she likes him better than me?'

Lil took my hand. 'She won't,' she said. 'Children know who their real parents are.'

There was a pause.

'Lil,' I said. 'I've got a bit of a confession.'

Lil gave me a fake shocked glance. 'Been naughty, have you?'

I chuckled. 'Yes, a bit,' I said. I took a breath. 'When I said I wasn't going to look into your past any more, I did mean it, honestly. But there was a mix-up at work and my colleague requested the court papers and well, I read them.'

Lil stared at me, all smiles gone.

I carried on, babbling a bit now because Lil hadn't really reacted in the way I'd expected.

'I read about what you were accused of doing during the war and I think you're wonderful. What you did for those women? If you did it, that is. That was amazing. And I know you were punished back then, and I understand why you might not want to talk about it, but you should be celebrated, Lil. You did good things. And I want to hear your side of the story.'

Lil looked at me with such disappointment in her eyes that I stopped talking straight away. 'You researched me?' she said. 'Even though I'd told you I didn't want to remember those times?'

'Accidentally,' I said, knowing I was stretching the truth a bit. A lot.

Lil nodded. 'Fine,' she said. 'I'll tell you what we did. And then I want you to leave.'

Chapter 38

Lilian

July 1944

Flight Captain Rogers was a small woman in her forties, with a large bottom and an enormous chest. She was much shorter than me and I could look down at the top of her salt and pepper hair, but she still terrified me.

'Miles,' she barked at me as I knocked on her open office door. 'Come in or go out, don't lurk.'

I sidled in. 'Someone said you needed to speak to me?' I said, annoyed at how my voice quivered.

She nodded her head towards the chair opposite where she sat and I lowered myself into it. My heart was beating faster; I'd never been asked to sit before.

'Is something wrong?'

She looked at me, her face stern. 'Something is very wrong,' she said.

I breathed out nervously and waited.

'Someone has made an allegation about you,' she said. 'A very serious allegation. Depending on what you tell me, I may have to inform the civilian police.'

I started to sweat. Bloody, bloody Rose. Bloody Will.

'One of the pilots came to see me; she was very upset,' Rogers began. 'She confessed that she and one of the mechanics had sneaked into the back of a plane for a bit of a cuddle. I shall, of course, deal with that in my own time. Though she will not tell me the name of her partner in all this.'

I snorted and turned it into a gasp.

'They fell asleep, and when they woke up, they discovered the plane had taken off. You were the pilot,' she carried on. Rogers pursed her lips. 'When the plane arrived in Lincolnshire, the pilot in question tried to find you to explain what had happened. She saw you going into town and she followed.'

I tried to look shocked and surprised. 'She followed me into town?' I said carefully. 'Then she'd have seen that I met an old friend there. I don't remember seeing any of our girls, though.'

If Rogers pursed her lips any tighter they'd disappear altogether.

'Indeed,' she said. 'For reasons that remain unclear, the pilot decided to eavesdrop on your conversation with your friend.'

'We were just talking,' I said. 'We weren't doing anything wrong.'

'No,' Rogers said. 'But this pilot alleges you were discussing the friend's unwanted pregnancy and that you had made arrangements for her to seek an illegal termination.'

'Goodness me,' I said, forcing a laugh. 'How silly. We did chat about pregnancies – that's true. My friend had been worried she had been caught, but she was telling me she had been mistaken.'

I looked down at my feet. My boots needed polishing. 'She was very ashamed of herself,' I added for good measure, thinking of Mary's unapologetic manner. 'She won't get herself in that situation again.'

Rogers watched me carefully. 'You are saying the pilot is mistaken?' she said.

232

'I am,' I said, pleased that my voice wasn't quivering any longer. This was far too important to show any weakness.

'Does Ro – erm, the pilot, have any proof? Because I really think she must have misunderstood what we were saying.'

Rogers nodded. 'That's what I said. But she was adamant.'

'So there is no proof?' I said, thanking God we'd always been so careful. 'There can't be, because I wasn't doing anything wrong.'

I was thinking fast. Annie had the letters women wrote us, safely locked in the PO box in town. There wouldn't be any in any of our belongings, because we never left anything lying around. And from the sound of it, Annie and Flora were in the clear anyway.

Confident there was nothing to be found, I raised my eyes to Rogers' face. 'Search my locker if you need to,' I said. 'You can even have a look in my billet. I have nothing to hide.'

'We will,' she said. 'At the moment you are free to go. Please remain on base for now. I will alter the flight schedule accordingly.'

Heart thumping, I nodded and turned to go.

'Miles?' Rogers said.

I looked back.

'If you've got nothing to hide, there is nothing to fear.'

I nodded again and left the room, forcing myself to walk and not run as I wanted to.

Outside, it had started to rain and I was glad because it meant no one would see I was crying. Was I in the clear? Or was this the end of my time in ATA?

And then I saw Rose. Hurrying along ahead of me. Had she been eavesdropping? Listening to my conversation with Rogers?

Filled with fury, I speeded up and caught her shoulder. 'Rose,' I said.

'Oh, Lilian,' she said, feigning surprise. 'Is everything all right?'

I was almost spitting with rage. 'No, it bloody well isn't all right,' I said.

'I've just done my duty,' she said dripping with piety.

We were about the same height, Rose and me, though I was scrawnier than she was. We were almost nose to nose, squaring up to each other like prize fighters. I had never wanted to hit anyone more than I wanted to hit her at that moment. Never.

'Why do you care?' I hissed.

'Because you're doing a bad thing,' said Rose. 'And you shouldn't. What you're doing is immoral and dangerous.'

'I know,' I said. 'But it's necessary. These women are desperate, Rose. They are bloody desperate and God knows what they would do if we weren't there to help them. Kill themselves, perhaps. Go mad. I don't know. But this is important.'

Rose shrugged. 'It's against the law,' she said simply. 'I don't see why women like you should swan around, acting like butter wouldn't melt, and being all holier than thou, when the rest of us are playing by the rules.'

I stared at her, bewildered once again by the vitriol she felt towards me.

'Seducing men whenever you like, breaking the law whenever you want – it's not right and you shouldn't be allowed to get away with it.'

I shook my head. 'You've hated me since school,' I said. 'What did I ever do?'

Rose didn't speak. She just looked at me, hatred burning in her eyes.

'Is this all about Will?' I said, almost laughing at the ridiculousness of it all. 'Is this all because you're sweet on some man?'

Rose looked slightly shame-faced. Only slightly, mind you.

I couldn't believe that she was going to bring the whole thing down, and ruin countless women's lives, because she liked Will and he liked me. Ruth was watching me, waiting for me to act but I couldn't speak; my mind was racing as I tried to work out a way to rescue our network. To save everything we'd worked so hard to put in place.

I'd been completely confident when I'd told Rogers she could search my locker. I knew we'd not been silly enough to leave any evidence lying around.

And yet.

I narrowed my eyes as I stared at Rose.

Her accusations may come to nothing, but the whiff of suspicion would remain. Rogers, and the other officers, would watch us like hawks. Me and Flora and Annie. It would be impossible for us to carry on. Rose would have got her revenge, though in a very different way to how she intended. I shook my head. This couldn't happen. Not after everything we'd done.

Rose laughed. But it was more like a bark. 'You can shake your head all you like,' she hissed. 'It won't change anything. I've got you bang to rights, Lilian.'

I met her hate-filled gaze as an idea took root. Rose was determined to get her ridiculous revenge on me; that was clear. But perhaps I could somehow make it all about me and not involve the others. If I confessed to helping Mary, made it all about that one mistake, then this might not be the end. Annie and Flora would be off the hook and the network could carry on.

I took a deep breath.

'You're right,' I said simply. 'I was helping Mary get rid of her pregnancy. I knew someone who could help her and I put them in touch. That's all it was.'

Rose eyed me suspiciously. 'I heard her ask you about others,' she said.

I shrugged. 'You must have misheard,' I lied. 'There are no others. Mary is an old friend and I wanted to help her.' I lifted my chin. 'Just her.'

Rose narrowed her eyes. 'What about Flora and Annie?' she said. 'Are they involved?'

'God, no,' I said. 'Flora? Never. She's a Presbyterian.'

'And Annie?'

I shrugged. 'She's a good person too. She'd not break the law. Not like me.'

'It sounded like you'd done this a lot,' Rose said, frowning. 'It sounded professional.'

'Professional?' I scoffed. 'I was just helping out an old friend.'

'I think you're lying.'

'Think what you like,' I said. 'You can't prove it.'

Rose started to talk and I stopped her by holding up my hand.

'Listen,' I said. 'I will fall on my sword if that's what you want. I will go back to Rogers right now and admit that I arranged the termination for Mary, and that I was wrong. I expect I will be discharged and my career in the ATA will be over.'

I swallowed the sob that rose up in my throat at the thought of never flying again.

'You and Will,' I said the name like it made me sick, which it did a bit. 'You and Will can live happily ever after together for all I care. You've won, Rose.'

'You'll go and confess, right now?' Rose said.

I nodded. 'Right now.'

Rose nodded, triumph gleaming in her eyes. 'Fine,' she said. 'Good.'

Shaking like a leaf, I turned away from her and headed back to find Flight Captain Rogers.

Chapter 39

Helena

July 2018

'I want you to go,' Lil said again.

I stared at her, not understanding. 'If you're tired, we can come back another time,' I said.

'I don't want you to come back,' she said, her voice calm, but determined. 'I will tell you what you want to know, and then I want you to go.'

I wasn't sure what she meant. Did she really mean she wanted me to go and never come back? Surely not. I knew I'd not done as she asked, but refusing to see me again was overkill. That couldn't be what she meant. And she was offering to tell me what had happened so she couldn't be too upset …

I took her hand. Her fingers lay limply in mine.

'Please tell me what happened,' I said. 'It all sounds incredible.'

'It wasn't,' she said. 'It was frightening and dangerous and it was horribly necessary. But it wasn't incredible.'

I didn't speak; I didn't want to interrupt her.

'I lived near an airfield at the beginning of the war,' she said. 'Near Kelso.'

I nodded.

'I was bored and lonely, and interested in the planes. I started hanging round and asking questions and generally making a nuisance of myself. I was determined to learn how to fly, but of course I wasn't allowed.'

I smiled. That sounded like Lil.

'The ATA was mostly well-to-do girls at first,' she carried on. 'But in 1943 they expanded and one of the pilots saw an ad in *Aeroplane* magazine and suggested I apply. And that was that. I loved flying. I really loved it.'

She paused.

'But then there was the other side of my life in the ATA.'

I leaned forward a bit. I didn't want to miss anything.

'That all started when a girl from the base had a fumble with a soldier,' Lil began. 'Well, it was less of a fumble and more …'

She looked right at me, but it was like she wasn't seeing me. I bit my lip.

'Anyway, a few weeks later, she realised she was pregnant. She couldn't have a baby. Not then. Not like that. My friend Flora knew someone in Manchester who'd helped a friend of hers. We did a bit of digging. We got it sorted. And because of that, and …' she paused '… some other things that happened, we realised there were women all over the country, helping other women.'

'An underground network,' I breathed. 'Just as they suspected.'

'Exactly that. We tapped into it. We knew we were in a position to put women in touch with people who could help them because we travelled all over the country and met all sorts of people. We could arrange transport. We even arranged adoption for those who were too late to sort things out another way. The adoptions were great. We loved those. Finding families that wanted a baby and giving the woman a way out. I'd have liked to have kept in touch with those ones, found out how it was all going.'

'But you didn't?'

She shook her head. 'Too risky,' she said. 'These weren't legal adoptions. It was fraud, I suppose. But during the war, people lost everything. Family, homes – and all their paperwork. It was easy to say someone was someone else, or a baby belonged to another family. And the women we helped – they were desperate, Helena. They couldn't do things properly. They had no choices left.'

'Lil,' I began. 'This is wonderful. Do you see how wonderful it is? You saved those women.'

'Not all of them,' she said.

'How do you mean?'

'There were some we couldn't help. If they contacted us too late, or we couldn't get to them, or I remember one girl just never showed up to the meeting point – I don't know what happened there.'

She paused and looked up at me.

'It was dangerous. The girls with money, they could pay for real doctors. But in all the time we were doing it, I only remember one girl having enough to fork out for a man in Harley Street. Mostly it was older women, you know the types? They'd delivered all the babies round their way, they knew how things worked – and how to stop them.'

I shuddered. 'What did they do?' I whispered.

'Depends,' she said. 'Mostly they'd use a sort of douche, to wash them out.'

'Christ.'

'I think they all had their favourite concoctions,' Lil said. 'Soap, often, sometimes other things if they couldn't get hold of soap – it was rationed of course, which made it harder to come by. I heard about someone using turpentine. Cod liver oil. They'd pack them with gauze and send them home – but sometimes the bleeding was too heavy.'

I wanted to cry, thinking about how desperate these women had to have been to go through that. But Lil wasn't finished.

'Some of them used knives,' she said matter-of-factly. 'To puncture the sac. That was riskier because of the infection.'

'Did anyone die?'

Lil nodded. 'We lost one early on,' she said. 'Bet, her name was. I'll never forget that. She was nineteen years old.'

Now I was crying, one tear after another sliding silently down my cheeks.

'And there was another. Emily Page. She lived in Edinburgh and I was there when she haemorrhaged. That's another thing I'll never forget. The sight of her sheets, soaked in blood.'

'Did she die?'

Lil shrugged. 'I don't know,' she said, a slight crack to her voice. 'We took her to the hospital but we never heard what happened after that. I wish I knew.'

'There were a few of you?' I asked. 'It wasn't just you alone?'

She nodded. 'There was me, and my friends Flora and Annie,' she said. 'We organised things. We had another friend in Scotland, Jemima, who helped a lot. There was a midwife up there called Katie, who was wonderful. And Flora's contact in Manchester was a big help. Every time we helped someone we made new friends and new contacts. It grew so fast, it almost had a life of its own.'

'Why did you do it?' I asked. 'Why did you help?'

I wondered if she'd tell me that someone had helped her in her lowest moment and that was why, but she didn't.

'It was the right thing to do,' she said. She looked directly at me again. 'That's why I did it.'

There was a pause as I wrestled with the idea of asking her straight out if she'd had a baby. And then I chickened out. 'What happened with the court martial?' I asked instead.

Lil's expression darkened. 'A couple of folk at the base had a bit of a grudge against me.'

'And they grassed you up?'

She nodded. 'One was a girl I knew from school. She just

disliked everyone. She was one of those types who always feels hard done by, you know?'

It was my turn to nod. I'd met plenty of people like that.

'And the other was someone I'd thought was a friend.'

'They knew what was going on?'

'We'd not told them of course, but Rose Smythe – she was the one who thought the world owed her a living – she'd always had a particular bee in her bonnet about me. I tried to ignore her most of the time, but she just wouldn't leave it alone. She'd watched us round the base, chatting about arrangements. She'd listened in to conversations, and spied, and she'd got it in her head that I was selling stuff on the black market – cigarettes, gin, that sort of stuff. Then she roped Will in.'

'Will?'

Lil's frown deepened. 'He was a friend,' she said. 'At least I'd thought he was a friend. But he went along with Rose. They followed me to a meeting.'

'They thought you were smuggling, and instead they found out you were arranging an abortion?'

'Exactly,' Lil said.

'Rose went straight to an officer and accused me. But we'd been careful. We'd always tried to cover our tracks. There was very little evidence against me, but Rose's accusations were all that was needed to court-martial me. It wouldn't have stood up in a civil court. I didn't get into trouble with the police, thankfully. I admitted arranging one termination and I was dishonourably discharged.'

'And what about Flora? And Annie? Did they get into trouble?'

Lil gave a slight smile. 'Not one bit,' she said. 'I knew if I took the rap, then they'd not do any more digging. I fell on my sword; Rose was satisfied, because she just wanted rid of me. And the officers were happy because it was all dealt with neatly without any scandal really ...'

I could barely take in the enormity of what she'd done.

'Did Flora and Annie carry on?'

'They did,' Lil said.

She paused.

'That was the plan at least. And I heard bits and pieces, from Jemima in Scotland. But we'd agreed not to stay in touch – if anyone got wind of us being friendly then the network could be at risk. They even carried on after the war, I believe. And Flora in particular was a campaigner for abortion to be made legal back in the 1960s. I remember seeing her name in the papers at the time.'

'But you weren't tempted to get in touch?'

Lil shook her head. 'Too much water under the bridge,' she said.

'Why do you think they did it? Why did Rose and Will follow you and get the proof about what you were doing?'

Lil shrugged. 'They both told me I was doing a terrible thing,' she said.

'But you think they were really doing it to get at you?'

'I know that's why they did it,' Lil said. 'Rose even said as much. She told me I needed taking down a peg or two.'

'And Will?'

Lil took a breath. 'Will had been sweet on me,' she said. 'He asked me out to a dance and I went along and we had a great time. But I wasn't one for romance back then.'

Or ever, I thought. As long as I'd known her, Lil had never had a partner.

'I let him down gently, and I thought he'd understood. I explained …'

She trailed off and I waited, wondering again if she'd mention anything about having a baby.

'I thought he'd understood,' she said again. 'But he betrayed me.'

I reached out to cover her hand in mine, but she pulled away from me.

242

'And now you've done the same,' she said sharply.

'What?' I said, confused.

'You betrayed me,' she said. 'You dug around in my life, in my memories, without thinking of the consequences.'

'I didn't do it for myself,' I said. But I trailed off. I couldn't tell her I'd done this for Dad. I couldn't put the blame on to him. If Lil was angry with him, she'd never tell him the truth.

'You're not the person I thought you were, Helena,' she spat.

I looked at my feet.

'I want you to go now,' Lil said. 'And I don't want you to come back. Not ever.'

She ruffled Dora's hair. 'Maybe you can come and see me with Granny,' she said.

'Granny,' agreed Dora. 'Love Granny.'

'But, Lil,' I said, horrified at how blunt she was being. 'Lil ...'

'Goodbye, Helena.'

Chapter 40

Lilian

November 1939

A couple of days after I'd climbed the hill and seen the airfield far below, gripped with cabin fever because Ruth was watching me like a hawk and wouldn't let me out of her sight, I crept into the hall and started pulling on my thick coat. The sky was steel grey and I knew snow was on its way, so I wanted to hike up the hill and have a look at the planes once more before the weather got too bad. I wound my scarf round my neck and lowered myself on to the stairs to pull on my boots.

'Oof,' I gasped as I squished my bump and the baby kicked me in revenge.

'Where do you think you're going?' Ruth stood in the doorway to the living room, holding a bundle of clothes. I groaned inwardly. I'd thought she was in the garden, digging up the last of the potatoes before the ground froze completely. I'd obviously been wrong.

'Walk,' I muttered.

Ruth smiled at me. 'I know you're bored,' she said. 'But Katie

244

is coming in half an hour to check on you. Remember, Jemima's friend? The one who's going to help.'

Defeated, and with only one boot half on, I slumped against the stairs and wiggled my foot until the boot came off. 'I forgot,' I said.

Jemima was a funny one. She kept herself to herself most of the time. Ruth had told me that her marriage hadn't been a very happy one and her husband had been a lot older than her. I thought maybe it had been hard for her, coming from down south and starting again in a place where her husband was local. She knew everyone in Kelso but she was very particular about who she spent any time with. She'd opened my eyes to a sort of underground network of women who could and would help each other out, no matter how much risk there was to themselves. Katie, her friend who was coming to visit, was one of those women.

We didn't have to wait long. Jemima drove up in her battered farm van, and opened the door to help Katie out. Jemima was as tall and Amazonian as Katie was slight and pale. She looked like a little girl clambering down from the van and I felt a moment of fear as I watched. Was this who we were relying on? Had we made a terrible mistake?

But when Katie and Jemima came into the kitchen I realised I'd been wrong. Katie was older than I'd first thought. Probably in her late forties or even her fifties like Jemima. Her pale hair was streaked with grey and her light blue eyes were kind.

Jemima made the introductions, then busied herself making tea. Ruth and I sat in the living room, waiting awkwardly for Katie to speak.

'Right then,' she said, realising we just wanted her to get on with it. 'Let's have a look at you, shall we?'

She opened her bag and pulled out a stethoscope and slung it round her neck. Then she rubbed her hands together to warm them up.

'It's bitter out there,' she said. 'Lie back.'

Obediently Ruth stood up and I lay back on the sofa. Katie lifted my top up and gently felt my bump.

'There's baby's bum,' she said, prodding the top. 'And his or her head is down, which is good.'

The baby wiggled at her touch and she smiled.

'Ooh he's not happy about me poking him,' she said in her soft borders accent. 'But he's a good size. Everything looks fine. Shall we have a listen?'

Ruth was watching, an odd expression on her face. I thought again how hard this must be for her. After all, she'd been pregnant too. Her baby would have been almost the same age as mine.

'What will happen?' she said as Katie put the stethoscope in her ears and breathed on the end so it wasn't so cold. 'When the baby comes?'

Katie held up her finger to indicate that Ruth should pause while she listened. She moved the end of the stethoscope around my tummy a little bit then nodded and listened for a few seconds.

'Good strong heartbeat,' she said. 'Do you want to hear?'

Did I? I shook my head. 'Ruth might.'

Holding the end of the stethoscope against my skin, Katie pulled the earpieces out with one hand and held them out to Ruth. She knelt down next to me, put them in her own ears, and gasped as she heard, I assumed, the baby's heartbeat for the first time.

'Oh, Lil,' she said. 'That's the baby.'

'Your baby,' I said. 'It's your baby.'

Her eyes filled with tears and I couldn't tell if it was with happiness that she was going to be a mother, or sadness that I wasn't.

Katie smiled. 'First babies are tricky to predict,' she said. I winced just a little bit at the implication that there would ever be a second baby.

'You're sixteen?' she continued and I nodded. 'My instinct is you'll go early.'

I closed my eyes briefly as I heaved myself back to sitting. The very thought of giving birth made me want to vomit, but I couldn't wait for all this to be over. To leave the house whenever I wanted. To be able to put my own boots on. To go home, even. Back to Kent. Though the thought of coming face to face with Mr Mayhew, or Mrs Mayhew, was even worse than the thought of giving birth, so perhaps not. Maybe, I thought, I could sign up. Or volunteer at the airbase. Maybe I could even learn to fly.

'Lil,' Ruth was saying. 'Katie's explaining what's going to happen.'

I forced myself to concentrate.

'When you think the baby's coming, get Jemima to fetch me,' Katie was saying. 'I'll come as soon as I can.'

A thought occurred to me. 'Who are you?' I asked, almost rudely. 'Why are you helping us?'

'Lilian,' Ruth chided, but Katie, who'd been kneeling down packing away her stethoscope, stood up again and then sat down next to me and took my hand.

'I think that as women we get a rough deal,' she said, half to me and Ruth, and half to herself. 'Men can make as many mistakes as they want, do as many wrong things as they like, and there are no consequences. But we're left holding the babies.'

I shifted on the saggy sofa, slightly uncomfortable at the way she was talking.

'The way I see it, no man is ever going to put himself on the line to help a woman.' She looked at me, her pale blue eyes sharp. 'Where's the dad?'

'I'm sorry?'

'Your baby's dad? Where is he?'

I flushed. 'He signed up,' I said, staring at her in defiance.

'And did he want the baby? Did he offer to help?'

Slowly I lowered my eyes. 'No,' I said. 'He's married.'

She shrugged as if I'd made her point. Which I supposed I had.

'We have to help each other,' she said. 'There are women like me all over the place.'

'Midwives?' Ruth said.

Katie nodded. 'I'm a midwife but I know some nurses do it too, and a couple of doctors.'

'Women doctors?' I was impressed.

'And men,' Katie said. 'And people like Jemima, helping us find each other.'

'And they all deliver babies and register them to a different mother?' Ruth seemed torn between awe and disgust.

'They do,' said Katie. 'And sometimes we do other things too. If a woman really can't have a baby.'

I looked blankly at her, not understanding, until I saw Ruth's expression and the penny dropped.

'You help them get rid of the babies?' I said quietly. 'That's illegal.'

Katie nodded. 'But it shouldn't be, in my opinion. We do things properly, though there's always a risk to the woman of course. But there are some butchers out there. I've seen girls die because of it.'

I felt bile rising in my throat. That could have been me, if it hadn't been for Ruth and Bobby.

There was an awkward pause, then Ruth gave an overly bright smile. 'So, when the baby arrives, you'll sign all the paperwork as though I am the mother. And we'll put my name on the birth certificate.'

'If that's what Lilian wants,' Katie said. 'There's no going back so she has to be sure.'

'What about Lil's health?' Ruth said, before I could answer. 'I don't want her in danger. What if she needs stitches? Or if she loses too much blood?'

'There is a doctor nearby who I can call in an emergency,'

Katie explained. 'He doesn't ask questions. And he's not interested in the paperwork anyway.'

'And afterwards?' Ruth was chewing her lip in concern. 'What about afterwards?'

'Feeding?' Katie said. 'That's up to Lil.'

I turned my head away, not wanting to think about breast-feeding.

'No need to decide now.' Katie squeezed my hand. 'About anything. You don't even have to say if you want to put Ruth on the birth certificate yet. Think about it for a while.'

But I didn't have to think. 'It's what I want,' I said.

Katie nodded. 'Then that's what we'll do.'

Chapter 41

Helena

July 2018

I was in a state of disbelief mixed with shock all the way home. I couldn't quite take in the fact that Lil had told me she never wanted to see me again. Surely she didn't mean it? But then I'd think about her face, and I'd realise all over again that she'd absolutely meant it. I was furious with Dad, and with Greg, and with the world.

My mind in a fug, I rang Miranda from the train on the way home and told her what had happened.

'Shit,' said. 'He just turned up? No warning?'

'No warning,' I said grimly.

'And Lil threw you out?'

'Well, not literally,' I said. 'But yes, she asked me to leave and never come back.'

'I'll come round,' she said.

I managed a smile. 'No,' I said. 'It's fine. Jack's coming.'

But as I was making some pasta for Dora's tea, Jack phoned.

'We're doing a bloody reshoot,' he said. He sounded annoyed.

'What does that mean?'

'It means that bastard Brice who's playing my right-hand man has groped too many women on set and he's been sacked.'

'Good,' I said. 'Sounds like he should have been sacked before now.'

'He definitely should have been sacked before now,' Jack agreed. 'But now he's been replaced, and we need to reshoot all the scenes he was in.'

'Shit,' I said. 'So I won't get to see you?'

'Sorry,' he said. 'We should be done by the middle of the week but until then it's long days and lots of early starts. They're putting us up in a hotel nearby.'

'Don't worry,' I said, forcing myself to sound much brighter than I felt. 'It's not your fault. We can catch up when you're done.'

'Are you okay? You sound a bit funny.'

Where to begin? Was I okay? Considering my daughter's father had just announced he wanted to see her after being away for more than a year, and I'd just upset my favourite aunt on behalf of my dad?

'I'm fine,' I said.

I gave Dora her tea and together we watched an actor who wasn't nearly as good as Jack, in my opinion, read the bedtime story on CBeebies. Dora obviously thought so too because she turned to me at the end, her little face creased in a frown.

'Where is Jack?' she said.

'He's at work, darling.'

'Jack read the story?'

'Not today.'

I put her to bed and tucked her in. On the wall next to where she slept, she had photographs of my parents, one of my sister Imogen and brother Andy – who was away so often she'd barely met him – one of Miranda and Freddie, and one of Greg. I'd put it there after he'd gone to Canada, even though we'd not parted on particularly good terms.

251

'Dora,' I said now, pointing to the photograph. 'Do you know who this is?'

'Daddy,' she said obediently.

'Would you like to see Daddy?'

She looked thoughtful. 'Yes, see Daddy,' she said.

I bit my lip. 'Maybe Daddy could read you a story,' I said. 'That would be nice.'

'Jack read the story.'

'Jack will definitely read you stories too,' I said.

Feeling drained, I ran myself a bubble bath. I got in the water, submerged up to my neck and closed my eyes. My mind was racing, and I hoped a long soak could help me work out how I'd got myself into this horrible mess.

What on earth was I going to do about Lil? That was the question. I felt like I was stuck between a rock and a hard place. If I left Lil thinking I'd done the research because I wanted to 'poke around in her memories' as she'd put it, then she'd probably never speak to me again.

That idea was unbearable.

But if I told her why I'd done it, there was still no guarantee she'd forgive me – and then I'd have dropped Dad in it too.

As far as I could tell it was lose/lose. I wished so hard that I'd never seen her name on that list.

Lil had always said family was the most important thing. From the day when she'd rocked up on our door when Mum was ill and sorted us all out, she'd always drummed into us that family was the constant; that everyone else in your life would come and go, but family would always stand by you. Was she right?

I felt a glimmer of hope breaking through my dark mood. Dora was my daughter and she always would be, but there was no reason why Greg – and yes, even Kimberley – couldn't love her too. He was her family, wasn't he?

I would send Greg a message and get him to come and visit,

I thought. I'd see if Fliss would let me work from home in the afternoon on Monday and get him round while Dora was at nursery. We could sort this out and then perhaps we could fetch Dora together and he could stay for tea. It could be the beginning of something.

But as for Lil? I still had no idea what to do for the best there.

The next day was Sunday so I took Dora to the park and then, bracing myself, I went round to see my parents.

Mum answered the door, wearing her coat.

'Are you going out?' I said.

She looked flustered. 'I'm going to see Lil,' she said. 'The care home rang – she's not very well and she won't eat.'

I felt awful. 'Oh, Mum, this is all my fault,' I said, feeling tears well up. 'I went to see her yesterday and I asked about her being discharged from the ATA.'

Mum bent to release Dora from her buggy, then she ushered me into the living room, where Dad was snoozing on the sofa.

'Robert,' she said sharply, making him jump. 'Helena's here.'

'Dad, I went to see Lil yesterday,' I said. 'And we talked about what she did, during the war. She was amazing, Dad. She helped so many women.'

Dad sat up a bit straighter.

'But she told me all the details and then she threw me out,' I said, starting to cry properly now. 'She told me she didn't want to see me again and that Mum should take Dora when she went to visit.'

Dad's brow furrowed in concern.

'I didn't tell her,' I said. 'I didn't say that you wanted to know – or why you wanted to know – and she didn't mention you. So that's good, isn't it? It's only me she hates.'

'Oh, Helena,' Dad said. 'You took the blame for me?'

'I couldn't tell her,' I said, sniffing. Mum, who was busy keeping Dora distracted but clearly listening intently, handed me a tissue.

'You're very kind, Helena,' she said. 'Robert, now do you see that we've gone about this the wrong way?'

Dad looked ashamed. 'I do see,' he said. 'I should have listened to you when you said it was a bad idea.'

Mum patted him on the knee. 'It's done now.'

'And now Lil is poorly?' Dad said.

'She won't leave her room, the care-worker said,' Mum explained. 'Says she's under the weather. She's not eaten since yesterday lunchtime.'

'That was when I visited,' I said, feeling dreadful. 'Oh, God, this is awful.'

'I'm going down to see her,' Mum explained. 'Taking her some bits that she likes to eat.'

'Have you got some pink wafers?'

Mum gave me a quick, worried smile. 'I have.'

Dad heaved himself up from the sofa. 'I'll come,' he said. 'I'll explain everything.'

'Absolutely not,' Mum said, fiercely. She stood in front of Dad, her feet planted squarely on the carpet like a boxer. 'We are not going to talk about this until Lil is back on her feet. She is an old woman, with a tricky past, and I am not going to let you upset her.'

Despite myself, I smiled. Mum could be very forceful when she wanted to be.

'Will you ring me?' I said. 'When you've seen her?'

Mum gave me a kiss and picked up her bag. 'Of course,' she said. 'I'm sure it's not as bad as you think.'

Chapter 42

I couldn't concentrate on work the next day. Mum had called when she got home and said Lil had been pleased to see her. She'd eaten a little bit of dinner, and some pink wafers, but she'd still not come out of her room. Mum sounded worried on the phone and it gave me chills.

And as for Greg, I'd messaged him and asked him to come to mine at 4 p.m. We could talk things through, I thought. He'd replied asking if Kimberley could come too and I'd agreed.

But first, I had to get through the morning researching the background of a former Premier League footballer. And persuade Fliss to let me leave early. Elly wasn't even in the office today, so I had no distractions, but I still couldn't concentrate properly.

Mid-morning I wandered to the kitchen and made myself a coffee, and when I got back to my desk, Fliss was there.

'Can I have a word?' she said. She looked serious. I followed her into her office.

'Shut the door,' she said and I felt my stomach twist with nerves.

'Helena, there's no easy way to say this,' she said. 'I've been worried you're not keeping on top of your research.'

'I am,' I said. 'I've done everything I should have.'

She shook her head. 'They're supposed to be filming Lady Jane Grey next week and you've not handed over the initial findings to the chap from Oxford,' she said.

'Shit.' It had gone completely out of my mind with all the other stuff that was happening.

'And when I looked at your research,' Fliss went on, 'I saw in the Jack Jones file that you'd requested court documents for someone named Miles.'

I stared at her.

'If you've been doing your own research and letting your work slide, now is the time to tell me,' she said.

I felt like a silly schoolgirl who'd not done her homework.

'You're right,' I admitted. 'I have been doing some of my own research and it's all got out of hand, and that's why I forgot to hand over the Tudor stuff.'

Fliss looked sympathetic. 'This isn't like you, Helena,' she said. 'I'd never have thought you'd have dropped the plates like this.'

'I know. It just all snowballed.'

She didn't say anything, just looked at me, disappointed. This was horrible. I felt like my entire life had fallen apart in one weekend.

'I'm so sorry,' I said. 'It was a family mystery and my dad talked me into it, and it just got bigger and bigger …'

'They always do,' Fliss said. 'That's why I'm so strict about not doing your own research with our resources. It becomes all-consuming.'

'I'll do Lady Jane Grey now,' I said, desperate to make amends. 'I'll have it done by the end of the day.'

But Fliss shook her head. 'No,' she said. 'I'm going to give you three weeks to sort yourself out. Take some time off, regroup, and then come back with your head together. I'll take over Lady Jane Grey.'

'Are you firing me?' I asked.

Fliss gave me a small smile. 'Not yet,' she said. 'This is your last chance, though. You're a great researcher, Helena. Passionate, measured, methodical, knowledgeable. But you're in a mess and you need to get it sorted out.'

I snorted; a mess was an understatement. 'So, what? I just don't come in tomorrow?' I said.

Fliss shook her head. 'Go now,' she said. She looked tired and I felt bad about giving her more to do. 'Just go.'

So I did.

I went home and I cleaned the house from top to bottom. I sorted out my bedroom, which was still showing the signs of Jack's visit, and carefully picked up my Audrey Hepburn print and wrapped up the broken glass, and threw it away. I rolled up the print gently and put it to one side. I'd get a new frame for it. I cleaned the bathroom, and stacked Dora's books in her bookshelf neatly, thinking of Jack as I picked up *The Gruffalo*.

I completely forgot that Greg was coming to visit. So when the doorbell rang at exactly 4 p.m., I was surprised.

I opened the door in the joggers and bleach-stained T-shirt I wore for cleaning, with my hair tied up in a scarf, and gasped when I saw him and Kimberley.

'Shit,' I said. 'I completely forgot.'

'Helena?' Greg said, sounding confused. 'I thought we'd arranged this.'

'We did,' I said. 'I've just had a bit of a day of it.'

'Is it still okay to meet with you?' said Kimberley. She looked so nervous that I felt bad.

'Of course,' I said, showing them in and thinking at least the house was clean. 'Come on in.'

This time I made tea, and acted the gracious hostess, despite my scruffy clothes. Then Kimberley and I sat together in the living room while Greg prowled about and looked at the photos on the mantelpiece, and Dora's toys in the toy box under the window, and generally made me feel uncomfortable.

'You've got it looking really nice,' he said. 'Dora must be very happy.'

'She is,' I said, wondering what he was getting at.

'I know this must be tricky for you,' Kimberley said.

My temper flared, just a bit. 'You know what?' I said. 'In terms of my relationship with Greg, this isn't really that tricky. Not compared to the day he told me to get an abortion because we were too young to have a baby.'

Standing by the fireplace, holding a photo of Dora dressed as an elf at Christmas, Greg winced, but I wasn't finished.

'And it's actually a breeze compared to moving all my stuff into my sister's spare room when I was pregnant,' I carried on. 'And let me see. Is it harder than giving birth by myself? Erm, nope. Or getting through the long, long newborn nights on my own? Nope, that was harder too.'

Now I'd started I found I couldn't stop.

'Hmm, and how about when he turned up with a bike as a first birthday present for Dora? A bike that – by the way – she's still too small for, and announced he was off to live in Canada?'

Greg looked embarrassed and ashamed and I was glad.

'So no. This isn't actually that tricky,' I said to Kimberley knowing I was being a bitch. 'In fact, compared to the shit he's brought to my door in the past, you're quite an improvement.'

'Oh, my,' Kimberley said to Greg. 'You told me she was quiet.'

'Quiet,' he said. 'But dangerous.'

There was a pause and then the corner of Kimberley's mouth twitched and she started to giggle.

I watched, not knowing how to react, as Greg nervously began to laugh too. And suddenly I found I was laughing as well.

'Dangerous?' I said. 'I'm not dangerous. I'm just really, really pissed off with you.'

Greg grinned. 'And you have every right to be,' he said, suddenly serious. 'I have been the biggest idiot and I owe you a massive apology, and I owe Dora a lot of love, and I also probably owe you about a gazillion pounds in child support.'

I shook my head. 'We're fine,' I said. 'We don't need your money, and Dora certainly doesn't need your love. I don't even need an apology.'

'I know,' Greg said. 'I understand.'

Kimberley spoke up. 'When Greg told me about Dora, I broke up with him,' she said. 'I couldn't understand how he could have a daughter who he didn't have a relationship with.'

I raised an eyebrow. I'd thought the same.

'Kimberley reacting as she did made me realise how wrong I'd got it,' Greg said. 'And when we got back together, I promised I'd make an effort to get to know Dora. That's why I put in for the transfer back to London. If you agree – and only if you agree – I'd really like to get to know her.'

It was all completely reasonable. I knew Dora would want to get to know her dad, even if she didn't understand what it all meant yet. And Kimberley, God love her, seemed to have been the making of Greg. But it didn't mean I was happy about it.

'Of course, I agree,' I said, forcing a smile. 'I need to go and get her from nursery now. Want to come?'

Chapter 43

We went to the park, the four of us. Greg even pushed Dora's buggy. And when she wriggled and squirmed and said 'out' like she always did, he said 'wait until we get to the park' just like I always did. Then he looked at me, a bit sheepish, and said, 'I just thought the road was a bit busy for her to be walking.'

I smiled, feeling impressed and undermined all at the same time. 'You're right,' I said.

When we reached the entrance of the playground, I unstrapped Dora and picked her up. 'Dora, do you remember who this is?' I asked her.

She looked at Greg, eyes screwed up. Then she put her little hand on his cheek. 'Daddy,' she said. ''Lo, Daddy.'

She wriggled in my arms so I put her down and she ran off to the climbing frame.

'She remembers me?' Greg said in wonder.

'She's got a photograph, next to her bed,' I said. 'That's why.'

Greg gave me a funny look, which might have been gratitude, and then he gestured towards where Dora was clambering up. 'Should I make sure she doesn't fall?'

I nodded. 'She's remarkably good at climbing, but probably for the best.'

'I've got it,' Kimberley said. She headed over to Dora.

'Wow,' I heard her say. 'You're so high up.'

I smiled. Always better to compliment Dora's bravery than ask her to be careful. That never ended well.

'Good at climbing, eh?' Greg – who had been a member of the climbing society at university and who bored anyone who asked about his adventures in the Lake District – said.

I grinned. 'You should see her with a bookcase and a mother who's not paying attention,' I said. I took a breath. 'Listen, why don't I go home and you can spend some time with Dora?'

'Really?'

'Not too long. Because she'll be getting tired. Shall we say an hour?'

'Thanks, Helena,' Greg said. 'I really appreciate how good you're being.'

I shrugged. 'Don't think it's easy for me,' I warned. 'Because it's not. But I know it's the right thing to do. See you at mine in an hour. Don't be late.'

I wandered off towards the other entrance of the park, close to my house. Halfway across the field, I stopped and looked back. Greg was laughing as Dora led Kimberly by the hand to the swings.

For a second, my heart lurched. They looked like a real family. A proper unit. Just as I'd thought Greg and I were going to be, that day when I found out I was pregnant.

I was no psychologist, but I knew that my desperation to give Dora a stable home life came from my own childhood. My mum was a wonderful grandmother, but when I was small she'd been absent – through no fault of her own – and that made me determined to be there for Dora. So when Greg had bailed, and I'd walked out, I'd never questioned my decision. If he was flaky, or uncertain, I knew I didn't want him in my baby's life.

The few times he'd seen her that first year had left me feeling wobbly. I had been pleased – for myself if not for Dora – that he'd gone to Canada, so I could carry on building a life for my child.

And I'd done it, I thought now, standing in the park watching them together. Dora was loved and she was happy, and she had a routine, and family around her. I had a job and enough money to pay for nursery and baby ballet, and the spaghetti hoops she liked. I would never forget to pay the electricity bill, or be so late to pick her up that she thought I wasn't coming.

At least, that's how my life had been.

It wasn't like that any more.

Suddenly, my job was uncertain and without that job I couldn't guarantee I would always be able to pay the bills. With Greg back on the scene, I could picture a future where Dora spent her weekends being shunted back and forth between our houses. Lonely Christmases where she spent the day with him and Kimberley, and no doubt the other kids they'd have now he was father of the year, and I would be left watching *Mrs Brown's Boys* with Lil.

My stomach twisted again.

Lil. She wasn't even talking to me.

I watched Dora put her arms up to Greg and I wanted to cry. How could my whole life have fallen apart? How could all the good, strong foundations I'd built it on suddenly have collapsed?

With an uncharacteristic flash of rage, I knew who to blame.

My father.

I spun round and marched towards the entrance. I had to walk past my parents' house to get home so I wasn't even going out of my way. I just hoped he'd be there because I needed to get a few things off my chest.

He was. And he wasn't in his studio luckily – we weren't allowed to disturb him when he was working, though the mood I was in, that wouldn't have stopped me. He was in the kitchen.

'Helena, lovely to see you,' he said. 'I was just making tea – would you like one?'

'No thanks,' I said. 'I can't stop. Greg's got Dora.'

Dad raised his eyebrows. 'He has?'

'Yes,' I said shortly. 'And it's your fault.'

Dad chuckled. 'Why is it my fault?'

I wasn't sure, not really. But I knew I was angry with Dad and I wanted to get it out. 'I've been suspended from work,' I said. I knew I was exaggerating but it felt like a suspension. 'Fliss has asked me to take three weeks off.'

Dad sat down at the table. 'Good Lord,' he said. 'She found out what you were doing?'

'She did.'

'Did you tell her you'd done it for me?'

I shook my head. 'What difference would that have made, Dad?' I said. 'It doesn't matter why I did it, I just made the wrong decision.'

I took a deep shaky breath.

'And the same with Lil. I did the wrong thing and now I'm paying the price.'

'I'll explain to Lil,' Dad said.

'No,' I almost shouted. 'How can you, now? How can you explain? Even me talking to her about the court case has made her ill. Imagine how she'll react if you rock up and start asking if she's your mother.'

Dad stayed quiet.

'Dad, I've messed everything up,' I said. 'I just wanted to give Dora a good childhood, you know. The sort of childhood …'

I stopped just in time but Dad knew where I was going. 'The sort of childhood you didn't have?'

I closed my eyes. 'Yes,' I whispered. 'I'm sorry.'

Dad reached across the table and took my hand. 'No,' he said. 'I'm sorry.'

His voice cracked a bit and I looked at him. He seemed wretched and suddenly very old.

'We've never really talked about it, have we?' he said. 'That time?'

'It wasn't so bad, for Miranda and me,' I said. 'We were older. It was the little ones who missed out.'

But Dad shook his head. 'It wasn't a picnic for you either. And that was my fault.' He slurped at his tea. 'When Sal – your mum – when she was ill after Immy was born, I went to pieces,' he said. 'I don't know what would have happened if Lil hadn't stepped in. You girls were taking care of me and you were so little. And Lysander was just a tiny thing. I'd never paid much attention when you were babies, and suddenly I had to make sure Imogen was fed and had clean nappies.'

His voice cracked again and I winced. It was hard to see my father this way.

'And then Lil turned up and made everything okay. She showed me how to be a dad. A proper dad, not just a dad who did the fun bits and then sodded off back to my studio.'

I nodded. 'She did,' I said. 'She was amazing. And we've let her down so badly.' I closed my eyes again, picturing Greg and Kimberley. 'And I've let Dora down.'

'Absolutely not,' said Dad, quite crossly. 'You have absolutely not let Dora down.'

'She's going to end up in a broken family,' I said. 'Spending weekends here and there.'

Dad shrugged. 'So?' he said.

'So, that's not what I wanted.'

Dad took my hand again. 'It's not a broken family,' he said. 'It's just a family. They come in all shapes and sizes.'

I looked at him, not convinced.

'Jack said that, remember?' he went on. 'That it's not to do with blood, it's to do with love? You told me.'

I nodded.

'I was very lucky to have parents as loving as Ruth and Bobby were,' Dad said. 'And I am lucky to have Lil in my life, still, whether or not she is my biological mother.'

I nodded again.

'And Dora is lucky to have a wonderful mum like you. And she'll be lucky to have a dad who loves her.'

'And a stepmother,' I said.

'And maybe a stepfather, one day,' Dad said softly.

I shook my head this time. 'It's too hard, Dad,' I said. 'I thought I could ease Jack into the family, but it's too hard.'

'Don't punish yourself, Helena,' Dad said.

I gave him a weak smile. 'What are we going to do about Lil?' I said.

Dad shrugged. 'I'm not sure,' he said. 'But we'll think of something. We'll put it all right.'

Chapter 44

Lilian

February 1940

I was terrified. More scared than I'd ever been in my life. More frightened than when I told Mr Mayhew I was pregnant, or the first time he'd pushed his hands up my skirt and told me I was precious. More frightened than when Bobby signed up, or when we saw German planes flying low over the villages back down in Kent at the beginning of the war.

The baby was coming.

'Don't panic,' Ruth was saying to me, over and over. 'Just keep breathing and it will all be fine.'

'Where's Katie?' I said, my voice shrill. 'Where is she?'

'Jemima's gone to fetch her,' Ruth said. 'They'll be here soon.'

Another pain gripped me and I doubled over, clutching my stomach.

'No, darling, breathe,' Ruth said. I wanted to hit her. How could she be telling me what to do, when she'd never been through this? How dare she? And then the pain subsided and I felt a wave of shame. How could I have thought such awful thoughts about caring Ruth?

I was in my bedroom upstairs, where Ruth had helped me when the pains started to come closer together. I'd found when the contractions started it was better to stand up and hang on to my metal bedstead but now they were gone again, I lowered myself on to the bed and leaned against the pillows. This was awful.

I burst into tears. 'I can't do it,' I sobbed. 'I can't have a baby. I'm only a girl. I can't do it, Ruth. Don't make me do it.'

Ruth had a bowlful of water at my side and now she wrung out a cloth and gently dabbed my sweaty forehead.

'Sweet Lil,' she said. 'It's nearly over. Keep going, brave girl.'

I carried on crying, but my sobs were quieter and outside I heard Jemima's van pull up.

'Thank God, thank God, thank God,' I said under my breath.

Jemima and Katie came into the room just as another pain arrived. I heaved myself up and gripped the bedpost tightly, Ruth rubbing my back.

'How far apart are the contractions?' Katie said.

'Two minutes,' Ruth said, 'and getting closer together all the time.'

Katie was all business. She waited for the pain to lessen then helped me back on to the bed. She was surprisingly strong for someone so tiny.

'Can I take a look?' she asked. I nodded, just wanting it to be over, and turned my head so I didn't have to watch.

'You're nearly there,' she said. 'Clever girl.'

Nearly, as it turned out, meant another two hours of contractions. I cried, and I shouted, and at one point I pulled off my nightie and threw it at Ruth. Until eventually Katie examined me and grinned.

'This baby's about to arrive,' she said. 'Next contraction, Lil, I want you to start pushing.'

'No,' I said. 'I can't. I'm too tired.' I wanted to curl up on the bed and die. Or sleep. Either one. I did not want to push.

'Come on, girl,' Ruth said. She was sitting next to me on the bed, arm round my shoulder. 'Come on. It's nearly over.'

I felt the wave of pain take over and I pushed with all my might.

'The head and shoulders are out,' Katie said in delight. 'Keep going.'

I screwed up my face and pushed hard, and with a gush of – something – I felt the baby slip out from between my legs. Katie scooped it up and there was a second where everything was quiet and then the tiny, purple creature she was holding began to cry.

'Oh, Lil,' Ruth sobbed. 'You did it.'

'It's a boy,' Katie said, holding him aloft like he was a trophy. 'A beautiful, bouncing boy.'

'A boy,' Ruth said. Jemima, who'd made herself scarce when things started to get too much, poked her head round the door and Ruth beckoned her to come in.

'It's a boy,' she said and Jemima nodded.

'Knew it,' she said.

Katie efficiently snipped the cord, then wrapped the baby in a blanket. I looked at the little bundle she was holding and then at Ruth's sweaty, tear-stained face.

'Give him to Ruth,' I said. 'Give the baby to Ruth.'

Katie paused. 'Are you sure?'

I nodded, feeling my heart pounding in my chest. 'He's Ruth's baby,' I said.

Carefully, Katie handed the tot to Ruth and she cradled him, looking at his face adoringly.

'He looks like Bobby,' she said. 'Oh you precious little mite, hello.'

The baby stopped crying.

'He likes you,' I said, my voice croaky. 'He knows you're his mummy.'

'Lil,' Ruth said, still looking at the baby's little face. 'Are you positive about this? You don't have to do it, you know.'

I shook my head. 'I can't be a mother,' I said, shakily. 'Not now. Not to this baby.'

Ruth stroked my hair with one hand. 'Do you want to hold him?'

Did I? To my surprise, I nodded and Ruth gave him to me. I looked down at his tiny features, searching for any sign of Mr Mayhew and feeling thankful when I couldn't see anything. Ruth was right; he did look like Bobby.

'Hello, baby,' I whispered. 'I'm sorry I can't be your mummy. But I know Ruth will care for you and love you so much. Much more than I can. And your dad is a wonderful man. The best man. I know he will be there for you too. He'll teach you to ride your bike and your mummy will teach you your letters and your numbers. She's very clever you know? And maybe one day, I can teach you how to play the piano?'

I spread out his little fingers, which were curled over on the blanket. 'You've got a good span,' I said. 'I think you'll make a wonderful pianist.' Very gently, I kissed him on the top of his soft, dark hair, and then I handed him back to Ruth. 'Thank you,' I said. 'Look after him.'

Ruth was still crying. 'Thank you,' she said. 'I will. I promise.'

Katie coughed politely. 'Ladies,' she said. 'I need to have a look at Lil and check she doesn't need any stitches. And we need to deliver the afterbirth, darling.'

'We'll leave you,' Ruth said.

'Take the baby,' I urged her but Katie shook her head.

'He needs feeding,' she said. 'Do you want to try?'

I closed my eyes briefly. 'I can't,' I said. 'Will he be all right if I don't?'

'We've got some baby milk downstairs,' Ruth said.

'And bottles,' Jemima added. 'I've sterilised them already. Boiled them in a pot.'

Katie nodded approvingly. 'He'll be fine,' she said. 'I can make you some tea with sage leaves, Lil. That will help to dry up your milk, and if Jemima can find me some cabbage leaves we can put them in your brassiere so it won't hurt so bad. Why don't you take him downstairs, Ruth, and sit by the fire with him. Give him a bottle but remember he's only tiny and he won't drink much.'

Her face glowing with happiness, Ruth agreed.

'Wait,' I said. 'Can I name him?'

'Of course.' Ruth looked a bit nervous and I thought she was worried I'd want to call him Ian.

'Robert,' I said. 'Call him Robert.'

'Robert,' Ruth said. 'That's perfect.'

She smiled at me, cuddled little Robert closer, and she and Jemima went downstairs.

'Let's patch you up, then,' said Katie. She looked at me, her expression soft. 'How are you feeling?'

'I feel like I've been knocked over by a bus,' I said.

'I meant inside. How are you feeling inside?'

I thought about it, thinking about Robert's little face and his pink fingers gripping the blanket, and then I smiled. 'I'm sad,' I said. 'And happy. And most of all, I'm relieved.'

Katie nodded. 'What are you going to do now?' she asked.

I looked out of the window at the leaden winter sky. 'Now I'm going to learn how to fly,' I said.

Chapter 45

Helena

July 2018

What I'd said to Dad about Jack was true. I'd been pushing the thought aside since Greg turned up but now it had planted itself right at the front of my brain.

Dora had enough going on in her life with Greg arriving the way he had. And I did too, with Lil, and Dad, and work. It just all seemed too difficult. And behind all my doubts was a niggle. The tiniest little niggle that said he'd talked me into doing Lil's research. It was all his idea. That he'd said I should look into it and use him as a cover story. Maybe I'd been wrong to blame Dad for the whole mess with Lil; maybe it was Jack's fault.

By the time he emerged from his reshoots, halfway through the following week, my house was shining because I'd cleaned it – again. My wardrobe was bare, because I'd cleared out all the clothes I didn't wear, my bookshelves were in alphabetical order, and Greg had picked Dora up from nursery every day.

'Shall I come round?' Jack said on the phone.

'Actually,' I said. 'I'll come to you.'

Greg and Kimberley agreed to babysit, so I took a bottle of wine and some posh crisps and went over to Jack's house.

When he opened the door and pulled me into an embrace I wanted to cry. Everything about him just felt so right.

He poured the wine, and opened the crisps and I found a bowl to put them in. And then we went through to the lounge and he took a deep breath. 'I've got some news,' he said.

I blinked. 'You have?'

'I got that job. In New York.'

'On the Netflix show?' I said, thrilled. 'They want you back? That's amazing.'

He grinned. 'It's totally amazing,' he said. 'It's eight episodes now, but it could even lead to more.' His face fell. 'The only thing that's not amazing, is that I need to go to the States.'

My heart was pounding in my chest. 'I think that could be a good thing,' I said, hardly able to believe I was saying the words. 'Let me tell you everything that's happened since I last saw you.'

First I told him about Lil. I explained that I'd gone to see her, and what she'd told me, and that now she wasn't talking to me.

'Bloody hell,' Jack said. 'This is one incredible story.'

'Totally incredible,' I said.

'But you need to tell her that it all came from your dad. It's not fair for you to take the blame like this.'

'Oh, I'm just getting started,' I said.

Jack topped up my wine.

'Fliss found out what I was doing,' I said. 'She was annoyed and concerned, and she's told me to take three weeks off to sort it out.'

'Shit,' Jack said. 'But you're not suspended or anything?'

'Not officially. But it feels like it.'

'Bloody hell,' Jack said again. 'I spend one weekend doing reshoots and it's all gone crazy.'

'And I'm not even finished,' I said.

I filled him in on Greg showing up unannounced and he grew stern and quiet.

'That's what you want is it?' he said. 'Greg back in your life?'

'He's not back in my life, not really,' I pointed out. 'He's in Dora's.'

Jack nodded. 'He hurt you so badly,' he said.

'He did,' I agreed. 'I won't ever forget that. But this isn't about me and him. He's engaged to someone else, and I'm … well, I'm moving on too. It's about him and Dora.'

'So when I left you the other morning, things were fine and now everything's fallen apart?' Jack said.

I forced a smile. 'Basically,' I said. I took a breath. 'And that's what I wanted to talk about.'

'Don't,' said Jack. 'Don't say it.'

'I think this New York thing could be good,' I said. 'It's a break, some time off, isn't it? It's what I need, Jack, to sort my life out. How long will you be gone?'

'Four months? Maybe a bit longer.' Jack's face was totally still. He stared straight ahead.

'Listen,' I said. 'You came into my life and I wasn't expecting you. You arrived and just created chaos.'

A muscle twitched by Jack's eye.

'And it's been amazing. And wonderful. But that chaos has spread through my whole life and my job, and my family. And I need to put it back together again and I can't do it if you're here.'

Jack was looking perplexed. I couldn't meet his eyes – his gorgeous, lovely brown eyes – because I knew if I did I would crumble.

'Helena, sweetheart,' he said. 'I can see why you might think this is a good idea. Because it was my idea, wasn't it? It was me who suggested you research Lil. You wouldn't have done it – none of this would have happened without me.'

My eyes grew hot with tears. He knew me so well; he under-

273

stood how I thought. But I shook my head. 'That's not it,' I lied. But Jack carried on.

'And I see now that it was wrong. We did the wrong thing when we carried on poking about in Lil's life,' he said. 'But you did it for your dad. That wasn't wrong. You were doing what you thought was best. Lil will understand that.'

I took a deep shuddery breath because from where I was standing it didn't look like Lil would ever understand that.

Jack was still talking. 'Fliss will come round,' he said. 'And Greg? Well, you can work that out.'

'It's not going to be easy,' I said.

'And that's why you need me on your side.'

'I can't do it,' I said. 'I can't think of you right now. My life is broken and I need to fix it.'

Jack sighed. 'I really don't think your life is broken, my darling. And if it is, then perhaps it needed to break – just a little bit.'

Stubbornly, I shook my head. 'It was fine,' I insisted. 'Dora was happy. My job was fine – it was great – and now I've been suspended. My family was great. My sister was wonderful. Lil was wonderful. It was exactly how I needed it to be.' I let out a sob. 'And now it's all different.'

'Don't be a martyr,' Jack warned. 'Don't dump me just so you can feel like you've done something to make amends.'

That was exactly what I was doing, I realised. I was punishing myself. But it was the only thing I could think of to do.

'I have to,' I said quietly. 'I don't know what else to do. I need to sort this out and you going to New York is an opportunity.'

'So what, we just don't speak?'

'I guess not,' I said. 'Four months, you said?'

He nodded. 'That's a long time,' he said. 'I don't want this, Helena. I want to be with you, helping you, supporting you.'

He leant his head against mine and I closed my eyes.

'I just want you with me.'

'It's only a few months,' I said, trying to be strong. I knew

274

this was the right thing to do, even if it didn't feel that way. 'And then, maybe, when you come back, things will be better and maybe we'll still like each other.'

I tried to smile again but this time I found I couldn't do it.

'Or maybe you'll have met someone else,' I said. 'That's a chance I'm going to have to take.'

'I'm not going to meet anyone else,' Jack said. 'I've met you.'

'I'm going to go,' I said.

Jack followed me to the front door and I opened it. He took my hand and kissed it, like a prince in a fairy story.

'For what it's worth,' he said. 'I think you're doing the wrong thing. I love you, Helena. I think you love me too. And I'm going to miss you a lot.'

I cried all the way home.

Chapter 46

Helena

August 2018

Listlessly I scrolled down the showbiz website, pretending I wasn't interested in what it had to say, while all the time scanning the stories for any mention of Jack. He was back in New York already, it seemed. And there were rumours he was heading to LA to do a pilot for another TV show that was tipped to be huge. I wondered if he'd move out to the States permanently. It seemed inevitable.

I jumped as my doorbell rang.

'Use your key,' I shouted, carrying on scrolling. 'I'm busy.'

A sharp knock on the window made me look up. Miranda stood there, scowling. Her arms full with a large box.

'Helena, let me in,' she mouthed through the glass.

Sighing, I threw back the blanket I'd been sitting under, and padded through to the front door. I opened it, and without bothering to say hello, I slunk back into the living room and took up my position under the blanket again.

'Hi, Miranda, so nice to see you. Your hair looks great,' Miranda sang as she came into the room.

'Hi, Miranda,' I said. I didn't bother looking at her hair. It always looked great.

'Why are you in your pyjamas?' Miranda said, putting the box down on the floor. 'It's the afternoon. Where's Dora?'

'She's with Greg,' I said. 'Again. And I don't have a job, remember? So I'm not going anywhere.'

Miranda looked at me in disgust. 'You are such a drama llama,' she said. 'It's Saturday, so you wouldn't be at work anyway. And aren't you back in the office on Monday?'

I ignored her and went back to my scrolling.

'Are you looking for pictures of Jack again?'

'No,' I lied, shutting the laptop. 'I was working, actually.'

'Really?'

I caved immediately. 'Yes, I was looking for pictures of Jack.'

'Anything?'

'No.'

'Right, well, let's get on, shall we?'

I stared at her. 'Get on with what?'

'Operation Closure.'

I threw back the blanket again and stood up. 'Miranda,' I said. 'I really appreciate you coming round to cheer me up. But I am sad, and missing Dora, and worrying about Lil, and I'm enjoying wallowing in my own weird way. So please, go away and let me wear my pyjamas and look for photos of my ex-boyfriend online.'

Miranda grinned. 'Nope,' she said. 'I've got something for you. Two things, actually. Shall I put the kettle on?'

Rolling my eyes, I followed her into the kitchen.

'Any biscuits?' she said, as she bustled about filling the kettle and getting mugs out of the cupboard.

'I ate them all.'

'Lucky I brought some more then,' she said, pulling a packet of chocolate hobnobs out of her bag with all the flourish of Paul Daniels cutting Debbie McGee in half.

'While I'm doing the tea, why don't you read this?' she added, handing me an envelope.

I gave her a puzzled look and slipped my finger under the flap to open it. It was a letter, handwritten, which never happened any more.

'Is this from Lil?'

Miranda nodded. 'Read it.'

I started to scan the letter and Miranda screeched. 'Out loud, for heaven's sake. I've managed to resist steaming it open, for a whole week. Would you bloody well read it out loud?'

'Dear Helena,' I read.

'I must apologise, my dear, for the way I treated you when you came to visit. I was shocked and upset that you'd uncovered my secrets. But I was wrong to ask you to leave, and please know I didn't mean it when I said I never wanted to see you again.'

Miranda smiled at me, and I felt a weight lift from my shoulders.

'My friend Hugh, the actorrrrr …'

I paused and looked up from the letter.

'She has totally written actorrrrr with five Rs,' I said.

We both chuckled and the weight lifted a bit more.

'My friend Hugh the actor once told me that keeping secrets causes them to fester and I can see now that he is right. Far better to have things out in the open.'

Miranda nodded. 'I agree with that,' she said.

'I've been happy in my life. Though not as happy as I might have been if things had been different. But I don't regret anything I've done and I hope you understand why I acted as I did.'

'And so, my dear, I send you this box full of odds and ends that I have collected over the years. I believe it might explain some things. I also have an inkling that your father was behind you researching my time during the war. If I'm right, then I think he needs to see what's in this box too. Though perhaps not yet.

'Please come and see me soon, and bring Dora, and her ponies.'

I reached out and took Miranda's hand.

'I remain your adoring aunt, Lilian.'

I burst into tears while Miranda grinned.

'She's the best,' she said. 'Tea's up.'

She handed me a mug, and with the biscuits under her arm led the way back to the living room, where I sat down, still sniffing. Miranda picked up the box she'd brought with her, and put it on the sofa in between us.

'I went down to see Lil last weekend,' she said. 'She gave me this to give to you. With very strict instructions that we were to open it together and I wasn't to peek before you saw it.'

'Have you peeked?'

'No!' Miranda sounded outraged. Then she gave me a sheepish grin. 'Well, I opened it, but when I saw what was inside I shut it again and didn't rummage. We need to do it together.'

'So this is the odds and sods?'

'Have a look.'

I studied the box. It was an old hat box with a twisted cord handle. I couldn't remember ever seeing Lil wearing a hat that would have come in a box like this. Gently, I eased the lid up and peered underneath. The box smelled musty and old. There were a few papers, and photographs, and even newspaper clippings inside.

I looked up at Miranda in confusion. 'What is this?'

'No idea,' she said, looking as bewildered as I felt. 'Shall we go through it?'

I suddenly felt nervous but Miranda reached inside the box and pulled out a photograph. 'Look, this is Dad when he was small,' she said, handing it to me. 'With Grandma Ruth.'

Dad, who looked to be about five years old in the photograph, was sitting on Grandma's lap, a toy aeroplane clutched in his little fat fingers.

'I wonder if that's the aeroplane Lil gave him?' I said. 'The one he told me about.'

I laid the photograph on the coffee table and reached into the box myself. This time I found a photo of a young Lil in uniform, arm in arm with two women about the same age. They were all laughing and they looked very carefree. Behind them was a plane and I wondered if they'd been about to fly away together when the picture was taken.

'Flora and Annie, I bet,' I said to Miranda, showing her.

'God, they were so young,' she said. 'Look at this one – must have been when Lil joined up.'

She showed me the picture she held, of Lil in uniform again, but this time posing for a formal photograph.

'She was beautiful,' I said. She was, though her expression was guarded and she wasn't smiling at the camera.

We leafed through the box and found all the pictures – which were mostly of Dad. There was one of Dad as a chubby baby, and regular ones of him growing up. Each with the date written on the back in Ruth's handwriting.

'Keeping her up to date,' I muttered, laying them out in order on the coffee table.

'Looks like it,' Miranda agreed.

She rummaged about some more, and found a few folded concert programmes from Dad's early days as a performer. There were school concerts and some church recitals. Again, Grandma Ruth had written on some of them.

'Beautiful performance,' she'd jotted along the top of one. 'Biggest round of applause of the evening,' she'd written on another.

My eyes filled with tears. 'Grandma Ruth was such a lovely person,' I said, showing Miranda the programmes.

She nodded, equally teary-eyed. 'I think from all this, it definitely looks like Dad is Lil's son,' she said, sniffing. 'I can't see why else she'd have all this stuff.'

'Any clues about his father?'

I leaned over so I could see inside the box. 'All that's left are a few more concert programmes and some newspaper cuttings,' I said. 'Nothing romantic.'

'No cinema ticket stubs or love notes?'

I shook my head. 'Just these.' I pulled out the bundle of programmes and yellowed cuttings, which were tied together with string. 'These are from recitals Lil did when she was young,' I said. 'Ooh and look, there's a write-up from the local paper.'

Carefully, I unfolded the soft newspaper page and smoothed it out. It showed Lil, at about fourteen, sitting on a piano stool with her hair in a long plait down her back. Standing next to her, was an older man – in his late twenties or early thirties – with swarthy good looks. He had his hand on Lil's shoulder and he was smiling down at her.

'Pianist Lilian Miles, fourteen, has been chosen to represent Kent schools at a county music masterclass later this year,' I read out. 'Lilian, pictured with her proud piano teacher Ian Mayhew, will travel to London to perform at Westminster Hall.'

'Impressive,' said Miranda. She reached out and took another cutting, spreading it out as I had done. 'Oh, this is from after the war,' she said, scanning it. 'Oh heavens, oh, Helena, look ...'

She held out the cutting and I took it. It was a report from a court case from the 1950s. Ian Mayhew was accused of raping one of his pupils.

'Oh shit,' I said.

Miranda looked grim. 'I know.'

'But hang on, this isn't Lil,' I said, reading on. 'This girl was fifteen in 1953. Lil was older than that.'

'Helena,' said Miranda gently. 'Do you think Lil kept this cutting for a reason?'

'Because she knew this Mayhew fellow?' I said.

Miranda shook her head.

'Because he did the same to her?' I said, realisation dawning. 'Oh no.'

I looked more carefully at the clipping, scouring the picture

281

of Ian Mayhew for any resemblance to Dad. 'He must have been injured in the war,' I said. 'Look, he's got scars on his face in the later photo.'

Miranda shrugged. 'Hard to feel sympathy.'

'Did he go to prison?' I asked. 'What are the other cuttings?'

Miranda was ahead of me, unfolding the small pieces of updates on the case, and then finally a bigger story.

'Here,' she said, giving it to me.

I read the piece quickly and then looked up at Miranda.

'He killed himself when he was found guilty,' I said, rolling my eyes. 'What a coward.'

'Justice of a sort, I suppose,' Miranda said. 'How awful.'

I felt a wave of guilt and disgust and sorrow all at once. 'No wonder she didn't want me poking about in her life,' I said. 'No wonder she just wanted to forget it all. This wasn't some teen romance; it was rape.'

Miranda looked grim. 'Grooming, I suppose,' she said. 'Only I can't imagine they called it that then.'

I shuddered. 'She was just a kid. If Dora …'

'Don't,' said Miranda, her eyes brimming with tears. 'Please, don't.'

We were both quiet for a while, leafing through the newspaper cuttings and thinking.

'Poor, poor Lil,' I said, thinking about the little girl with the long plait in the photograph we'd found. 'Think how frightened she must have been when she found out she was pregnant.'

'And poor Dad,' Miranda said. 'To have a rapist as a father.'

'Should we tell him?'

'Lil said in the letter we could take the box to him,' Miranda told me.

'She said not yet,' I reminded her. 'I think we need to make things right first. Don't you?'

Miranda spread her hands in a helpless gesture. 'We can't make this right,' she said. 'How can we ever make this right?'

'Easier, then,' I said. 'We'll make it easier. Better somehow.'
'What are we going to do?'
'I've got an idea,' I said.

Chapter 47

Lilian

August 1944

Rose had most definitely won, I thought a month later as I reflected on everything that happened. In the battle between us, which I hadn't even known about, she was the victor. And I was left with nothing.

I opened my locker door and peeled off the photograph of Ruth, Bobby and Robert. I was packing my things to leave. I had, as I'd predicted, been discharged.

It could have been worse, I supposed. Rose had given her testimony against me in my court martial, just as she'd threatened.

She'd calmly and clearly told the judge advocate what she thought she'd overheard when I met Mary, just as she'd told Flight Captain Roberts. She said I'd organised a network of back-street abortionists who I called on to help women in trouble. It chilled me how close she'd got to the truth. But when she was questioned about this she admitted she had absolutely no proof.

When it was my turn to speak, I admitted arranging a termi-nation for Mary. I said she was my friend and that she'd turned to me in a time of trouble. I said I'd used a contact I'd made on another trip to Lincolnshire, and that I wasn't sure who the woman who'd performed the procedure was. I lied that I'd never done anything like it before and that I never planned to do it again.

And fortunately I was believed.

I was charged with contravening standing orders, a sort of wishy-washy offence that meant I'd done something wrong that didn't really break any actual laws. And I was found guilty and dishonourably discharged from the ATA.

So, I was going. I'd been up to Scotland to say goodbye to Ruth and Robert, and I'd used one of my contacts to pull some strings and get me passage on a ship heading for New York. If I made it across the ocean safely, I was planning to find some jazz clubs that might take me on so that I could rebuild my life. The Allies were pushing back into Europe and for the first time it seemed like there would be an end to the war. I thought I'd ride out the last months over the Atlantic. Maybe I would come back, maybe I wouldn't. Maybe I'd go to Paris, or Rome, or Australia. The world was my oyster.

I slammed my locker door shut and jumped to see Flora and Annie standing there.

'You weren't going to sneak off without saying goodbye, were you?' Flora said.

I shook my head, even though that was exactly what I'd planned to do.

'She was,' said Annie, grinning.

'Lil, we've got a plan but we need to know you're all right with it,' Flora said. 'Can we walk?'

Arm in arm, with me in the middle, we strolled to the very edge of the airfield and began to follow the perimeter fence.

'We've been talking,' Annie began. 'We're really proud of everything we've done here.'

'Me too,' I said.

'And we want you to know how proud of you we are.'

I stopped walking and looked at them both in turn. 'Don't,' I said. 'I will cry.'

Annie tightened her grip on my arm. 'You started this,' she said. 'And now you've given up everything so we can carry on.'

On my other side, Flora squeezed me in affection. 'You should know what a brave, clever, inspirational woman you are.'

I swallowed a sob. 'I'm not brave,' I whispered. 'I'm bloody terrified most of the time. I'd never have done all this without you, girls.'

'We will keep going, as best we can, just the two of us,' Annie said. 'We've been working it out. It might be that we can't help as many women as we want, but we can do some good.'

'And when the war is over, we're thinking we might organise ourselves properly. I've been talking to some people about it,' Flora added.

I smiled at them both. Such brilliant, bold women that I was proud to call my friends.

'I'll help,' I said, all my plans for my new life in America forgotten. 'I won't be in New York forever. I'll come back and I'll help.'

But Annie shook her head again. 'That's too risky,' she said. 'You need to stay far, far away from all this.'

'No,' I said. 'I want to be involved. Not straight away, obviously. I'll leave it a few months.'

'I'm sorry to say – and believe me, I really am sorry – that you being involved makes the chance of the whole thing being uncovered much more likely,' Flora said. 'Don't you see?'

I hung my head as the enormity of my confession finally hit home. 'I do see,' I said. 'Of course, I see.'

We were approaching the most remote hangar on the field, and outside was a pile of tarpaulins. I slumped down on the pile and put my head in my hands. 'We can't stay in touch, can we?'

Flora and Annie both sat down next to me.

'I don't think so,' Annie said. 'We have to decide, really.'

'Choose between our friendship and the network?' I said.

Annie nodded, her lips tightly pinched together. 'It's not easy.'

'Nothing ever is,' I said bleakly.

There was a pause as we all looked at each other.

'We have to keep the network going,' I said. 'That's the right thing to do.'

'I agree,' said Annie.

'So do I,' Flora added.

'But I don't like it,' I said. I tried to smile but instead I felt the tears come again. 'I don't like it one bit.'

I gripped Annie's hand in one of mine and Flora's in the other.

'I'm very lucky that we met,' I said. 'Not just because of the network, though that's been so important to me. But because of you and your friendship as well. And what Rose did was awful and mean-spirited and the worst of it is that she has made me lose you.'

'Oh, stop it,' said Annie. 'You're making me cry.'

'I've never had friends like you two and I probably never will again,' I carried on. 'And I want you to promise that you will stay in touch on my behalf. So you'll still be a gang of three, even though there will only be two of you.'

Flora nodded. 'Of course,' she said in a squeaky voice.

'Try to stop us,' Annie added.

We slung our arms round each other's necks and hugged and cried a bit and then eventually I untangled myself and stood up, brushing the dust from my uniform skirt that I was about to take off for the last time.

'I have to go,' I said, swallowing yet another sob. 'Look after each other.'

'We will,' said Annie.

I blew them a kiss and then I walked away, without looking back.

Chapter 48

Helena

August 2018

I left it another two weeks to visit Lil. She was still under the weather, and I didn't want to set her back. I'd phoned her, though, and told her Miranda had delivered the box and I had a plan.

'What sort of plan?' she'd said suspiciously and I'd told her I hadn't worked it all out yet, but I would fill her in when I saw her.

Greg and Kimberley had gone back to Canada, leaving – I was surprised to realise – a bit of a gap in our lives.

Dora had enjoyed spending time with them and we'd arranged for Greg to FaceTime every weekend so she didn't forget them. Canada was a very long way away for a two-year-old whose world didn't extend much further than nursery and her grandparents' house.

I still wasn't completely fine with Dora having what Miranda called a 'Disney dad'. I'd raised my eyebrows questioningly when she'd called Greg that and she'd explained it was the term for a weekend father – who did all the good bits of parenting and not the drudge work.

'I'm not sure Kimberley would let him get away with that,' I'd said. I was slightly uneasy that she was the reason Greg had suddenly decided to play dad. I didn't completely trust him to follow through, and I wasn't convinced he would transfer to London, but for now, I was willing to give it a go. With a set routine in place, of course – my desire for stability in Dora's life wasn't going anywhere.

I'd gone back to work. I'd been terrified on my first day back, but Elly had bought me a croissant for breakfast, and Fliss had landed me with three new families to research and I'd thrown myself back into things.

And then I'd gone to her with an idea – something I was hoping to talk to Lil about later – and she'd loved it. I'd gone from the bottom of the heap to the top in no time at all. I found that bringing work home to do when Dora was in bed stopped me searching for Jack on showbiz websites, and stopped me thinking about him, and wondering what he was doing now.

And so, as summer faded into autumn, Dora and I got on the train again and headed down to see Lil.

I thought perhaps she looked a little frailer than before, but other than that she was in good spirits.

'I'm so sorry about upsetting you,' I said, giving her a hug.

She'd smiled. 'It's hard to remember things you've tried very hard to forget, but I think Hugh is right and it's always better to have it out in the open. A few months ago I'd have said that was nonsense, but it's remarkable how much lighter I feel knowing you know what happened.'

Dora was sitting on her lap, snuggling in to her. Lil wound one of Dora's curls round her finger.

'Was I right that your father pushed you into this?' she asked.

I bit my lip, and then nodded. 'But don't blame him,' I said.

'I understand the drive to know where you came from. I see it at work all the time. And Jack …'

I trailed off. I didn't want to talk about Jack right now.

'Dad just wanted to know the truth,' I said.

'Have you showed him the box?'

I shook my head. 'Not yet,' I said.

'Down,' Dora commanded. Lil let her slide off her lap, and I handed her the bag containing her ponies so she could get them out.

'Dad still doesn't know for sure,' I said.

'You didn't tell him?'

'It's not my story,' I said. 'You just need to talk to each other.'

'What on earth would I say?'

I shrugged. 'I don't think it matters,' I said. 'I think he just wants to know.'

Lil shook her head. 'I can't,' she said. 'What if he hates me for giving him away? What if it changes everything?'

'He doesn't hate you,' I said.

'If he's suspected for a while, why didn't he say anything?'

'He was scared of upsetting you,' I said. 'And he was worried he might be wrong, so he didn't want to just barrel in and ask if you were his mum. He thought you might be offended.'

Lil looked down at her feet. 'I have carried a lot of shame,' she said. 'And I know nowadays it doesn't matter – having a baby out of wedlock.'

I grinned. 'Oh, believe me, there are still some people who like to judge,' I said. 'But you're right, it doesn't matter. I've felt a lot of things about having Dora, but shame isn't one of them.'

'I've carried it with me for eighty years,' Lil said. 'I'm not sure I can let it go now.'

I felt my eyes fill with tears. 'None of this was your fault,' I said. 'Your piano teacher was a bad man, who preyed on young girls. He groomed you, Lil.'

She scoffed. 'Groomed? There was no such thing back then.'

'No, but the idea is the same. Befriending you, taking you to concerts, winning over your parents, and then ...'

'I thought I loved him,' Lil said. 'But I see now I was too young.'

'It was rape,' I whispered, hating the word. 'He raped you.'

Lil winced. 'I know,' she said.

'But he didn't break you, Lil.'

She made a face that suggested I was wrong.

'He didn't. Look at your life. Look at your amazing, incredible life. Think about what you did in the war and the difference you made – you and all the ATA pilots. Look at the women you helped, and look at Dad; he adores you. And he told me how happy his childhood was, and how wonderful his parents were. You did that, Lil.'

She nodded, slowly.

'And Dad's musical talent? He gets that from you.'

'I've often worried that came from his father,' she said. 'Mr Mayhew, I mean.'

I snorted. 'I doubt that.'

'I sometimes wonder if my life would have been different,' Lil said. 'If I hadn't been on the move all the time. If I could have been the star of the show, rather than a session musician.'

I didn't say anything. I hated to hear she had regrets.

'But then I remember what a wonderful time I had. The people I met, and the things I experienced.'

'Did you ever meet anyone?' I asked. 'Did you have relationships?'

'Men are trouble,' she said.

'They are,' I agreed. 'But not always.'

'There were a few over the years,' she said, her eyes thoughtful. 'There was Philippe in Paris, who'd wooed me for months.'

I smiled. 'Go on,' I said.

'I have very fond memories of playing piano in a basement bar – ooh it must have been in the late 1950s. I was living in a top-floor apartment back then. There was no lift in the building, and I'd come home in the early hours of the morning to find Philippe asleep on the stairs, waiting for me.'

'What happened to him?' I asked, delighted at the idea of Philippe waiting on the stairs.

Lil shrugged in a very Gallic fashion.

'Things got serious, so I moved on.'

'Was there anyone else?'

'There was a chap called Marc who I met on one of the cruises I played on. We spent a lot of time together while we cruised round the Mediterranean, and when we disembarked I was rather sad.'

'And?'

'We were both due to sail on the same cruise a few weeks later – and I got scared, so I changed my plans and went to work on a different ship instead. I never saw him again.'

'That's sad,' I said.

'It's too late for regrets now,' Lil said firmly. 'It is what it is.'

Dora was arranging all her ponies in a circle.

'Are they dancing?' Lil said.

'They are chatting,' said Dora. 'They are a family.'

'There's a lot of them for one family,' I said.

Dora looked at me in disdain. 'This family is different,' she said.

I laughed. 'They all are,' I said.

'So tell me, what's this plan of yours?' Lil asked, watching Dora fondly.

I paused. 'I'm not sure if you're going to agree but hear me out.'

Lil looked suspicious so I jumped straight in.

'I want to tell this story,' I said. 'Your story.'

'About Robert?' she said, looking alarmed.

'No, the network,' I said. 'I want to find out what happened later and I want everyone to know about what you did.'

'I'm not sure,' Lil said. 'We were breaking the law, and not just once, we were breaking it over and over again.'

'I can find out for definite, but I'm pretty certain you wouldn't get into trouble now.'

'How would you do it?' she said.

I shook my head slowly. 'I'm not completely sure,' I said. 'Sometimes the stories don't really show themselves until we've started doing the research.'

'Won't you get into more trouble at work?'

I grinned. 'I've spoken to Fliss about it already,' I said. 'She loves the idea and she's pitched it to the bigwigs. They're keen too. I've been given one day a week to work on it – if you give me your blessing.'

I paused. 'I've learned my lesson, Lil,' I said. 'I'm not sticking my nose into someone else's life without permission this time.'

Lil patted my hand. 'Do you know, Helena?' she said. 'I'd rather like that. I'd like to know what happened after I went to America.'

I nodded. 'Then that's exactly what I'll do,' I said.

Lil smiled. 'Let's make it quid pro quo.'

I had no idea what she was talking about. 'What do you mean? You don't have to do anything for me.'

Lil smiled again, a slightly mischievous grin that made her look much younger. 'Oh I think I do,' she said. 'Wait and see.'

Chapter 49

Helena

August – October 2018

'He won't go,' I said to Miranda on the phone later. 'I've asked him to go and speak to her, and he won't.'

I was tearing my hair out. I'd told Dad that Lil wanted to speak to him, but he was still digging his heels in.

'I'm just going to leave it a few weeks,' he said. 'Let the dust settle.'

'The dust won't settle if you don't let it,' I said. But he wouldn't budge.

'I've had an idea,' Miranda said. 'I think we should have a party.'

'What, like a "my great-aunt is really my granny" party?' I said.

'No.' Miranda was exaggeratedly patient. 'For Lil's ninety-fifth birthday.'

I sat up straighter. 'That's a brilliant idea. Would we have it at her place? They have parties in the lounge sometimes.'

'I think we should have it at Mum and Dad's,' Miranda said.

'Lil can stay over like she does at Christmas and we can just have a little do to celebrate her life. And Dad will have to talk to her because she'll be in his house.'

'Do you think Mum and Dad would mind?' I said.

'Mum's already agreed.'

'You're amazing.'

'I know.'

'So, her birthday is the end of October, that gives us roughly two months to arrange it all. Is that enough time?'

'Easy,' said Miranda. 'You do the guest list and the invitations, I'll do catering, Mum can do decorations.'

'Brilliant,' I said. 'What about presents?'

'Ah,' said Miranda. 'That's always tricky.'

I smiled to myself. 'Tell you what,' I said. 'Leave that to me. I've got something up my sleeve.'

'Really?' said Miranda. 'You know that makes me nervous.'

'Just let me see what I can do,' I said. 'And then I'll fill you in.'

We ended the call, and I pulled my notebook over to where I sat on the sofa. I thought I could track down Annie and Flora, and anyone else I could find from the old days, and invite them along to Lil's party. That was if they were still with us. She was a ripe old age, of course, and she'd been one of the young ones during the war.

And so I threw myself into the research, working every evening after Dora had gone to sleep, checking birth certificates and marriage certificates, and speaking to women's rights activists, and family planning experts, and eventually just a couple of weeks before Lil's party, I found Annie.

I rang her straight away and explained who I was, and what I wanted to do, and she sounded thrilled.

'You're Lil's niece?' she said. Her voice sounded young on the phone – I'd never have guessed her age if I hadn't known.

'I am. Well, great-niece. She asked me to find you.'

'Well I never,' Annie said.

She lived with her daughter in Hastings, so I arranged to go down to see her the following day – fortunately it was my allocated research day and Fliss was pleased when I told her what I'd discovered.

'Get some photos,' she said. 'See if she'll go on camera.'

'She might not be up for it,' I warned. 'She's very old.'

Annie, though, was delighted to talk. We sat in the sunny living room of her daughter's big white-painted house, overlooking the sea. Her daughter – Val – made us tea and cut thick slices of homemade lemon drizzle cake.

'How nice that you live with your daughter,' I said.

'Val's husband died five years ago, and she and her daughter Penny bought this house together,' Annie explained. 'I moved in a short while after that. And Penny's daughter Lucy is here too. She's fourteen.'

'Incredible,' I said, grinning. 'My daughter Dora – she's nearly three – she says families are all different.'

'She's right,' said Annie.

I got out my notebook and told Annie about how Lil had told me her story – I missed out the bit where I researched it behind her back, and I didn't mention my dad for now. And I explained what my job was, and how I was hopefully going to put together a documentary telling the women's stories.

'I think that's a wonderful idea, Mum,' said Val, who was in her late sixties or early seventies and looked just like Annie.

'I'm a nurse,' she told me. 'At least I was. I'm retired now. I worked in obstetrics for years and the things I saw back in the Sixties. Dreadful business.'

'I can imagine,' I said.

'I'd be honoured to help you with your programme,' Annie said.

'Thank you,' I said, touched that she was so keen. 'But actually, that's not the main reason I came.' I reached into my bag, and pulled out an envelope. 'I wanted to give you this.'

Annie opened the flap and pulled out an invitation to Lil's party. 'A party,' she said. 'Oh how wonderful. I'd love to come.'

'Val, you too,' I said. 'And bring Penny and her daughter as well, if they'd like to come.' I looked at Annie. 'It's going to be a surprise,' I said. 'Lil won't know you're coming.'

Annie clapped her hands in joy. 'Marvellous,' she said. 'I love surprises.'

I grinned at her. 'Tell me everything,' I said. 'About the network.'

'Do you know about Flora?' Annie said.

I nodded, sadly. 'I found her death certificate,' I said. 'Breast cancer?'

'Back in 1985,' Annie told me. 'I still miss her.'

'I'm sure,' I said. 'You were all such good friends.'

'We carried on,' Annie said. 'With the network. In fact, after the war, we stepped it up a gear.'

I scribbled frantically in my notebook. This was all amazing.

'The adoptions had to stop after the war,' Annie said. 'The paperwork was getting too complicated. But we did advise women who wanted to have their babies adopted and we helped them find places to go if they wanted to have them in secret.'

'Oh my,' I said. 'What about the other stuff?'

Annie lifted her chin, just a fraction, in pride. 'By the Fifties we had women in almost every town in Britain. There were hundreds of us. Nurses, doctors, women like me – fixers, Flora called us – putting people in touch with people. But it wasn't perfect. It was expensive still, and dangerous; things often went wrong, and lots of our contacts were arrested.

I shuddered. 'Was Flora a fixer too?' I asked. 'Lil said she'd seen her on the news.'

Annie grinned. 'Flora went legit.'

'Legit?'

'She studied law – in her own time, I mean; she didn't go to university. And she became an adviser to the politicians who were campaigning for abortion to be decriminalised. After the law changed, she and I helped set up a chain of clinics. Giving family planning advice and doing terminations.'

'Goodness,' I breathed. 'You should be so, so proud of yourselves.'

'We're proud,' Val said. 'Mum's work influenced my career choice, and Penny's too. She's a doctor.'

'Wonderful,' I said.

'Flora had a good lot of write-ups when she died,' Annie said, proudly. 'Obituaries in all the broadsheets. She even got a mention on Radio 4.'

I wrote that down too. I could track those down and use them. 'What about other people who Lil might know?' I asked. 'Do you think we can find anyone else to invite to her party?'

'She wouldn't want them at the party, but I imagine she'd like to know what happened to Rose Smythe,' said Annie thoughtfully.

'The one who grassed her up?' I said. 'I'm definitely not inviting her.'

'And Will Bates,' Annie said. 'I've often wondered what became of him.'

I scribbled a note to remind myself to look up what had happened to Rose and Will. 'Did Flora have kids?' I said. 'We could invite them.'

'Oh yes, three boys,' said Annie. 'I've got their details. I'll write them down for you before you go.'

'This is going to be such a lovely birthday present,' I said.

'I hope it's not such a shock seeing me after all these years that she keels over,' said Annie with a glint of mischief in her eye. 'She's no spring chicken.'

'Mum,' Val warned. 'Don't be cheeky.'

But I didn't mind. I liked Annie enormously and as she told me more about what the network had achieved over the years, my admiration grew.

'You should be given some sort of award,' I said.

'It all started because of Lil,' she said modestly. 'Back when we helped that very first woman, it was because of Lil. She said it was the right thing to do and that she was desperate.'

She looked up at me. 'Flora and I always thought – though Lil never said – that she'd been in that position once and someone had helped her. And that was why she was so determined to help everyone we could.' She paused. 'Were we right?'

I smiled at her. 'Lil will tell you everything when you see her,' I said.

I gathered all my things, and we said our goodbyes. I was already looking forward to meeting Annie and Val again at the party.

'I've thought of someone else you should find out about,' Annie said. 'A woman we helped who ended up in hospital. Lil went to find her in Edinburgh and she was in a terribly bad way. We talked endlessly about what happened to her and we never knew.'

'Emily someone?' I said. 'Lil mentioned her. I've got her name written down. I'll definitely try to find out what happened to her.'

Annie gripped my hand. 'Thank you,' she said. 'For being interested.'

I kissed her cheek. 'Thank you,' I said.

Chapter 50

Helena

October 2018

The day of the party was foul. A horrible autumn day with strong winds, and blustery rain, and a real feeling that winter was on its way.

I was in a mood anyway, because I'd 'accidentally' looked at Jack's Instagram feed and seen a photo of him and that one from *Game of Thrones* with the hair, and it had made me think about watching it together and him doing an impression of the dragon woman to make me laugh, and the thought of never seeing his rubbish impressions again had plunged me into gloom.

'Come on,' I said to myself in the shower. 'It's been weeks. You should be over him by now.'

And yet I wasn't.

Still, at least I had the party to distract me. I had a new dress to wear, with a flouncy skirt and pockets, and Dora had new rainbow-striped tights to wear under her super-cute cord pinafore. We were all set.

Pietr had gone to Surrey to collect Lil. He was bringing her back to Mum and Dad's and she and Dad were going to talk before the party began – at least Miranda and I hoped that was going to happen. They were both so bloody stubborn I wasn't convinced.

Imogen was back in London, for good this time. She'd decided to train as a singing teacher and Dad was thrilled that finally one of us was doing something musical. And Andy had made a video message for us to play for Lil at the party, because apparently the site he was digging, which had been there for a thousand years, couldn't be left alone for one weekend.

Annie was going to be arriving later, with Val. And I had lots of things to tell Lil about people from her past. I hoped she'd be pleased.

Dora and I arrived at Mum and Dad's just as Pietr was helping Lil out of the car.

'Hello, you,' I said, giving her a kiss. 'Happy birthday.'

'Look at my tights,' said Dora, giving her a twirl. 'They have all the colours.'

'They're smashing,' said Lil.

We bustled up the path against the wind and into the warm house.

Dad stood in the hall, looking nervous.

'Hello, Robert,' Lil said.

He bent and kissed her.

'Hello,' he said.

Miranda was behind him and she gave me a quizzical look. I shrugged. I'd not thought about what happened next.

'Everything's done,' Miranda said. 'So why don't we all go into the lounge and have a sit-down before the guests arrive?'

We all went into the lounge and sat down, staring at each other expectantly.

Dad cleared his throat. 'Lil,' he began.

But she put her hand up to stop him. 'Let me,' she said.

There was a pause. I pulled Dora on to my knee in case she

started singing or running around and broke the moment. Freddie, bless him, sat quietly, his eyes round like saucers.

'Robert,' Lil said. 'I wanted to tell you …'

Dad got up and went over to her. Miranda had been sitting next to Lil, but she swiftly got up and Dad sat down instead. He took Lil's hand and I felt my eyes fill with tears.

'Robert,' Lil tried again. 'I'm your mother.'

Dad patted her hand. 'I'm very pleased to hear it,' he said.

Miranda and I exchanged glances. She was just as teary as I was. So was Mum. And Imogen. And, I thought, so was Pietr, though he was staring out of the window and pretending not to be interested.

'Do you remember when I was about five, you came to visit and you brought me a plane?' Dad said.

'I remember it well,' Lil said, smiling. 'I had a friend called Gareth, who was a mechanic on the airbase. He made it for you.'

'I loved it,' he said. 'But mostly I loved it because you gave it to me.'

Lil smiled again.

'I always looked forward to your visits,' Dad went on.

'I'm glad,' Lil said. Her voice was shaky.

'I understand,' Dad said. 'I understand why you had to give me to Mum and Dad. I also wanted to say thank you. For giving me the two most wonderful parents.'

Lil blinked at him. 'Do you know, in all this time I'd never considered you would thank me for giving you away,' she said.

'In many ways, I was lucky because Mum and Dad gave me a happy, stable home life and you gave me dreams,' Dad said.

Lil smiled. 'I knew you were talented the very first time I sat you at a piano,' she said. 'I remember how your tiny hands felt in mine that day.'

'You showed me how music could take you places,' he said. 'I chose my career because of you.'

Lil scoffed. 'You did that yourself.'

'And when I really needed you, Lil, you were there.'

Lil looked away. 'That's not true,' she said. 'I missed your concerts, your first day at school, your first steps.'

'Honestly, Lil,' Dad said. 'When Sal was ill after Immy was born, you turned up and you made everything okay. And you showed me how to be a parent.' He looked up at his mother. 'Looking back, that was when I started to wonder if you were my mother, even if I didn't realise it at the time.'

Lil said nothing.

'But Ruth was my mother too,' he said.

'She was a wonderful mother,' said Lil.

'Ruth will always be my mum and you will always be my Lil,' Dad said. 'I don't want things to change between us. Can we carry on as we have?'

Lil nodded.

A ring on the doorbell made us all jump.

'Guests,' said Miranda, clapping her hands.

Lil and Dad smiled at each other and Dad squeezed her hands.

'I'll let them in,' I said.

It was Annie and Val.

'Wait here,' I said after kissing them hello.

I went into the lounge, where the sombre mood of before had lifted. Freddie was tickling Dora, who was laughing uproariously. Dad was playing the piano, and Lil was watching him proudly. Mum was handing round drinks and Miranda had a plate of canapés. There was a bit of a party atmosphere, suddenly, as though the mood had lightened thanks to Dad and Lil's conversation.

'Lil,' I said. 'I hope you don't mind, but I've got a surprise for you. It's a birthday present of sorts.'

She looked at me, intrigued, and I helped her to her feet and gestured for Annie to come into the room.

Lil and Annie stood and stared at each other for a minute.

'Hello, Lil,' Annie said.

'Hello, Annie.'

Annie reached out to Lil and they hugged for a long time. I realised Lil was crying, and so was Annie – and so was I. But they were happy tears.

'Oh, my lovely Lil,' Annie said. 'I'm so very pleased to see you.'

'Why are you here?'

'Helena invited me,' she said, nodding towards me. 'She tracked me down.'

Lil looked at me. 'I thought you were going to tell me when you found something out,' she said.

I shrugged. 'Thought the surprise was better,' I said, smiling.

Lil linked her arm through Annie's. 'Come and have a drink,' she said. 'We've got a lot to catch up on.'

'More than seventy years,' Annie said with a grin.

They both sat down on the sofa, and I perched on the arm.

'Lil, there are some other things I need to tell you,' I said.

'Good heavens,' Lil said. 'Flora?'

I shook my head, sadly. 'She died,' I said. 'In the Eighties.'

Lil looked disappointed.

'But she had three boys,' I said, hating to see her glum again. 'And they're all coming with their families.'

'They are? How lovely.'

Lil looked a bit overwhelmed and I wondered if I should go on, but she nudged me impatiently.

'What else?'

'I found Rose,' I said. 'Rose who ratted on you.'

'Is she still alive?' Lil said.

'She's not,' I told her. 'She married Will, you know. After the war.'

'Poor bloke,' Lil said and I smiled at her barbed comment.

'They both died in the early 1950s, in a car accident,' I said. 'No kids.'

'Gosh, that's sad,' Lil said. 'I feel bad now.'

Annie nudged her. 'She was a cow, though,' she said and they both chuckled. I had a glimpse of what they must have been like as young women in the ATA.

'And I found Emily Page,' I said. 'The woman you helped in Edinburgh.'

Lil and Annie both looked up, apprehensive.

'She lived to a ripe old age,' I said. 'She only died in 2001. She married, and she had two children – a boy and a girl. Obviously, I didn't ask them along today. But I thought you'd want to know she survived.'

'Thank you, Helena,' Lil said. She gripped Annie's hand. 'Robert is my son,' she said, looking at her friend. 'I had him when I was just sixteen and my brother and sister-in-law brought him up.'

Annie nodded slowly. 'I wondered,' she said. 'I always wondered. It must have been hard for you.'

'No regrets,' Lil said.

'Are you happy?' Annie asked.

Lil looked round at us all. 'I believe I am,' she said.

Epilogue

Helena

November 2018

Lil's party was deemed an enormous success. She and Annie were having a wonderful time rekindling their friendship and poor Val seemed to spend half her time on the motorway driving Annie to Surrey to visit.

My research for the documentary was going brilliantly, thanks to Annie's help. I'd uncovered more of the network and found more women who helped others. I'd spoken to midwives and doctors, and the women they'd helped, and there was so much more to do. Fliss was thrilled. And even more so when we pitched another documentary – this time about the women who flew for the ATA – and that was commissioned too. Lil was chuffed that the stories of her brave colleagues would be heard.

I, on the other hand, felt flat and miserable.

Everything was working. In theory. Dora and Greg were building a relationship across the ocean, with their FaceTime chats, and Greg was planning to visit for her third birthday in December. Work was great. My house was tidy. I'd even reframed the shattered Audrey Hepburn print. In short, things were back to normal.

But I missed Jack.

When I'd broken up with Greg, I'd been shocked. I'd felt as though someone had thrown a bucket of icy water over me with no warning. But once the initial horror wore off, I felt strange, undoubtedly, but also slightly relieved. Like I'd been walking on eggshells or clenching my teeth and now I could relax. And of course, I'd had my pregnancy to distract me, which had been a blessing.

This time, though, it was different. Memories of the short time I'd spent with Jack kept rolling through my mind like some sort of terrible romantic film montage. I kept thinking 'oh I'll tell Jack that' about silly things from the new season of *Stranger Things* going up on Netflix, to discovering a new coffee place that made the best flat whites. All in all, I just felt really, really sad and I couldn't seem to shrug it off.

One Friday evening, well into November, when the weather was shifting from autumnal to full-on wintry, I felt especially low. Dora was in bed, and though it wasn't especially late it was properly dark already. Feeling in need of comfort, I put on an episode of *Gilmore Girls*, ordered some takeaway, poured myself a glass of red wine, and started sorting out my list of interviewees for the documentary.

When the doorbell rang, I jumped to my feet and padded through to the door in my socks. I was starving. But it wasn't my dinner. Well, it was the dinner, but it wasn't the Deliveroo driver I was expecting – instead it was Jack who stood there, clutching the bag of food.

'I met your driver outside on my way up the path,' he said. 'Is there enough for me? I'm really hungry.'

I blinked in surprise. 'There's plenty,' I said. 'I always order too much.'

We stared at each other for a second.

'So, can I come in?' Jack said eventually, and awkwardly. 'It's freezing out here.'

Silently, I stepped back and let him into the hall, where he stood looking just as awkward as he had outside.

'I need to tell you something,' he said.

'Do you want to go into the lounge?'

'No, I want to say it now, because I've got it all right in my head and if I leave it too long I'll forget.'

'Okay …'

Jack handed me the bag of food and took a breath.

'I think you're wonderful,' he said. 'And I have been miserable without you. More miserable than I've ever been, I think. I was in bloody LA, surrounded by glamorous people, and Hollywood megastars, and all I thought about was you. I was in a restaurant and I saw that chap from *Game of Thrones*, the one you like. And my agent introduced me, and he was nice, you know, but all I wanted was to take his photo and send it to you and say "look he does know something after all" and I couldn't.'

'Is this what you practised?' I said. 'Because it's a bit rambling.'

Jack punched me gently on the shoulder. 'No, it's not what I practised,' he said. 'I've gone off track a bit.'

'Go on,' I said, beginning to grin. I knew where this was going.

'You're wonderful, and I've been miserable,' he said. 'And I know for a fact you've been miserable too.'

I narrowed my eyes at him. 'Have you spoken to Miranda?' I said.

He shook his head. 'I spoke to Lil.'

My mouth fell open. 'Lil?'

'She said you were moping and I needed to come back,' Jack said. 'She said that you were being a martyr and that a life filled with regrets was no life at all.'

'She said that?' I said, impressed. 'That's quite poetic.'

'Have you been miserable?'

I stepped closer to him. 'I have,' I said.

308

'Do you know what we can do to make it better?'

I stepped closer still. Our bodies were almost touching now and I could smell his familiar smell.

'Maybe ...' I said. And suddenly we were kissing, right there in my hall. The food bag still clutched in one of my hands, and the front door open with fallen leaves blowing in with the rain.

There was a noise at the top of the stairs and we broke apart. Dora stood at the top, her hair wild from sleep. She was leaning over the stair gate and she looked very cross.

''Lo, Jack,' she said, waving her battered copy of *The Gruffalo* at him. 'Where you been?'

Acknowledgements

Mary Ellis, the last surviving pilot from the Air Transport Auxiliary, died aged 101 while I was writing this story. Lots of Lilian's experiences as a pilot were really the experiences of Mary and her friends in the ATA. I owe a big thank you to the wonderful exhibit *Grandma Flew Spitfires* at the Maidenhead Heritage Centre for bringing the stories of these brave women to life.

I must also thank my editor Nia and everyone at HQ, my agent Felicity, and my husband Darren for all their support. And of course, thank you to my readers. You're all brilliant.

Dear Reader,

Thank you so much for taking the time to read this book – we hope you enjoyed it! If you did, we'd be so appreciative if you left a review.

Here at HQ Digital we are dedicated to publishing fiction that will keep you turning the pages into the early hours. We publish a variety of genres, from heartwarming romance, to thrilling crime and sweeping historical fiction.

To find out more about our books, enter competitions and discover exclusive content, please join our community of readers by following us at:

🐦 *@HQDigitalUK*

𝗳 *facebook.com/HQDigitalUK*

Are you a budding writer? We're also looking for authors to join the HQ Digital family! Please submit your manuscript to:

HQDigital@harpercollins.co.uk.

Hope to hear from you soon!

ONE PLACE. MANY STORIES

**Turn the page for an extract from
Kerry Barrett's enchanting *The Girl in the Picture* ...**

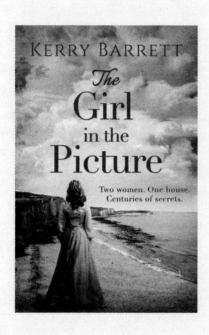

Chapter 1

Present day

Ella

'It's perfect,' Ben said. 'It's the perfect house for us.'

I smiled at the excitement in his voice.

'What's it like?' I asked. I was in bed because I was getting over a sickness bug but suddenly I felt much better. I sat up against the headboard and looked out of the window into the grey London street. It was threatening to rain and the sky was dark even though it was still the afternoon.

'I'll send you some pictures,' Ben said. 'You'll love it. Sea view, of course, quiet but not isolated …' He paused. 'And …' He made an odd noise that I thought was supposed to be a trumpet fanfare.

'What?' I said, giggling. 'What else does it have?'

Ben was triumphant. 'Only a room in the attic.'

'No,' I said in delight. 'No way. So it could be a study?'

'Yes way,' said Ben. 'See? It's made for us.'

I glanced over at my laptop, balanced on the edge of my dressing table that doubled as a desk, which in turn was squeezed into the corner of our bedroom. We'd been happy here in this

317

poky terraced house. Our boys had been born here. It was safe here. But this was a new adventure for us, no matter how terrifying I found the thought. And just imagine the luxury of having space to write. I looked at my notes for my next book, which were scattered over the floor, and smiled to myself.

'What do the boys think?' I asked.

'They're asleep,' Ben said. 'It's pissing down with rain and we're all in the car. I rang the estate agent and he's on his way, so I'll wake the boys up in a minute.'

'Ring me back when he arrives,' I said. 'FaceTime me, in fact. I want to see the house when you do.'

'Okay,' Ben said. 'Shouldn't be long.'

I ended the call and leaned back against my pillow. I was definitely beginning to feel much better now and I'd not thrown up for a few hours, but I was glad I'd not gone down to Sussex with Ben because I was still a bit queasy.

I picked up my glass of water from the bedside table and held it against my hot forehead while I thought about the house. It had been back in the spring when we'd spotted it, on a spontaneous weekend away. Ben had a job interview at a football club in Brighton. Not just any job interview. THE job interview. His dream role as chief physio for a professional sports team – the job he'd been working towards since he qualified. Great money, amazing opportunities.

The boys and I had gone along with him at the last minute and while Ben was at the interview, I'd wandered the narrow lanes of Brighton with Stanley in his buggy and Oscar scooting along beside me. I had marvelled at the happy families I saw around me and how my mood had lifted when I saw the sea, twinkling in the sunshine at the end of each road I passed. That day I felt like anything was possible, like I should grab every chance of happiness because I knew so well how fleeting it could be.

The next day – after Ben had been offered the job – we'd

driven to a secluded beach, a little way along the coast, and sat on the shingle as the boys ran backwards and forwards to the surf.

'I love it here,' I said, shifting so I could lie down with my head resting on Ben's thigh and looking up at the low cliffs that edged the beach. I could see the tops of the village houses that overlooked the sea and, on the cliff top, a slightly skew-whiff To Let sign.

'I wish we could live here,' I said, pointing at the sign. 'Up there. Let's rent that house.'

Ben squinted at me through the spring sunshine. 'Yeah, right,' he said. 'Isn't that a bit spontaneous for you?'

I smiled. He was right. I'd never been one for taking risks. I was a planner. A checker. A researcher. I'd never done anything on a whim in my entire life. But suddenly I realized I was serious.

'I nearly died when Stanley was born,' I said, sitting up and looking at him. 'And so did Stanley.'

Ben looked like he was going to be sick. 'I know, Ella,' he said gently. 'I know. But you didn't – and Stan is here and he's perfect.'

We both looked at the edge of the sea where Stanley, who was now a sturdy almost-three-year-old, was digging a hole and watching it fill with water.

'He's perfect,' Ben said again.

I took his hand, desperate to get him to understand what I was trying to say. 'I know you know this,' I said. 'But because of what happened to my mum I've always been frightened to do anything too risky – I've always just gone for the safe option.'

Ben was beginning to look worried. 'Ella,' he said. 'What is this? Where's it come from?'

'Listen,' I said. 'Just listen. We've lived in the same house for ten years. I don't go on the tube in rush hour. I wouldn't hire jet skis on our honeymoon. I'm a tax accountant for heaven's sake. I don't take any risks. Ever. And suddenly I see that it's crazy to live that way. Because if life has taught me anything it's that even

319

when you're trying to stay safe, bad things happen. I did every-thing right, when I was pregnant. No booze, no soft cheese – I even stopped having my highlights done although that's clearly ridiculous. And despite all that, I almost died. Oscar almost lost his mum, just like I lost mine. And you almost lost your wife. And our little Stanley.'

'So what? Three years later, you're suddenly a risk taker?' Ben said.

I grimaced. 'No,' I said. 'Still no jet skis. But I can see that some risks are worth taking.' I pointed up at the house on the cliff. 'Like this one.'

'Really?' Ben said. I could see he was excited and trying not to show it in case I changed my mind. 'Wouldn't you miss London?'

I thought about it. 'No,' I said, slowly. 'I don't think I would. Brighton's buzzy enough for when we need a bit of city life, and the rest of the time I'd be happy somewhere where the pace of life is more relaxed.'

I paused. 'Can we afford for me to give up work?'

'I reckon so,' Ben said. 'My new job pays well, and …'

'I've got my writing,' I finished for him. Alongside my deathly dull career in tax accountancy, I wrote novels. They were about a private investigator called Tessa Gilroy who did all the exciting, dangerous things I was too frightened to do in my own life. My first one had been a small hit – enough to create a bit of a buzz. My second sold fairly well. And that was it. Since I'd had Stan, I'd barely written anything at all. My deadlines had passed and my editor was getting tetchy.

'Maybe a change of scenery would help,' I said, suddenly feeling less desperate when it came to my writing. 'Maybe leaving work, and leaving London, is just what I need to unblock this writer.'

That was the beginning.

Ben started his job at the football club, commuting down to Sussex every day until we moved, and I handed in my notice at work. Well, it was less a formal handing in of my notice and more a walking out of a meeting, but the result was the same. I was swapping the dull world of tax accountancy for writing. I hoped.

My phone rang again, jolting me out of my memories.

'Ready?' Ben said, smiling at me from the screen.

'I'm nervous,' I said. 'What if we hate it?'

'Then we'll find something else,' said Ben. 'No biggie.'

I heard him talking to another man, I guessed the estate agent, and I chuckled as the boys' tousled heads darted by.

It wasn't the best view, of course, on my phone's tiny screen, but as Ben walked round the house I could see enough to know it was, indeed, perfect. The rooms were big; there was a huge kitchen, a nice garden that led down to the beach where we'd sat all those months before, and a lounge with a stunning view of the sea.

'Show me upstairs,' I said, eager to see the attic room.

But the signal was patchy and though I could hear Ben as he climbed the stairs I couldn't see him any more.

'Three big bedrooms and a smaller one,' Ben told me. 'A slightly old-fashioned bathroom with a very fetching peach suite ...'

I made a face, but we were renting – I wasn't prepared to risk selling our London place until we knew we were settled in Sussex – so I knew I couldn't be too fussy about the décor.

'... and upstairs the attic is a bare, white-painted room with built-in cupboards, huge windows overlooking the sea, and stripped floorboards,' Ben said. 'It's perfect for your study.'

I couldn't speak for a minute – couldn't believe everything was working out so beautifully.

'Really?' I said. 'My attic study?'

'Really,' said Ben.

'Do the boys like it?'

'They want to get a dog,' Ben said.

I laughed with delight. 'Of course we'll get a dog,' I said.

'They've already chosen their bedrooms and they've both run

321

round the garden so many times that they're bound to be asleep as soon as we're back in the car.'

'Then do it,' I said. 'Sign whatever you have to sign. Let's do it.'

'Don't you want to see the house yourself?' Ben said carefully. 'Check out schools. Make sure things are the way you want them?'

Once I would have, but not now. Now I just wanted to move on with our new life.

'Do you want to talk to your dad?'

'No.' I was adamant that wasn't a good idea because I knew he'd definitely try to talk us out of it. I'd not told him anything about our move yet. He didn't even know I'd handed in my notice at work – as far as he was aware, Ben was going to stick with commuting and I'd carry on exactly as I'd been doing up until now.

I got my cautious approach to life from my dad and I spent my whole time trying very hard not to do anything he wouldn't approve of. I'd never had a teenage rebellion, sneaked into a pub under age, or stayed out five minutes past my curfew. I'd chosen my law degree according to his advice – he was a solicitor – and then followed his recommendations for my career.

This move was the nearest I'd ever got to rebelling and I knew Dad would be horrified about me giving up my safe job, about Oscar changing schools, and us renting out our house. And even though moving to Sussex would mean we lived much nearer him, I thought that the less he knew of our plans, the better.

'We could come down again next weekend,' Ben was saying. 'When you're feeling well?'

'No,' I said, making my mind up on the spot. 'I don't want to risk losing the house. We were lucky enough that it's been empty this long, let's not tempt fate. Sign.'

'Sure?' Ben said.

'I'm sure.'

'Brilliant,' he said, and I heard the excitement in his voice

322

again, along with something else – relief perhaps. He would be pleased to leave London.

'Ella?'

'Yes?'

'I've been really happy,' he said softly. 'Really happy. In London, with you, and the boys. But this is going to be even better. I promise. It's a leap of faith, and I know it's scary and I know it's all a bit spontaneous, but if we're all together it'll be fine.'

I felt the sudden threat of tears. 'Yes,' I said.

'We're strong, you and me,' Ben said. 'And Oscar and Stan. This is the right thing for us to do.'

'I know,' I said. 'We're going to be very happy there.'

Chapter 2

From then I barely had time to draw breath, which was lucky really. If I'd had time to think about what we were doing I'd have changed my mind, because the truth was I was absolutely terrified about the move.

On paper, the house was perfect and I trusted Ben's judgement. And it wasn't as if I hadn't been involved, I told myself, when all my worries about how I'd not even seen our new home surfaced. I'd spotted it first. I'd seen it on FaceTime and on the estate agent's website. I'd been part of the decision-making from the start.

So, I concentrated on the fact that we'd found a tenant for our London house with almost indecent haste. I worked out whether our battered sofa would fit in the new lounge, and if the boys would need new beds, and I dreamed of having my own study, a haven, tucked away in the attic room.

The one fly in the ointment was Dad. I had to tell him we were moving of course. So one day, a week or so before we finally went and just before I finished work, I took a half-day and drove down to Kent to see him and my step-mum, Barb.

'I thought we could go for a late lunch at the pub,' I said when I arrived, thinking that if I told Dad the news in public, it might go better. I breathed a sigh of relief when Barb and Dad agreed, so we all strolled along the road towards their local. Truth be told, I had no idea how Dad would react because I'd never done anything he didn't agree with before.

'He might be fine,' Ben had said. 'I think you're overthinking this. He just wants you to be happy.'

But I wasn't sure. I was scared my whole relationship with my dad was conditional on me doing what he wanted me to do. I knew he would be nervous about the risk we were taking, and he'd expect me to listen to his concerns, and then announce he was right and change my mind. But I wasn't going to do that this time – and that's why I was so worried.

I'd grown up, with Dad, in Tunbridge Wells. Dad didn't live in the same house any more because he and Barb – who I loved to bits – had moved when they got married, soon after I started university. It wasn't far from where we'd lived when I was a kid, but far enough, if you see what I mean.

'So how's Ben's job going?' Dad asked, as we settled down at our table.

'Good,' I said. 'Really good.'

'Dreadful commute,' Dad said.

'Awful,' I agreed. 'And that's why we've made a decision.'

Dad and Barb looked at me as I took a breath and explained what we were doing.

'It's a lovely house,' I said. 'And we're just renting, though Ben says the landlord mentioned he'd be willing to sell if we like it.'

Barb smiled at me.

'It sounds wonderful,' she said. 'But won't it mean you commuting instead?'

There was a pause.

'Well,' I said. 'Actually.'

Dad took his glasses off and rubbed the bridge of his nose and I felt my confidence beginning to desert me.

'Actually?' he prompted.

'Actually, I've handed in my notice,' I said. I picked up my sparkling water and swigged it, wishing it was gin.

Barb and Dad looked at each other.

'That's a big decision,' Barb said carefully.

'It is,' I said. 'But we're confident it's the right thing to do. Ben's salary is good enough for us to live on, and I've got my writing.'

Dad nodded as though he'd reached a decision. 'You'd be best taking a sabbatical,' he said. 'What did they say when you asked about that? If they said no, you've probably got cause to get them to reconsider. I can speak to Pete at my old firm, if you like? He's the expert on employment law …'

'Dad,' I said. 'I didn't ask about a sabbatical, because I don't want to take a sabbatical. I'm leaving my job and I'm going to write full-time. It's all planned.'

Dad looked at me for a moment. 'No, Ella,' he said. 'It's too risky. What if Ben's job doesn't work out? Or the boys don't settle? Have you checked out the school for Oscar? He's a bright little lad and he needs proper stimulation. And don't even think about selling your house in London. Once you leave London you can never go back, you know. Not with house prices the way they are.'

'Dad,' I said again. 'It's fine. We know what we're doing.'

'I'll phone Pete, now,' Dad said. 'Now where did I put that blasted mobile phone?'

'Dad,' I said, sharply this time. 'Stop it.'

Dad winced. 'Keep your voice down, Ella,' he said. 'What's wrong?'

I shook my head. 'I knew this is how you'd act,' I said. 'I knew you wouldn't want me to give up work, or for us to move house.'

'I just worry,' Dad said.

I felt a glimmer of sympathy for him. Of course he worried. But I wasn't his little girl any more and we didn't have to cling to each other like we were drowning, like we'd done when I was growing up.

'Don't,' I said, more harshly than I'd intended. 'Don't worry. I'm fine. Ben's fine. The boys are fine.'

Barb put her hand over Dad's as though urging him to leave things there, but Dad being Dad didn't get the message.

'I think I should phone Pete,' he said. 'Just in case.'

I pushed my chair back from the table and stood up. 'Do not pick up your phone,' I said. 'Don't you dare.'

Dad and Barb both looked stunned, which wasn't surprising. I'd never raised my voice to Dad before. I'd never even disagreed with his choice of takeaway on movie night.

'Ella,' Dad said. 'I think you're over-reacting a bit.'

But that made me even more determined to put my point across.

'I'm not over-reacting,' I said. 'I want you to understand what's happening here. I'm leaving my job, and we are moving to Sussex. Which, by the way, means we will be nearer to you than we are now. I thought you'd be pleased about that.'

My voice was getting shriller and I felt close to tears, but as Dad stared at me, shocked into silence, I continued. 'I know it's risky, but we have decided it's a risk worth taking. Because, Dad, you know better than anyone that things can go wrong in the blink of an eye. You know that.'

Dad nodded, still saying nothing.

'So it's happening. And I knew you wouldn't approve. And I'm sorry if this makes me difficult. Or if me doing something that you don't like means you don't want me in your life any more. But it's happening.'

'Ella …' Dad began. 'Ella, I don't understand.'

'Oh you understand,' I said, all my worries about the move and about telling him spilling over. My voice was laden with venom as I leaned over the table towards him. 'You understand. I've always been a good girl and done what you wanted me to do, haven't I?'

Dad still looked bewildered and later – when I went over and over the conversation (if you could call it a conversation when it was really only me talking) in my head – I saw the genuine confusion in his face, the hurt in his eyes, and it broke my heart. But at the time, all I thought of was that I'd been proved right.

'For the first time in my whole life, I'm doing what I want to do,' I said. 'And it's not what you want me to do but I'm going to do it anyway.' I picked up my bag. 'And you can't send me away this time – because I'm going.'

Ignoring Dad's shocked expression and Barb's comforting hand on his arm, I threw my coat over my shoulder and marched out of the pub, and down the road to my car, where I sat for a while, sobbing quietly into my hands. I wasn't sure what had just happened and I had a horrible feeling that I'd got everything wrong.

The next book from Kerry Barrett is coming in 2019

DIGITAL HQ

If you enjoyed *The Hidden Women*, then why not try another exciting read from HQ Digital?